A deliciously passi
leave her reputa
and her hear

Virgin
UNDONE BY THE BILLIONAIRE

Three fantastic novels from favourite
authors Jennie Lucas, Susan Stephens
and Anna Cleary

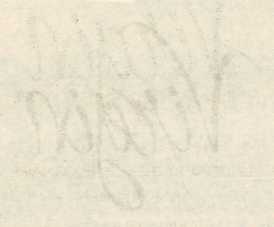

Virgin

UNDONE BY THE BILLIONAIRE

JENNIE LUCAS

SUSAN STEPHENS

ANNA CLEARY

MILLS & BOON

Mills & Boon, an imprint of Harlequin (UK) Limited, Eton House, 18-24 Paradise Road, Richmond, Surrey TW9 1SR

VIRGIN: UNDONE BY THE BILLIONAIRE
© Harlequin Enterprises II B.V./S.à.r.l. 2011

The Innocent's Dark Seduction © Jennie Lucas 2009
Count Maxime's Virgin © Susan Stephens 2008
Untamed Billionaire, Undressed Virgin © Anna Cleary 2008

ISBN: 978 0 263 89664 0

011-0112

Harlequin (UK) policy is to use papers that are natural, renewable and recyclable products and made from wood grown in sustainable forests. The logging and manufacturing processes conform to the legal environmental regulations of the country of origin.

Printed and bound in Spain
by Blackprint CPI, Barcelona

The Innocent's Dark Seduction

JENNIE LUCAS

Jennie Lucas grew up dreaming about faraway lands. At fifteen, hungry for experience beyond the borders of her small Idaho city, she went to a Connecticut boarding school on scholarship. She took her first solo trip to Europe at sixteen, then put off college and travelled around the US, supporting herself with jobs as diverse as gas station cashier and newspaper advertising assistant.

At twenty-two she met the man who would be her husband. After their marriage, she graduated from Kent State with a degree in English. Seven years after she started writing, she got the magical call from London that turned her into a published author.

Since then life has been hectic, with a new writing career and a sexy husband and two babies under two, but she's having a wonderful (albeit sleepless) time. She loves immersing herself in dramatic, glamorous, passionate stories. Maybe she can't physically travel to Morocco or Spain right now, but for a few hours a day, while her children are sleeping, she can be there in her books.

Jennie loves to hear from her readers. You can visit her website at www.jennielucas.com, or drop her a note at jennie@jennielucas.com

To the Watermill girls—Rachael, Carol, Becks, Susan, Francesca, Rachel, Kerstin and, most of all, Sharon Kendrick— in memory of that fabulous week we hatched story plots, drank wine and ate chocolate during the creative writing workshop in Posara, Italy.
You guys rock.

CHAPTER ONE

SPARKLING white lights twinkled beneath the soaring, frescoed ceilings of the grand ballroom of the Cavanaugh Hotel. All the glitterati of New York were sipping champagne, gorgeous in tuxedos and elaborate gowns for the Black and White Ball, hosted by the illustrious—and mysterious—Countess Lia Villani.

"This isn't going to be as easy as you think," Roark's old friend whispered as they moved through the crowd. "You don't know what she's like. She's beautiful. Willful."

"Beautiful or willful, she's just a woman," Roark Navarre replied, raking back his black hair with a jet-lagged yawn. "She'll give me what I want."

Casually Roark straightened the platinum cuff links of his tuxedo as he looked around the packed ballroom. His own grandfather had once tried to force him to live in this wealthy, stuffy, gold-plated cage. He still couldn't believe he was back in the city. Roark had spent the past fifteen years building massive land projects overseas, most recently in Asia, and he'd never thought he would come back.

But this was the largest piece of land in Manhattan to come on the market in a generation. The five sky-scrapers Roark planned to build would be his legacy.

So he'd been furious when he heard Count Villani had beaten him to it. Fortunate for Roark the canny Italian aristocrat had died two weeks ago. He allowed himself a grim smile. It was lucky indeed that Roark was now dealing with the count's young widow instead. Though she still seemed determined to follow her husband's last wishes and spend most of his enormous fortune to create a public park in New York, the young gold digger would soon change her mind.

She would succumb to Roark's desires. Just like every woman.

"She's probably not even here," Nathan tried again. "Since the count died…"

"Of course she's here," Roark said. "She wouldn't miss her own charity ball."

But hearing the awed whispers of the countess's name around them, Roark wondered for the first time if she might be some small challenge. If he might actually have to make an effort to get her to accede to his demands.

An intriguing thought.

"There are rumors," Nathan whispered as he followed Roark through the crowds, "that the old count died in her bed of too much pleasure. His heart couldn't take it."

Roark gave a derisive laugh. "Pleasure has nothing to do with it. The man was sick for months. My heart will be fine. Believe me."

"You haven't met her. You don't know. Christ." Nathan Carter wiped his forehead. His old friend from Alaska was vice president in charge of Navarre Ltd.'s North American holdings. He was normally cool and confident. It shocked Roark to see him look so nervous now. "She's hosting this benefit to raise money for the park. Why do you think she'll sell the land to you?"

"Because I know her type," Roark ground out. "She sold her body to marry the count, didn't she? He might have wanted to leave the world with one magnificent charitable act to make up for years of ruthless business deals, but now he's dead she'll want to cash in. She might appear like some kind of do-gooder, but I know a gold digger when I see…"

His voice trailed off as he focused on a woman entering the ballroom. He sucked in his breath as he watched her descend the sweeping stairs.

Lustrous black hair curled over pale, bare shoulders. Her eyes were hazel green, the color of a shaded forest, fringed with black lashes. She wore a white gown that displayed the hourglass shape of her curvaceous body to perfection, sleeveless and tight over her breasts, the skirts widening out into a mermaid shape below her knees. She had the face of an angel, but with a bite: blood-red lips stood out starkly, rich and full and delectable, luring a man's kiss.

Strangely shaken, Roark breathed, "Who is that?"

Nathan glanced behind him and gave a sardonic smile. "That, my friend, is the merry widow."

"The widow…" Roark looked back at her. The

woman was the most beautiful he'd ever seen. Curvy, saintly, wicked. She was a cross between Rita Hayworth and Angelina Jolie. For the first time in Roark's life, he fully understood the ramifications of the word *bombshell*.

Maybe there was something to the rumors that the old count died in her bed of too much pleasure.

Roark stared at her, stunned. He'd had many women in his life. He'd seduced them easily across every continent. But at this moment it was as if he'd never seen a woman before.

Woman?

He swallowed. Countess Lia Villani was a *goddess*.

It had been too long since he'd felt like this. Too long since he'd been so intrigued—or aroused. He'd crashed the countess's party to convince her to sell him the land. The sudden thought came to him: if she was receptive to his proposal to sell him the land for a huge amount of money, perhaps she would be equally receptive to the suggestion that she share his bed to seal the bargain?

But he wasn't the only man who wanted her. Not by a long shot.

Roark watched as a white-haired man in a sleek tuxedo hurried up the sweeping steps to her side. Others, not quite so bold, stood watching her from a distance. Already the wolves were circling.

And it wasn't just her beauty that drew every eye in the room, the longing, wistful gazes of every man, the envy of every woman's annoyed glare. She had power in the dignity of her bearing, in the cool glance she gave her new suitor. In the teeth she flashed in a smile that didn't meet her eyes.

Wolves circling?

She was a she-wolf herself. This countess wasn't some weak simpering virgin or clinging, cloying debutante. She was powerful. She wielded her beauty and will like a force of nature.

And Roark suddenly wanted her with an intensity that shocked him.

With one glance the woman set fire to his blood. As she moved down the stairs, her curvaceous body swaying with each step, he could already imagine her arching naked in his bed. Gasping out his name with those pouty red lips as he plundered her full breasts and made her tremble and writhe beneath his touch.

This woman that every other man wanted, Roark would take.

Along with the property, of course.

"I am so sorry for your loss, Countess," Andrew Oppenheimer said earnestly, bending over to kiss her hand.

"Thank you." Numbly, Countess Lia Villani stared down at the older man. She wished herself back at Villa Villani, mourning quietly in her husband's overgrown rose garden, enshrouded by medieval stone walls. But she'd no choice but to attend the benefit she and Giovanni had spent the past six months planning. He would have wanted her to be here. The park would be his legacy, as well as her family's. It would be twenty-six acres of trees and grass and playgrounds, in eternal remembrance of the people she'd loved.

They were all dead now. First her father, then her sister, then her mother. Now her husband. And in spite of the warm summer night outside, Lia's heart felt as cold and unbeating as if she'd been lowered into the frozen ground with her family long ago.

"We'll find some way to cheer you up, I hope." Andrew stood back from her, still holding her hand gently.

Lia forced herself to form her mouth in the semblance of a smile. She knew he was just trying to be kind. He was one of the park trust's biggest donors. The day after Giovanni had died, he'd written her a check for fifty thousand dollars.

Strange how, in the past two weeks, so many men had suddenly decided to write large checks for the benefit of the park.

Andrew held on to her hand, not allowing her to easily pull away. "Allow me to get you some champagne."

"Thank you, but no." She looked away. "I appreciate your kindness, but I really must greet my other guests."

The ballroom was packed with people; everyone had come. Lia could hardly believe that the Olivia Hawthorne Park in the Far West Side was going to become a reality. The twenty-six acres of railyards and broken-down warehouses would be transformed into a place of beauty, right across the street from where her sister had died. In the future, other kids staying at St. Ann's Hospital would look out their windows and see a playground and acres of green grass. They'd hear the wind through the trees and the laughter of playing children. They'd feel *hope*.

What was Lia's own grief and pain compared to that? She pulled her hand out of his clasp. "I must go."

"Won't you allow me to escort you?" he asked.

"No, I really—"

"Let me stay by your side tonight, Countess. Let me support you in your grief. I know it must be hard on you to be here. Do me the honor of allowing me to escort you, and I will double my donation to the park. Triple it—"

"She said no," a man's deep voice said. "She doesn't want you."

Lia looked up with an intake of breath. A tall, broad-shouldered man stood at the base of the stairs. He had dark hair, tanned skin and a hard, muscular shape beneath his perfectly cut tuxedo. And even as he spoke to Andrew, he looked only at her.

He had a gleam in his dark, expressive eyes that made her feel strangely hot all over.

Warmth. Something she hadn't felt in weeks, in spite of the June weather.

And this was different. No man's gaze had ever burned her like this.

"Do I know you?" she whispered.

He gave her a lazy, smug smile. "Not yet."

"I don't know who you are," Andrew interrupted coldly, "but the countess is with me—"

"Could you go and get me some champagne, please, Andrew?" she said, turning to him with a bright smile. "Would you mind?"

"No, of course I'd be delighted, Countess." He gave the stranger a dark look. "But what about him?"

"Please, Andrew." She placed her hand on his slender wrist. "I'm very thirsty."

"Of course," Andrew said with dignity, and went down the stairs toward the waiters carrying flutes of champagne.

With a deep breath, Lia clenched her hands into fists and turned back to the intruder.

"You have exactly one minute to talk before I call security," she said, walking down the stairs toward him, facing him head-on. "I know the guest list. And I don't know you."

But when she stood next to him on the marble floor, she realized how powerfully built the dark stranger truly was. At five-seven, she was hardly petite, but he had at least seven inches and seventy pounds over her.

And even more powerful than his body was the way the man looked at her. His gaze never moved from hers. She found herself unable to look away from the intensity of his dark eyes.

"It's true you don't know me. Yet." He moved closer, looking down at her with an arrogant masculine smile. "But I've come to give you what you desire."

"Oh?" Struggling to control the force of heat spreading through her body, Lia raised her chin. "And just what do you think I desire?"

"Money, Countess."

"I have money."

"You're spending most of your dead husband's fortune on this foolish charitable endeavor." He gave her a sardonic smile. "A shame to waste money after you worked so hard to get your hands on it."

He was insulting her at her own party! Calling her a gold digger! And the fact that it was partially true…

She fought back tears at the slight to Giovanni's memory then looked at the stranger with every ounce of haughtiness she possessed. "You don't know me. You don't know anything about me."

"Soon I'll know everything." Reaching forward, he gently ran a finger along the edge of her jawline and whispered, "Soon I'll have you in my bed."

Men had said such ridiculous things to her before, but this time she couldn't scorn the arrogance of his words. Not when the brief touch of his fingertip against her skin caused a riot of sensation to sear her whole body.

"I'm not for sale," she whispered.

He lifted her chin. "You'll be mine, Countess. You'll want me, as I want you."

She'd heard about sexual attraction, but thought she'd lost her chance to experience it. Thought herself too cold, too grief stricken, too…numb.

Feeling his hand on her was like a burst of hot sunlight, causing warmth and light to sparkle prisms of diamonds across her frozen body. Warmth unfurled in her. Melted her.

Against her will, she moved closer.

"Want you? That's ridiculous," she said hoarsely, her heart pounding. "I don't even know you."

"You will."

He took her hand in his own, and she felt the strange

warmth racing up her fingertips and her arm. To her breasts and the core of her body.

She'd been so cold for so long. Outside, the streets of New York were sweltering in the first real heat wave of the summer. Back at her adopted home in Tuscany, the high mountains were warm and lush and green. But for Lia time had stopped in January, when she'd first learned of Giovanni's illness. Since then, in her heart, the ice and snow had only risen higher and higher, burying her in its cold waves.

Now she felt the dark stranger's heat almost painfully. Desire struck her with the sharpness of its heat, and blood rushed through her with a sudden burning intensity and throbbing pain, as frozen limbs came back to life.

"Who are you?" she whispered.

He pulled her slowly into his arms and looked down at her, his face inches from her own.

"I'm the man who's taking you home with me tonight."

CHAPTER TWO

HAVING his larger hand wrapped around her own caused a seismic boom to spread shock waves through Lia's body. As he pulled her into his arms, she felt his hands touch her back above her gown. Felt the brush of his sleek tuxedo against her bare skin, felt the hardness of his body against her own.

Her breath suddenly came in short, quick little gasps. She looked up at him, bewildered by her overwhelming sensation and need. Her lips parted, and…and…

And she wanted to go with him. Anywhere.

"Here's your champagne, Countess." Andrew's sudden return broke the spell. Scowling at the dark stranger, he barged between them and gently placed a Baccarat flute into her hand.

Across the room Lia suddenly saw the other board members of the park trust trying to get her attention. Saw discreet little waves, donors heading her way. Realized that three hundred people were watching her, waiting to talk to her.

She could hardly believe she'd actually considered

running off with a stranger to heaven knows where, and doing heaven knows what.

Clearly grief had taken a toll on her sanity!

"Excuse me." She pulled away from the stranger, desperate to escape the intoxicating force of him. She raised her chin. "I must greet my guests. My *invited* guests," she added pointedly.

"Don't worry." The sardonic heat in the man's dark eyes caused a flush to spread down her body. "I'm here as the guest of someone you *did* invite."

Meaning he was here with another woman? At the same moment he'd very nearly convinced Lia to leave with him? She tightened her hands into fists. "Your date won't be pleased to see you here with me."

He gave her a lazy, predatory smile. "I'm not here with a date. And I'll be leaving with you."

"You're wrong about that," she flashed defiantly.

"Countess?" Andrew Oppenheimer's lip curled into a snarl as he glared at the other man. "May I escort you away from this…person?"

"Thank you." Putting her hand on Andrew's arm, Lia allowed him to steer her toward the many well-heeled, elegantly dressed socialites and stockbrokers.

But as Lia sipped Dom Perignon and pretended to smile and enjoy their chatter—recognizing every park trust donor, knowing every person, their income and their place in society—she couldn't block out her awareness of the dark stranger. No matter where he was in the enormous hotel ballroom, she always felt his presence.

Without looking around, she felt his gaze on her and knew exactly where he was.

Filled with a strange, humming tension, she felt her reason start to melt like an icicle dripping water in the sun.

She'd always heard that desire could be bewildering and destructive. That passion could destroy a woman's sanity and cause her to make ridiculous choices that made no sense. But she'd never understood it.

Until now.

Her marriage had been one of friendship, not passion. At eighteen, she'd married a family friend she respected, a man who'd been kind to her. She'd never once been tempted to betray him with another.

At twenty-eight, Lia was still a virgin. And at this point in her life, she'd assumed she would stay a virgin till she died.

In some ways, it had been a blessing not to feel anything. After losing everyone she'd ever cared about, all she'd wanted was to remain numb for the rest of her life.

But now…

She felt the tall, dark stranger every instant. As she made her opening speech on the dais, thanking her donors and guests with a champagne toast while tuxedoed men hovered around her like sharks, all she could feel was the stranger's hot glance throbbing through her veins.

Making her feel alive against her will.

He was handsome, but not with the dignified elegance that Andrew and the other New York blue bloods had. He didn't have the milk-fed look of someone born with a silver spoon in his mouth. No.

In his midthirties, muscular and rough, he had the look of a hardened warrior. Ruthless, even cruel.

A shiver went through her. A liquid yearning in her veins that she fought with all her might, telling herself it was the result of exhaustion. Illusion. The trick of too much champagne, too many tears and not enough sleep.

But when the guests all sat down to their assigned seats for dinner, she looked again, and realized the stranger had disappeared. All the intense emotion that had been singing through her veins like crescendoing music abruptly ended.

She told herself that she was glad. He'd made her feel strange and uneven and half-drunk.

But where was he?

Why had he gone?

Dinner ended, and a new dread distracted her. The emcee, a prominent local land developer, went to the dais with his gavel.

"Now, the fun part of the night," he said with a grin. "The auction you've all been waiting for. The first item up for bid…"

He started the fund-raiser with a 1960s crocodile Hermès bag that had once been owned by Princess Grace herself. Lia listened to society mavens placing enthusiastic bids around her. The increasingly astronomical bids should have delighted Lia. Every penny donated tonight would go to the park trust, for playground equipment and landscaping costs.

But as she heard the items get auctioned off one by one, she felt only a trickle of building fear.

"It's a perfect idea," Giovanni had said with a weak laugh when the party planner had first suggested it. Even from his sickbed, he'd placed his trembling hand over Lia's. "No one will be able to resist you, my dear. You must do it."

And even though Lia had hated the idea, she'd eventually agreed. Because Giovanni had asked her.

She'd never thought his illness would take a sudden turn for the worse. She hadn't expected that she would be here to face this all alone.

One by one the auction items sold. The dress-circle box at the Vienna Opera Ball. The month-long stay at a Hamptons beach estate. The vintage 1966 Shelby Cobra 427 in pristine condition.

And every punch of the gavel caused the tension to heighten inside her. Getting closer and closer to the final item for sale…

After the twenty-carat Cartier diamond earrings were sold for $90,000, Lia heard the crack of the gavel. It was like the final blow of a guillotine.

"Now," the emcee said gleefully, "we come to our last item up for bid. A very special item indeed."

A spotlight fell on Lia where she stood alone on the marble ballroom floor. A titter rose from the guests, who'd all heard whispers of this open secret. She felt the eager eyes of the men, the envious glares of the women. And she longed more than anything to be back in her cloistered Italian rose garden, far from all this.

Oh, Giovanni, she thought. *What have you left me to?*

"One man will win the opening dance tonight with

our own charming hostess, Countess Villani. The bidding starts at $10,000—"

He'd barely gotten the words out before men started shouting out their bids.

"Ten thousand," Andrew began.

"I'll pay twenty," a pompous old man thundered.

"Twenty-five," cried a teenage boy, barely out of boarding school.

"Forty thousand dollars for a dance with the countess!" shouted a fortysomething Wall Street tycoon.

The bidding continued upward in slow increments, and Lia felt her cheeks burn and burn. But the more humiliated she felt, the straighter she stood. This was to earn money for her sister's park, the only thing she had left in her life that she believed in, and, damn it, she would smile big and dance with the highest bidder, no matter who the man was. She would laugh at his jokes and be charming even if it killed her—

"A million dollars," a deep voice cut in.

A shocked hush fell over the crowd.

Lia turned with a gasp. The dark stranger!

His eyes burned her.

No, she thought desperately. She'd just barely recovered from being in his arms. She couldn't be close to him like that again, not when touching him burned through her, body and soul!

The emcee squinted to see who'd made such an outlandish bid. When he saw the man, he gulped. "Okay! That's the bid to beat! A million dollars! A million, going once…"

Lia cast around a wide, desperate glance at all the men who'd so eagerly been fighting over her the moment before. Wouldn't any of them meet the offer?

But the men looked crestfallen. Andrew Oppenheimer just clenched his jaw, looking coldly furious. But the last bid before the stranger's had been a hundred thousand dollars. A hundred thousand to a million was too big a leap, even for the multimillionaires around her.

"A million going twice…"

She gave a pleading smile at the very richest—and very oldest—men. But they glumly shook their heads. Either the price was too high, or…was it possible they were afraid of challenging the stranger?

Who was this man? She'd never seen him before tonight. How was it possible that a man this wealthy could crash her party in New York, and she'd have no idea who he was?

"Sold! The first dance with the countess, for a million dollars. Sir, you may collect your prize."

The dark eyes of the stranger held her own as he crossed the ballroom. The other men who'd bid for Lia fell silent, fell back, as he passed. Far taller and more broad-shouldered than the others, he wore his dark power like a shadow against his body.

But Lia wouldn't allow any man to bully her. Whatever she felt on the inside, she wouldn't show her weakness. He obviously thought she was a gold digger. He thought he could buy her.

You'll be mine, Countess. You'll want me as I want you.

She would soon disabuse him of that notion. She lifted her chin as he approached.

"Do not think that you own me," she said scornfully. "You've bought a three-minute dance, nothing more—"

For answer, he swept her up in his strong arms. The force of his touch was so intense and troubling that her sentence ended in a gasp. He looked down at her as he led her onto the dance floor.

"I have you now." His sensual mouth curved into a smile. "This is just the start."

CHAPTER THREE

THE orchestra started playing, and a singer in a black sequined dress started singing the classic song of romantic yearning, "At Last."

Listening to the passionate lyrics of love long awaited and finally found, Lia's heart hurt in her chest. The handsome stranger spun her out on the dance floor, causing her white mermaid skirt to flare out as she moved. The sensation of his fingers intertwined with her own held her more firmly than chains on her wrists. The electricity of his touch was a hot current that she couldn't escape, even if she'd wanted to.

He pulled her closer against his body. She felt his muscles move beneath his crisp, elegant tuxedo as his body swayed against hers, leading her in the rhythm. She lost all sense of time amidst the sensuality of his body against hers. He smoothly controlled her movements, and his mastery over her caused a tension of longing to build inside her.

Raising one hand to gently move her dark hair off her shoulders, he leaned down to speak in her ear. She felt the whisper of his breath against her neck, causing prickles to spread up and down her body. The flicker of his lips, the tease of his tongue against her sensitive earlobe, ricocheted down her nerve endings.

"You're a beautiful woman, Countess."

She exhaled only when he moved back from her.

"Thank you," she managed. She raised her chin, desperately trying to hide the feelings he was creating in her. "And thank you for your million-dollar donation to the park. Children all over the city will be—"

"I don't give a damn about them," he said, cutting her off. His dark eyes sizzled through hers. "I did it for you."

"For me?" she whispered, feeling her whole body go off-kilter again, growing dizzy as he moved her across the dance floor.

"A million dollars is nothing." He gave a sudden searching look. "I would pay far more than that to get what I want."

"And what do you want?"

"Right now?" He pulled her close, holding her hand entwined with his larger one against his chest. "You, Lia."

Lia.

No man had called her by her first name like that. Acquaintances called her Countess. Giovanni had called her by her full name, Amelia.

Hearing her dance partner's lips caress her name as his hands caressed her body caused a shiver to scatter her soul.

But the heat in his dark eyes was steady. Controlled. As if the overwhelming desire that was ripping her self-control to shreds was nothing more than of passing interest to him. A momentary pleasure in his life that was full of pleasures—like a single sip of champagne, hardly to be noticed in the endless crystal flutes.

But it was new to Lia. It made her knees weak. Made her dizzy, filling her with longing and fear.

He held her tightly, swaying in time to the scorching passion of the song. Lia was dimly aware of all New York society watching them. She could feel the stares, hear the first whispers at the impropriety of this dance. Holding her as he was, without even a sliver of space between them, he held her like a lover.

As if no one in the world mattered to him but her.

She knew she should push him away. She was, after all, a new widow. Allowing him to hold her like this not only disgraced Giovanni's memory, it caused injury to her reputation. And yet his powerful control over her senses caused her body to betray her mind's commands.

She tried to put some distance between them.

She could not.

She didn't even know this man, but something about the way he held her made Lia feel she'd been waiting for this moment all her life.

He spoke in a low voice for her ears only. "I knew it from the moment I saw you."

"What?" she whispered.

"What it would feel like to touch you."

She trembled. Did he know what he made her feel? Did he have any idea how he affected her?

She forced herself to toss her head, to act as if nothing were wrong. "I feel nothing."

"You're lying." He ran his hand down her glossy black hair, stroking the bare skin of her shoulders.

The tremble deepened, making her knees shake. She had to get ahold of herself. Before the situation was too far out of her control. Before she was utterly lost! "This is just a dance, nothing more."

He stopped suddenly on the dance floor. "Prove your words."

All the bravado left her when she saw the intent in his eyes. Here, on the dance floor, he meant to kiss her—staking his claim of possession for the entire world to see.

"No," she gasped.

Ruthlessly he lowered his lips to hers.

His kiss was demanding and hungry. It seared her to the core. His lips moved against her own, suffusing her with his heat. Against her will, she fell against him, surrendering to the sweet languorous stroke of his tongue.

She wanted him. Wanted *this*.

She wanted it like a drowning woman wanted air.

As she felt him move against her, his strong hands moving against the soft skin of her naked back, a low moan escaped her. His power and warmth enveloped her as his sensual lips seduced her, allowing her to hold nothing back.

How long had she been drowning?

How long had she been all but dead?

Her breaths came in little shallow gasps as his kiss deepened. She heard the shocked hiss and jealous mutters of the crowds around them. "Crikey," one man muttered, "I would have paid a million for *that*."

But as Lia tried to pull away, he only held her more forcefully, plundering her lips until she again sagged in his arms. She forgot her name. Forgot everything but her desire to give anything—anything at all—to keep his heat and fire hard against her. She wrapped her arms around his neck, pulling him close against her body as she kissed him back with the ravenous hunger of fresh new life—

Then he released her, and her body instantly fell back into the icy breath of winter.

Opening her eyes, she looked into the face of the man who'd so cruelly brought her to life only to discard her. She expected to see smug, masculine arrogance. After all, he'd amply proven his point.

Instead he looked shocked. Almost as dazed as she felt. He gave his head a slight shake, as if clearing the fog from his mind.

Then his expression again became arrogant and ruthless. Leaving Lia to wonder if she'd just imagined a momentary bewilderment to match her own.

She touched her still-throbbing lips in shock. Oh, my God, what was wrong with her? With Giovanni not two weeks in his grave!

With the commanding force of the handsome stranger's kiss, he'd made her forget everything—her grief, her pain, her emptiness—and surrender herself completely. It was like nothing she'd ever experienced before. And even at this moment she wanted more of him. Thirsted for him like a woman abandoned in the desert...

She took another short breath, gasping for air, for sanity and control.

Putting her hands on her head in despair, Lia backed away from him. "What have you done?" she whispered.

His dark gaze sharpened on her own. His eyes were hot enough to melt glass, skewering her heart. *Burning her.*

"The dance isn't done." The deep fiber of his voice commanded her, compelling her to return to his arms.

"Stay away from me!" Turning too quickly in a jerky, uneven movement, she nearly slipped on the hem of her white satin gown in her desperation to flee. Cheeks aflame, she ran through the crowded ballroom, leaving behind the winter fairyland of black lattice trees and twinkling white lights.

She raced past the shocked guests, past her horrified society friends, past everyone who tried to grab her, who tried to ask questions or offer back-handed sympathy.

She had to escape. Had to get away from the dark stranger and all the unwilling tumult of scandalous desires he caused within her.

Glancing back, she saw him in grim pursuit.

And she didn't hesitate. Didn't think. Kicking off her four-inch stiletto heels, she just *ran.* Ran down the hallway of the hotel, ran until her whole body burned, as she hadn't done since her school days when she'd competed fiercely on the track team.

And yet still he gained on her! How was it possible?

Because she wasn't the lithe, fit girl she'd been ten years ago, she realized. Years of inactivity in Italy, of long days sitting by Giovanni's bedside, and nights of crying alone in her bed with a broken heart, were finally catching up with her.

And so was the stranger.

Panting, she dashed into the hotel lobby. Wealthy tourists in polo shirts and chic little summer dresses stared at her with their mouths agape as she stumbled across the marble floor and pushed violently out through the revolving door into the summery violet of dusk.

The doorman cried out when she nearly knocked him over. "Hey!"

"I'm sorry!" she cried back at him, but she didn't stop. She couldn't. Not with the man so close behind her.

In the distance she could see a subway entrance. She ran for it with all her might.

She was fast. But he was faster. She heard the heavy echo of his footsteps on the sidewalk behind her. She weaved through a crowd of tourists browsing the shop windows along Fifth Avenue. She saw a taxi pull in front of Tiffany's, right behind a dog walker surrounded by dogs of all sizes.

She leaped over the man's tangled leashes like a hurdle. She heard the rip of her white satin gown as she landed on the other side. Panting, she flung herself into the taxi over the back of the exiting passenger.

Behind her, she heard the stranger curse aloud, caught up in leashes, dogs, and tourists loaded with shopping bags.

"Go!" she shouted at the taxi driver.

"Where, lady?"

"Anywhere!" Looking back through the window at

the approaching stranger, she gasped and held up the hundred-dollar bill she always tucked in her bra. "There's someone following me—get me out of here!"

The taxi driver glanced in the rearview mirror, saw the hundred-dollar bill and the panicked expression on her face, then stomped on the gas pedal. The car roared away, its tires scattering water from the nearby gutter as they ducked into the evening traffic.

Turning around to look out the back window, Lia saw the diminishing figure of the dark stranger behind her. Wet with water, he stared after her in repressed fury, his mouth a grim line.

She'd escaped him. She nearly cried with relief.

Then she caught her breath and realized she'd just fled her own party. What had she been so afraid of? What?

His fire.

Her body shook with suppressed longing as she sank her head against her hands…and really cried.

CHAPTER FOUR

ROARK returned to the ballroom empty-handed, furious and soaking wet. He took a towel from a beverage cart and grimly wiped the grimy water from his neck and the shirt and lapels of his tuxedo.

She'd gotten away.

How was it possible?

He scowled in fury. He'd never had any woman turn him down before for anything. He'd never had any woman even *pretend* to resist.

Lia Villani had not only resisted him, she'd outrun him.

Crumpling the wet towel angrily, he tossed it on the empty tray of a passing waiter. Clenching his jaw, he looked across the ballroom.

He saw Nathan on the crowded dance floor, swaying with a plump-cheeked girl with honey-blond hair.

Roark ground his teeth. He'd been chasing the fleet-footed countess all over Midtown, nearly breaking his neck and getting soaked in the process, while Nathan was flirting on the dance floor?

His old friend must have felt his glower across the

ballroom, because he turned and saw his boss. At the expression on Roark's face, he excused himself from his pretty blond dance partner, kissing her hand after walking her off the dance floor with visible reluctance.

When Nathan was close enough to see Roark's wet hair and tuxedo, his jaw dropped. "What happened to you?"

He ground his jaw. "It doesn't matter."

"That was quite the show you put on with the countess," Nathan said brightly. "I hardly know which scandalized everyone more—the million dollar bid, your make-out session on the dance floor, or the way you both ran out of here like you were in some kind of race. I didn't expect you to return so quickly. She must have agreed to sell you the property in record time."

"I didn't ask her," Roark snapped.

Nathan's jaw fell open. "You paid a million dollars to get her alone on the dance floor, and you didn't even ask her?"

"I will." He furiously pulled off his wet tuxedo jacket, tucking it over his arm. "I promise you."

"Roark, we're running out of time. Once the deed is signed over to the city—"

"I know," Roark said. He opened his phone and dialed. "Lander. Countess Villani left the Cavanaugh Hotel in a yellow cab five minutes ago. Medallion number 5G31. Find her."

He snapped the phone shut. He could feel the elite families of New York edging closer to him. Most of them looked at him with bewilderment and awe.

Who was he? their glances seemed to say. Who was

this stranger who would bid a million dollars for a dance…and then ruthlessly kiss the woman that every other man wanted?

He tightened his jaw. He was a man who would soon build seventy-story skyscrapers on the Far West Side. A man who would start a new business district in Manhattan, second only to Wall Street and Midtown.

"I know you."

Roark turned to see the white-haired blue blood who'd brought Lia her champagne. He had to be in his sixties, but powerful and hearty still. "I know you," he repeated, furrowing his brow. "You're Charles Kane's grandson."

"My name," Roark stared at him coldly, "is Navarre."

"Ah, yes," he mused, "I remember your mother. She had that regrettable elopement. A trucker, wasn't it? Your grandfather could never forgive—"

"My father was a good man," Roark said. "He worked hard every day of his life and didn't judge anyone by the money they made or the school they attended. My grandfather hated him for that."

"But you should have been at his funeral. He was your grandfather—"

"He never wanted to be." Folding his arms, Roark turned away from the man dismissively.

The emcee of the auction hurried forward to get his attention. Roark recognized Richard Brooks, a Brooklyn land developer who'd once worked for a Navarre subsidiary.

"Thank you so much for your bid, Mr. Navarre," the

emcee gushed. "The Olivia Hawthorne Park Foundation thanks you for your generous donation."

Just what Roark needed—a reminder that he'd just pledged a million dollars toward the very project he was trying to destroy! His lip curled into a snarl. "My pleasure."

"Will you be in New York for long, Mr. Navarre?"

"No," he said sharply, and before the man could ask him any more questions, he pulled a checkbook from his tuxedo coat pocket and swiftly wrote a check for a million dollars. He held out the check, not allowing a single bit of emotion to appear on his face.

"Oh, thank you, Mr. Navarre," the man said, bowing as he backed away. "Thank you very much."

Roark nodded, his face cold. He hated these little obsequious toadies. Fearing him. Wanting his money, attention or time. He glanced at all the women staring at him with frank longing and admiration. Women were the worst of all.

Except for Lia Villani. She hadn't tried to lure him.

She'd run away.

Faster and more determined than Roark, she'd managed to get away from him in spite of his best efforts.

Why had she run?

Just because he'd kissed her?

That kiss. He'd seen how it had affected her—damn close to the way it had affected him. It had shaken him to the core. It shook him still.

He hadn't intended to kiss her. He'd meant to convince her to sell him the property before he seduced her. But something in her defiance, in the way she'd resisted him as they danced, had taunted him. Something in the way she'd tossed her long, lustrous black hair. In the way she'd licked those full red lips, moving her curvaceous body to the music, had maddened his blood.

She'd defied him. And he'd responded.

It was just a kiss, nothing more. He'd kissed many women in his life.

But he'd never felt anything like *that.*

So? He argued with himself. Even if it was desire stronger than any he'd known, the ending would still be the same. He would take her to his bed, satiate his lust and swiftly forget her. Just like always.

And yet…

He scowled.

Somehow Lia Villani's beauty and seductive power had made him forget the most important thing on earth—business. He'd never forgotten it before. Certainly not for a woman. And because of that mistake, he might now lose the most important deal of his life.

Nathan had been right all along. Roark had been underestimating the countess. She was far more powerful than he'd ever imagined.

But instead of being furious, Roark was suddenly intoxicated by the thought of the hunt. The takedown.

He would take her property.

Then he would take *her.*

His body hurt with need for her. He couldn't forget how she'd trembled in his arms when he kissed her. Couldn't forget the softness of her breasts against his chest, the curve of her hip against his groin. Couldn't forget the shape of her. *The taste of her.*

He had to have her. He wanted her so badly that it made his body shake.

His cell phone rang. He snapped it open.

"Lander," he said, "give me the good news."

Lia slammed the door of her silver Aston-Martin Vanquish convertible with a weary thump. Every muscle in her body ached. It had been a long twelve hours. She'd stopped at her town house in New York just long enough to get her passport and change into a knit dress and a cashmere shawl. She'd taken the first flight out of JFK Airport, connecting first in Paris then in Rome, before she'd reached Pisa. Even flying first class, the trip had been exhausting and long.

Maybe because she'd spent the whole time crying. Looking over her shoulder, half expecting the man to pursue her.

But he hadn't. She was still alone.

So why didn't that make her feel happier?

Looking up at the medieval castle on the edge of the forested mountain, she took a deep breath. But she was home. The medieval Italian castle, carefully refurbished over fifty years and turned into a luxurious villa, had been Giovanni's favorite retreat. Over the past ten years, it had become Lia's home, as well.

"Salve, Contessa," her housekeeper cried from the doorway. Tears shone in her eyes as she added in accented English, "Welcome home."

Welcome home. Walking through the front door of the Villa Villani, Lia waited for the feelings of solace and comfort to rush over her as always.

But nothing happened. Just emptiness. Loneliness.

A fresh wave of grief washed over her as she set down her bag. *"Grazie,* Felicita."

Lia walked slowly through the empty rooms. The valuable antique furniture blended with the more-modern pieces. Every room had been scrubbed clean. Every window was wide-open, letting in the bright sunshine and fresh morning air of the Italian mountains. And yet she felt cold. She might have been enveloped in a snowdrift...or a shroud.

The memory of the stranger's kiss ripped through her, and she touched her lips, still remembering how his touch had seared her last night. How his warmth had burned her with a deep fire. And she felt a sudden sharp pang of regret.

She'd been a coward to run away from him. From her feelings. From *life...*

But she would never see him again. She didn't even know the man's name. She'd made her choice. The safe, respectable choice. And now she would live with it.

She barely felt the hot water against her skin as she took a shower. She dried off with a towel and put on a simple white smock dress. She brushed her hair. She washed her teeth. And she felt dead inside.

The loneliness of the big castle, where so many generations had lived and died before she was born, echoed inside her. As she went into her bedroom, she glanced down at Giovanni's diamond wedding ring on her finger.

She'd just kissed another man wearing her dead husband's ring. Shame ricocheted through her soul like a bullet.

Tears threatened her as she briefly closed her eyes. "I'm sorry," she whispered aloud, as if Giovanni were still alive and in the same room to hear her. "I never should have let it happen."

She looked back down at the diamonds sparkling on her finger. She didn't deserve to wear it, she thought with despair. Slowly she pulled the ring off her finger.

Going into Giovanni's old bedroom down the hall from hers, she opened the safe behind the painting of Giovanni's beloved first wife. Lia tucked the ring inside the safe and closed the door.

After locking the safe, she stared at the pretty woman in the painting. The first *contessa* was laughing, sitting on a swing and kicking her feet. Giovanni had loved Magdalena so much. It was why he hadn't minded marrying Lia. He'd said he already knew he would never love again. He'd loved a woman once, and he would love her forever.

That kind of love was something Lia had never experienced—and never would. She took a deep breath. She felt cold, so cold.

Would she ever feel warm again?

"I'm sorry," she whispered one last time. "I didn't mean to forget you." And she went outside into the sunlight of the rose garden.

The riotous multitude of roses in red, pink and yellow filled the space, surrounded by ancient stone walls that were seven feet high. This had been Giovanni's favorite place. He'd grown the roses himself. He'd spent hours carefully taming and tending the garden.

But the garden had been neglected for months. The flowers were now overgrown and half-wild. The blooms now reached up into the warm blue sky, some as tall as the stone walls that had been built from the ancient Roman foundations.

She leaned forward to smell one of the enormous yellow roses. Yellow for memory. No wonder it had the strongest scent. She missed Giovanni's warmth, his kindness. She felt so guilty that she'd forgotten him, even for a moment. For the length of a kiss…

She closed her eyes, breathing in the fragrance, listening to the wind in the trees above, feeling the warmth of the Tuscan sun on her skin.

"Hello, Lia," a voice said quietly.

She whirled around.

It was him.

His dark eyes gleamed as he stared at her through the wrought-iron gate. Pushing it open, he slowly entered the garden. His black shirt and black jeans stood out starkly against the profusion of colorful half-wild roses. There was a predatory grace in his body as he approached her like a stalking lion. She felt the intensity of his gaze from her fingers to her toes.

Somehow, he was even more handsome here than he'd been in New York. The man was as wild and savage as the forest around them. As unrestrained in his masculine beauty as the sharp-thorned roses.

And they were alone.

He stood between her and the garden door.

This time there would be no taxi. No escape.

She instinctively folded her arms over her chest, trying to stop herself from trembling as she backed away. "How did you find me?"

"It wasn't difficult."

"I didn't invite you here!"

"No?" he said coolly. He reached for her, twining a black tendril of her hair around his finger as his dark eyes caressed her face. "Are you sure?"

She couldn't breathe. Birds sang beyond the medieval stone walls once built to keep invading marauders out. The same walls that now kept her *in*.

"Please leave me," she whispered, shaking with desire for him. For his warmth. For his touch. For the way he made her feel alive again and young and a woman. She licked her dry lips. "I want you to go."

"No," he said. "You don't."

And, lifting her chin, he kissed her.

His lips were so hard and soft and sweet, she could hear the buzz of honeybees in the medieval garden, their secret world hidden behind the crumbling stone walls. The fragrance of overgrown half-wild roses drenched her senses. And she felt dizzy. She was lost, lost in him. *And she didn't want it to ever end.*

He pushed her back against a wall that was warm with sunlight and thick with twisting vines of wisteria. He kissed her again, more forcefully. Teasing her. Taking. Demanding. Seducing…

Giovanni's chaste peck on her forehead at their wedding hadn't prepared her for this. All night on the lonely plane ride across the Atlantic, she'd tried to convince herself that her passionate reaction to the dark stranger's kiss had been a moment of madness, a one-off that could never be repeated. But the pleasure was even greater than before, the sweet agony only increasing with the hard tension of her longing. All her grief and loneliness and pain fell away. There was only the hot demand of his mouth, the pleasurable caress of his hands.

What he wanted he took.

She tried to resist. She really did. But it was like trying to push away Christmas or happiness or joy. Like trying to push away life itself.

Though she knew she shouldn't, she wanted him.

She returned his kisses hesitantly, then with a hunger that matched his own. She trembled at the brazen force of her own desire as he encouraged her every tremulous touch, murmuring appreciation at her slightest attempt at a caress.

She felt him pull off her little white shift dress, then her bra. She gasped as her naked breasts were bathed in the warm glow of sun.

With a groan, he lowered his mouth to suckle her nipple, and she cried out. Cupping her other breast in his hand, he licked and stroked her flesh. Caressing her hips, he pulled down her panties, dropping them to the grass.

And she couldn't stop shaking.

"Lia," he said hoarsely. "Ah, Lia. What you do to me…"

He picked her up in his strong arms. She stared up at his handsome face, at the intensity in his deep dark eyes.

She suddenly knew this fire could consume them both.

He gently laid her down on the soft grass. Covering her body with his own, he moved slowly against her. She moaned, wanting something, not even sure what she wanted but wanting it *now*. Unzipping his pants, he spread her naked thighs apart with his own. She felt his hard shaft demanding entrance, and she quivered beneath him, tense and yearning.

He lowered his head to kiss her, his lips and tongue intertwining passionately with her own.

And he filled her with a single deep thrust.

Pain stabbed through her, making her gasp.

He froze, looking down at her, shock rippling over his handsome face.

"How is it possible? You're a *virgin*?"

CHAPTER FIVE

Lia, a virgin?

Roark was in shock.

She was the most beautiful woman he'd ever seen. Every man desired her. She'd been married for ten years. How could she be a virgin?

How was it possible that Countess Lia Villani, the woman whose beauty seduced and entranced men beyond reason, had never been bedded until now?

But there was no mistaking the physical signs. Her earlier hesitation and awkward response to his first kiss, which he had taken as evidence of her pride, were cast in a new light.

Lia was innocent. Or at least, she had been.

Until Roark had possessed her.

A surge went through his blood. As he looked at her lying on the fallen rose petals, her hazel-green eyes so clear and so deep, he felt a strange breathless rush.

The intensity of the feeling reminded him of skydiving. Flying high above the clouds in Alaska, Roark remembered opening the door of the plane. Staring into nothing but air, he'd heard a buzzing in his ears as he threw himself headfirst off the edge.

He'd fallen with the wind howling in his ears, whipping painfully against his skin in a freefall. He'd felt the dizziness and danger as the earth approached at 130 miles an hour.

The adrenaline that ripped through him was the same now.

Lia was dangerous.

More dangerous than he'd ever realized.

But knowing he was the only man who'd ever had her, fierce pride and possessiveness went through him. Dangerous or not, he could not let her go.

He was still hard inside her. He knew he should pull away. He'd never taken any woman's virginity but knew instinctively that it had just changed them both forever. They would always be connected by this, and that scared him.

She licked her full red lips.

"Why didn't you tell me?" he ground out.

"I don't want you to stop," she whispered, reaching up to stroke his cheek with a small trembling hand. Her eyes were as many shades of hazel as the rose vines and soft earth beneath them. "You make me feel warm. I want you inside me…"

He groaned aloud.

He slowly drew back and thrust again inside her, this time more deeply. The pleasure was intense for him, and he had to sharply keep himself in control. He stifled her second gasp with a fierce kiss, seducing away her fear until she melted back in his arms. Until she moaned with pleasure, tossing back her head as he pressed her against the grass. He kissed her throat, sucking on the tender flesh of her ear. Her full breasts bounced softly as he thrust into her, moving with agonizing gentleness.

Holding back like this was killing him…

She cried out, clutching her nails into his back. He heard her intake of breath, felt the building tension of her body. He thrust into her, moving his hips side-to-side against her. He stroked her skin, riding her on the soft green grass, beneath the warm sun and the sweet scent of roses.

Then he heard her harsh gasp. She arched against him with a sharp cry that never seemed to end.

At that, he lost all control. Pushing into her, he thrust just three times before his world exploded in a burst of light.

Beautiful…rare…*angel*.

It was like nothing he'd ever felt before. His eyes remained closed as he held himself inside her, struggling for breath. It seemed to take years before he slowly came back to earth.

When he finally looked down at Lia's beautiful face, her eyes were still closed. Her parted lips turned up sweetly, as if she were still in heaven. He looked down at her naked body, at the full breasts and wide hips and slightly curved belly of a 1940s pin-up girl. She was so lush and impossibly desirable. He could feel himself growing hard again as he looked at her.

Then he realized something. *He hadn't used a condom.* He'd just risked getting her pregnant.

He swore beneath his breath.

Furious at himself, he pulled away from her.

Lia's eyes opened—her luminous hazel eyes with depths that seemed to go on forever. He watched her long, dark lashes flutter against her pale skin with a blush like roses on her cheeks.

He took a deep breath.

"Are you on the Pill?"

She blinked at him. "What?"

"Are you on the Pill?"

She shook her head. "No, why would I be?"

Why indeed? A cold sweat broke out over his body. He stood up and readjusted his clothes, righting his pants over his hips.

He could hardly believe he'd been so stupid.

Lia had some power over him that he didn't understand. How could he have acted so foolishly—as mindless as a rutting bull driven half-mad with the scent of lust.

The overwhelming force of his desire for her felt too dangerous. Too *close.*

He didn't want to care about anyone ever again.

A flash went through him, the memory of red flames, white snow and a desolate black sky. The sobbing. The crash of the fire and crackle of burning timber. Then, worst of all, the silence.

He pushed the thought away. Business. He had to think of business.

He cursed himself under his breath. Damn it, he still hadn't asked her to sell him the New York property!

"The New York property…" he muttered, then stopped.

"What about it?"

Turning his head, he said hoarsely, "How is it possible that you were a virgin? You're a widow. Every man desires you. They say the old count died of pleasure in your bed—"

She stiffened. "That's not true!"

"I know." He lifted her to her feet. Her naked body was a vision before his eyes, and even now, when he should have been satiated, he couldn't stop looking at her. "But you were married. How can you be a virgin?"

"Giovanni was good to me," she whispered. "He was my friend."

"But never your lover."

"No."

And Roark was fiercely glad. He reveled in it.

But why? Why did he care that he'd been her only lover? What difference did it make?

Still naked and dazed in the sunshine of the garden, she took a breath and licked her full red lips. She was so beautiful he ached to take her inside the castle, find a wide bed and enjoy her body again at his leisure. To take his time and show her how long pleasure could last....

Why was she having such a strange effect on him? He took a deep breath, desperate to regain control over his body and his mind. Business. *Ask her about the land!* he ordered himself.

But his mouth wouldn't follow his orders. He couldn't stop looking at her.

It was because she was naked. It had to be. Once she was covered up, he would be able to think again.

Bending to pick up her discarded white dress and panties from the grass, he handed them to her.

"Why did the count marry you, if not for your body?"

Looking dazed and disoriented, she stared at him, clutching the fabric in her hands. "He married me to be kind."

"Right," Roark said sardonically, forcing himself to look away. It was easier to be distant when he couldn't see her or touch her. "That's why men get married. To be *kind*. I had business dealings with Count Villani once or twice. The man was ruthless."

"He was my father's friend." From the corner of his eye, he saw her slip on her dress, pulling up her panties beneath. "My father's shipping company was stolen by a heartless corporate raider, and a few months later he died of a heart attack."

Roark looked at her sharply.

"Giovanni came to L.A. for the funeral," she continued simply. "He saw my sister had no money to pay for her treatment. He saw my mother was mad with grief. And he tried to save us." She shook her head as tears filled her eyes. "But it was too late for them."

A shipping company. Los Angeles. It was all starting to sound too familiar.

The Olivia Hawthorne Park Foundation thanks you for your generous donation.

Roark hadn't paid attention to the name before. Now, a sick feeling went through his chest. "What was your father's name?"

"Why?"

"Humor me."

"Alfred…Alfred Hawthorne."

Roark swore silently.

Just as he'd feared. Her father was the same man who, ten years ago, had mortgaged himself to the teeth trying to fight Roark's hostile takeover of his shipping company. He had heard the man had died a few months later, followed to the grave by his teenage daughter who'd had some kind of brain tumor. Then the mother committed suicide with sleeping pills.

Only their oldest daughter had lived. Amelia.

Lia.

And she'd just given him her virginity.

Roark clenched his hands. She'd only done it because she didn't know his name. By some miracle he'd managed not to tell her. But if she knew…

Once she knew, he wouldn't have a shot in hell of getting her to spit on him to save him from burning to death, much less getting her to sell him the New York property.

"Did you know my father?" she asked softly, looking up at him.

"No." And in a way it was true. He'd never really known the man. He'd just taken his poorly managed company and broken it into parts, destroying the docks and selling the valuable oceanfront property in Long Beach for a brand-new condominium development.

"I wish you had. I think you would have liked each other. Both powerful men, focused on success."

The difference being that Roark always won, while

her father had been a weak failure, a third-generation heir of a company he didn't know how to properly run.

Roark managed not to point this out to her, however.

He had to convince Lia to sell him the New York property before she found out who he was.

Walking away from her, he took some papers out of the black leather briefcase he'd left beside the garden gate. The gate creaked loudly as he closed it and returned to her. "I want you to do something for me."

"What is it?"

"A favor."

"A favor?" she teased, smiling. "A bigger favor than giving you my virginity?"

He gave her his most charming smile in return. "It's a small thing, really." He paused. "Build your park somewhere else besides New York."

Her jaw dropped. "What?"

"Transfer your purchase rights to the property site to me. I will make it worth your while. I'll pay you ten percent over the asking price. Call it a finder's fee." He spread his arms in an expansive gesture. "Build the park in Los Angeles to honor your sister. Let me build skyscrapers in New York."

She looked up into his face, her skin the color of ash. "That's what this was all about? That's why you kissed me in New York? Why you followed me to Italy?"

He ground his jaw. "It wasn't the only reason…."

She shoved his chest, pushing him away very, very hard as she looked wildly over the rose garden. "That's why you paid a million dollars to dance with me at the charity ball." Her eyes glittered as she raised her chin. "That was why you seduced me. Just to get the land from me?"

He was losing the deal. He could feel it slipping through his fingers.

Looking at her, he shook his head. "Of course I want the land. More than you can possibly know. I can build five skyscrapers on that property that will last hundreds of years. The biggest project I've ever done. It'll be my legacy." He took a deep breath. "But that has nothing to do with making love to you. Taking you like this was…a moment of pure insanity." He reached for her, trying to bring her back into his arms, back under his control. "If I'd known you were a virgin…"

"You know everything about me now, don't you?" she said bitterly. "My name. My family. Where I live. And I still know almost nothing about you." Evading his grasp, she clenched her hands into fists. "I don't even know your name."

If she heard his name, all was lost. "What difference does my name make? Think of the deal I'm offering you."

She raised her chin, and her dark-hazel eyes glittered. "I want to know your name, you cold-hearted bastard."

"I'm offering you a fortune." He pushed the land-transfer contract into her hands. "Just look at these numbers…"

"Tell me your name!" she shouted.

And he couldn't lie to her. His honor was more important than anything—even than the deal of a lifetime. He took a deep breath.

"My name," he said quietly, "is Roark Navarre."

CHAPTER SIX

LIA stared at him. "Roark...Navarre?"

She still remembered her father's cry that lovely June morning, long ago. "He's done it, Marisa. Roark Navarre has ruined us." Lia had just graduated from high school and was still reveling in being accepted by Pepperdine, an expensive private university in Malibu she'd attend in the fall. Olivia had just started a promising experimental treatment with a new doctor. And their mother, who always switched so quickly between ecstasy and despair, had been happily painting the distant Santa Monica pier with watercolors on canvas. The California sunshine had been bright and warm against their three-story beach house.

Then her father had come home in the middle of the morning, staggering into her mother's arms as if he'd just received a heavy blow.

"He's done it, Marisa. Roark Navarre has ruined us."

Roark Navarre.

Now Lia whirled on him, trembling and hot with fury. "Your name is Roark Navarre?"

"So you do know me."

"Of course I know you. You destroyed my family!"

"It wasn't deliberate, Lia. It was just business."

"Business," she spat out, tossing her head with a derisive sneer. "Just like it was for the sake of business that you seduced me?"

"Lia, I didn't realize who you were until just now."

"Right." She shook her head furiously. "Why should I believe a word you say? You caused my father to lose his company—"

"He would have lost it to someone, if not to me. Hawthorne was completely inept. A typical third-generation heir bumbling his way through a business he didn't understand."

"How dare you!" She paced, then stopped, covering her mouth with her hands in a horrified gasp. "I let you take my virginity."

"Yes," he said. "Thank you. I enjoyed it very much."

She sucked in her breath, crumpling the contract he'd given her, twisting and strangling it in her hands.

"Get out." She threw the contract at him. It bounced off his chest and fell to the grass. "The land is going to be a park, across the street from the hospital where my sister died. I would die before I let you put skyscrapers on Olivia's park!"

Clenching his jaw, he shook his head. "You're making this personal. It's *business*. If you don't have any fond feelings for me, fine. Take me for every penny you can. Force me to double my offer—"

"It's too late." She suddenly felt the insane urge to

laugh. "Before I left New York, I signed the papers that turned the land irrevocably over to the trust. I sent it by messenger. It's been too late for hours. The property is permanently out of your reach."

She saw something like grief and fury cross his face. She'd hurt him. She'd prevented him from having something he really, really wanted.

And she was glad. She wished she could do more. She wished she could hurt him a fraction of the way he'd hurt her.

"Because of you, my father lost every penny we had," she whispered. "My sister had to go for months without treatment. My mother couldn't take the anguish of losing her husband and her daughter. They all died. And it's your fault!"

"It was your father's fault," he said coldly. "Your father was the failure. He was a fool. A man shouldn't have a wife or children if he can't even take decent care of them—"

Lia slapped him.

Looking shocked, Roark touched his cheek.

She stared up at him with hatred. "Don't you dare call my father a failure." She felt tears rising to her eyes, and she fought them with all her might. She would die before she would let him see her cry! "You seduced me for the sake of skyscrapers that will never, ever love you back. And you call my father a failure? You call him a fool? *He loved us.* He's a better man than you will ever be."

Roark straightened, holding his hands stiffly clenched at his sides. For several seconds their eyes locked. Lia could hear the pant of her own anguished breathing and the sound of the birds overhead, a warm breeze rattling the leafy fullness of the trees.

Then his jaw clenched.

"I've already had your body," he said. "And since it's too late to buy the land, we have nothing else to discuss. Nothing about you is interesting enough to deserve another second of my time." His eyes were like black ice as he tossed back callously, "Let me know if there's a baby, won't you?"

Picking up his briefcase, he turned and left through the garden gate.

Shocked, she listened to the departing sound of his footsteps. It wasn't until she was alone in the rose garden that Lia allowed herself to collapse into sobs. Putting her face in her hands, she fell to her knees on the soft grass and cried. For her family. For herself.

She'd just given her virginity to the man who'd destroyed her family.

Four months after that horrible day they'd lost everything, her father had died of a heart attack in the little two-bedroom Burbank apartment they'd rented after their beach house was sold for debt.

Thank God for Giovanni. Her father's old friend had come from Italy for the funeral. He'd seen eighteen-year-old Lia trying to support her sick younger sister and a mother who was silent and half-mad with grief. The next morning he'd proposed marriage.

"Your father once saved my life in the war, when I was barely older than you. I wish I'd known about your troubles—I wish he'd told me," he'd said with tears in his eyes. "But I can take care of you all now. Marry me, Amelia. Become my countess."

"Marry you?" she'd gasped. As kind as Count Villani was, he was three times her age!

"In name only," he'd clarified, his cheeks turning red. "My wife of fifty years died last year. No one will ever replace Magdalena in my heart. I'll never ask anything from you but your company, your friendship and the chance to repay my debt to a man who's dead. He was my friend, and I didn't even realize his business was in trouble. Your mother is too proud to accept my help, but if she believed this was truly your choice…"

So Lia had married him, and she'd never had reason to regret it. She'd been happy with him. He'd been a good man. But her marriage ultimately hadn't saved her sister and mother. It had been too late to pursue the experimental treatment in L.A., so they'd moved to New York where Olivia could be a patient at St. Ann's, the best pediatric brain cancer facility in the country. But in spite of her determination and bravery, Olivia had died at fourteen. A week later their fragile mother had died from an overdose of sleeping pills. Lia still wasn't sure whether her mother had deliberately taken her life, or just been desperate for one night's sleep to escape the grief. She almost didn't want to know.

If Roark hadn't ruthlessly taken her father's business and left him a broken-down man with oceans of debt, Alfred might have found new investors. Perhaps he would have saved the company instead of being swallowed by the stress of his failure. Olivia could have continued her experimental treatment and it might have worked.

Or maybe Olivia would have died anyway. Her treatment in California had been experimental with only a slight chance of success.

But now Lia would never know.

She only knew that if not for Roark, her whole family might still be alive. Her father. Her sister. Her mother.

Roark Navarre. His name caused a surge of hatred to tighten her hands, crushing a red rose between her fingers. A thorn drew blood on her thumb.

And as if he hadn't done enough already, he'd deliberately taken her virginity for the sake of a business deal! Did the man have no conscience at all? Did he have no soul?

The bastard. The ruthless bastard.

With a soft curse, she sucked the blood off her thumb.

Lia went into the castle to take a shower, desperate to wash the scent of him off her skin. She tried not to remember the feeling of his naked body against hers. The hoarse whisper of his voice, "Ah, Lia. What you do to me…."

She leaned her head against the cool tiles. Standing beneath a stream of water so hot it burned her skin, she was overwhelmed with guilt and shame. She'd betrayed Giovanni's memory in the worst possible way. Taking pleasure in Roark's arms, she'd betrayed her whole family. She knew it was the worst moment of her whole life.

She was wrong.

Three weeks later she discovered she was pregnant.

CHAPTER SEVEN

Eighteen months later.

MARRIED.

Roark still couldn't believe it. Nathan was getting married.

They'd met in Alaska, both working their way through college. For fifteen years they'd enjoyed the lifestyle of commitmentphobic, workaholic bachelors, earning huge fortunes and dating an endless succession of beautiful women.

He'd never thought Nathan would settle down. But he'd thought wrong. His friend was getting married today.

Roark waited for him at a table in the bar of the Cavanaugh Hotel, where he'd been slowly nursing his scotch for the past ten minutes.

He wondered if it was too late to talk Nathan out of it. Grab the poor bastard and force him to run before it was too late.

Roark rubbed the back of his head, still jet-lagged from his long flight from Ulaanbaatar. He'd finished the project in Mongolia yesterday and arrived in New York just an hour ago. His first time in the city in a year and a half, and he almost hadn't come. But he couldn't let his old friend face the firing squad alone.

One week before Christmas, and the sleek, modern hotel bar was filled with businessmen in dark, expensively cut suits. There were a few women scattered here and there, a few in suits but most wearing slinky dresses and red lipstick as fake and carefully applied as their bright, flirtatious smiles.

It could have been any expensive bar in any five-star hotel in the world, and as Roark took another sip of the exquisite forty-year-old Glenlivet, he felt disconnected from everyone and everything. He glanced down at the half-filled tumbler. The scotch was just a year older than Roark was. In a year he'd be forty. And though he told himself life was only getting better, there were times…

He heard a buxom blonde burst into shrieking laughter at the joke of the short, balding man nearby. He watched them sip pink champagne cocktails and pretend they were in love.

All fake. So fake.

Roark couldn't believe he was back in New York. He wished he was back on the building site, sleeping on a hard cot in a tent in Mongolia. Or working in Tokyo. Or Dubai. Or even back in Alaska.

Anywhere but New York.

Was she here for Christmas?

The thought sneaked into his mind, unbidden and unwelcome. Scowling, Roark took another sip of scotch.

All the places he'd been in the last year and a half jumbled together. He'd been working hard. Constantly. Trying to forget her.

The only woman who'd ever brought him such pleasure.

The only woman who'd ever left him wanting more.

The only woman to hate him with such intensity.

Deservedly?

Her accusations still burned through his soul, no matter how many sixteen-hour days he worked or how many hours he spent riding horses along the Mongolian plains, the cold desert wind whipping his skin.

"You seduced me for the sake of skyscrapers that will never, ever love you back. And you call my father a failure? You call him a fool? *He loved us.* He's a better man than you will ever be."

Roark pressed the cool glass against his forehead. He'd made his choice. He wanted no wife. He wanted no children.

He'd had a family once, people who'd loved him. And he hadn't saved them. Better to have no one to love than to fail them. Easier. Safer for everyone.

Too bad Nathan didn't realize that.

He loved us. He's a better man than you will ever be.

"Roark?" he heard Nathan say. "Christ, you look bad."

Relieved to be interrupted, Roark looked up to see his old friend standing by the bar table. Nathan beamed at him, looking hale and hearty in jeans and a sweater.

"And I've never seen you so happy," Roark admitted. He held out his hand. "You're even getting fat!"

With a grin, Nathan shook Roark's hand. Sitting down at the table, he ruefully patted his belly over his sweater. "Emily keeps feeding me. And after today, it's only going to get worse!"

Roark looked straight at him. "So run."

"Same old Roark," his old friend said with a laugh. He shook his head. "I'm just glad you made it. Trust you to fly in from Mongolia with an hour to spare."

"Last chance to talk you out of it."

Nathan signaled to the waitress for a drink. "If I'd thought you actually meant to come to the wedding, I would have made you best man."

"And if I'd been your best man, I'd have convinced you not to get married. Stay free."

"Believe me, when you find the right woman, freedom is the last thing you want."

Roark snorted. "Right."

"I'm serious."

"You're crazy. You've only known the girl for what, six months?"

"A year and a half, actually. And we've just had some news to make this truly the happiest day of our lives." Nathan leaned over the table with a grin. "Emily's pregnant."

Roark stared at him. "Pregnant?"

Nathan laughed at his expression. "Aren't you going to congratulate me?"

Pregnant. His old friend wasn't just settling down with a wife, he was going to have a child. And it made Roark feel every one of his thirty-nine years. What the hell was wrong with him, anyway? He had the perfect life as a bachelor, the life he wanted!

"Congratulations," Roark said dully.

"We're looking for a place in Connecticut. I'll commute to the city for work, but still have a nice house with a yard for the kids. Emily wants a garden…."

A garden. Roark had a sudden memory of an Italian garden full of roses. Blooms in red, yellow, pink, hidden from the world by a medieval stone wall seven feet high. The feel of the hot sun, the buzzing of honeybees and the wind rattling the trees. And the taste of her skin. Oh, God, the sweet taste of her…

"And to think I only met Emily because of that West Side land deal," Nathan continued. "Do you remember it?"

Roark put down the half-empty glass and said evenly, "I remember that we lost it."

The loss was still sharp for Roark. It was the only time he'd ever lost anything.

No. There'd been another time. When he was seven years old and his mother had dumped him in the snow in the middle of the night. Her face had been black with soot, streaked with terrified tears. She'd run back into the cabin for her husband and older son. Roark had waited, but they'd never come out….

"It was at the Black and White Charity Ball that I first met Emily." Nathan nodded his thanks at the cocktail waitress who'd brought his drink. "She works for Countess Villani. You remember the countess, don't you?" He whistled through his teeth. "That's a woman no man can ever forget."

"Yes, I remember her," Roark said in a low voice. No matter how hard he tried to forget Lia, he remembered. He remembered the way she'd felt in his arms when he kissed her at the ball. Remembered the tremble of her virginal body when he took her in the garden. Remembered the explosive way he'd desired her.

The way she'd looked at him with wonder as they made love—then hatred when she learned his name.

All things he didn't want to remember. Things he'd spent the past year and a half trying to forget.

He'd never seen a woman her equal. And he'd only had her once, taking her with frenetic, desperate passion. He'd wanted more. He'd wanted to take her again and again, to slow down, take his time, to enjoy her.

She was the only woman who'd ever denied him the chance to take his pleasure for as long as he desired.

Forget her? How could he, when Lia was the one woman every man wanted—and he was the only man who'd ever touched her?

At least, he *had* been the only one. He suddenly wondered how many men had taken Lia to bed in the last year and a half.

Roark's hands tightened around the glass.

"Although the countess doesn't hold a candle to my girl," Nathan said. "Emily is so warm and loving. The countess is beautiful, definitely, but so cold!"

"Cold?" Roark muttered. "I don't remember her that way." She'd been nothing but fire and heat and warmth, from the passion of their first shared kiss to the fierce intensity of her hatred.

"She caught you in her web, didn't she?"

Roark looked up, saw the amusement in Nathan's eyes.

"Of course not," he retorted. "She's just the woman who put a park where my skyscrapers should have been. Other than that, she means nothing to me."

"I'm glad to hear that," Nathan said gravely. "Because she's obviously forgotten you. She's been seeing the same man for months. Her engagement is expected any day."

A cold shock burned through Roark's body.

Lia...*engaged?*

"Who is he?"

"A wealthy lawyer from an established New York family."

The cold turned to ice. "What's his name?"

"Andrew Oppenheimer."

Oppenheimer.

The white-haired, powerful man who'd known Roark's grandfather.

Him? Lia's husband?

And Roark knew this marriage wouldn't be celibate as her first one had been. Oppenheimer wanted her...as all men did.

As Roark did.

He took a deep breath as the colors and sounds of the bar swirled around him. He realized that eighteen months of hard physical work hadn't changed his desire for Lia Villani. Not at all.

He wasn't done with her. Not by a long shot.

He still wanted her.

And even if Lia hated him...Roark would have her.

CHAPTER EIGHT

"You know I care for you, my dear." Andrew's arm tightened around her shoulder as they sat in the church pew. "When will you say yes?"

Lia looked up at him, biting her lip. "Andrew…"

"I love Christmas, don't you?" he murmured, tactfully changing the subject. "The presents. The snow. Isn't this place romantic with the candles and roses?"

The cathedral was indeed very romantic, decked out for Christmas with holly, fir boughs and red roses lit by a multitude of candles. The wedding was aglow with all the breathless magic of a winter's night.

But it didn't make Lia want a Christmas wedding of her own. It only made her yearn for her baby daughter, who was already tucked into her crib for the night beneath the watchful eye of her nanny.

And the red roses made Lia think of a black-haired, broad-shouldered man who had set her world on fire, then cut her to the heart.

"Marry me, Lia," Andrew whispered. "I'll be a good father to Ruby. I'll take care of you both forever."

She licked her lips. Andrew Oppenheimer was a kind man. He'd make a good husband and an even better father.

So why couldn't she say yes? What was wrong with her?

"What do you say?"

Swallowing, she looked away. "I'm sorry, Andrew. My answer is still no."

He watched her for a moment, then patted her hand gently. "It's all right, Lia. I'll wait for you. Wait and hope."

Lia flushed guiltily. She liked Andrew. She kept hoping that she would fall for him, or be able to accept a marriage of friendship, like her first marriage had been.

But one night of passion with Roark had ruined her forever. Now she couldn't imagine marrying a man without that fire.

She knew she was being stupid. Her daughter needed a father. And yet...

She looked away. The church pews were packed full of friends of both her friend and employee Emily Saunders, and the bridegroom, Nathan Carter. She heard a late arrival come into the pew behind her, passing by other guests to find a spot directly behind her.

"I'd like to take you someplace for New Year's Eve," Andrew continued, holding her hand. "The Caribbean. St. Lucia. Or skiing in Sun Valley. Anywhere you like..."

Andrew bent his head and kissed her hand.

She heard a low cough in the pew behind her. She glanced behind her. Then looked again as time suddenly froze.

Roark.

He was sitting behind her, looking straight at her. Wearing a black shirt, a black tie and black pants, he looked more handsome and alluring and wicked than the devil himself—the only man who'd ever made her feel hot and alive. The only man she hated with every fiber of her being!

"Hello, Lia," he said coolly.

"What are you doing here?" she blurted out. "Emily said you were in Asia—said you wouldn't possibly make it!"

"Haven't you heard?" he said lazily. "I'm magic." He nodded at Andrew. "Oppenheimer. I remember you."

"And I remember you, Navarre." Andrew's eyes darkened. "But times have changed. You won't be taking another dance from me."

For answer, Roark looked back at Lia. His dark eyes tore through her and he really seemed to be magic, because with a single glance he changed the winter into summer. He ripped off her prim gray silk Chanel dress and she felt the heat of his naked body pressed against her skin.

Even after a year and a half, the memory of him making love to her amid the roses was as intense and sharp as if it had just happened an hour ago.

She'd told herself she'd erased him from her memory. But how could she, when every morning she woke up to those same dark eyes shining from her baby's chubby, adorable face?

Ruby.

Oh, my God, what if he found out?

Fear stabbed down her spine. After nearly nine

months of pregnancy and nine months of her baby's infancy she'd thought they were finally safe. That Roark would never come back to New York. He would never find out she'd had his baby.

Everyone in society believed that Ruby was the count's posthumous child—a miracle born nine months after his death. She couldn't disgrace Giovanni's memory now or give the man she hated any reason to interfere in their lives!

"You are more beautiful than ever," he said.

"I hate you," she replied, turning away.

She heard him give a low, sensual laugh in reply, and a tremble went through her.

What was he doing here?

What did he want?

How long would he stay?

He's just here for the wedding, she told herself. *He's not here for me.*

But the way he'd looked at her…

It had been like a Viking looking at a long-sought treasure he'd come to plunder. He'd looked at her as if he intended to possess her. To make her moan and writhe beneath him again and again until Lia's senses sucked her under and she screamed with the intensity of her unwilling pleasure….

The harpist began to play the bridal music and all the guests stood in the pews, craning their heads to see the bride at the end of the aisle.

Lia's knees trembled beneath her as she stood. She watched as Emily, luminous in her white tulle bridal gown and veil, walked down the aisle on her father's arm. Their faces were beaming.

Emily deserved happiness, Lia thought. For the past two years, Emily Saunders had been more than a secretary for her park trust foundation—she'd become a close friend.

But even as she smiled encouragingly at Emily, Lia couldn't stop feeling Roark's presence behind her.

His warmth.

His heat.

He stood behind Lia with nothing but the polished wood pew between them. She could have touched him by lifting her hand a few inches. But she didn't have to touch him to feel him all over.

She felt Roark's nearness as she sat back down on the pew next to Andrew. Felt it as the minister performed the wedding ceremony. Felt it as the bride and groom kissed, then rushed happily from the cathedral, their faces glowing with joy.

Watching them leave, starting their new lives together, Lia suddenly felt a pain in her heart.

She was happy for Emily, she truly was. But their love only made her feel more alone. She wanted love like that. She wanted to give her precious baby daughter the family she deserved. A loving home. An adoring father.

Better to have no father than a cold-hearted bastard like Roark Navarre, she told herself fiercely. If he found out she'd had his baby, what would he do? Demand to spend time with Ruby, barging in on their lives? Use custody of her precious daughter as a weapon against her? Introduce their child to an endless succession of his temporary girlfriends and one-night-stands?

He'd already destroyed Lia's parents and sister. She wouldn't give him the opportunity to destroy her baby's life, as well.

She couldn't let him find out about Ruby. Especially since Roark, of all people, would know the baby couldn't possibly be Giovanni's child!

Andrew took Lia's limp hand and led her out into the aisle, moving from the pews with the other departing guests. She saw Roark and sudden cowardice shook her. She ducked behind Andrew's slender frame.

Roark stepped in front of them. His dark eyes looked past Andrew, seeking hers with unerring force. "I'll walk with you to the reception, Lia."

"Back off, Navarre," Andrew said. "Can't you see she's with me?"

"Is that true?" he said, still looking down at her. "Are you with him?"

She'd been dating Andrew for several months now, and all he'd done was kiss her hand and her cheek. He'd wanted to do more, but she hadn't allowed it. She kept hoping she'd want him to kiss her, that she'd feel some kind of passion. She knew he'd make a good husband. A good father. He was exactly what she and Ruby needed.

Except he wasn't.

Lia swallowed. "Yes, I'm with Andrew." She clasped the older man's hand more tightly. "So if you'll excuse us…"

Somewhat to her surprise, Roark let them go. But her

breathing had barely returned to normal at the reception held at the Cavanaugh Hotel two blocks away, before she saw him watching her across the ballroom. The same hotel ballroom, decorated with white twinkling lights. But now red poinsettias and green Christmas trees decorated the festive room. She held Andrew's hand as the just-married couple were introduced to their guests. Sat with him as dinner was served. He squeezed her fingers as they watched Emily and Nathan share their first dance as a married couple.

And all Lia could think about was the last time she'd been in this ballroom. The man who had kissed her then. Who was here again now.

I shouldn't be holding Andrew's hand like this. Not when she couldn't stop thinking about the dark, dangerous man watching her. The man she hated.

The man she desperately wanted.

"Would you like to dance?" Andrew asked, and Lia nearly jumped. Even holding his hand, she'd nearly forgotten he was there. Not trusting her voice, she nodded and allowed him to escort her onto the dance floor.

Every moment she felt Roark watching her. Wanting her. Intending to have her.

The orchestra started to play the next song, and her heart jumped in her chest as she recognized the opening notes of "At Last," the same song she and Roark had shared during the Black and White Ball, the song that had played the first time Roark had kissed her on the dance floor in front of everyone.

How many men would have been so bold? So ruthless, to want a woman and just kiss her?

She felt Roark's dark hungry gaze watching her from the edge of the dance floor, and she knew he was remembering it, as well. Her cheeks went hot. She stopped on the dance floor even as other couples whirled around them.

"What's wrong, Lia?" Andrew asked with concern. "You look ill."

She backed away. Everything felt so confused. "I'm just feeling a little dizzy," she whispered, her teeth chattering. "I need some air."

"I'll go with you."

"No. I need a minute—alone." She turned and ran, desperate to make it out of the ballroom and out of the hotel long enough for a few deep cold breaths. She needed to feel the wintry air to cool her hot cheeks and freeze her heart to the way it was before Roark had returned to New York.

But she was only halfway down the hallway before Roark was upon her. He pushed her into a broom closet. He shut the door with a bang, locking out the world behind them, cloaking the small room in darkness.

"Roark," she gasped. "We can't—"

"Have you slept with him?" he demanded tersely.

"Who?" she gasped.

"That old man," he said harshly. "And all the others who lust after you. How many men have you taken to your bed since I left you?"

She stiffened. "It's none of your damned business—"

"Answer me!" His hands gripped her shoulders painfully in the darkness. *"Have you given yourself to any other man?"*

"No!" she cried, twisting beneath his hands. "But I wish I had. I wish I'd slept with a dozen men, a hundred, to get the memory of your touch off my skin—"

He pulled her against him with a hard, unyielding kiss. His hands moved over her silk dress, caressing her backside as he crushed her breasts against the hard muscle of his chest.

Her skin sizzled where he touched. A soft whisper of a moan escaped Lia as she felt her bones melt and her body turn to butter in his arms.

CHAPTER NINE

HAD she ever wanted anyone like this?

Ever wanted *anything* like this?

As he kissed her, plundering her lips with insatiable hunger, Lia wanted more. She reached her arms over his shoulders and gripped him to her. She could hear the rush of blood in her ears as he flicked his tongue against hers, kissing her deeper still. She felt the strength of his body in the darkness and felt as if she was floating. Flying. Every inch of her body was tense with the agony of longing.

She wanted him so badly, she thought she'd die if he stopped kissing her now....

"I can't take this, Lia." She felt Roark's ragged breath against her skin, the roughness of his cheek against her own. "I can't take being without you."

Her breasts were tight, her nipples taut against his chest. His every move caused a new explosion of her nerve endings in her breasts and between her thighs. She felt him hard and ready for her. She closed her eyes in the darkness, swaying against him with a quick, shallow intake of breath.

She felt as if she'd been sleeping her whole life. Waiting for this—only this. Her whole body was exploding like fire.

She'd been waiting for Roark since the day she was born.

"Tell me you're mine," he said hoarsely. "Just mine."

Lia's eyes flew open.

Oh, my God, what was she doing in Roark's arms? Allowing him to touch her—allowing him to kiss her in a broom closet? Had she lost her mind? With Andrew still waiting for her in the wedding reception down the hall!

"Let me go!" She struggled to be free of Roark's grasp. "I don't want you—"

He cut her off with a hungry kiss. His lips were hot and tight on hers, bruising her, searing her tongue with his own. The more she tried to resist his embrace, the more forcefully he convinced her. Mastering her. Enslaving her. Until her hatred changed to furious passion and the unyielding force of mutual need.

She wrapped her hands up around his back, kissing him with all the pent-up anger and longing of the past eighteen months.

"I hate you," she whispered against his mouth. "I hate you so much."

"I'm tired of wanting you. Tired of hungering for what I can't have." His voice was a deep whisper in the darkness. The stubble on his chin was rough against her skin. "I've spent the past year trying to forget how your body felt against mine. Hate me all you want. But I'm still going to have you."

He slowly kissed down her throat, moving his hands over her breasts, over the silky smoothness of her shirtdress.

Then she felt him fall to his knees in front of her. For a moment he didn't touch her, and she felt adrift in the darkness; then she felt his strong hands moving slowly past her knee-high black boots, up her bare thighs.

She trembled and shook. "Roark…what are you…?"

"Shhh."

He stroked the outside of her legs to the curve of her hips. He ran his fingertips along the lace edge of her silken panties. He lifted her skirt. She felt his hot breath on the inside of her thighs.

"Roark," she gasped.

He moved forward to kiss and lick her thighs. Then his kisses climbed higher. He moved his hand over her panties, cupping her, stroking the moistening spot between her legs. He kissed her through the sliver of fabric, pulling at the silk gently with his teeth.

She sucked in her breath. He yanked her underwear to the floor, rolling it like a whisper down her legs. He reached between her naked thighs, stroking her with his fingers until she was sopping wet.

Then he took his first taste of her.

She gasped, arching her back against the wall of the broom closet. She gripped his shoulders.

"You can't…we mustn't—"

But he didn't listen. *He didn't stop.*

Holding her firmly, he pressed her legs apart, lifting her knee over his shoulder. He tipped her body back against the wall. She felt his hot breath between her legs.

Her breath came in short, shallow gasps as she trembled.

"No," she whimpered, even as she involuntarily arched to meet his mouth.

He leaned forward and took a long, deep taste between her legs, at the same moment thrusting a thick finger inside her. She writhed against the wall, flinging her head from side to side as he held her.

"You're so sweet," he whispered. "Like sugar."

Spreading her wide with his fingers, he lapped her with a full stroke of his tongue. She cried and gasped, but he didn't let her go.

Pleasure ripped through her body, making her nipples into hard, aching peaks. He reached one hand up to squeeze her breast; with his other, he thrust two fingers inside her, teasing her as he swirled her sensitive nub with his tongue, leaving her wet as she twisted beneath his mouth, sobbing for release.

"Please," she cried. "No more…"

"Say you're mine," he whispered. She felt him push another finger inside her, swirling her harder and faster with his tongue until she twined her hands through his hair, pulling him closer still.

"I'm…yours," she sobbed.

He nibbled and sucked and thrust inside. She threw her head back with one loud, final shriek as the darkness all around her burst into sudden vibrant color….

"Hello?" a man's voice said tremulously. "Lia? Are you in there?"

As she still panted for breath, struggling to regain control of her wildly flailing senses, she watched with horror as the broom closet door started to open!

She stumbled down off Roark's shoulders and he rose unsteadily to his feet. She pushed down her dress. And blinked in the bright light as she saw Andrew standing in the doorway.

"Lia?" He looked in shock at Roark. "What are you doing in here?"

"I took the dance from you," he replied coolly.

With a sob, Lia stepped forward. "I didn't mean for this to happen, Andrew. I am so sorry. Forgive me."

She saw him blink hard, take a deep breath. "All I've ever wanted was for you to be happy, Lia." He swallowed. "I see now that you will never be happy with me."

"Andrew—"

"Good-bye, Lia. Good luck." Turning away, he paused in the doorway. She heard him say quietly over his shoulder, "I hope you find what you're looking for."

And he left, closing the door behind him.

Lia stared after him in horror.

"Oh, my God," she whispered. "What have I done?"

"It was inevitable." Roark wrapped his arms around her waist, turning her to face him. "It's best for him to know the truth."

"The truth? You mean that I have no self-control?" She gave a harsh, bitter laugh, then shook her head. Her throat hurt. Her whole body hurt with the shame of what she'd done. What she'd let Roark do to her. "Why do you keep doing this to me? Why do I let you?"

"I'll tell you why." He stroked her cheek. His voice was dark and deep, mesmerizing in its power and intensity. "Because you want to belong to me."

CHAPTER TEN

ROARK'S words still haunted her as she got dressed for work in her town house the next morning. Lia glanced at herself in the mirror of her elegant, solitary bedroom. Just remembering what he'd done to her last night caused her hands to shake as she buttoned her sleek Armani jacket. Her dark hair was swept up in a glossy chignon, and with her black suit, dark-patterned stockings and high-heeled boots, she looked like any capable businesswoman heading to work.

Only the dark hollows beneath Lia's eyes gave away the truth.

She hadn't slept at all last night. She'd fled that broom closet like the hounds of hell were snapping at her heels. She'd run from the wedding without even saying farewell to Emily or wishing her joy as a married woman. Instead Lia had scrambled headlong from the hotel, flagging down a taxi with the same panic she'd had at the Black and White Ball eighteen months earlier.

What was it about Roark Navarre that turned her into such a coward?

"Yes, a coward," she said accusingly to the outwardly serene woman in the mirror. "A total fraud."

She could still feel Roark's hands on her body. Could still feel his hot breath, the sleek possessive force of his tongue. She looked again at her face. Her cheeks had turned red.

She hated him.

But that didn't stop her from wanting him.

What was wrong with her? Knowing what he'd done to her family, knowing the kind of man he was, how could she possibly want him? And yet she did. She had absolutely no self-control where he was concerned.

Thank God she'd never see him again. Now that Emily and Nathan were on their way to their honeymoon the Caribbean, Roark would go back to Asia. Lia hoped he was already halfway over the Pacific on his private plane, on his way to some remote country, never to return. Then she could never again be tempted by the most selfish, arrogant, devastating man she'd ever met.

And he would never know she'd had his baby.

She rubbed her hands against her temples. He must never know. And the only way to make sure she kept her secret was to stay away from him. She no longer trusted herself when he was around. Madness seized her. She'd already surrendered her body; what would keep her from giving up her secrets? Just thinking of the way she'd let him rip off her underwear in the broom closet last night, lifting her thigh over his shoulder to lick and thrust inside her with his tongue…

She shivered, then clenched her fists. She'd been weak. And poor Andrew had been hurt as a result.

She'd already sent Andrew a note of apology. She realized now that their relationship would never have worked, but the thought of how it had ended still made her blush with shame.

Lia heard her baby laugh from the kitchen downstairs. In spite of everything, her heart lightened at the sound. Hurrying from her bedroom and down the stairs, she found Ruby enjoying an extremely messy breakfast in her high chair. Her nanny was unloading the dishwasher, putting the china away in the cupboard as she made silly faces to make the baby laugh.

"Good morning, Mrs. O'Keefe."

"Good morning, Countess," the plump, kindly woman replied with an Irish lilt.

"And good morning to you, Ruby," Lia said, wiping a clump of strained peaches off her chubby cheeks tenderly. "And how are you enjoying your breakfast this morning?"

Ruby gurgled at her happily, waving a spoon.

Lia kissed the baby's forehead, feeling a wave of love. As always, she hated the thought of leaving her daughter, even for just a few hours. Even for such a good cause.

"She'll be fine, my dear." Mrs. O'Keefe said with a smile. She leaned forward to tickle the baby's tummy through her pajamas, making the baby shriek with glee. The capable Irish widow had cared for them since before Ruby was born, watching over the whole household as if they were her own daughter and granddaughter. "We'll have a lovely morning, reading stories and playing with blocks, then her morning nap. You'll be gone such a short time. She won't even miss you."

"I know," Lia said numbly. Ruby would be fine. It was Lia who always had a hard time. "It's just that I was already away from her for the wedding last night…"

Mrs. O'Keefe patted her shoulder. "I'm glad you got out. About time, I think. Your husband was a good man. I mourned my own, as well. But you've been mourning him long enough. The count wouldn't have wanted you to take on so. You're a beautiful young woman with a wee baby. You deserve a night out for a bit of fun."

A bit of fun? Lia thought of Roark pressing her legs apart, his hot breath on her thighs. The feel of his tongue as he tasted her.

Her whole body trembled as she tried to push the memory away. *It's over,* she told herself desperately. *He's gone. I'll never see him again.*

But she couldn't stop trembling.

She'd spent ten years being faithful to Giovanni in a marriage of companionship. After his death, she'd found out she was pregnant with Roark's child and she'd never had the chance—or the inclination—to sow any more wild oats. She was twenty-nine years old and she'd had only one sexual experience in her whole life. Only one lover.

Roark.

No wonder he held such power over her.

Lia's hands shook as she put on her white wool overcoat with the princess-style collar. Even hating him, she couldn't resist. This fire for Roark had burned inside her for far too long, unstoked but hot beneath the ash.

Her only hope was to never see him again.

Lia put on her white gloves and scarf, then hugged her peaches-happy baby. "I'll be back before noon."

"No hurry, love," Mrs. O'Keefe said placidly. "She'll likely sleep till two."

Picking up her Chanel handbag in her gloved hands, Lia gave her daughter one last kiss, then took a deep breath and left. As she came out of her town house she looked up at the acres of empty space on the other side of the street.

She'd bought this new town house last year because of the location. No one had understood why she would want to live in the Far West Side of Manhattan, away from the more exclusive Upper East Side where most of her friends lived; but this was the only place in the city that made her feel a sense of home.

Her sister's unfinished park was across the street, holding the silence of winter in the snowy, sparkling morning. The railyards and broken-down warehouses had cleared. The park waited breathlessly for spring, when the frozen earth beneath the snow would soften and warm, and grass, flowers and trees could be planted. The Valentine's Day fund-raiser would pay for much of that.

"Good morning."

She nearly jumped when she saw Roark standing at the bottom of her town house steps. Seeing him was like seeing a ghost. She'd already decided he was long gone, on his private plane flying across the Pacific.

She swallowed. "What are you doing here?"

His dark eyes gleamed as he looked at her, and she felt her heart quicken and pound, making her cheeks hot. Making her hot all over. "Waiting for you."

He came up the steps and took her hand. Even through her gloves she felt his touch sear her skin, his heat causing sparks all over her body.

"I thought you were going back to Asia," she whispered.

His gaze traced her hungrily. "Not till this afternoon."

She'd been so sure he was gone. But now, with his hand holding hers, all she could think about was how glad she was to see him, how intoxicating it was to be near him again.

Then she remembered Ruby.

Her sweet laughing baby, eating peaches and rice cereal in her town house. Lia glanced behind her, then clenched her hands.

She had to get Roark out of here.

"I'm on my way to work." Ripping her hand from his grasp, she started walking quickly down the steps.

"I didn't know you had a job."

"I'm still doing fund-raising for the park." Stopping on the sidewalk, she looked each way down the quiet street. "It's not as easy as you might think."

"I'm sure," Roark said, sounding amused. "What are you doing? Looking both ways before you cross the street?"

"Hailing a cab," she said, annoyed.

"You'll never get a cab this time of the morning. Where's your driver?"

"It was an unnecessary expense. I let him go when I had…" *When I had a baby.* She coughed, coloring. "Lately, I've been working more from home."

"I can help." Roark indicated the black Rolls-Royce that was waiting discreetly at a distance. "My driver can take you wherever you need to go."

She ground her teeth. "I am not one of your floozies, Roark, waiting breathlessly for your assistance. I can get my own cab."

He lifted his hands in surrender. "Go ahead."

She looked first one way, then the other down the quiet street. A few cars went by. She lifted her arm as several taxis passed—all of them already filled with passengers. And she felt Roark's amusement.

She glowered at him, reaching into her handbag. "I'll call a car service."

He placed his hand over hers. "Just let me take you."

She swallowed as she felt his heat through her white gloves. Why did his slightest touch always have such an effect on her? "You'll take me straight to work?"

"Yes. I promise." He stroked back a tendril of hair that had escaped her chignon. "Right after breakfast."

Breakfast? Was that a metaphor for a morning of hot, fiery sex? She licked her lips. "I'm not hungry."

He gave her a slow-rising grin that she felt to her toes. "I think you're lying."

She sucked in her breath, tried to regain control. "I told you, I need to go to work."

"And I'll take you there. After breakfast."

"Breakfast?" she whispered. "You mean breakfast at…at a restaurant? With food?"

"That is how breakfast is usually done." His eyes gleamed wickedly, as if he knew exactly what she was thinking. He glanced up at her town house. "Unless you want to invite me inside." He stroked her inner wrist beneath her glove, making her tremble all over in a flash of heat. "I rather like the idea of you cooking for me."

Swallowing, she glanced back at the town house, where her baby was playing with Mrs. O'Keefe. Oh, my God. At any moment, the widow could come out with Ruby for their morning walk.

She had to get Roark out of here!

She whirled to face him, ripping her hand away from his touch. Her eyes glittered. "If I made you breakfast, I'd dump salt in it, boxes and boxes."

He gently stroked her chin. "You don't mean that."

"Count yourself lucky it wasn't rat poison!"

His smile broadened. "You're quite a woman, Lia."

"And you're quite a rat. Don't ever try and push me into another broom closet. If you even think of—"

"No more closets, I swear." But even as she exhaled in relief, he finished in a low, dark voice, "The next time I take you, Lia, you'll be in my bed."

CHAPTER ELEVEN

LIA took another sip of the fragrant strong coffee, rich with cream and sugar, from a tiny cup painted with pale-blue flowers and traced in twenty-four-karat gold.

The owner of the expensive French café sprang forward to refill her cup as she set it down, but she covered it with her hand. "No more for me, thank you, Pierre. I'll just finish this, then go."

The manager nodded sagely. "*Oui, madame.* Of course. But," he said with a *tsk*, "we've missed Mademoiselle Ruby today. I hope she is well?"

Lia nearly choked on her coffee. She felt Roark watching her.

"She's very well," she managed. "She just...couldn't make it today."

"I'm glad to hear that, madame." Bowing, he backed away respectfully.

"Who's Ruby?" Roark inquired.

Lia's teeth chattered. When Roark had allowed her to choose the restaurant, she'd picked her favorite place. She'd thought it would make her feel comfortable, that it would make her feel calm and strong enough to face Roark.

How could she have failed to consider the fact that Pierre served her and Ruby brunch every Sunday? He adored the baby. He always brought her little origami cranes which he made for her out of the linen napkins.

Rattled, Lia scraped the last of her syrup on the very last bit of waffle and stuffed it all in her mouth.

"Ruby's a friend," she mumbled. "Just a good friend."

A very good friend indeed. The darling of Lia's life, the cutest baby in the world, who'd just learned to crawl. Swallowing the lump of waffle, she stood up so abruptly that her napkin fell to the floor. "I'm done. Let's go."

Lia almost expected Roark to fight her, to insist that she stay. Or worse—to pick her up in his strong arms and drag her to some hotel room.

But he didn't. He just paid the bill, took her hand and escorted her back to where his driver awaited them outside.

As the Rolls-Royce edged slowly through the midmorning traffic, she slowly started to breathe again. Was it really that easy? By some miracle, would he leave her like he'd promised?

"Right up here," she told the driver. Relief flashed through her when she saw the nineteenth-century building that contained her tiny West Side office. She'd made it!

"Goodbye, Roark," she told him, opening her door. "Thanks for breakfast. Good luck in Asia."

"Wait." He grabbed her wrist. She took a long, shuddering breath, then turned back to face him. He looked up at her. "Invite me inside."

"To my office? Why?"

He gave her a wicked grin that made her hair curl, that made her body feel sweaty all over even as her breath froze like smoke in the cold winter air. "I want to help you."

"Help me?" she whispered. "How?"

"I want to donate money for your park."

The same park he'd done his best to destroy? The colossal cheek of the man! Fury raced through her.

"You lying bastard!" she burst out. "Do you really think I'm stupid enough to believe you want to help me?"

He snorted, giving her a lazy half smile. "I think I can see why you're having a hard time raising money."

"Of course I don't talk to real donors that way. But you're not serious!"

His eyes met hers, all trace of his smile gone. "What would it take to show you how serious I am?"

She chewed her lip.

She did need donations for the park. They were still twenty million short, and it would be a miracle if they could get that much together by March, when the landscaping bids would be completed.

But getting Roark out of New York before he found out she'd had his baby was even more important than raising money for the park.

She could just refuse him, of course. But every time she'd run away from Roark, it only made him pursue her more. Like any dangerous wolf or bear, he seemed maddened by the sight of prey running away.

So what if she didn't run away?

What if instead she gave him exactly what he wanted? Wouldn't that make him lose interest? The only reason he continued to pursue her was because she didn't want him. In a world where every other woman on the planet lived to serve him in every way possible, he must have found Lia's hatred an intriguing novelty.

But if she'd actually wanted to be his girlfriend, a playboy like Roark wouldn't have been able to run from her fast enough. Throwing herself at him would be the easiest way to get rid of him.

But…throw herself at him? The idea terrified her. *She couldn't do it.*

She would just have to allay his suspicions, accept his money and then pray he would leave.

"Fine," she ground out, turning away with ill grace. "You can come into my office long enough to write your check."

"Very generous of you," he said, getting out of the Rolls-Royce behind her.

He followed her into the building, up the rickety old elevator to the rooms on the third floor that Lia had rented for her foundation. There were two offices—one for Emily, one for Lia—and a front waiting room that held some chairs where their receptionist answered the phones.

The girl looked up breathlessly when she saw Roark. He smiled at her casually, and Lia could see the effect it had on Sarah. She gawked at dark, handsome Roark as if she'd never seen a man before.

For some reason it annoyed Lia. "Good morning, Sarah," she said. "Do you have the preliminary list?"

"Hmm?" It took several seconds before the receptionist even seemed to realize Lia was with him. "Um. Right. Yes, I have it, Lia. Here it is."

"This is Roark Navarre," Lia said over her shoulder, as she headed to her office with the papers in her hands. "He's here to write a check, then he's going to leave."

"Hello, Mr. Navarre," she heard Sarah giggle, and Lia suddenly wanted to smack her. Sarah Wood was a graduate of Barnard with a degree in economics, but a single smile from Roark had turned her into a puddle of giggly femininity!

"Do you need a pen?" the girl was cooing.

"No, thank you, Miss…?"

"Call me Sarah," the pretty blonde sighed.

"No, thank you, Sarah. I see a pen right over there."

Lia stomped into her office, throwing down her coat, scarf and gloves across her leather sofa with a growl. She forced herself to turn away from Roark and Sarah and look over the names on her list. She'd need to call Mrs. Van Deusen and Mrs. Olmstead first. The old society mavens would take offense if she didn't.

She heard Sarah giggle again. Grinding her teeth, Lia tightened her hands around the papers. If she heard Sarah sigh and coo over Roark once more, she wouldn't be responsible for the consequences!

"Why do you have a playpen in here?"

Lia whirled around to see Roark in her doorway, staring at the playpen that was tucked in the far corner behind her sofa. Oh, no! Before Ruby had learned to crawl and developed an intense dislike of confinement,

Lia had brought her to the office for a few hours a week. She'd forgotten the playpen was still there, filled with baby toys!

Roark stepped further into her office, looking around curiously as he took a pen off her desk. "Is it for Emily? You waste no time, do you? They only just found out she was pregnant yesterday."

She wiped two beads of sweat off her forehead. "Emily? Yes. Of course," she stuttered. "It's for Emily's baby."

And it wasn't even a lie, since the gorgeous, barely-used playpen would likely be moved over to the adjacent office after Emily finished maternity leave. Assuming Emily even came back. Assuming she didn't decide to be a stay-at-home mom in a charming Connecticut house with a white picket fence, making dinners and ironing shirts for an adoring husband who loved her, making cookies for their happy, growing brood of children...

"Lia?"

She blinked as her wistful thoughts evaporated. "What?"

He held his checkbook in his hand. "How much do you need?"

"For what?"

"For the park."

She stared at him unblinkingly. "Oh. Right." She took a deep breath. "Our next fund-raiser is a masquerade ball on Valentine's Day. You won't be in New York, of course." *And thank God for that,* she added silently. "But if you wanted to buy an individual ticket and donate the seat, it would be a thousand dollars. Or if you wanted to sponsor a whole table—"

"You don't understand." He put his hands on her shoulders. "How much would it take for you to be completely done with fund-raising?"

"What are you talking about?"

"How much would cover everything?"

She shook her head. "But you don't care about the park. You told me so yourself. You said you didn't give a damn about the kids."

"I still don't."

"Then why?"

"Just tell me what you'd need to be free. Give me the number."

She licked her suddenly dry lips. "Trying to buy me, Roark?"

"Would it work?"

She swallowed. "No."

"Then it seems I have no choice but honesty." Looking down at her, he stroked her cheek. "I want you to leave New York. With me."

To leave…with Roark?

Her heart was pounding as she whispered, "Why would I want to do that?"

"I'm tired of trying to forget you, Lia," he said softly. "Tired of chasing you in my dreams." He stroked the inside of her palm with his thumb. "I want you with me. And since I can't stay, you must come."

"Roark, this is crazy. We can't stand each other—"

He stopped her with a kiss. At the seductive, powerful

touch of his lips, his arms wrapped around her as he held her tight against his chest. The floor of her office swayed beneath her feet. When he finally pulled away, she felt so dazed that all she knew was that she wanted to stay in his arms for the rest of her life.

Stay in his arms for the rest of her life?!

What was wrong with her? She hated Roark! He'd destroyed her family. Was she going to give him the opportunity to ruin her baby's life as well?

Where was her loyalty?

Where was her sanity?

And if he knew about the baby, he'd never forgive her. He might even try to take Ruby away from her....

"No, thanks," she said stiffly, stepping back a safe distance. "I'm not interested in traveling with you. I like being home. And in case you've forgotten, we have absolutely nothing in common except rose gardens and broom closets."

"Lia—"

"Just go, Roark," she said, turning away even as her heart ached beneath the weight of her longing. "My answer is no."

He stood silently for a moment, then turned on his heel. She heard him talk to Sarah, who'd no doubt been listening breathlessly to every word. Lia's cheeks flamed. She'd likely even heard Roark kiss her!

She heard him say in his most charming, seductive voice, "Sarah, how much money does your boss need to finish the Olivia Hawthorne park?"

"About twenty million," the girl said cagily. "Ten

mil for landscaping, another ten mil as capital for our pledged part of future upkeep."

"I'd really love to see the park." Roark paused. "If someone would just show me the park, I'd be willing to donate twenty million dollars to cover all expenses. For the sake of the children of New York." Lia felt his eyes on her and flushed. He continued smoothly, "I just need someone to show me what I'm paying for. And maybe share some lunch. Twenty million dollars for lunch and a tour. Does that seem a fair deal to you, Sarah?"

The girl nearly fell out of her chair.

"I'll get my coat," she gasped out. "I'll show you everything, Mr. Navarre. I'll serve you lunch personally. Even if it takes all night—I mean, all day."

Suddenly Lia's irritation exploded, although she couldn't exactly say why. Letting Sarah go in her place would have been a perfect solution to his obvious manipulation. And yet she couldn't allow it.

Not because she was jealous, she told herself. She just wanted to make sure he actually paid up the twenty million dollars!

"It's all right, Sarah. I'll do it," Lia bit out, grabbing her coat and handbag. She bared her teeth in a smile at Roark. "I'll be delighted to show you the park."

"I'm flattered."

"For twenty million dollars, I would have lunch with the devil himself!"

As Sarah sighed in obvious disappointment, Roark gave Lia a sharply possessive smile, and she knew this had been his intended outcome all along. "Let's go."

"I won't be your mistress, Roark," she whispered as they left the building. "I'll give you a tour of the park. I'll even treat you to lunch. But you're nothing to me but a big fat wallet. I look at you and see sprinklers and playground equipment, nothing more!"

"I appreciate your honesty." He stopped her on the sidewalk. "So let me return the favor."

He gave her a cheeky grin, rubbing the back of his head. His gorgeous, thick, full black hair. She remembered how silky it had felt in her hands last night when his head had been between her legs. Her cheeks went hot.

He looked down at her. As people hurried past them on the sidewalk, she didn't hear car horns honking. She didn't see anything but his handsome face.

Scattered snowflakes tumbled from white clouds moving swiftly across the bright blue sky.

"I have everything I've ever wanted," he said quietly. "Money. Power. Freedom. I've had everything any man could want. Except one thing. One dream that keeps slipping through my fingers. And I'm not going to let it get away this time."

"What is it?" she whispered.

"Don't you know?" He took her face in his hands, looking down into her eyes with such fierce intensity it almost broke her heart. "It's you, Lia."

CHAPTER TWELVE

PRISMS of scattered snowflakes swirled like diamonds in the sparkling sunlight as Roark stood next to her on the edge of the large white field.

He didn't touch her. He hadn't touched her in the Rolls-Royce, either, on the ride from her office. They hadn't spoken a word since he'd told her he wanted her.

Even now, his hands were tucked into his black wool coat, as if to keep himself from pulling her into a kiss. But the brightness of the snow and blue sky caressed his tanned face, tracing his Roman nose, the strong cut of his jawline and his impossibly chiseled cheekbones.

Every time she looked at him, his dark gaze was on her, sizzling her blood, electrifying her to the core.

But he didn't touch her. And every moment, she felt the space between them get smaller, drawing her inevitably closer. How long could she resist this? How?

She looked away, trying to remember her loyalty to her dead family and her need to protect her baby daughter.

Roark didn't want to settle down and raise a family.

He wanted a mistress who would toss aside everything to spend her life in endless pleasures around the world.

The image flashed through her of what it would be like to be Roark's mistress. The luxury. The freedom from responsibility. A life of adventure without constraints. Sleeping in his bed every night…

Swallowing, she pushed the thought aside. She was a mother. And even if she hadn't been, that sort of life wouldn't have appealed to her for long. She wanted—needed—a home. She needed someplace in the world to call her own.

Yet she remembered his words: "I've had everything any man could want. Except one dream that keeps slipping through my fingers. And I'm not going to let it get away this time…"

"It's beautiful."

Startled, she looked up at his voice. From the northern edge on top of a snowy hill, Roark was looking out at the wide emptiness of the park. In the distance behind him she could see the sparkle of the Hudson River. "Not as beautiful to you as ten million square feet of office space, though, is it?"

His dark eyes cut through her.

"Not as beautiful to me as you are," he said in a low voice. "I meant what I said. I want you to be with me, Lia. Until we're sick of each other. Until I have my fill of you. No matter how long it takes." He gave a light laugh. "Who knows. It might take forever."

Her heart pounded. Just when she thought she

couldn't take the dark intensity of his gaze for another moment, he looked away.

"I've never liked this city. But your park..." He took a deep breath. "It almost feels like home."

"You have a home?" she blurted without thinking.

Glancing at her, he gave a harsh laugh. "You're right. I don't. But the place I'm thinking of is northern Canada." He looked back over the snowy park. "My father was an ice trucker. He drove supplies across frozen lakes and rivers in winter. My mother met him when she was heli-skiing over spring break. They had three dates and that was it for both of them."

"She was Canadian?"

"American. The only child of a wealthy New York family." His lips pressed together as if holding back some emotion. "When I was seven, I came to live here with my grandfather."

She stared at him. "You grew up in New York?"

He gave a harsh laugh. "Yes. I grew up fast. My grandfather was a cold man. He disinherited my mother at nineteen for eloping. He never forgave her for marrying a trucker. Nor did he think I was worthy of being his grandson."

"But...but he was your grandfather!" Lia gasped. "Surely he loved you!"

Roark looked out at the wide vista of the snowy park. In the distance, a swirl of wind picked up a scattering of snowflakes and sent them whirling to the sky. "He said he'd spoiled my mother and wouldn't make the same mistake raising me. He fired a new nanny every six months. He didn't want me to get too attached to any of the servants, he said. He was afraid I'd get soft—or show my low-class origins."

His emotionless words struck at her heart. Her throat hurt as she whispered, "Oh, Roark."

He shrugged. "It doesn't matter. I've had the last laugh. I've made a fortune ten times the size of the one he left to charity when he died. He disinherited me, of course. The day I turned eighteen, I left New York, and he was furious. Said he'd wasted his time raising me. He was thrilled to send me back to the gutter where I belonged."

"He couldn't have meant it!"

"You don't think so?" Roark's lips curved into a humorless smile. "He said I should have died with the rest of my family. He said I should have burned in the fire."

"That's how your parents died?" she whispered. "In a fire?"

For a moment she thought he wasn't going to answer. Then he turned his bleak eyes on her. "Not just my parents. My brother, as well. The curtains caught fire from the space heater in the middle of the night. My mother woke me up and carried me from the cabin. My father was supposed to wake up my older brother. When they didn't come out, she went back for them."

Lia sucked in her breath. Without thinking, she placed her hand over his, desperate to offer comfort. "Oh, Roark…"

Without moving his hand, he looked away. "It was a long time ago. It doesn't matter now."

"But it does. I know how it feels." She took a deep breath, blinking back tears. "I'm so sorry."

He glanced down at her hand so tightly clasping his.

"I'm the one who's sorry, Lia." His dark eyes seemed haunted as he looked up. "I never meant to hurt your family when I took your father's company. If I'd known…" He gave a harsh laugh and ripped his hand from hers. "Christ, maybe I'd still have taken it anyway. You're right. I am a selfish bastard."

Staring at him now, so troubled as he looked out over the snowy winter wonderland of the unfinished park, she felt her heart in her throat. It hurt too much to speak.

"But you have to know one thing," he said in a low voice. "Making love to you in Italy had nothing to do with any business deal. I just wanted you. Wanted you beyond reason. I've always known I didn't want children, yet I was so far gone that I forgot to use a condom." He shook his head fiercely. "Do you know that for months after I left you, I waited for you to contact me with the news we'd conceived a child?"

Suddenly the truth was pounding in her throat. She wanted to tell him. She *had* to tell him.

She took a deep breath. "Would that have been so terrible," she whispered, "if I'd gotten pregnant with your child?"

Raking back his hair, he gave a harsh laugh. "It would have been a disaster! I'd be no good as a father. The responsibility. The pressure. Lucky for us you weren't pregnant, wasn't it?"

She choked down the ridiculous hope that had been building in her heart.

"Yes," she said dully. "Very lucky."

He looked out over the sparkle of the snow, the endless white fields bare of trees. "I know this thing between us can't last. You're right. We're nothing alike. You want a home and I must have my freedom."

She watched his handsome face, her heart breaking.

Then he turned to face her. "Do you know you're the first woman who ever turned me down? I admired you the moment I saw you. Your beauty, your grace. Your pride. You challenged me. Unlike most women, you never needed me to save you. And I admired that most of all."

She swallowed the lump in her throat. "I'm not nearly so strong as I look. Since Giovanni died, I've been alone."

"Alone? How can you think that?" He shook his head in amazement. "Don't you see how the whole world loves you?" He moved toward her, gently tucking a dark tendril behind her ear that the wind had blown in her face. He didn't touch her skin, and yet the closeness of his caress sent every nerve in her body spinning. "You spend your life taking care of other people. You are the most intriguing woman I've ever known. Sexy as hell. But your courageous spirit—that was what caught me. Your strength. Your goodness. Your honesty."

Honesty? Oh, my God. The enormity of her secret was pounding in her brain, making her whole body hurt.

"You insulted me to my face so gleefully," he continued, "I knew you'd always tell me the truth, even if it hurt me." He rubbed his cheek wryly. "Especially if it hurt me."

She felt her own cheeks go hot. "I was wrong to slap you that day."

"No, I deserved it." He looked down at her. She could feel the heat from his body, and yet still he didn't touch her! He said softly, "If I hadn't taken your father's business, your life would have been so different."

Silence fell between them. She heard the sad caw of birds high overhead, flying south so late, so late. She heard the crunch of the fresh snow beneath his shoes as he turned away.

He blamed himself. And after all this time of blaming him, somehow, knowing he blamed himself…broke her heart.

"It wasn't your fault really," she heard herself say in a small voice. "My father's heart was weak. My sister's treatment was experimental. My mother was fragile. Maybe it had nothing to do with you. Maybe…I never should have blamed you."

Roark's eyes closed as he took a long, deep breath. When he opened his eyes, they shone—with unshed tears?

Roark?

"Thank you." He reached out to stroke her cheek. The sensation of his touch, after waiting so long for it, caused a deep shudder to go through Lia. Her knees went weak.

Suddenly the air between them changed. Electrified. He ran his thumb along her sensitive lower lip.

"Come to my hotel," he whispered. "Don't make me wait. I can't wait anymore. I need you now."

Yes, she thought desperately, then thought of Ruby and turned away.

"I can't."

"Come to my bed once of your own free will," he asked quietly. "After that, if you decide you don't want me, I won't pursue you again. But give me one chance to persuade you. One chance to show you what I can offer. What our life together could be."

She looked at him, dazed by the gentle seduction of his touch. She felt dizzy, overwhelmed. And she knew she couldn't bear for him to leave. Not yet. She couldn't bear the thought of him letting her go, setting her adrift again and alone in the cold winter. Not without one last chance to be warm…

"If I come to your bed, you'll let me go?"

"Yes," he said in a low voice. "If that is what you truly desire. But I will do everything I can to convince you to stay. To come away with me. To be my love."

"Your…love?" she said softly.

"My mistress." He held her in his arms, looking down at her. "I'm not offering love, Lia. I'm not offering marriage. I know this fire between us cannot last. Let's just relish every moment that we have."

Closing her eyes, she silently pressed her face against his coat. She could feel the cold, blustery wind against her face, but the rest of her body felt hot. And warm. His arms were wrapped around her as he held her tightly. Her breasts felt hard and aching, her body rising toward him with every quick, panting breath.

He wanted long-term pleasure. No commitment. No emotional entanglement.

That wasn't what she wanted from a man. Not as a husband and not as her baby's father.

And yet...

One afternoon in his bed. Then Roark would return to Asia, and Ruby would be safe forever. He need never know he had a daughter. He need never feel a burden of responsibility he didn't want, or interfere in their lives. He could continue his endless travels and never look back.

He would never have the opportunity to fail Ruby as a father. And Lia wouldn't be forced to watch Roark replace her in his life with an endless parade of new mistresses when he tired of her.

They were wrong for each other. She saw that clearly. She wanted a family and a home. She wanted a steady man who would love her forever and love their children.

She wanted a life like Emily had. But since she couldn't have that...

One afternoon in Roark's bed.

One time to try to satiate her craving for him and then she'd forget. She'd send him on his way and start a new life with her baby. She would forget him.

She *would*.

Her heart pounded as she turned her face upward, looking into his eyes. The sun was behind his head, giving his black hair a halo like a dark Renaissance angel. He dazzled her. His masculine power and beauty blinded her.

And she heard herself whisper, "I need to be home by two o'clock."

He took a deep breath and held her fiercely, kissing her forehead, her hair.

"You won't regret it," he vowed. "I'll make sure you never regret it."

A few hours. Just a few hours, Lia told herself. As he lowered his head to claim her lips with a passionate kiss, she knew she'd burn each caress onto her memory. She would make these next few hours last forever.

Then…she would let him go.

CHAPTER THIRTEEN

As THEY went up the elevator of the Cavanaugh Hotel to the $20,000-a-night presidential suite, Roark realized he was shaking.

Oh, my God, when had he ever wanted a woman like this?

When had he ever wanted *anything* like this?

He stopped in front of the hotel room door, looking down at her. Her hazel eyes were clear and serene, like pools of cool water in a Canadian forest, reflecting the green and brown of the wilderness and vivid blue of the sky.

Unable to look away, he lifted her into his arms and carried her over the threshold. He closed the door behind them with a kick.

He carried her across the marble floor of the foyer, beneath the enormous crystal chandelier, and across the six-room suite into the master bedroom. He set her gently to her feet. Through the tall floor-to-ceiling windows behind her, he could see the stark beauty of

Central Park. Black trees twisted patterns against the white expanse of snow.

He took off his black coat. He peeled off her white wool coat and gloves and scarf, dropping them to the floor. He started to take off his black shirt, but found himself distracted when she started to do the same right in front of him.

Her hazel eyes never left his as she slowly unbuttoned her black jacket, revealing a lacy black bra beneath. She unzipped the back of her skirt and let it fall. He saw black lace panties and black stockings held up by a garter belt.

Stockings? A garter belt…?

Who was this woman? She was modern, young, a countess. And yet she was an old-fashioned fantasy, a 1940s bombshell. The more time he spent with Lia, the more he wanted her.

It was why he'd realized he wanted her for longer than just a night. He wanted her in his life until he'd had his fill.

For the first time, ever, he wanted to keep a woman with him on his travels.

Roark swallowed, and his hands stilled on the buttons of his shirt as he watched her. Lia was truly a woman who'd be feverishly desired by every man, no matter the age or time.

Kicking off her black high heels, she put one small foot on the bed and unclasped the first garter. Without looking at him, she rolled the black stocking slowly down her leg.

His breath came in hoarse little gasps.

Dropping the first stocking to the carpet, she repeated

the process with the other leg. He licked his lips, unable to look away.

She finally turned to face him. She took a deep breath, and for the first time, he saw the blush on her cheeks, the tremble of her hands. She was nervous.

Somehow that was the sexiest thing of all.

Lia clasped her hands together, tucking them behind her back. Then she looked up at him with a sensual smile, a mischievous gleam in her eyes.

Roark's heart pounded. How was it possible that he was the only man who'd ever touched her—this most desirable woman on earth? A woman so powerful and yet so vulnerable. So strong and proud and mysterious, yet utterly honest.

How was it possible that a woman like this existed anywhere beyond the realm of male fantasy?

She took a deep breath, suddenly shy. "What…what do I do now?"

It was all the invitation he needed.

Roark ripped off the last buttons of his shirt, pulled off all his clothes. With a growl, he lifted her up in his arms. "I'll take it from here."

He placed her tenderly on the soft bed. He moved down to kiss her lips, stroking her bare arms. He kissed down her throat, stroking every inch of her body with his sensitive fingers. She touched him back, timidly at first, then with greater confidence. He relished feeling her hands on his skin.

He relished it far too much.

But after eighteen months of frustrated desire, he

wanted to take his time, to enjoy her. To take her slowly. Until he was utterly satiated with this complicated, sexy-as-hell, mysterious woman....

How long would that take?

She had to come with him to Hawaii and Tokyo. He would convince her. He had no choice. One day would not be enough. He'd kill any man who tried to take her from him now.

At this moment Roark never wanted to let her go.

He stroked and kissed her shoulders, her belly. Cupping her breasts together with his hands, he pressed his face between them. She moaned softly beneath him.

He pulled off the black lace bra.

He unhooked the garter belt.

Slowly he rolled her black panties down her thighs and dropped them to the floor. She closed her eyes. He could feel her tremble beneath his hands.

She was in his power. The thought intoxicated him.

He had taken her virginity so brutally and breathlessly in Italy. Now he had a second chance to be the lover she deserved. For the next few hours she was his prisoner in this hotel suite, and he was determined to make her feel better than she'd ever felt in her life.

He would show her what making love could really feel like.

Roark kissed her hard, and she matched him with passion of her own. When he drew away, he stared down at her. Licking his fingertips, he swirled them against her breasts, making smaller and smaller circles until he centered on the peak of her taut nipples making her gasp. He lowered his mouth to taste her, suckling each side. He kissed down her flat belly, stroking the inside of her thighs with his powerful hands, making her tremble beneath him.

"Oh, Roark," she choked out.

He wrapped his hands beneath her backside, holding her close to him. Pushing her legs apart, he flicked his tongue inside her, making her twist and sway. He felt the hot sweat of her skin, heard the quick pant of her breath.

And he smiled. Sliding on a condom, he lifted his body above hers.

But he didn't push inside her, not immediately. Instead he teased her. He felt her body arch to meet his as she instinctively tried to bring them closer, but he resisted. Beads of sweat formed on his forehead with the effort of not thrusting inside her. He moved slowly against her, tempting her until she gasped and pleaded wordlessly for release.

Finally, when she could take it no longer, he pressed inside her, inch by agonizing inch. But he didn't close his eyes at his own wave of pleasure.

Instead he watched her.

Watched the way she sucked in her breath, biting her full bottom lip. Her mouth was smeared with red lipstick, bruised with hard kisses.

He watched the way her eyelids fluttered. Her beautiful face turned up blissfully as if she heard choirs of angels. He watched the fervent movement of her lips as she soundlessly gasped his name.

With each slow thrust, sliding his hips in rhythm to the center of her pleasure, he watched her. Until she started to tense and shake beneath him. Then he rode her. Deeper. Faster. He never closed his eyes. He never looked away from her. When she finally cried out her release, their eyes locked, and lightning went through Roark's body, exploding him into a million chiming pieces.

His angel.

Being with her was like nothing he'd ever felt before.

Afterward, he held her. He wanted to be close to her. He stroked her as she dozed in his arms.

He'd never wanted a woman to sleep in his bed.

He himself had never been unable to sleep because he wanted to just stare at the woman he'd bedded.

Lia's beauty and power and goodness held him. He watched the slanting warmth of the afternoon sun leave a glow on her closed eyes, on her lips curved in a gentle smile.

She was perfect, he thought. The perfect woman. The perfect mistress. The perfect wife.

Wife?

He'd never thought he would marry, but looking at her now, he had the sudden desire to possess her forever. To keep her solely for his own use and pleasure. To make sure no man could ever, ever touch her. Permanently.

For the first time in his life, he could understand why a man would want to take a wife.

He'd never wanted any woman like this. Roark had always been determined to stay free.

Now, for the first time, ever, he suddenly had found

a woman who wouldn't commit to him. And all he wanted to do was pin her down.

He tried to push the thought away. He couldn't get married. He wasn't the marrying sort. And even if he was, Lia wouldn't marry him.

She wanted a home. She wanted a child. She wanted love.

What could he possibly offer her to compensate for everything he wouldn't—couldn't—give her?

"Lia," he whispered, stroking the inside of her bare arms. Her eyes fluttered open, and he saw her face light up with a smile on sight of him. And something inside his heart beat faster.

"Lia," he repeated, then swallowed.

Marry me.

Give up your desire for home and a family and love. Be mine. Give yourself to me.

"Yes?" she said, stroking his rough cheek and looking up into his eyes tenderly.

But he couldn't speak the words. Him, marry? Roark, take a wife? The idea was ridiculous! He'd spent his whole adult life avoiding commitment and emotional attachment. He wouldn't give that up now for some momentary lust.

Asking Lia to travel with him was already more than he'd ever asked any woman. It would be enough. It had to be enough.

He would make it be enough.

And he lowered his head to kiss her.

* * *

Lia had barely caught her breath from their first love-making session when he woke her.

But as he kissed her now, moving his hands against her naked breasts, she felt her body tense with instant desire. He was already rock solid against her. She timidly reached down to explore the most masculine part of his anatomy in a way she never had before, and he jumped beneath her touch. With a growl, he picked her up as if she weighed nothing at all.

Sitting up in bed, he placed her on his lap facing him. Sliding on a condom, he lifted her up in his strong arms, then lowered her over him, impaling her slowly, inch by inch. He held her tightly in his lap, with her legs wrapped around his body. He rocked back and forth, causing her breasts to brush against the dark hair of his chest. She felt her sensitive core slide slickly against his lower belly as he moved deeply inside her. Almost immediately, she tensed and cried out.

"Thirty seconds," he said, sounding amused as he brushed away the strands of hair stuck to her sweaty forehead. "Let's see if we can make you last longer than that."

For the next hour he tortured her with pleasure.

He rolled her on top of him on the bed, showing her how to find her own rhythm, to control the pace and the intensity of his thrust. He tipped her back onto the bed and lifted her leg over his shoulder to show her how deep he could be inside her. He tasted her with his tongue. Played her with his skilled fingers. Made her writhe...made her *beg*.

But every time she would start to tense and feel the deep

shake coming from within, he would abruptly stop. And he would move away, changing the rhythm. Until she was nearly weeping with the frustration of agonized desire.

He teased her like this for a full hour. And the entire time, he was rock hard and huge for her. How could any man last like this? How?

And how long did he intend to torture her?

"Please," she finally begged, tears streaming down her face. "Just take me!"

He looked down at her with dark eyes full of tenderness and gave her a wicked half grin. "I think you can handle another few hours."

"No!" she said fiercely, and then with sudden strength, she pushed him back against the bed. She climbed over him and lowered herself upon him. She held his wrists back against the pillow as he gave a soft gasp.

"My turn," she whispered in his ear. Using all the skills he'd taught her, she started to ride him. He tried to protest, but she ignored him, forcing him to thrust inside her again and again until he, too, started to tense and writhe.

Finally he breathed, "Lia, stop. Lia, I can't keep on like this. Slow down…oh, my sweet girl…" But against his protests, she kept riding him, moving her hips faster and forcing him deeper inside with every thrust. Until finally he tossed his head back and with a mighty roar he exploded inside her, shaking and trembling beneath her. In the exact same instant, she cried out as the spiraling pleasure took her so high that it nearly made her pass out.

With a shuddering breath, she collapsed against him.

For a long time, she wasn't even sure how long, he just held her. But gradually she came back to awareness. She felt him stroking her back. She opened her eyes and saw that he was awake, staring at her. As if he couldn't get enough of her.

And she wanted him.

Not just in bed.

But in her life.

Forever.

She realized with a sudden shock: *she was falling in love with Roark.*

No! she thought in desperation. *I can't fall in love with him!* She desperately tried to remember all the reasons she had to hate him.

But all she could think of was the stark vulnerability she'd seen in his face when he'd told her how his family had died in the fire. How his own grandfather had despised him and not even allowed him to love a nanny. How since he was seven years old he'd never had a real family or home…

But he doesn't want those things! she told herself fiercely. *He doesn't want a wife. He doesn't want a child!*

It was so hard to keep silent about their baby. She wanted to tell him so badly that it was choking her.

But she couldn't risk Ruby's happiness on a father who didn't want her. And she didn't want to force Roark into a responsibility he didn't want.

If she were truly starting to care for Roark, she told herself, she had to keep the secret. She had to give him the freedom he wanted.

And, a tiny voice whispered, *if he knew how you've lied all these months, he would hate you.*

She closed her eyes, unable to meet his gaze that ripped through her defenses, that ripped through her soul.

She was falling in love with Roark.

And she had to let him go.

She glanced at her diamond-crusted Piaget watch. "Two o'clock," she whispered. Ruby would be waking up from her nap. She took a deep breath. "It's late. I have to go."

"Late?" He moved beneath her. "Our flight across the Pacific doesn't depart for two hours."

"No." She started to sit up. "I'm sorry. This afternoon is all we can ever have. I can't travel with you. I can't risk…"

Can't risk my child's heart on a father who doesn't want her.

Can't risk you hating me if you knew what I hid from you.

He stared at her. "Lia, don't do this."

She briefly closed her eyes, gathering her strength. "You said if I came to your bed of my own free will, you'd let me go."

He grabbed her wrist. "Lia, wait." He took a deep breath, then looked her straight in the eyes. "If you won't be my mistress…then be my wife."

CHAPTER FOURTEEN

BE HIS wife?

Lia stared at him in the luxurious hotel suite, her heart pounding.

"You…want to marry me?" she whispered.

"I want to have you in my life." His eyes were dark, intense. "At any cost."

She took a deep breath. So nothing had changed. He still didn't love her. He was merely willing to marry her just to get his own way.

But how long would that kind of marriage last?

And if he knew about Ruby…

He didn't want a baby. And whatever he said now, he didn't want a wife, either. A man like Roark would never settle down with anyone.

He admired Lia because he thought she was honest and good. If he ever found out how she'd lied all this time—lied to his face—lied to him as she surrendered her body to his…

He didn't love her, and he never would.

And if he ever knew the truth, he would hate her.

Hot tears rose to her eyes as she grabbed up clothes from the floor. "I have to go."

She dressed quickly, then turned to go.

"Lia."

He rose before her, naked and strong and powerful. Her heart was in her throat as she remembered every inch and taste of his body. The way he'd felt against her.

"I know you want a home and family of your own," he said quietly. "Those are things I can't give you. But I'm offering you everything I have. More than I've ever offered anyone. I want you, Lia. Come with me. Be my wife."

She swallowed back the pain of wanting him. Perhaps if she weren't a mother, she might have been willing to sell herself short for the promise of the life he offered her.

But she *was* a mother. She had to put Ruby first.

Lia had already made a mistake by sleeping with a man who had no desire to be a father. She wouldn't compound the mistake now by marrying him.

"I've made my decision," she whispered. "Goodbye."

"No!" He took her hand.

She turned away. "You gave me your word."

Sucking in his breath, he dropped her hand.

"Yes," he said dully. "I promised."

"Goodbye." She started running for the door so he wouldn't see the tears streaming down her face.

But after she'd gotten into the hallway, slamming the door behind her, she leaned back against the door, wracked with silent sobs as she said goodbye to the only man she'd ever kissed. The only man she'd been tempted to love. The father of her child.

I'm doing the right thing, she told herself as she pressed the elevator button with a sob. *The best thing for all of us.*

So why did it feel so wrong?

She'd left him.

Roark couldn't believe it. He'd been so certain that she would be his.

He'd just asked her to be his wife.

And she'd refused him.

Perhaps it was for the best, he told himself. He rubbed his head wearily. He'd been a fool to impulsively blurt out the offer. He would have tired of her in a week. In a day. Lia had done him a favor turning him down.

Hadn't she?

The penthouse, with all its exquisite furnishings, echoed with silence. Marble, crystal, expensive hardwoods—all cheap and ugly now that she was gone.

His phone rang as he got out of the shower.

"The plane's ready for takeoff, Mr. Navarre," his assistant said respectfully. "Straight to Lihue with a brief fueling stop in San Francisco. I've had the driver pull around the front of the hotel. Shall I send someone up for your things?"

"Don't bother," Roark said dully. "I'm traveling light."

Traveling light. Just as he liked it. He put on his black shirt. His platinum cufflinks. His black pants and black coat of Italian wool.

But as he stuffed a few items into his leather suitcase, he felt strangely numb in a way he hadn't felt in a long time. Not since that frozen winter day so long ago when he'd lost so much in the fire.

It's for the best, he told himself again. It was no good to get too attached. And Lia was the type of woman a man could get attached to. He didn't want that. They would have driven each other crazy. And yet...

His hands clenched around the handle of his suitcase. He still couldn't believe that he'd lost her.

Downstairs at the reception desk, he spoke briefly to his assistant who would be following him to Tokyo in a few days' time. The main floor of the Cavanaugh Hotel was decorated with a thirty-foot-tall Christmas tree that was covered with red glass ornaments. All the joyful faces and colorful lights in the lobby irritated Roark, setting his jaw on edge.

As Murakami handled the hotel bill, Roark went outside. He blinked for a moment in the darkening winter afternoon, his breath turning to white clouds of smoke in the frozen air.

"Sir?"

Without a word, Roark handed the bag to his driver and got in the back seat. As the Rolls-Royce pulled away from the hotel circle, turning south on Fifth Avenue, his chauffeur said, "Did you have a nice visit in New York, sir?"

"My *last* visit," Roark muttered, looking out the window.

"I hope you'll be spending Christmas someplace warm, sir."

He remembered the heat of Lia's body, the warmth in her eyes.

The world is full of women, he told himself angrily. He would replace her easily.

And she would replace him. She would find a man who could give her more than Roark ever could. Maybe just some regular guy with a nine-to-five job who would come home every night to their snug little house. A man who would be faithful to her. A man who would be father to her children.

Roark's body hurt with need for her.

But he'd given her his promise. He'd never thought he would have to keep it. But she'd made her choice to turn him down. He had to respect her decision.

And yet…

He suddenly realized he'd forgotten to give her the twenty-million-dollar check.

The thought whipped through his body, making him sit straight up in the leather seat. "Turn right up here," he barked out.

"Sir?"

"Thirty-fourth and Eleventh," he ground out. "As fast as you can."

When his driver pulled up in front of the old building that held Lia's office, Roark jumped out of the car. He was too impatient to wait for the slow, rickety elevator, so he raced up the stairs, taking three at a time. He reached the third floor and pushed open the door. His heart was pounding, but not from exertion.

Sarah the receptionist looked up at him in surprised pleasure.

"Mr. Navarre. Did you forget something?" She

smiled. "Did you, um, did you want me to take you on the park tour after all?"

Lia wasn't here. She wasn't even here. His jaw clenched with suppressed disappointment as he took his checkbook out of his coat's inner pocket.

"The countess already showed me the park. But she left before I could give her the donation."

Bending over the table, he wrote a check for twenty million dollars to the Olivia Hawthorne Park Trust and handed it to her.

Sarah goggled at it in her hands. "I'll get you a receipt."

"It's not necessary," he said. He'd promised Lia he'd never contact her again, then he'd found a loophole to get around his own word of honor. And she wasn't even here.

Nice, he mocked himself.

"The countess would insist," Sarah said breathlessly. She quickly wrote out a receipt for a twenty million dollars. "How do you want this announced?"

"What are you talking about?"

"We'll send out a press release announcing your charitable donation, of course. Do you want this ascribed to you personally, or to your company?"

"Don't mention it. Don't mention it to anyone," he said grimly.

"Ah. Anonymous. Gotcha." She winked. "You're quite the do-gooder, Mr. Navarre. Families will enjoy this park for generations to come."

He growled at her, then turned to go. As he reached the door, he heard her sigh, "Lia will be so sorry she wasn't here to see this. But she always likes to be home when her baby wakes up from her nap."

Roark froze, his hand already on the doorknob.

"Baby?"

"She's the cutest little thing."

Roark went straight back to the desk. Her eyes went wide as she saw the fierce expression on his face.

"How old is she?" he demanded.

"That's the most romantic part," she replied with a sigh. "Ruby was born nine months after the count died. A miracle to comfort Lia in her grief. And Ruby is the sweetest little thing. She's crawling like crazy... Where are you going?"

But Roark didn't answer. He pushed open the door, rushing down the stairs in a fury.

A baby.

Lia'd had a baby.

And she'd never told him. She'd deliberately kept it a secret.

He remembered how nervous she'd been when he ambushed her outside her town house that morning. At the time, he'd thought she was just afraid he might try to invite himself into her bedroom. But she'd been nervous he might find out the truth.

Perhaps the baby had been born nine months after the count died, but the man couldn't be her father. It was impossible. Lia had been a virgin when Roark had first touched her!

She had told him herself at the wedding reception, there had been no one else since. He remembered the way the waiter at the café this morning had said, "We've missed Mademoiselle Ruby today."

"Who's Ruby?" Roark had asked.

A friend, she'd answered. Just a good friend.

God, he'd been stupid! Thinking he could trust a beautiful, clever, willful woman like Lia Villani!

He'd overestimated her good heart.

He'd underestimated the depths of her deceit.

She'd lied to him. She'd hadn't even given him the choice to be part of their child's life. Instead she'd been so ashamed of her baby's true parentage that she'd lied about it. Rather than admit that Roark was the one who'd fathered her baby, she'd told everyone her elderly husband had risen from his sickbed to father a child days before his death!

Fury made Roark's hands shake. *She'd tricked him.* Lied to him for a year and a half. All the time he was traveling the world, dreaming of her against his will at night, she'd been having his baby. Choosing to keep it a secret. Lying about the baby's father.

Lying to his face.

Lying to him in bed.

Roark clenched his hands.

And to think he'd actually intended to let Lia go.

He'd meant to keep his promise and leave her alone, no matter what it cost him. He'd actually intended to try and be noble. To give up his own selfish desires for the sake of respecting her wishes.

Noble. He nearly laughed at that now. He climbed into the back seat of his Rolls-Royce.

As the driver made his way to her town house, Roark stared out at the passing traffic. His lips curled back as he barked a cold laugh. He'd admired her. He'd thought she was special. He'd thought she was honest and good. Now?

He would keep her in his bed. She would stay there, his prisoner, for as long as he desired her.

The world was a selfish place. A man had to take what he could, when he could. And screw the rest.

CHAPTER FIFTEEN

"WELL, I'm off then," Mrs. O'Keefe said, picking up her purse and giving her employer a doleful stare. "If you're sure you don't want me to stay…"

"I'm sure," Lia said, wiping her eyes. She tried to smile at her baby, who was sitting next to her on the Turkish carpet in the front room playing with blocks. "I'm fine, really," she insisted. "I just…I'm a little sad."

"My dear, it's been a year and a half since he died. He wouldn't want you to take on so."

Of course, Mrs. O'Keefe thought Lia was weeping over Giovanni. How could she explain that she was heartsick over Ruby's real father, a man who was very much alive but who had no interest in having a daughter, loving a wife or settling down in a home?

"That's not why I'm crying," Lia said, wiping her eyes. "It's…someone else."

"Someone else?" The Irishwoman's eyes met hers. "Who?"

Lia shook her head. She was crying over a man who

would never, ever forgive her if he ever found out how she had lied.

But he would never find out. Roark was on his way to the Far East, never to return. She should be glad, right? She should be thrilled.

But she wasn't.

When she'd first found out she was pregnant, she'd hated Roark with such passion she'd thought the only way she could completely love her baby would be to forget the man who'd fathered her.

Now, every day for the rest of her life, Lia would look into her daughter's eyes and be reminded of an emotion entirely different from hatred. She'd be reminded of the way Roark had tenderly asked her to stay with him. And the way Lia had refused him.

The way she'd lied.

Stop it, she told herself, wiping her eyes fiercely. *Stop it.*

Ruby gurgled happily, handing her mother a wooden block with the letter *L.* Lia smiled through her tears as she looked down at her daughter.

"*L* is for love," she whispered, giving the block back to her.

She hugged her baby. Ruby would always have the best of everything. The best schools. The best homes in both New York and Italy. The best clothes. A mother who loved her.

There was just one thing that Lia couldn't give her.

"Don't feel bad to be the one who's left behind," Mrs. O'Keefe said softly. "Don't feel guilty. Your count will not blame you from heaven if you find someone else to love. You're young. You need a man of your own. Just as your wee girl needs a father who's alive on this earth to love her."

Lia stared at her. Then looked at her baby.

Ruby already had a father who was alive…

Oh, my God, she thought suddenly. *What have I done?*

She'd told herself that she'd kept Roark and Ruby apart for their own good.

But what if that had been a self-serving lie?

Roark was capable of change. He'd proven that today. He'd said he never wanted to get married…but he'd proposed to her.

Roark had also said he didn't want to be a father. But he might have changed his mind about that, as well. He might have taken one look at Ruby and wanted to be her dad.

What if Lia had just made the biggest mistake of her life—sending Roark away—not because she thought he would abandon Ruby, but because Lia feared he would hate her for keeping her a secret?

She took in a sudden breath.

Lia's own feelings meant nothing, compared to her daughter's needs. She had to put her child first. And no matter how Roark might hate Lia, if there was a chance he might want to be Ruby's father, she had no choice.

She had to tell him the truth.

"I hope you don't mind me speaking to you like this," Mrs. O'Keefe said, tears sparkling in her kind eyes. "I think of you as the daughter I never had. I don't want you to make the same mistake I did…"

Slowly Lia rose to her feet.

"Thank you," she whispered. "You're right."

The doorbell chimed. Mrs. O'Keefe cleared her throat awkwardly. "I'll get the door. It's likely that new stroller I ordered from the shop."

Nodding absently, Lia grabbed the phone on the elegant table. She dialed the operator and asked to be transferred to the Cavanaugh Hotel. She waited with her heart in her throat.

"I'm afraid Mr. Navarre checked out an hour ago," the hotel receptionist said.

Hanging up the phone, Lia felt like crying. *She was too late.*

"Yes?" Mrs. O'Keefe inquired at the door.

"I'm here to see the countess."

Roark's voice! He couldn't be here—couldn't be!

With a gasp, Lia dropped the phone from her suddenly numb hands. It clattered on the hardwood floor.

The gray-haired widow looked at him, then glanced back at Lia. "Ah," she said with a sudden grin. "So you're what all the fuss is about. You'll do well, I think. Come in."

And she held open the door.

He took two steps inside the foyer. He filled Lia's foyer with masculine energy, his black coat whirling around him as he came inside her house.

"What are you doing here?" Lia whispered. "You

said you'd never contact me again. I thought you were gone for good…."

"Goodbye, then!" Mrs. O'Keefe sang as she left, closing the door behind her.

"I didn't come here for you," Roark said. He looked at the baby sitting on the expensive carpet in front of the marble fireplace, playing with wooden blocks. "I came for her."

She sucked in her breath. "How did you find out?"

His jaw was hard as he turned on her savagely.

"Why did you tell the whole world that she's the count's baby? Why did you never tell me I had a child?"

Her mouth suddenly went dry. "I wanted to tell you."

"You're lying!" he said furiously. "If you'd wanted to tell me, you would have done it!"

"What was I supposed to do, Roark? You said you didn't want a child! You said you never wanted to be a father! And I hated you. When you left me in Italy, I never wanted to see you again!"

"That was your excuse *then*. What about yesterday, at the wedding? This morning, when we had breakfast? When you showed me the park? When we made love at the hotel? Why didn't you tell me then?"

"I'm sorry," she whispered. "I should have told you then. I was afraid you'd hate me."

His dark eyes froze right through her.

"I do hate you."

He went into the front room and got down on his knees. He handed a block to the baby, who smiled and chattered nonsense syllables, waving the block at him happily. He looked at her. And looked.

Then he picked the baby up in his arms.

"What are you doing?" she cried.

"My plane is waiting to take me to Hawaii and Japan," he said coolly. "And I don't trust you."

"You can't think of taking her from me!"

He narrowed his eyes and his lips curved into a cold, cruel smile.

"No. You will come, as well. You will travel with me wherever I wish to go. You will remain in my bed until I am finished with you."

"No," she gasped. Be in his bed, have her body possessed by a man who hated her? "I'll never marry you!"

"Marry?" He barked a laugh. "That was when I thought you were an honest woman with a good heart. Now I know you're nothing more than a beautiful, treacherous liar. You aren't worthy to be my wife. But you will be my mistress."

"Why are you acting like this?" she whispered. "You never wanted to be a father. Why are you acting like I kept something precious from you, when we both know that all you've ever wanted is your freedom?"

He just drew his lips back into a snarl.

"You will agree to my demands, or I will take you to court. I will fight you for custody with every lawyer I possess." He gave her a grim smile. "Believe me, you will run out of lawyers long before I will."

A cold shiver went through her. She looked at her baby in Roark's arms. Seeing them together, Roark tenderly holding his child, caused a crack in her heart. It was just what she'd always dreamed of.

Then he looked back at Lia, and all tenderness disappeared from his eyes. Instead she saw only hatred.

Hatred—and heat.

"Do you agree to my terms?"

She couldn't let him win. Not like this. She wasn't the kind of woman to surrender without a fight.

She lifted her chin. "No."

"No?" he demanded coldly.

"I won't travel with you as your mistress. Not with our child living with us. It's not decent."

"Decent?" His dark eyes swept through her like a storm. "You've never thought of decency before. In the rose garden. In the broom closet. In my hotel suite."

"That was different." Tears rose to her eyes, tears she despised as she glared at him. "If Ruby is with us, that changes things. I'm not going to set that kind of example for her, or give her that kind of unsettled home life. It's marriage or nothing."

"You'd rather show her the example of selling yourself in marriage without love—not just once, but twice?"

She flinched.

"I will accept your terms, Roark," she said hoarsely. "I will sleep in your bed. I will follow you around the world. I will give myself up to your demands." She swallowed. "But only as your wife."

He stared at her for a long moment. Then he bared his teeth into a smile.

"Agreed."

He put out his hand.

She reached out to shake on the bargain. The touch of his skin against her fingers sizzled her as he jerked her close.

"Just remember—becoming my wife was your choice," he whispered in her ear. He reached his other hand to stroke her cheek, looking into her eyes. "It was your mistake."

Roark married Lia in a drab little affair at city hall that evening. Mrs. O'Keefe held Ruby and acted as one of the witnesses; his assistant, Murakami, acted as the other witness. No family was in attendance. No friends. No flowers. No music.

Lia wore a cream-colored suit she'd pulled hastily out of her closet. Roark didn't bother to change out of his black shirt and pants. Why should he act like this wedding meant anything to him at all?

He didn't smile as they were married. He didn't look at her. He didn't even kiss her at the end. He just put a plain gold band on her finger as the judge proclaimed them man and wife.

And he would make his wife pay for what she'd done.

They left city hall for the downtown heliport in a Cadillac SUV. His assistant sat in the front passenger seat, next to the driver, with Roark directly behind him. As they discussed the current financial details of the Kauai and Tokyo build sites—the price of steel was going through the roof—Roark couldn't stop glancing at Ruby, who was in the baby seat next to him.

He had a daughter.

He could still hardly believe it. As Murakami droned on about the rising costs of concrete, a situation that normally would have been of the utmost importance to Roark, he barely paid attention. He couldn't take his eyes off his baby. She was yawning now, sucking sleepily from a bottle.

There could be no doubt she was his child. Her eyes were as dark as Roark's, with the same coloring he'd inherited from his Spanish-Canadian father. She looked just like him.

But she also looked like Lia. She had the same full mouth, the bow-shaped lips. She had the same joyful laugh, holding nothing back.

Roark would just have to ignore that. He despised Lia and didn't want to be reminded of her features in his baby's face.

He had the strangest feeling in his heart every time he looked at Ruby. He didn't know if it was love, but he already knew he would die to protect her.

A totally different feeling than he had for his baby's mother.

In the third row of the SUV sat Lia and the nanny, who seemed like a sensible, trustworthy sort of woman. But Roark would have her references investigated just in case.

He ground his jaw. His instincts were clearly not as sound as he'd once believed.

God, he hated Lia.

When he remembered the pathetic way he'd lowered his guard at the snow-filled park and spoken of how his family died—something he'd never discussed with anyone—his cheeks went hot. He'd even told her about his humiliating upbringing with his grandfather. The way Charles Kane had despised his low-class blood. The way he'd fired the nannies as soon as Roark began to love them. The way he'd tried to toughen Roark up as a boy, stamping out his childish, desperate yearning for his dead family with harsh lessons and cold comfort.

Roark had revealed himself to Lia in a way he'd never done with anyone in his life.

He had laid his soul bare to her.

Now, remembering how he'd been so determined to blow her mind in bed, practically begging her to run away with him, Roark was overwhelmed with anger and shame.

He would enjoy punishing her. Their marriage vows would be the chains he'd use to destroy her. He would make her regret eighteen months of lies.

She had made Roark want her. The thought still made him furious. She'd made him think she was special, a smart, sexy, loving woman different from the rest. She'd almost made him care.

And all along she'd been playing him for a fool.

"Thanks for coming," he heard Lia whisper behind him.

"It's no bother," Mrs. O'Keefe replied softly, settling back noisily against the leather car seat. "I couldn't let you and wee Ruby fly off into foreign lands without me, now could I?"

He realized the woman saw more of the truth about the relationship between Lia and Roark than she was letting on. She knew something wasn't right about this marriage, and didn't want Lia and her baby to face it alone.

For Ruby's sake, Roark was glad the woman had agreed to leave New York with them. He'd offered to double her salary for the inconvenience. He wanted his child to receive the best of care. He didn't want her to be separated from her caregiver, as he'd been as a child.

But he disliked the thought of Lia having a friend. He didn't want her to have any comfort.

He wanted her to suffer.

But not at the cost of Ruby's happiness.

The chauffeur parked the Escalade outside the Pier 6 heliport, following with their luggage and the baby seat. Murakami stayed behind as Roark's chief bodyguard, Lander, awaited them on the tarmac and escorted them to the helicopter.

After a seven-minute helicopter ride, they touched down at the small Teterboro Airport and boarded Roark's private plane. It was comfortable and luxurious. Roark, Lia, Ruby and Mrs. O'Keefe were the only passengers, waited on by three bodyguards, two copilots and two flight attendants, one of whom brought crackers and juice for Ruby as the other offered Lia a glass of champagne before takeoff.

"Congratulations, Mr. Navarre," the first flight attendant said, then turned to beam at Lia. "And best wishes to you as well, Mrs. Navarre."

Mrs. Navarre. The name went through Roark's soul with a shudder.

He had a wife.

A wife he hated.

Lia paled. As she took the champagne flute in her hand, she glanced uneasily at Roark.

He could see the question in her eyes. What did he intend to do with her?

He coldly looked away. Carrying his briefcase, he passed her without a word. He paused only to kiss the top of Ruby's tousled head, then went to the couch in the back cabin. He didn't want to see his wife's beautiful, troubled face.

She was meaningless to him, he told himself fiercely. Meaningless.

And so she would remain until they arrived in Kauai, where the beach house awaited them with a massive master bedroom overlooking the Pacific.

Then she'd learn her place in his life.

CHAPTER SIXTEEN

WITHIN an hour of landing on the beautiful Hawaiian paradise of Kauai, Lia knew she'd just arrived in hell.

Warm tropical winds swayed the palm trees above the tarmac. Lia had never been to Hawaii before, but it was lovely. The morning was fresh and bright as the dawn broke over the eastern hills. She took a deep breath, cuddling her baby as she descended the steps from the plane.

Two convertible Jeeps waited for them. Roark approached her, his eyes glittering and bright. For a moment she thought he meant to say something to her, but he only took Ruby from her arms and snapped the sleeping baby into the car seat in the back of the first Jeep.

"Come with us," he invited Mrs. O'Keefe. "I'm driving this one."

But he didn't say a word to Lia.

It was like a stab to her heart. And there was no way she was going to be left in the second car with the bodyguards and other staff. Raising her chin, she defiantly climbed into the back seat of Roark's Jeep, next to Ruby. She waited for him to insult her or tell her to leave.

He did something worse.

He ignored her. As if she wasn't there. As if she was a ghost.

Mrs. O'Keefe climbed into the front passenger seat. With a smile at her, Roark started the car and drove north on the narrow highway that twisted along the coast. The intense, fierce, demanding billionaire looked so different in this light. He wore a white T-shirt that revealed the hard-muscled shape of his body, casual jeans and sandals.

Lia had changed clothes, as well, into a tiny knit halter dress and high-heeled sandals that she'd brought in her suitcase, that she'd foolishly hoped might please him. But he hadn't even looked at her.

He was now speaking courteously to Mrs. O'Keefe, pointing out the sights as they traveled through quaint little surfing towns clinging to the edges of white sand beaches and rocky cliffs.

Mrs. O'Keefe glanced back at Lia several times, as if struggling to make sense of the obvious tension between the newly married couple. Lia shook her head with a smile she didn't feel, then tucked back her wind-tossed hair behind her ear as she stared out at the Pacific Ocean.

They passed resorts, pineapple stands and tiny Hawaiian villages. As they traveled north, the land became more lushly green. The coastline became more wild.

Wild and rocky like Lia's breaking heart.

Mrs. O'Keefe eventually fell asleep, lulled by the

roar of the sea and the hum of the Jeep's engine. Roark drove silently, looking straight ahead.

Lia stared at the back of his head. Tears welled in her eyes once again. She yearned for him to glance at her in the mirror. To yell at her. To insult her. Anything.

Anything but ignore her.

By the time they arrived at the large estate an hour later, Lia's heart had turned to stone in her chest. The caravan pulled through a gate, past a guardhouse into a private lane that led to a gorgeous estate. She saw an enormous, palatial beach house. She saw koi ponds edging a wraparound lanai and elegant, slender palm trees waving in the clear blue sky.

Roark stopped the Jeep in front of the beach house. He turned off the engine and walked around the other side of the truck, passing by Lia without a single glance.

He opened the front passenger door. "Mrs. O'Keefe," he whispered, shaking her gently on the shoulder. "Wake up. We're here."

The Irishwoman woke up and nearly gasped when she saw the tropical estate. "It's beautiful! This is your home?"

"For a few days." Roark unbuckled his sleeping baby from the car seat and tenderly took her in his arms, holding her against his strong chest.

Lia's heart ached with the vision of seeing their daughter held so lovingly in Roark's arms. How long had she yearned for just this moment? Since she'd found out she was pregnant, she'd wished she could give her daughter a father. A home.

And now, seeing their baby held this way by Roark

made her want to weep. It was the fulfillment of one dream.

But never once had Lia thought if that dream came true, another cherished dream would die.

She'd been married twice. Her first husband had wed her out of obligation; her second husband had wed her to punish her. She would never know what it felt like to really love a man and be loved by him in return.

One dream gained; the other gone forever.

Or was it?

Was there any way he might someday forgive her? Any way to earn back his trust?

"The housekeeper will show you to your room," Roark said to Mrs. O'Keefe.

"Shall I put the baby to bed, Mr. Navarre?" the nanny replied. "She hardly got any sleep on the plane…"

He shook his head, then glanced down at his sleeping daughter with a smile. "I'll put her to bed. I've never gotten the chance to do it before."

Lia could hear the blame in his voice, even though he didn't look at her.

He greeted the waiting housekeeper and staff with a few brief words, then passed them through the sliding door.

Leaving Lia behind without a single glance or word.

A hard lump formed in her throat as she slowly followed her husband and child inside. She really was starting to question her own existence, so she nearly jumped when the housekeeper greeted her, "Aloha, Mrs. Navarre."

"Aloha," Lia sighed, looking around her in amazement. "This place is beautiful. I didn't even know that Roark had a home in Hawaii."

The housekeeper cleared her throat. "Actually, this vacation house belongs to Paolo Caretti. They're friends. He loaned it to Mr. Navarre."

"Oh." Of course. Of course this house didn't belong to Roark. Even a place as incredible as this couldn't tempt Roark to want to settle down. Her husband only liked to create buildings that he sold to others. Then he always moved on.

And whatever she might wish, he probably wouldn't stick around long enough to raise Ruby, either. Even if he loved his daughter, he would still leave her. Because that's just how a man like Roark lived—with no commitments. Neither to places nor to people.

She squared her shoulders and took a deep breath. Perhaps it was a good thing to remind herself of that, then. She'd already started to fall for him hard. She'd felt her heart break at the stark pain in his eyes when he'd spoken about losing his family. She'd felt her body explode with joy when he'd made love to her at the hotel penthouse.

So having him ignore her was a kind of gift, wasn't it? It would keep her from loving him. Wouldn't it?

She went inside the front door and saw a man-made waterfall that flowed into an indoor pond. Glancing down at the pond, she saw orange and gold fish swimming beneath the water. She walked though the Japanese-influenced design and modern architecture, crossing the pyinkado hardwood floors and through the shoji sliding doors.

She followed the sound of his footsteps through the cool, darkened house. She stopped in the doorway of a nursery and watched as he carefully set their sleeping baby down in a sleek, simple crib, still holding her cuddly blanket and wearing her soft knit clothing set.

"Do you need any help?" she whispered, because she couldn't bear the silence any longer.

"No." He spoke without looking at her. "Your room is down the hall. I'll show you."

After hours and hours of silence, he'd finally acknowledged her presence! That was something, wasn't it? In spite of everything, she felt a tiny flame of hope in her heart as she followed him down the hallway.

He pushed open the sliding doors and revealed a large bedroom with a balcony overlooking the private beach. Sunlight sparkled over the bright blue Pacific like waves of diamonds over sapphires.

"It's beautiful here," she said.

"Yes."

She felt him put his hands on her shoulders.

Questions trembled on her lips. *Roark, can you forgive me? Can you change your wandering soul and stay with us?*

But she didn't dare ask the questions because she feared his answers. She closed her eyes as a breeze blew in from Hanalei Bay, warm against her skin. His body pressed against her back.

"It's time for bed," he said in a low voice.

The intent in his voice was unmistakable. Was it possible that he'd realized why she'd kept Ruby a secret and forgiven her? That he wanted and desired her as he had in New York—with a simple fierce longing that had led him to ask her to travel with him around the world?

Roark turned her around in his arms and she saw the harsh truth in his dark eyes.

No.

He still hated her. But that wasn't going to stop him from taking her body. He intended to coldly possess her.

And as he lowered his head to claim her lips in a fierce, bruising kiss, God help her but she couldn't deny him what he wanted. The heat and force of his embrace overwhelmed her senses. As he stroked her body, untying the back of her halter dress and dropping it to the floor, her longing was so sharp it edged between pleasure and pain.

He lowered her to the enormous bed. He looked down at her. He pulled off his jeans and silk boxers. She heard the roar and crash of the surf outside their open window, the warm breeze blowing in the hibiscus-scented air.

Then he possessed her roughly, without tenderness. But as she gasped with the joyful force of her pleasure, she could have sworn she heard him whisper her name as if it was torn from deep within his soul.

They settled into a pattern of sorts over the next four days.

Busy with work, overseeing the extensive remodel and expansion of a luxury resort on Hanalei Beach, Roark ignored her during daylight hours.

In the evenings he would come home for an elegant

dinner prepared by the mansion's chef. He spoke courteously with the staff and pleasantly with Mrs. O'Keefe. His handsome dark features glowed as he played with Ruby and read her a story before putting her to bed. But it was as if Lia didn't exist.

At least not until dusk.

She existed only to pleasure him in the dark. And every night it was the same. No tenderness. No words. Just a fiercely hot possession taken by an unloving lover.

Roark came home early one afternoon, and as usual it was as if Lia were invisible. Lia watched him play with the baby on the private white sand beach, helping Ruby make a sand castle. When it grew too hot, he cradled the baby against his tanned, naked chest and carried her into the ocean to feel the water against her skin.

For a moment, the baby looked nervous and glanced back at Lia, as if considering whether to cry and reach her arms for her mother.

"You're all right, little one," her father said to her softly. "You're safe with me."

Ruby looked up at him, and her expression changed. She didn't cry for her mother after all. Instead, she clung to Roark, giggling as her toes splashed in the water.

No one could resist Roark Navarre for long.

Watching them, Lia, sitting alone on the beach in the perfect sunshine of a Hawaiian day, felt her heart break a little more.

He was punishing Lia. Cruelly. Deliberately taunting her with what she'd never have.

And what she was starting to realize that she desperately wanted.

His attention.

His affection.

His love.

Lia tried to tell herself that she didn't care. The next day she went on a catamaran with Mrs. O'Keefe and Ruby, circling the island to see the sharp black cliffs of Na Pali, known as the Forbidden Coast. As the crew set up fresh pineapples, papaya and mango with chocolate croissants and a full breakfast, Lia sat with Ruby, who was wearing a baby-size life jacket. She stared out at the ocean.

Bottle-nosed dolphins followed in the wake of the boat, and in the distance she could see sea turtles swimming in the warm water. The brilliant Hawaii sun was hot against her skin. It was paradise.

It was hell.

Tonight I won't let him take me, she promised herself.

But when he came to her that night after she'd fallen asleep, waking her with his lips against her mouth even as his hands reached beneath her nightgown to stroke her naked body, she trembled and obeyed.

Not because he forced her.

Because she could not resist.

Some nights he didn't even bother to kiss her, but tonight he did. She heard the thwap-thwap-thwap of the ceiling fan above them as he pulled off her nightgown and panties in the darkness. She couldn't see his face. She could only feel his hands, rough and seductive against her skin. She felt her body start to rise, even as her heart split in her chest.

"Please," she cried hoarsely. "Please don't do this to me."

For answer, he kissed down her naked body, nuzzling her breasts. She felt the rough hair of his legs against hers, felt his hard muscles against her soft body. Her body cried out for his touch, like an addiction she couldn't control.

Stroking her hips, he spread her legs and tasted between her thighs. Her breathing became shallow, quick gasps.

She wanted him. Wanted *this*. So much it was killing her.

But it wasn't enough. She wanted more.

She wanted all of him.

She was in love with him. In love with the man who was so loving to their daughter. Who for one afternoon had been kind to her, as well.

She'd fallen in love with her tormentor. Wasn't there a name for that?

Marriage.

"Please, just let me go," she whispered. "Roark. Just let me go."

A trick of moonlight traced his cruel, sensual mouth as he gave her a smile.

"You're my wife. You belong to me."

He thrust into her, and she gasped as her whole body arched to meet his with the shock of unwilling pleasure. And she knew she loved him. Wanted him. Wanted everything.

She loved a man who only wanted to punish her.

And as he left her to sleep alone, she knew she'd just lost herself, body and soul, in hell.

The next morning she was surprised to see him at the breakfast table. Drinking black coffee and reading a Japanese-language newspaper, he didn't even bother to look up when she sat down across from him.

Then he said, "We'll be leaving for Tokyo today."

Leaving Hawaii? Lia should have been relieved. She should have been *thrilled*.

Instead she felt sad. These four days could have been a romantic honeymoon. A chance to make a wonderful memory as a family. Instead she would look back on their days in Kauai and remember only pain.

"Tomorrow's Christmas Eve," she pleaded, ignoring the painful lump in her throat. "Couldn't we at least stay here until…"

"We leave within the hour," he said coolly. And, throwing the newspaper down on the glossy wood table, he left her to eat alone, and salt her own bitter coffee with tears.

CHAPTER SEVENTEEN

CHRISTMAS morning, their luxurious Tokyo hotel suite was filled with mountains of presents organized and wrapped by Roark's personal staff. The bright silver Christmas tree decorated in blue had also been designed by his staff. Everywhere they went, they were serviced by the vast network of servants and employees around the world who existed to make Roark Navarre's life easier.

Lia hated it.

He'd ignored Lia's plea for a real green tree that she could decorate herself. She'd wanted to have her old family Christmas heirlooms shipped from Italy. But Roark had refused that, as well. He didn't want her to do anything for him. Ever.

Except, of course, at night. When he cruelly broke her spirit and her heart with her body's own desires.

Lia sucked in her breath as she saw Roark, wrapped in a black robe, enter the room carrying two Christmas gifts he'd obviously bought himself. No self-respecting member of his staff could have done it—the presents had been impatiently wrapped with rough, clumsy edges, and no bows or cards.

But as he came toward the couch where Lia sat with Ruby and Mrs. O'Keefe, she wanted one of those hand-wrapped presents more desperately than she'd ever wanted anything from Santa as a child.

But, of course, neither gift was for her. The first one was for Ruby—a handmade doll that he'd personally ordered from a tiny village in Peru. The second was a Himalayan cashmere scarf for Mrs. O'Keefe.

But as Lia pulled her cotton robe tighter over her nightgown, furiously swallowing back grief and disappointment, he miraculously pulled a box from his pocket.

"For me?" she whispered. As Ruby crawled around the floor in her footsie pajamas, gleefully ripping the wrapping paper, Lia placed the box carefully on her knees. This gift had obviously been professionally wrapped with its tinsel paper and big blue bow, but still…

Hope rushed into her heart.

He'd gotten her a gift. Could he be starting to care for her? To feel even a fraction of what she felt for him?

Was he starting to forgive her?

She looked up at him with a tremulous smile. "What is it?"

He placed his hand on her shoulder. "Just open it."

Holding her breath, she slowly opened the gift. Inside the silver wrapping paper was a flat velvet box. Inside the box was an expensive diamond necklace.

At least fifty carats of cold facets glittered at her.

Diamonds as cold as his heart when he took her body in the darkness.

Taking the necklace from her, he wrapped it around her neck like a slave's chain.

And for Lia, that was the end of Christmas.

They weren't in Tokyo for long. The heavy weight of the diamonds felt like an iron shackle worn by a sultan's harem girl while Lia acted as his hostess for a lavish New Year's Eve party in Moscow. While she listened to him speak in Russian, a language she didn't understand, and watched him flirt with beautiful, blond, hungry-eyed women.

He was slowly killing her.

The diamond necklace was a symbol of her captivity. He'd trapped her as certainly as any slave girl. He'd trapped her with the bond visibly building between him and their daughter. Trapped her with the love she felt for the man he'd been in New York. The man he still was, with everyone but her.

He would never forgive Lia for lying about Ruby. He would certainly never love her as she loved him.

Did he know how she felt? Did he know how it affected her when he took her body, without offering her even a tiny sliver of his heart?

Perhaps he did, she thought with a tearful shiver. He was doing it deliberately; it was his revenge.

But she stayed with him.

Because she'd given him her marriage vow.

Because she'd given him a child.

Because she loved him.

But as the months passed, as they traveled around the world checking on the various massive build sites of his projects, she felt a slow steady burn of anger rise inside her.

Staying in luxurious hotel suites—the Ritz-Carlton in Moscow, the Burj Al Arab in Dubai, then back to Tokyo—she acted the part of perfect hostess for his parties and business dinners. She often felt the eyes of other men on her. But the one man she *wanted* to look at her never did. Not with love. Not even with admiration. He ignored her.

Except at night.

It was too much. Finally, when they returned to Dubai, Lia snapped.

She hadn't slept much on the all-night flight from Tokyo. Roark had held her in his bed on the private plane. The memory of his sensual lovemaking, possessing her night after night like a punishment throughout their marriage, still blistered her skin. Every night, he taunted her with his skilled touch, teasing and withholding what she wanted most.

His admiration. His respect.

His love…

And when Roark again ignored her the morning they arrived in Dubai, going straight to his skyscraper building site and leaving Lia, Ruby and Mrs. O'Keefe to go to the hotel alone, she finally snapped.

Usually Lia would have unpacked his clothes and tried to make their family comfortable, to make their ultraluxurious hotel suite feel a little more like home.

But today, as she opened his suitcase, *she couldn't do it*. She couldn't unpack one more time.

Funny to think she'd once loved the idea of travel. Now she hated it. Everything about it. Even flying on a private plane, staying in five-star hotels and traveling with a full staff. Her mother had grown up in a wealthy family and had told them stories of traveling like this. It had sounded so exotic to Lia as a child. So luxurious.

Exotic? Luxurious?

She hated it. She wanted a *home*. She wanted friends and a job and a life of her own. Instead she had servants and a husband who despised her.

No.

She closed his suitcase with a snap. She'd had enough.

Lia dressed carefully in the hotel suite, in a scarlet wrap-dress with a plunging neckline. She brushed her dark hair until it gleamed over her shoulders. She called to make arrangements and when she hung up the phone she put on deep-red lipstick and glanced at herself one last time in the mirror. She took a deep breath. Her knees shook as she took the elevator downstairs and traveled into the booming city.

From the back seat of her chauffeured Rolls-Royce, Lia looked up at Roark's new skyscraper. The unfinished building looked like an ice pick wrapped in a dragon's claw. The walls hadn't been added yet, so the hot desert wind howled between the empty floors and steel beams.

After making sure the lunch had been arranged, Lia waited on the twentieth floor, shivering, alternating between fear and hope.

Throughout the months of their marriage, Roark had never wanted her company in private. He'd required her to host his cocktail parties, yes, but he'd never asked her to spend time alone with him.

Unless they were in bed. But that didn't count. He never asked her permission, he simply took her body as his due. And she couldn't resist. To be honest, she hadn't even tried. Because no matter how little regard he had for her soul, she still melted beneath his touch. And part of her had hoped that somehow, someday, if she tried hard enough, he would grow to care for her.

Hope made her heart pound faster in her chest as she waited for Roark now. Could she change his mind? Could she convince him to want a home after all?

A home…a family…a wife?

She glanced down at her exquisite platinum Cartier watch. *High noon.*

The elevator gave a ding.

Roark strode out, looking around him impatiently. He wore a sleek white suit, showing his sophisticated taste and perfect physique. The blindingly bright sun over the Persian Gulf cast Roark's black hair in a halo. He wore aviator sunglasses that made it impossible to see his eyes, and he had stubble on his hard, tanned jaw. The tiny imperfection somehow only made him more impossibly handsome. He looked to her more like a dream than a flesh-and-blood man.

"Roark," she called softly.

He turned and saw her. His jaw hardened.

She rose to her feet, trembling in her sexy leopard-print heels.

"What is this?" he asked coldly, looking at the little table with the tiny gleaming lights sparkling amid roses. She'd arranged for their chef to provide them with lunch, including all his favorite dishes per her instruction.

She steadied her shaking hands, clasping them behind her back. "We need to talk."

He didn't bother to appreciate the lunch she'd carefully arranged. He didn't even glance at the dress she'd so breathlessly chosen, hoping to please him. He just turned away. "We have nothing to discuss."

"Wait," she cried, blocking him. "I know you think I betrayed you, but don't you see I'm trying to make it right? I'm trying to make us a real family!"

He ground his jaw, looking away from her. "I'll fire Lander for this. He said I was needed up here."

"You are needed. By me." Taking a deep breath, she held out a key. "I want you to have this."

"What is it?"

She looked up into his darkly handsome face. "It's the key to my favorite place in the whole world. My home."

"Your home in New York?"

She shook her head.

"Italy," she whispered.

He stared at her, and for a moment she knew that he, too, was remembering the way they'd conceived their baby in the medieval rose garden. Remembering the heat between them. Before the hurt.

His face hardened.

"Thank you," he said coolly, taking the key from her. "But as you are my wife, it is an empty gesture. Since we married I've taken all of your possessions under my control."

Anger surged through her.

"Don't do this. We could be happy together. We could have a real home together…"

"I'm not a settling-down kind of man, Lia. You knew that when you married me."

She shook her head. "I can't bear to keep traveling like this," she whispered. "I can't."

Roark lifted her chin, looking down at her with a hot, sensual glance. "You can. And you will." He gave her a mocking smile. "I have faith in you, my dearest wife."

She shook her head. "You don't have faith in me," she said tearfully. "You don't even like me. While I—"

I love you, she'd wanted to say, but he cut her off.

"You're wrong." He pulled off his sunglasses, tucking them into his white jacket. "I do like you. I like the way you host my parties. You add glamour to my name. You raise my child. And most of all—" he looked down at her, sweeping her up into his arms "—I like the way you fill my bed."

"Please don't do this," she whispered, trembling in his arms. "You're killing me."

He smiled down at her. His handsome eyes gleamed darkly in the unforgiving sunlight. "I know."

And lowering his head, he kissed her.

He had such restraint, holding her loosely in his arms even as the passion of his kiss lit fires inside her body.

She felt herself start to surrender against him. Her will started to falter beneath the force of her desire. As always.

But this time…

No.

With a huge effort, she pulled away.

"Why are you deliberately trying to hurt me? Why?"

"You deserve to be hurt. You lied to me."

And suddenly she knew. Memories of their time together in New York flooded through her, echoes of his voice.

I want you to be with me, Lia. Until we're sick of each other. Until I have my fill of you. No matter how long it takes…. Who knows. It might take forever.

With a deep breath she shook her head. She raised her chin defiantly, looking him straight in the eye.

"You're the liar, Roark. Not me. *You.*"

His lips curved into a snarl. "I never lied to you."

"You're not punishing me because I kept Ruby a secret. You're punishing me to keep me at a safe distance. You asked me to be your mistress, and I refused. Then you found out about Ruby, and it was one more thing you feared to lose. Why don't you admit it? You love Ruby. And you could love me. But you're afraid to risk loving anyone—because you can't risk the pain of losing them. The truth is, you're a coward, Roark. A coward!"

He grabbed her hard by the arms, his fingers tightening painfully into her flesh. "I'm not afraid of you or anyone."

She shook her head desperately. "I know what it feels

like to love someone and lose them. I understand why you wouldn't want to face it again. That's why you're pushing me away. But you're not as heartless and cruel as you'd like me to believe. I know in your heart…you're a good man."

"Good?" he gave a harsh laugh. "Haven't I proven it to you by now? I'm a selfish bastard to the core."

"You're wrong," she whispered. "I saw your true heart in New York. I saw the soul of a man who was in pain. A man who—"

"Stop it, Lia. Just stop it."

Briefly closing her eyes, she leaped off the cliff.

"Roark, I—" she took a deep breath "—I've never said these words to anyone, but Roark…I'm in love with you."

He froze, staring at her.

"Be mine," she said softly. "As I am yours."

His jaw hardened. "Lia—"

"You're the only lover I've ever had. You saved me when I thought I'd never feel anything ever again. I love you, Roark. I want a home with you. I was wrong to keep Ruby a secret, and I'll always regret that. But can you forgive me? Can you be my husband, Ruby's father, share a home? Can you ever love me?"

The hot desert wind whipped tendrils of hair across her face as he stared at her in silence.

Then he finally spoke.

"No."

No. His answer went through her like a funeral dirge, like the doleful tolling of a church bell summoning mourners to grieve.

Tightening her hands into fists, she shook her head.

"Then I can't be your wife. Not anymore."

"You're my wife forever," he said coldly. "You belong to me now."

"No, I don't." Tears streamed unchecked down her face. "I wish I did. But if I can't be your real wife, I can't stay and pretend. No matter how much I love you. I can't stay and live in this twisted marriage with you."

"You have no choice."

"You're wrong." She lifted her head. "I'll never prevent you from seeing Ruby. Our lawyers will work out some arrangement of joint custody. And when I'm back in New York—I'll set the record straight. I'll tell everyone that you're her real father."

"Really?" His voice dripped scorn. "You will ruin your reputation? Be mocked as a slut and branded a liar?"

"I don't care about that anymore." She gave a harsh laugh. "A lost reputation is nothing, compared to being tortured by you this way, having you ignore me every day and make love to me every night, all the while knowing you will never love me. I won't let Ruby think this is a normal marriage. A normal way to live. She deserves better." She looked at him fiercely. "We both do."

"I can stop you from leaving."

"Yes," she said. "But you won't."

Straightening her spine, she walked toward the elevator door, not looking behind her. And her bravado paid off. He didn't grab her. He didn't stop her. She walked right into the elevator and the doors silently closed behind her.

I'm free, she repeated numbly to herself as the elevator sped swiftly down the twenty floors of his bare steel skyscraper. *Free.*

But she knew that was a lie. She'd lost the only man she had ever loved; the only man she ever would love. And she realized now that she was like Giovanni had been. *Love once, love forever.* She loved Roark, and she'd lost.

She would never be free again.

CHAPTER EIGHTEEN

Lɪᴀ blinked wearily as she stepped out of the plane. Mrs. O'Keefe was behind her carrying the diaper bag as Lia cuddled her crabby little girl in her arms. Ruby hadn't slept at all on the seven-hour journey from Dubai, and the baby was exhausted.

She wasn't the only one.

Outside, Lia saw the sun setting to the west over distant mountains. The tiny private landing strip was surrounded by forest that was the gold-green of spring. The evening was still warm, caressing her skin.

She saw her Mercedes SUV and driver awaiting her on the tarmac. Lia tucked Ruby into her baby seat in the back as Mrs. O'Keefe climbed in next to them. With a tip of his hat and a respectful greeting in Italian, her driver started the engine. Lia leaned back in her seat, staring blankly out the window.

Spring had come early in northern Tuscany. The air was surprisingly warm, racing gleefully from the clutches of winter. Cold streams ran rampant over the hills from melting snow, and the mountains were already green in the sunshine.

As they drove down the winding road, Lia's heart lifted in spite of everything. She knew these little villages and mountains and forest so well. They soothed her heartache. She knew the people here. They were her friends.

Friends. Lia thought of all the friends she'd left behind, both here and in New York. Everything she'd given up for Roark, hoping to make him forgive her. Hoping to make their marriage work.

All for nothing. It still hadn't been enough for him.

The driver finally turned down the private road, and Lia saw the place she'd missed for far too long.

Home.

The medieval castle rose from the evergreens and budding trees of the green-gold forest. It stood on a rock, built above the ancient foundation of a Roman fort.

"Home," she whispered aloud, her heart in her throat. Mrs. O'Keefe patted her hand as the Mercedes stopped in the courtyard. Lia carried Ruby out of her baby seat and Mrs. O'Keefe followed them to the front door, where they were rapturously greeted by Felicita.

"Finally you come for a visit!" the housekeeper cried joyously in Italian. She kissed the baby's cheeks. "You haven't been here since the wedding! At last, Ruby, *bella mia!*" The housekeeper swooped the bleary-eyed baby from her arms. "Welcome home! Are you hungry? Ah, no, I see you are tired…."

As the two older women hurried inside with the baby, Lia paused at the door, glancing behind her.

The setting sun was still warm, streaking pink and violet behind the green-and-gold mountains. She was home.

But everywhere she looked, she still saw Roark's face.

"Contessa?" The housekeeper peeked back out the door. She looked past her with a frown. "But where is your husband?" she asked in puzzled Italian.

Coming inside the castle, Lia leaned back numbly against the door, closing it behind her.

"I have no husband," she said in English.

She'd lost Roark. She'd lost her love. And for the rest of her life, she would know he was still alive, out there somewhere in the world, working, laughing, seducing other women.

Not loving her.

"Shall I give Ruby a bath? Poor lamb's too tired to eat. Shall I just give her a bottle?" Mrs. O'Keefe called down the hall.

"Contessa, I'm afraid dinner will be cold tonight," Felicita said in rapid, mournful Italian. "The old wiring, it has been having problems. There was smoke in the kitchen this morning, so I ordered the electrician. He was delayed and will come tomorrow morning."

It was all too much. Lia trembled, feeling cold all over. Feeling too numb to weep. She'd tried. She'd failed.

She'd lost the man she loved. She'd lost him forever. All she had now was her dignity to keep her warm. And her child...

"Mrs. Navarre?"

"Contessa?"

Lia jumped. "Yes, give Ruby a quick bath, please," she called back to Mrs. O'Keefe, then turned to the housekeeper. "Tomorrow's fine for the electrician."

"Do you want to put Ruby to bed, or shall I?" Mrs. O'Keefe called from upstairs.

"I'll be up in a minute." Lia pressed her face against the cool glass of the window, watching the last trace of scarlet sunset disappear behind the darkening horizon.

She'd escaped Roark's punishing captivity. But at what cost, when it had made her lose all hope?

"Va bene," the housekeeper said. "Shall I get you a cold sandwich for your dinner? A salad perhaps?"

Food was the last thing on Lia's mind. "No, *grazie.* I just want to go to bed."

As Lia tucked Ruby in her crib with kisses, both Mrs. O'Keefe and Felicita went to bed in their own suites in the servants' wing. Lia felt heart-stoppingly alone as she went to her own bedroom. The main wing of the castle was empty and silent. The air was as stifling as a tomb.

She put on her nightgown, then stared at her antique bed. The bed she'd slept in when she was a virgin wife, sharing this home and friendship with Giovanni.

She'd slept in this bedroom for ten years. And now she was back. As if nothing had changed.

She couldn't sleep here again.

Trembling with exhaustion and grief, Lia grabbed a pillow and blanket and went back to the nursery. The air still felt stifling. The baby's room was dark. Lia turned on the little nightlight inside the door, but with a crackle and burst, the light bulb exploded. Crazy old wiring, she thought, and tried not to cry.

Creeping through the darkness, Lia stretched out on top of the rug near the crib. She grew sleepy beneath the pool of moonlight listening to the sweet, steady rhythm of her baby's breathing.

A pity the electrician didn't come today, Lia thought with a yawn. But tomorrow would just have to do.

It wasn't a life-or-death matter, after all.

CHAPTER NINETEEN

ROARK couldn't sleep.

He sat up straight in his bed, disoriented. His head was pounding. He stared around him at the shadows of the luxurious suite in the Burj Al Arab hotel, the suite he'd expected to share with his wife.

Something was wrong.

He knew it by the way ice crept down his spine. By the sudden tremble of his hands—hands that were full of energy, wanting to act. But to do what? To fight for what?

Lia had left him.

So what? he told himself angrily. This jittery feeling, the way his hands clenched for an unknown fight and his belly coiled with fear, had nothing to do with her. Perhaps there was a business problem at one of the build sites. The complex architecture of the half-finished skyscraper in Dubai would give any land developer nightmares.

Yes. That had to be it. He was worried about the build site. Nothing to do with Lia. Or the way her expressive dark hazel eyes had looked at him a few hours ago with adoration when she'd asked him to love her. The beauty in her gaze, the love in her tearful eyes had knocked the air out of his chest.

It had made him more determined than ever to push her down. Push her back. *Push her away.* To show her the kind of uncaring, selfish bastard he really was. So she'd quit trying to lure and tempt him into the deep abyss of raw emotion that made men drown....

He couldn't forget the pain in her eyes when she'd called him a coward.

With a muffled curse, Roark tossed the blanket aside and got out of bed. As he took a shower, he felt the hot water envelop his body and he leaned against the tile, closing his eyes. He couldn't stop thinking about Lia's rapt expression when he'd come out of the elevator on the twentieth floor. Her beautiful face had been breathless with hope. She'd thought he might actually want to settle down with her in that old pile of rocks in Italy and make it a permanent home.

And then he'd finally crushed her.

He'd had his revenge, hadn't he? He'd finally punished her for her lies. Every night he'd held her in the darkness, every morning he'd seen the longing in her eyes, every day she'd wanted more of him than he could possibly give any woman.

Now, refusing her love, he'd punished her so badly that she'd never look at him that way again. He'd won.

And yet...

Somehow she'd snuck past his defenses.

The way he'd treated her over the past few months,

she knew the worst of his vengeful, selfish character. But that hadn't stopped her. She loved him anyway.

She was braver than he would ever be.

The traitorous thought made his whole body ache. Toweling off after the shower, he went into the bedroom. He wrapped himself in a towel as he opened the closet door. Empty. Where were his clothes?

Of course. When he'd finally gone to the hotel last night, he'd scowled and barked at everyone. He'd shouted off the hotel's butler who'd attempted to unpack his clothes; his own staff, who knew better than to be anywhere in firing range when he was in this sort of mood, had made themselves scarce. But for the past few months, even when he acted like an ass, servants had always invisibly managed to get into his bedroom and unpack his suitcase.

No. Not servants. Lia, he realized. She'd been the one unpacking for him all this time. Why? She was a countess, a seductive beauty, a busy mother, the sort of woman who always had a million friends. Why would she go to the trouble to unpack Roark's suitcase, quietly, privately, without even telling him about it?

The answer flashed on him immediately. *To make wherever they were seem more like home.*

Still wrapped only in a towel, he sat back on the unmade bed, stunned. Eyes wide, he looked back at the empty closet. He looked at his full suitcase.

Then he lowered his head in his hands, rubbing his temples. This exquisite hotel suite felt as empty and cold as a graveyard. He missed Lia and their baby. He remembered Ruby's laugh, the warmth of Lia's eyes. He wanted them. *Needed* them.

He cursed aloud. Lia had been right.

He was a coward.

Slowly he looked up.

He'd been afraid to love them. Afraid of ever loving someone again with all his heart, only to feel that heart shatter in a million pieces.

He remembered the sudden agonizing loneliness of that snowy night in northern Canada, watching as the fire burned the cabin to the ground.

"Stay here," his mother had said to Roark when her husband and older son never came out. Her desperate face was covered with tears and smoke as she looked at her seven-year-old son who was barefoot in the snow, shivering in his pajamas. "I'll be back, baby."

But she'd never come back. None of them had. Roark had waited as he'd been told. As the fire consumed the cabin, he'd yelled out their names. He'd tried to go inside the front door, but the fire had eaten away the porch, turning it into a fiery inferno. In panicked desperation, he'd run barefoot across the snow to the nearest neighbor's house two miles away.

For all his life, he'd thought it was his fault they'd died. He hadn't saved them. Maybe if he hadn't obeyed his mother and waited. Maybe if he'd immediately run for help, his parents and brother could have been saved.

Maybe if his mother hadn't saved him first, maybe if he'd never been born, his family might have lived.

But now he realized that even if he'd disobeyed his mother and run straight into the fire, he couldn't have saved them. He only would have died with them.

Roark stood up from the bed.

He'd thought all this time that he didn't want a home.

But against all expectation, a home had wanted him.

There was a reason the past three months had been the most settled of his life, no matter how often far or fast he ran away. Against his will, he'd found a home.

Lia.

Her steady heart, her courage, her will.

Lia and Ruby were his family. *They were his home.*

And he'd punished her. For what? For keeping Ruby a secret. He had been so infuriated at the sting of that rejection…but why?

Lia'd had no reason to trust him. He'd destroyed her father by taking his business, the catalyst that had ended in her family's deaths and forced Lia to marry an old man she didn't love.

Christ, Roark had told Lia outright he didn't want a child. Why wouldn't she believe that? But when he'd found out the truth, he'd punished her with coldhearted kisses and ignored her when he should have gotten down on his knees and begged her for a chance to be Ruby's father.

Begged Lia for the chance to be her husband.

Men all over the world would have killed to marry Lia, to have her in their bed, to have her love. And what had Roark done? He'd ignored her by day, and taken her body by night.

How was it possible she'd fallen in love with him? What had he ever done to deserve such a miracle?

Roark pulled a T-shirt and jeans out of his suitcase. Lia had swallowed her pride—which was almost as stubborn as his own—for months. Then she'd outright asked him to love her. She'd asked him to forget all their old hurts and to start a new life. A new home. A family. To love each other.

And he'd thrown it back in her face.

He didn't deserve her. He never had.

But…he could spend the rest of his life trying.

Opening his phone, he called Lander. "Get the helicopter to the airport. Get the fastest plane. Borrow one if you have to. Find out where she is."

"I already know," Lander said quietly. "At her castle."

Of course, Roark thought. Italy. Her home. The home he'd so callously thrown back in her face. He gripped the key she'd given him and tucked it carefully into his jeans pocket.

Seven hours later Roark's plane touched down in a private airport in Tuscany. Dawn was just starting to break over the green mountains. He took a deep breath of the clear mountain air. The morning was still dark and fresh with dew. New spring. New dawn. New chance.

The air was warm against his bare arms as he strode toward the red Ferrari parked and waiting for him on the tarmac. Starting the car, Roark gunned the motor. He pushed the car to the limit, squealing the tires as he barreled down the paved road and up the tiny winding highway.

He'd spent his whole life traveling as fast as he could,

always trying to escape his past. Now, for the first time in his life, he was trying to catch something.

Faster…faster… He drove at dangerous speeds off the highway and onto the gravel road. He heard the crackle of rocks hitting the Ferrari, ruining the paint as he skidded on the winding road that wended invisibly through the Italian mountains.

A smile traced Roark's mouth as he pictured how Lia would react when he woke her. Her hair, dark as a raven's wing, would be mussed from sleep. She'd wake and smile at him, her deep hazel eyes widening. Then she'd remember she was angry, and she'd tell him off.

He'd stop her anger with a kiss. And he wouldn't stop kissing her until she agreed to forgive him. He wouldn't stop until she let him love her for the rest of their lives.

Then he would make love to her with aching tenderness as the sun burst brilliantly over the green mountains….

Lia, I love you.

Lia, I'm sorry.

Lia…I'm home.

Roark looked up with a pounding heart as he finally arrived at the castle. He took a long deep breath of the fresh air.

Then slammed on the brake.

The same ice he'd felt seven hours ago stabbed through him. But instead of a trickle down his spine, the fear hit him like a tidal wave.

He saw a pale cloud drifting upward from one of the castle's second-floor windows, lifting towards the gray sky like a ghostly mist. Leaving the Ferrari with the keys still in the engine, he ran for the castle with his heart in his throat.

He knew that smell.

Smoke.

But the front door of the castle was locked!

Roark's hands trembled as he tried to use the key that Lia had given him, the precious key to her home. The home she'd begged him to share.

But his hands shook too much in his desperation. Finally he dropped the key and kicked down the door. It took three kicks before the heavy oaken door finally splintered apart at the lock and fell open.

He raced inside as the burglar alarm went off.

"Lia!" he shouted. "Ruby! Lia, where are you?"

He could smell the smoke more strongly than ever, but couldn't see where it was coming from. Where was the fire?

Where was his family?

He passed the expensive antiques, running on the newly gleaming floor. He saw a wide staircase.

"Mr. Navarre?" He saw Mrs. O'Keefe running toward him from the shadowy hallway in a thick flannel night-gown. Behind her, he could see an older woman in a white sleeping cap. "What's happened? The alarm—"

"There's a fire in the castle," he said tersely.

"Fire!" the Irishwoman gasped. "Oh, my God. Lia and the baby—"

"Where are they?"

"Upstairs, in the family wing. I'll show you—"

"No," he said harshly. "Get out. Call for help. Is there anyone else in the castle?"

"Just us." Mrs. O'Keefe glanced back at the woman behind her, who was speaking words in panicked Italian that Roark couldn't understand. The nanny's face was frightened as she looked upstairs. "Mrs. Navarre's room is at the top of the stairs, the baby's room to the right. Hopefully the alarm already woke her and she's on her way down…"

"Right. Hurry," he ordered them, and ran up the wide stairs, taking three steps at a time.

He had to find his wife and child.

This time he'd save his family—or he'd die with them.

Upstairs, heavy gray smoke hung like a thick cloud over the hallway. He found a bedroom at the top of the stairs with an antique bed. It was empty. The pillows and top blanket had been taken from the four-poster bed.

Lia hadn't slept here.

She had to be with their baby.

Roark whirled around and raced down the hall. But as he crossed to the next doorway on the right, the heat became palpable, almost unbearable.

He touched the door.

It was burning up.

"Lia!" he cried, coughing. "Lia!"

But there was no answer. No baby's cry. Just a whooshing sound, the crackle of flame.

His hand still on the hot door, Roark closed his eyes. His baby. His wife. His family.

He crouched close to the floor, where the air was better. Then pushed the door open with his shoe.

Waves of heat hit his skin.

The nursery was on fire. He saw flames leaping up through the edge of the floor, crawling along the far wall like a living monster.

He looked at the crib.

Empty.

The nursery was empty.

The relief that rushed through him nearly caused him to stagger as he rose to his feet. "Lia?" he cried out just to be sure. "Are you in here?"

No answer.

"Thank you," he whispered to no one in particular. Slamming the nursery door shut behind him, he ran down the hall, shouting for his wife and child.

And five minutes later he found them.

CHAPTER TWENTY

DREAMING in the cool garden, Lia was curled up with her baby on a blanket spread over fresh green grass. She was having such sweet dreams amid the roses, dreaming that Roark had come back to her.

I love you, Lia. I want to be your husband. I want to give you a home.

Something brushed her shoulder, but Lia didn't want to wake up. She didn't ever want to end her dream. Holding her sleeping baby tenderly in her arms, she turned her face away from whatever was trying to wake her.

"Lia!"

Tremulously Lia opened her eyes.

She saw Roark's handsome face above her, silhouetted against the reddish-pink sky of dawn.

"Roark?" she whispered, confused by the melding of dreams and reality. She sat up, holding her head.

"Oh, my love." He fell to his knees. Gathering Lia in his arms with a shuddering gasp, he kissed first Lia and then Ruby, who woke up and started to cry. He took Lia into his arms and held her fiercely and long, as if he never wanted to let her go.

When he pulled away, she saw tears in his eyes.

"Roark," she gasped, "what's wrong?"

He shook his head with a laugh at her shocked expression, then wiped his eyes. "I was a fool," he said hoarsely. "I almost lost you. For a few minutes I thought I did. And all because of my stupid pride. You were right, Lia. I was a coward. I was afraid…afraid to love you."

Her heart started to pound. Reaching up, she stroked his rough cheek. "Your face is covered with soot…"

"Later. Let's get you out of here." He picked up Ruby in one strong arm, cradling the baby to his chest, and reached for Lia's hand with his other. His hand felt so right in hers. She walked with Roark across the dewy rose garden and through the gate, never looking away from his handsome face. Afraid that if she did, the magic spell would end and she'd wake up.

Then she saw the fire truck parked awkwardly in the gravel driveway. Firefighters were busy putting out a fire inside the castle. Mrs. O'Keefe and Felicita were pacing frantically. When they saw Roark with Lia and Ruby, they ran to them with a joyful cry. It took several minutes before the two kindly women believed Lia's assurances that they were all right.

Lia stared in shock at the smoke still rising from the castle.

"It started in the nursery," Roark said quietly, standing beside her. "I spoke with one of the firemen. They think it was some problem with the wiring."

"Wiring," she repeated numbly. She shook her head. "Felicita told me there was a problem. I never should have…"

"A freak accident. There's no way you could have known."

"But we were in the nursery," she whispered. "Neither of us could sleep right. It was just too stifling and hot. So I grabbed the blanket and brought us outside. To get some fresh air." She looked at him. "I missed you. I thought in the garden I could pretend… Oh, Roark. You came back for us."

He took a deep breath, holding her hand tightly.

"I was a fool to ever let you go. I'll never do it again. Ever. You are my home, Lia."

She looked up into his face, saw the tracks of tears across his handsome, sooty face.

"I love you," he said. His dark eyes seared her soul. "I would go to the depths of hell for you. I'll spend the rest of my life trying to win back your love—"

She gave a choked sob. "You have it. Oh, Roark…"

Still holding Ruby with one arm, Roark wrapped his other around Lia's shoulders. Pulling her close, he kissed her, a kiss so sweet and true that she knew it would last forever.

He loved her, and she loved him.

Finally…they'd come home.

Three months later, Lia had her dream wedding to the man of her dreams.

As Lia stepped out of the horse-drawn carriage, she

looked out at the perfect June morning. It was lush and warm and lovely. The sky was blue, the birds were singing. The rose garden of the Olivia Hawthorne Park in New York was in full bloom.

Lia, too, was blooming. The night after Roark had found her in the castle garden, they'd conceived a baby. Just in time to not fit into her wedding dress, she thought ruefully. Only three months along, and she'd already gained fifteen pounds. She rubbed her belly with a grin. What could she say? Her baby had acquired a taste for the most fattening foods from all over the world. And so, it seemed, had Lia.

But it was nothing compared to the taste she'd acquired for being Roark's wife.

He was the one who'd suggested that they have a real wedding and renew their vows in front of all their friends. Nathan and Emily Carter, Mrs. O'Keefe and Lander—all their friends and staff had been invited to witness their joy.

As Lia reached the rose garden, wearing her dream dress of white beaded silk and holding a simple bouquet of red roses in her hand, she saw all the guests rise to their feet. The solo guitarist began to thrum an acoustic version of "At Last."

Her eyes met Roark's, and her heart leapt in her chest.

Their song.

Their wedding.

Their park. She thought of her sister, her parents, Giovanni. They'd all created this place. All the families of the city had a new park of their own, a place to run and play. The hospital across the street had a bright new view.

We did it, she thought, closing her eyes and remembering the people she'd loved and lost. *We did it.*

She felt the sun beam down warmly against her skin.

Opening her eyes, she looked at Roark standing at the end of the makeshift aisle of grass and flower petals, holding their one-year-old daughter. His handsome face was full of love and adoration for all the world to see.

He'd confided last night that he'd started a new development project: rebuilding their castle in Italy. "It'll be the same as before," he'd told her, "just better." And she believed him. She didn't see how on earth he could do it, but she knew that he would. "I'm going to make you happy, Lia," Roark had whispered last night before he kissed her. "I'll make you happy forever."

And she knew he would do that, as well. Because Roark was magic. *He was hers.*

Their life had only begun. A life with everything she'd ever wanted—and more.

With a smile on her face and grateful tears in her eyes, she took a deep breath and started walking toward the man and baby who were waiting for her—waiting to celebrate their love in front of all their friends, in a garden of red and gold roses beneath an endless blue sky.

Count Maxime's Virgin

SUSAN STEPHENS

Susan Stephens was a professional singer before meeting her husband on the tiny Mediterranean island of Malta. In true Modern™ romance style they met on Monday, became engaged on Friday and were married three months after that. Almost thirty years and three children later, they are still in love. (Susan does not advise her children to return home one day with a similar story, as she may not take the news with the same fortitude as her own mother!) Susan had written several non-fiction books when fate took a hand. At a charity costume ball there was an after-dinner auction. One of the lots, 'Spend a Day with an Author', had been donated by Mills & Boon® author Penny Jordan. Susan's husband bought this lot and Penny was to become not just a great friend but a wonderful mentor, who encouraged Susan to write romance.

Susan loves her family, her pets, her friends and her writing. She enjoys entertaining, travel and going to the theatre. She reads, cooks, and plays the piano to relax and can occasionally be found throwing herself off mountains on a pair of skis or galloping through the countryside. Visit Susan's website: www.susanstephens.net—she loves to hear from her readers all around the world!

For my friends, Danielle and Cathy,
and of course for la belle France.

CHAPTER ONE

THE men in the bar of the fancy London hotel had laughingly agreed that Tara should get out more. The better-looking of the two, a tall, powerfully built man called Lucien, with striking dark looks and thick nut-brown hair, argued with Tara's older sister, Freya, that there was no such thing as 'too quiet', and if Tara didn't want to party hard, why should she? Having flashed him a grateful glance, Tara sank back into the shadows with relief.

To get close to her sister was all eighteen-year-old Tara had ever wanted, but she was beginning to wonder if it was possible to get close to a flame that burned as bright as Freya. Maybe this was the way, Tara reflected later as she squeezed into some of her sister's clothes. The two girls had returned to their bedsit alone and were preparing to go out with the men they'd met earlier. Freya was always encouraging Tara to socialise, and tonight Tara felt it was a chance for her to prove she would do pretty much anything to win Freya's approval.

But not *that*, Tara thought, as the face of the man who had defended her earlier swam into her mind. Lucien's dark chocolate voice and black amused gaze had made her feel so nervous. He belonged to that other, more exciting world, the world Freya yearned to inhabit, the world in which Tara knew she didn't fit.

Freya thought nothing of talking to men they didn't know, but it was agony for Tara, who had hardly raised her eyes during the whole embarrassing encounter. She had felt so tongue-tied and gauche, so fat and so plain in her charity shop clothes, perched next to a glamorous older sister who drew attention wherever she went. She had wanted to disappear, and had only looked up once more when she'd been forced to answer the Lucien's direct question: 'Shouldn't you be studying?'

Instead of picking up men in a bar, she had presumed he meant. She had told him she did study, but by then, of course, Freya had moved the conversation on, wanting nothing to detract from the flirtatious tone she'd set. When Tara mentioned the remark later, Freya had laughed it off, saying Tara mustn't let it get to her, and that she had the rest of her life to study, and must use her youth to snare a man…

Tara's face was burning with humiliation as she thought about this now, though in fairness Freya had been partly right, for whatever he'd said about studying, Lucien, with the exotic accent, whose knowing gaze had sent flames of heat pulsing through her secret places, had asked Freya to make sure her little sister accompanied her to the party tonight.

Why had he done that? Tara wondered, going hot and cold as she thought about it. She already felt ridiculous, sitting here in their draughty bedsit, drenched in Freya's French perfume and wearing a body control underskirt Freya had said she must to create the right first impression. The second impression didn't bear thinking about. She'd have to be cut out of this top, just for starters.

'Stop fiddling with that top, Tara,' Freya insisted, breaking off from skilfully applying false eyelashes to admonish her. 'It cost a fortune—'

'Sorry…' Freya had insisted she must wear something glamorous tonight, and had pushed the spangled top into her hands. She was about to stop fiddling as instructed when Freya snatched it back.

'I've decided to wear it. You can have this one—'

'Thank you…' It was such a relief to exchange the glittery top Freya had picked out for her to wear, for an older, duller boob tube with a much more modest neckline.

'I hope you know your man's a count?' Freya pouted in the mirror as she applied her lip gloss.

'A count?' Tara's heart rate doubled. 'Really?' No wonder Lucien, the man who made her pulse race, was so confident and commanding. But since when was he *her* man? And if he was *her* man, what on earth was she supposed to do with him, never mind the fact that he was a count! She would never think of a thing to say to interest a man like that.

'You're a very lucky girl. It's up to you to make the most of tonight. Who knows…?'

Who knew what? Tara wondered, struggling to heave the Freya-sized Lycra top over her head. She raised a hesitant smile to please her sister. One thing was sure, she didn't know *anything* about *that* stuff, although her determination to better herself was no less than Freya's. There might not be room for a desk in their tiny room, but the books she was studying were kept safely under the bed.

'Here, put this wrap on—' Freya tossed what looked like a fabulous genuine fur in her direction.

'I'd rather not—' Tara shrank from the deep white pelt. In her imagination it still carried the faint scent of fresh air and freedom.

'Why ever not?' Freya demanded impatiently.

'I might spill something on it—' She hoped Freya was convinced by her excuse.

'Oh, all right then.' Freya pulled a face as she sorted through the tumble of clothes on her side of the bed. 'Take this shawl instead.'

Tara thought the pale blue shawl much prettier than the fur. Stroking it appreciatively, she thought about Freya's explanation for this fabulous collection of expensive things. 'Men like to buy me presents,' Freya had said, 'and what's wrong with that?' Nothing, Tara thought now, smiling fondly at her beautiful sister. Who wouldn't want to buy Freya gifts? When you lived like this and looked like Freya, no wonder her poor sister yearned for something better.

'What's that sigh for?' Freya demanded suspiciously as Tara started clearing up Freya's discarded tissues.

'Nothing…' Realising Freya had thought her sigh a complaint, Tara rushed to lay out her sister's coat and bag.

'See to yourself,' Freya snapped. 'I left that skirt out for you specially. Come on, Tara,' she chivvied as Tara viewed the tight skirt dubiously, 'we mustn't be late. And you can leave those cushions,' Freya snapped, bringing Tara to a standstill. 'They don't need plumping. I don't know why you bought them in the first place. No one's going to see them. For goodness' sake, stop tidying the room. You'll get all hot and bothered and we don't want that.'

What Freya did want from tonight made Tara very nervous. She knew she was destined to be a failure, because Lucien wasn't interested in her, and anything nice he'd said was just him being kind. That hadn't stopped her daydreams, which had a very dark edge to them, for they contained a lot of kissing and touching, which she knew was wrong.

She wasted some precious time fighting with the back zip on the skirt Freya had lent her, which was at least two sizes too small. In the end, she was forced to give up. Flashing a guilty glance at Freya, who thankfully hadn't noticed, she left the skirt open an inch or two at the top and folded the fabric over.

'Ready?' Freya demanded, snatching up her smart new red patent bag.

Ready to try not to show Freya up, Tara thought anxiously, straightening her tights. She hoped she could manage that much.

'Damn, it's so cold in here,' Freya said, rubbing her arms briskly. 'Come on, it's probably several degrees warmer outside.'

'If your fingers weren't half frozen you'd have been ready ages ago,' Tara said, laughing nervously in an attempt to cheer up her sister. She so loved to see Freya smile, but Freya was tense tonight, and Tara didn't need her sister to tell her that a lot hung on the outcome of their meeting with the two men.

Freya soon confirmed these thoughts. 'Don't worry, little sister; I don't plan to be living here much longer.'

Tara blinked at the horror of being separated from Freya. 'What do you mean?'

'I mean there's a big, wide world out there with a lot of wealthy men inhabiting it, men who want a woman just like me.'

'Oh…' Tara bit her bottom lip nervously. Of course

Freya deserved a better future, but as her own future rose like an empty canvas in front of her Tara wondered if she would ever get over being separated from her sister. They were orphans and Freya was the only family she had.

'You can always stay on here,' Freya said, continuing to touch up her hair as she spoke. 'Well, it's a start for you, isn't it?' she added, glancing at Tara. 'I'll sign the lease over to you before I go, as, most likely, I'll be living in the south of France—'

Tara knew it was the life her beautiful sister deserved, even if it left her feeling hollow inside. She brushed these selfish thoughts away. 'You always think of me.' She smiled, getting off the bed to give Freya a hug.

'Mind my make up,' Freya warned, backing away hastily. 'Now, listen to me,' she began firmly. 'You must make sure that count of yours takes you to his place tonight. He mustn't see this dump—'

'He isn't *my* Count,' Tara ventured, 'and I definitely won't be going home with him—'

'I wouldn't be so sure about that.' Freya turned and studied Tara keenly. 'You might be overweight, but you clean up well…'

'Not as well as you…'

'Ah, well…' Freya sighed with satisfaction as she took one last look at herself in the mirror. 'Hurry, hurry, hurry,' she exclaimed, spinning on her five-inch heels. 'We can't risk anyone poaching our men…'

He was restless as he waited for the two girls to arrive. This outing was a first for him. He never accompanied his brother, Guy, on his hunting expeditions, and yet here he was in a high-class pick-up joint, which his brother had persuaded him was the 'in' place that season.

After the encounter with the two women that after-noon he hadn't been able to shake the image of a timid young girl who had wanted to disappear into the shadows. And would have done if he hadn't coaxed her out of them, he remembered, flashing a glance at his watch, wondering what was keeping Tara. An occasion he had been so sure would bore him had acquired piquancy, thanks to her. Tara Devenish must be at least ten years younger than he was, Lucien reflected, though her sister's colourful reputation suggested Tara was no innocent. His body warmed at that thought, and right on cue the door of the exclusive supper club opened and in she walked.

The Count of Ferranbeaux drew the attention of the whole room as he rose to his feet. People sensed the dangerous edge to Lucien's mature elegance and it stopped conversation dead. Lucien was accepting of his physical needs, and after a week of non-stop business meetings even he would have admitted that his libido was in the danger zone, though he could not know that the miasma of testosterone cloaking his muscular frame was almost palpable.

Lucien made a silent note to add a London home to his ever-growing property portfolio. Entertaining in nightclubs wasn't for him, especially not on an evening like this. Tara was even lovelier than he remembered. She was quirkier and a good deal more outlandishly dressed too. Her pencil skirt had clearly been borrowed from her much slimmer sister, and the way she'd been forced to hitch it up had left it a good four inches short of respectable. Her ample breasts were stuffed for the occasion into a tight boob tube that revealed some tempting pale flesh, which for some reason she was trying to cover with a pale blue shawl. Surely, his cynical self calculated, shouldn't she be putting her wares on view rather than hiding them away?

He noticed nothing other than Tara as she walked towards him. He felt her aura of innocence, fear and excitement sweep over him, and when she stopped in front of him and gazed up tremulously he reached for her hand. Bowing over it, he raised it to his lips and, as her gaze sought his face, he felt her tremble.

The evening passed in a blur. The Count was at least ten times more attractive and a good deal more worldly-wise than Tara had remembered. Dressed in an impeccable dinner suit with a crisp white shirt, highly polished shoes and fine black socks, he looked like a film star and couldn't have attracted more attention from all the ladies present had he tried.

Which he didn't, and that was one of the nicest things about him. Even nicer than that was the way he looked after her. It was a little unnerving to begin with, because he was so much older than she was and her imagination insisted on working overtime, conjuring up all sorts of forbidden possibilities, but somehow he managed to make her relax. Then it was like a fairy tale. In her dreams she had always favoured the dark, flashing Latin looks of a Mediterranean hero, and Lucien Maxime, the Count of Ferranbeaux, or Lucien, as he had insisted she must call him, took Latin to the extreme.

As he turned to order another bottle of champagne, she stole a proper look at him. Lucien was very tall and very tanned, with hair the colour of roast chestnuts. It was thick and wavy, glossy hair, which he wore a little long, and as the evening progressed Tara decided that with the rough black stubble on Lucien's face, combined with those dark flashing eyes, he looked like a dangerous pirate. A pirate dressed by Savile Row, of course.

'Are you all right?' Lucien enquired, sensing her interest.

Better than all right. But as the keen black stare remained fixed on her face she went all wobbly inside and quickly folded her hands primly in her lap. 'Yes, thank you,' she replied politely.

Her simple remark prompted the wickedest look, as if Lucien knew her innocent pose covered some very naughty undercurrents and she gasped as his hand covered hers, though it was barely there for a moment. When he took his hand away she gazed down, certain his print would be branded there. She remained quite still after that, hardly able to believe the Count of Ferranbeaux had actually touched her. Then Freya said something and the spell was broken as Lucien turned away to take part in Guy and Freya's far livelier conversation, leaving her to watch his sensual lips move as he spoke, and dream more dreams as she inhaled his fabulous cologne.

How was she to guess he would turn so quickly and catch her looking at him? It was a relief when he said nothing to embarrass her, but, as one of his ebony brows peaked, she guessed he knew exactly what she'd been thinking.

Turning away to hide her burning face, Tara retreated into her thoughts, where she could have the luxury of the most frenzied fantasies. The conversation buzzed around her, but she was oblivious to it. She was too busy revelling in a fantasy world where a much older man was about to introduce a young, untried girl to a range of forbidden pleasures.

Freya's voice jerked her rudely out of this happy state. 'Come on, Tara, drink up,' she insisted impatiently.

Tara's cheeks flamed red as everyone turned to look at her. She had been trying so hard to keep up with Freya's drinking, for fear of being ridiculed, but had failed miserably. She had resorted to pouring her champagne into a conveniently placed plant pot when no one was looking, but now had no alternative other than to drain her glass.

Taking her by surprise, Lucien lifted it from her hand. 'We shouldn't kill too many plants,' he murmured discreetly, drinking it down, 'or they might not let us come here again—'

'Would that upset you?' Tara exclaimed, instantly concerned that she had offended him.

'Not a bit,' he confided, leaning close so that her face tingled with his warmth.

Of course he pulled away again, but not before she had felt a glow of happiness at sharing this private moment with him. She knew it was going nowhere, but made an extra effort to look good when he turned away. She smoothed her skirt and tried to tug it down to appear respectable, but it was Freya's and Freya liked to wear her skirts short. Adjusting her position on the banquette, Tara tried again. It was suddenly very important to her that Lucien shouldn't be ashamed of being seen with her. He was so elegant and she already liked him far too much to show him up.

She mustn't let these daydreams get out of hand, Tara's sensible inner voice warned. It was clear to everyone that Lucien Maxime was only trying to make her feel at ease and would barely register her existence by tomorrow.

Realising her restlessness had caused a pause in the conversation, Tara listened to her own good advice and remained very still. It would suit her best to be invisible for the rest of the evening, she decided.

They moved on to a restaurant, where Tara watched closely to make sure she was using the correct cutlery for each course. Lucien was kind again, arranging her napkin and spreading paté on her toast when she had been about to attack it with a knife and fork. She reached for some more bread, but quickly withdrew her hand when Freya gave her a warning look. They had agreed that Tara mustn't put on any more weight.

'You haven't finished your meal, I hope?' Lucien smiled at her as she scrunched her napkin anxiously. 'Here, try this… No…? A spear of asparagus won't hurt you.'

Asparagus with butter dripping from it? Tara shook her head a second time, but Lucien insisted on feeding the succulent spear to her himself, even mopping her chin with his own napkin when butter smeared her lips. And, as if that wasn't bad enough, he blotted some of the juice with his thumb sucking it whilst holding her gaze. This had an alarming effect on her, coaxing endless little pleasure pulses out of those secret places she wanted him to touch. Deciding a man like Lucien would surely know that made her cheeks fire up again. If there was a more sensual message a man could deliver to a woman, Tara couldn't imagine what it might be. But how she was supposed to respond to such advances remained a mystery to her.

She must be joined to Lucien by some invisible chain, Tara decided as her gaze kept wandering to him. Perhaps she was bewitched by him for, rather than wishing the evening could be over with, or that she could be invisible, she wanted the night to last for ever.

Freya soon put a stop to that, announcing that it was time to move on to an all night jazz club.

'Don't look so worried,' Lucien reassured Tara, seeing how concerned she was. 'You're coming home with me…'

Tara's face lit up. She was so grateful to Lucien. An early night, safe and alone with her dreams, was exactly what she wanted.

CHAPTER TWO

TARA was so relieved to hear that Lucien was taking her home she relaxed immediately and threw him a grateful glance. Then she saw how delighted Freya was and realised she'd missed the meaning behind Lucien's message. Going home with him meant going back to his hotel room.

She felt such a fool when they arrived outside the grand entrance to Lucien's magnificent penthouse suite, and only fear of upsetting Freya prompted her to follow him inside. Freya's insistent whispering before they'd parted—that everything was going so well for her and Guy that Tara mustn't screw things up now—was ringing in her head. Her fate was sealed, Tara realised the moment Lucien closed the door, for if there was an eighteen-year-old who could resist the Count of Ferranbeaux's brutally masculine charm it wasn't her.

She stepped cautiously across a cream-coloured carpet with pile so deep it felt like a mattress and gazed in awe at antique mirrors framed in gold, and at grand vases in matching pairs as tall as she was. The furniture was antique and both fabrics and walls were decorated in ivory and cream, as if dirt wouldn't dare to intrude here. The ceilings were high and decorated with gilt and plasterwork, and there was a heady fragrance in the air which she couldn't place at first, and then she realised it was wealth.

She was so entranced that Lucien had to take her by the elbow and lead her into the next room. This room was equally ornate, with arched windows dressed in heavy soft gold silk and a fire burning silently behind a glass screen.

'It's fake,' Lucien murmured, seeing her staring at the fire.

Of course she knew that, Tara pretended, reddening as she gave a little self-conscious laugh. It was a gas flame fire; she could see that now. She turned away quickly, though how she was supposed to act nonchalant amidst all this luxury, she had had no idea. She was standing in the middle of an intimate sitting room of a type she had no idea existed in hotels. It was a home away from home for the super-rich, she surmised, with magazines on the table, books on the shelves and an assortment of fruit that looked as if it had been picked that very morning. There were pictures on the walls that might have been original works of art and, instead of wallpaper, fabric—silk— glowing softly in tones of rich bronze and…

'Come over here and sit down before you fall over,' Lucien prompted.

She turned to see him smiling at her. What a country bumpkin he must think her. She pulled herself together quickly and crossed the room, trying to look confident, but there were so many lamps and tables she hardly knew where to tread and, in her usual clumsy way, she managed to stumble over a chair leg. Gasping with alarm, she reached out, only to feel strong arms catching her.

'Better now?' Lucien commented good-naturedly, steadying her back on her feet.

She had felt so safe in his arms that perhaps she didn't move as quickly as she ought to have done, and his next words proved it. 'I was going to order champagne,' he murmured against her hair, 'but I've changed my mind...'

She stared up at him, and his knowing half-smile sent ribbons of seduction rippling through her. She closed her eyes and just for a moment allowed herself to believe he was as captivated by her as she was by him and that now was the moment when he would sweep her off her feet...

'I've some freshly squeezed orange juice in the fridge,' he said casually, setting her aside so he could move towards the smart built-in bar. 'Or perhaps you would prefer me to call down for a hot drink...' He turned at this point. 'Cocoa, perhaps?'

Cocoa? Freya would not be pleased. Tara gulped unhappily. She could think of nothing to say. But how would she ever explain this mess to Freya?

'Why don't I make myself comfortable,' Lucien suggested, 'while you make up your mind?'

He was doing everything he could to make this easy for her, Tara realised, but she still couldn't relax. Her throat felt so dry she couldn't have spoken a word to him even if she could have thought of something to say. One look from Lucien was all it took to make her nipples pucker, so she crossed her arms over her chest and remained where she was, dithering in the middle of the room.

Lucien shrugged off his jacket, and his look of amusement caught her mid-gulp as she weighed up the width of his shoulders. She turned away, but not before registering the fact that his fingers were supple and capable as he deftly untied his bow-tie, and this only stirred more rebellion in her lower regions, which she could have well done without. Leaving the tie hanging, he next freed some buttons at the neck of his shirt. Sneaking glances at him, she now decided he looked exactly like a man in an advertisement for some high end luxury product, though far more handsome, of course. She went all dreamy again as she imagined touching that smooth tanned flesh and feeling it warm beneath her hands until the jangle of Lucien's heavy gold cuff-links hitting a glass bowl on the table jerked her back to reality.

'Won't you at least take your shawl off?' Lucien encouraged. 'Here, I'll put it somewhere safe for you…' He held out his hand.

She stared at him foolishly. By now he was folding back his sleeves, revealing powerful forearms shaded with black hair. 'I was just about to take it off,' she lied, wondering how a single inch of Lucien's fabulous suite could be called safe while he was in it. She took off her shawl, conscious that an acre of untoned naked flesh was now on show. Freya's hours at the gym had paid dividends for her, but Tara didn't have the time between jobs to follow suit, and would have felt too embarrassed to strip down in front of everyone, anyway.

'Come and sit here with me,' Lucien invited, beckoning her over to one of the sofas.

She chose the couch facing his and perched tensely on the edge of it. She was careful to sit very straight and lift her ribcage as Freya had shown her, in order to prevent herself looking too plump. But, as she did so, Lucien murmured, 'Impressive…'

Did he mean to give her confidence? She gulped in

horror, realising too late that he must think she was displaying her breasts for his approval. She quickly hunched her shoulders and lowered her gaze.

'Do I make you so nervous, *ma petite*?'

Risking a glance at him, she garbled something unintelligible that made him laugh.

'I don't think I am succeeding at putting you at your ease, am I?' Lucien demanded softly, 'though I'd very much like to do so…'

By sitting next to her? By draping his arm across her shoulders? She was about as far from at ease as she had ever been. In fact, she was quivering all over, wondering what Lucien expected of her.

'Relax,' he murmured, making her ear tingle with his warm, minty breath.

There was something so soothing in his voice she leaned into him. It felt so good just for a moment to rest her head against his firm chest and listen to the steady beat of his heart. Lucien made her feel so secure, and just for once she longed for rock instead of shifting sand, but when he brushed some errant strands of hair from her brow with his lips, she stirred self-consciously.

'Relax,' Lucien insisted.

She tried so hard to do what he wanted, but all the time her inner voice was warning her that this was no dream and was far more reality than she could handle.

'What would you like me to do next, little one?' Lucien murmured.

Her gaze flickered up, only to discover that Lucien's had darkened from sepia to black. Did that mean the world of wicked thoughts in her head was an open book to him? His knowing look suggested that was exactly the case, and his next words confirmed it. 'Shall we go to the bedroom?'

As he spoke Lucien touched his forehead to hers. It was such an intimate thing to do, her dreams took flight again. Oh, yes, she wanted to say, let's go there now, but she heard herself reply, 'I'm quite comfortable here, thank you.' Her voice had grown very small, and she knew that at this point she was supposed to sound breathy and provocative, as Freya had taught her.

'Then we'll stay here,' Lucien agreed with a shrug.

He didn't seem the least bit disappointed in her, Tara noticed with relief.

'Don't look so worried,' he insisted, cupping her chin. 'I won't bite…'

Or, at least, if he did, she would enjoy it, Tara thought as Lucien's lips tugged in a wicked half-smile. Sensation streamed through her at this thought, which he must have sensed because the hand that wasn't caressing her jaw began trailing a path of fire down her neck to her breastbone and, from there, unbelievably, incredibly, and quite fantastically, on to her bosom. She was transfixed. Whatever she had imagined about sensation, this was so much more—so much better. She hardly dared to breathe in case she distracted him as Lucien's sensitive fingers continued to tease and coax and cajole. Smiling faintly whilst holding her gaze, he murmured something in his own language. She didn't know what he said, but she could imagine and it made her groan.

'I think you like that,' he observed, continuing to abrade the tip of her nipple.

So much, he could have no idea. No one had ever touched her there before, and she doubted anyone could have coaxed so much feeling out of her. And yes, she liked it; she liked it a lot. Added to which, Lucien's stern voice was strumming her senses and causing the ache between her legs to grow until she could hardly remain still.

'You do like that,' he approved as she groaned once more beneath his skilful touches. She wouldn't know where to begin telling him how much. Her breathing was fast and shallow and her eyes were locked onto his burning gaze. She had no idea how to put her thoughts, her needs into words, though she was desperate to communicate them to him. Her biggest fear was that Lucien would tire of this and let her go. Unsure as she was of their final destination, she wanted to experience everything Lucien could teach her along the way. She was grateful when the flimsy top she'd had so much trouble tugging on proved no barrier to Lucien's explorations. He drew it over her head quite easily and then stared openly at her naked breasts, making a sound with his tongue against his teeth and shaking his head in disapproval when she tried to cover them.

'You should wear a bra,' he said at last.

'Should I?' she said anxiously, even as his stern command sent a pulse of arousal darting to her core. Something else she'd got wrong.

'Of course you should,' Lucien murmured with amusement, 'because that way there'd be more layers for me to unwrap, and I enjoy the process…'

She was beginning to understand the game, Tara realised, risking an uncertain laugh as Lucien peeled off her skirt.

'You must never, *never* apologise,' Lucien insisted. 'Certainly not for your magnificent breasts.'

He weighed them appreciatively in his big hands as he said this and, rolling her head back, she sighed, thrusting them towards him for more of his delicious attention.

She wanted as much of this as Lucien had to give her, but the moment he turned away to reach for something in a drawer she took the opportunity to tug off her shabby knickers. Lingerie was the one thing she had put her foot down over. Freya had wanted her to wear an uncomfortable lacy thong, while she preferred her tried and trusted comfortable knickers. But they were very old now, and she couldn't bear for Lucien to see them. By the time he turned back to her she had rolled them up in her discarded skirt.

Dipping his head, Lucien buried his face in her cleavage before rasping his stubble against her supersensitised skin, and by the time he tugged on her nipples again she could only cry out with abandonment. 'Oh, Lucien, I can't bear this...'

'Can't bear what?' he demanded sternly. 'This?' He suckled fiercely on one nipple, teasing the other between his thumb and forefinger. 'Or this...?' His voice was firmer still as he slipped a hand between her thighs, teasing the silky curls.

'Both,' she cried out in a voice that begged him for more. 'I can't choose... I don't know...'

By this time she was crazy for him and squirmed shamelessly beneath his touch. She had no idea how to ease the frustration mounting inside her, and only knew that she must... 'No!' she cried wildly when Lucien stopped touching her.

Lifting his handsome head, he studied the effect he was having on her with slumberous intent. 'No?' murmured.

'No, don't stop!' she explained frantically. Burying her fingers in his thick hair, she brought him back to her. Nothing—*nothing*—must stop this feeling inside her... *It* was going somewhere wonderful, though she didn't know where. Lucien had awoken appetites she had never guessed she had, and these appetites were sucking out the common sense from her head and replacing it with hot, hungry need.

He had anticipated her skin was like silk that carried the faint aroma of summer meadows, but he had not expected his fingertips to tingle with awareness like this. He took his time to trace each smooth pale inch of her, marvelling as he did so at the way her breasts filled his palms as if they had been made to fit there. Wherever he touched made her groan with pleasure, and whenever she groaned he found some new place to explore and increase that pleasure. Long before he had been ready to undress her she had started wriggling out of her wretched skirt, and he'd only had to help her to remove it. When he'd turned back to her after securing protection for them both, she had attacked his shirt without any of her former timidity, tugging it out of the waistband of his trousers and pushing it from his shoulders with a gasp of admiration. He wasn't a vain man, but he had always made time to work out. As she whimpered and reached for him, he realised he had never known a woman so hungry for love before. She was moving and clutching and sighing and even parting her thighs for him before he had thought of preparing her. 'Not so fast,' he warned. 'You'll enjoy it so much more if you learn to take your time…'

He had intended this to be a lingering seduction, but it seemed to him that Tara's intentions were very different. Perhaps she had been instructed to snare him fast? Perhaps those were her orders from her sister, Freya? Freya had hinted as much to him with her knowing looks and lascivious smiles in the direction of her younger sister, though if he had sensed Tara was at all unwilling he would have acted quite differently. Reluctantly, he was coming to the conclusion that Tara was part of a sophisticated double act in which she played as crucial a role in padding out the family finances as her sister.

There was an upside to this. It gave him the freedom to enjoy her, and he would make it worth her while. He was disappointed in her, he couldn't deny it, but the thought of sinking into that moist, plump flesh…the thought of pleasuring her, was irresistible.

But he would not make Guy's mistake and imagine this was more than it was.

'Lucien?'

He was instantly distracted by a voice as sweet and as innocent as Freya could have wished for. 'What is it, *ma petite*?' He had to hand it to Freya—she had trained her sister well. 'Tell me, *chérie*,' he encouraged. Tara was still new enough at this for him to want to take care of her.

She pouted prettily, a device no doubt learned from her sister. Tara might lack Freya's polished skills, but that didn't stop her throwing everything she had into this pursuit of her wealthy target. 'You have forgotten me, Lucien,' she complained.

'Never,' he murmured, soothing and petting her. But it wasn't enough; she wanted more. Of course she did. She had been told she must return to Freya like a hunter with her prize of a wealthy lover in the bag.

Even at the age of eighteen and a virgin, Tara knew the danger signals and had chosen to ignore them. She believed this was her one and only chance to live the fairy tale and have an incredible-looking man like Lucien Maxime make love to her. But, more importantly, she felt safe with him, and she had never felt safe before. In his eyes she could see the reflection of a sophisticated, smooth-running world where everyone was safe. She longed to be part of that world, under Lucien's protection, and knew she never could be, though for this one night she could pretend…

At the touch of his fingertips on her naked arms she exhaled raggedly. Lucien could communicate so much through touch. He promised so much pleasure, and she wanted to experience that pleasure. She wriggled shamelessly into a position where his hand must encounter her breast again. She might be plain, but she had seen men look at her chest before, and knew they liked it… If she could just keep Lucien's thoughts on the pleasures her body could afford him, perhaps he wouldn't turn away just yet…

She was perfect. Her breasts were a feast of perfection and he thought her lovely. This might be going nowhere, but he could lose himself for now. Tara was doing everything she could to make this possible for him and in return he would take her to paradise and back. If there was one thing he understood about a woman, it was her body and how to make it sing.

He lavished attention on every smooth and perfect inch of her, kissing and caressing her as he made her wait so that her senses sharpened. When that moment came and she couldn't wait any longer she grabbed his hand, guiding him to the sweet swell of her belly and pushing his hand down between her legs again. She parted those legs as if it was the most natural thing on earth to her, and even lifted her knees to encourage his exploration.

Moving down the bed, he tasted her and found her more than ready, but it pleased him to hold her back a little longer, knowing her pleasure would increase if she would only wait. She called to him during all this time with little whimpers of desire, which he answered by parting those swollen lips to find the receptive little bud trembling in anticipation of his touch. At the first lash of his tongue she shrieked his name. He caught her as she bucked and held her firmly in place to make sure she derived maximum pleasure from the experience. Far from subsiding in his arms when it was over, she clung to him and begged for more.

'Of course, *ma petite*...' He reasoned that she would want him to go 'all the way' so she could report back to Freya that she had bagged the Count as instructed. And she had, he thought a little sadly, knowing he was being manipulated. With his appetite, it was hardly likely that one night of excess with such a voluptuous young woman would be enough for him. His only hope of salvation was that by morning he would wake to find reason had returned.

Having protected them both, he slipped a pillow beneath her hips to tilt her into the most receptive position. Moving over her, he paused. The anticipation of sinking into that warm, throbbing flesh was so intense he wanted to hold back and savour the moment, but she wouldn't have it and, drawing up her knees as far as she could, she looked at him plaintively. He feasted his gaze on somewhere other than her face before testing himself inside her. They both exhaled sharply, which told him that neither of them could possibly have predicted this level of sensation. Even with his experience, this was a revelation. He withdrew completely, only in order to enjoy entering her again. He went deeper this time, taking her slowly and gently, conscious that he was stretching her. Whatever he thought of her, and whatever her level of experience, he was so much stronger than she was and honour demanded that he must treat her with care. When he thought he might be hurting her he stopped, but she urged him on, clamping her fingertips into his buttocks and working with him.

'Please Lucien…don't stop now,' she begged him when his impulse was to soothe her. But she was very tight, and he was very large, which made him move with the utmost care. Finally it seemed she relaxed again, and as her pleasure built her mouth fell open, and it pleased him to hear her sob in ecstasy.

He could see she was consumed by pleasure as he set up a regular pattern. He stared deep into her eyes to ensure she enjoyed this on every level. Her answer was to urge him on, straining to meet every stroke he dealt her as she closed her muscles around him to draw him deep.

It was more important for him to please Tara than he could possibly have imagined, though the sane part of his brain continued to warn that she had been well trained to please a man. He could see it all now. The Devenish sisters had set out that night in a wholly calculated manner to land a double prize, but whereas Freya might have succeeded, Tara's future remained in her own hands.

She lay next to him, watching Lucien sleep. The fantasy might be over, but she was determined to imprint every fragment of it on her mind. Biting down on her lip, she remembered the sharp pain that had marked the end of her innocence. But even that pain was precious because it was the only gift she had to give to Lucien.

Though the shock when he had taken her…

He had stretched her beyond anything she could have imagined possible. But he had also reassured her, and it was Lucien's care and gentle treatment of her that would stay in her mind.

She had been full of lust, Tara remembered, smiling shyly down at him, but Lucien had turned it into more than that, and for that she would never forget him or this night of passion. Whatever life held for her in the future, this precious memory of Lucien Maxime, the Count of Ferranbeaux, would remain safely locked away in her heart.

Which would have to be enough for her, Tara told herself sensibly, settling down in bed a respectful distance away from Lucien. She might have fallen for a man called Lucien, but the man lying beside her was the mighty Count of Ferranbeaux, and she wasn't silly enough to imagine he felt the same.

CHAPTER THREE

Two years later.

STORM clouds, unusual for the time of year in the far south of Europe, threatened rain as Lucien Maxime, the Eleventh Count of Ferranbeaux, halted his Aston Martin outside one of his many grand country hotels. Opening the car door, Lucien unfolded his powerful frame, retrieved his pale summer-weight jacket and threw it on. Sensing he was being watched, he glanced up. An unremarkable plump young woman with an infant in her arms was looking down at him from a wrought iron balcony.

Tara Devenish.

The shock of seeing Tara again was like a battering ram to his solar plexus and time melted away as he stared back at her. Was it only two years since that night? He'd lost a brother and gained a niece in that time. Guy and Freya had been married little more than a year when they had been killed in a horrific car crash, and the baby in Tara's arms was their orphaned daughter.

The sight of his niece lifted his heart, but to see Tara holding Guy's innocent child sickened him. He could only think of that night when Tara had ground her hips so shamelessly against him. She'd been good—better than good, she'd been practised, she'd been excellent—and he had later learned his brother had thought so too.

With a sound of disgust he slammed the car door, remembering how, shortly before the fatal crash, Freya had publicly denounced Tara for sleeping with her husband. Who knew what Guy's state of mind had been when he'd embarked on that tragic car journey? The way he saw it, Guy's blood was on Tara's hands and if she thought that touching cameo of her holding Guy's child would soften him she was out of luck. Someone should have warned her he was not as gullible as Guy—he was a different man, a very different man. He couldn't believe he had misjudged her character so badly.

Uniformed doormen, in the claret and gold of the aristocratic Ferranbeaux family, raced to open the door for him, but he got there first. Swinging the door wide, he acknowledged each man in turn by name. He might loathe the fuss and deference many men in his position so avidly courted, but believed that was no reason to brush people off.

Today, with little time to spare, he moved swiftly on. He didn't need the heraldic shield emblazoned on each man's jacket to remind him why he was here. The honour of the family was once more under siege, another scandal pending; another situation for him to deal with before the rumours got out of hand. Guy's death had opened Pandora's box and now Pandora herself, or that young ingénue, as he had once so foolishly thought of Tara Devenish, was here at his command. She had been easy to manipulate, wanting to see where Poppy would live before agreeing to sign the adoption papers. He suspected she had seen this as one last chance to follow her sister's lead in securing a wealthy husband. Why else had it taken a single phone call to her lawyer from his for her to agree to this meeting?

His hand strayed to the cheque already made out to Tara in his breast pocket. It was an amount large enough to cover her expenses for Poppy to date, and to buy Tara out of their lives for good. Everything he did for his brother's child would be above reproach and on his terms. Uproot, unsettle and unmask was the way he had dealt with every scrounger who had plagued him since Guy's death and he saw no reason to change his modus operandi now. Tara Devenish might think she was very clever, in her sensible shoes and neat suit, wisely deciding to cut a very different figure to her wayward sister, but it would take more than a costume to convince him she was not the double-dealing slut Freya had declared her to be.

Tara could evoke surprisingly strong feelings in him, Lucien realised as thunder rumbled an ominous sound-track to his thoughts. Two years ago he had thought her worth saving, and wanting to help out, he had left money for her on the night stand—lots of money, in the hope that she would use it to make a better life for herself. Now he felt he had been duped. He only had himself to blame. It wasn't even as if the signs had been unclear. Tara had been drenched in cheap scent and plastered in make-up, wearing an outfit designed to seduce. He could only conclude that his brain must have been lodged below his belt that night.

As the hotel manager hurried across the lobby to greet his Count, Lucien Maxime dealt swiftly with the formalities before making straight for the private sitting room where he had arranged for his meeting with Tara to take place. Lucien gave the room a quick once-over to check that everything was as he had requested. He had specified no flowers, no refreshments—no softening touches of any description. He would not allow Tara to imagine she had him in her sights again.

Having sent the manager to fetch her, he paced the room. Was it the prospect of seeing Tara or his niece that stirred such unaccustomed feelings in him? The truth, he accepted reluctantly, was that Tara had occupied far too great a part of his mind for the past two years. He had even considered looking for her to check on her progress, until of course the world's media had done that for him. The rage he'd felt then, when he'd read the newspaper reports documenting Tara Devenish's affair with his brother...

Even now it was all he could do to contain his anger. He shut that anger out, only to have another and even more disturbing image intrude on his thoughts—Tara, as she had looked in his bed.

He still wanted her.

That was the true torment.

As the minutes ticked by and there was still no sign of Tara, Lucien's expression darkened. She knew he was waiting for her to come down. At the very least, good manners demanded she should be on time for this appointment. Two years ago he had been prepared to indulge her, but no longer. Two minutes more and then he would go upstairs and bring her downstairs. An English court might have awarded Tara Devenish temporary custody of their niece, but both baby and Tara were under his jurisdiction now.

Seeing Lucien again was like a miracle—a miracle that made every part of her feel alive. She had forgotten

how beautiful he was and felt a shy embarrassment remembering how well they knew each other. When he
quit the car and the wind caught his hair, her body
reacted powerfully. When he straightened up all she
could think was how safe she had felt in his arms. But
when he looked at her and she saw the cold disappointment in his eyes her dreams collided with reality and she
rushed to shut that cruel look out.

She was too naïve for her own good, Tara reasoned,
walking across the room to put her sleeping niece down
to sleep. She could talk herself into believing anything:
that he had missed her; that he was coming to sweep her
up in his arms; that he was as eager to see her as she was
to see him…

That he had forgiven her never even came into her
thinking, because surely he must know the lies that had
been told about her couldn't be true…

Get real, Tara, she told herself impatiently. The
sordid facts were these: the first time she'd seen Lucien
in daylight was ten minutes ago. They'd met in a supper
club and had moved on to Lucien's hotel room, where
they'd had sex. At least, that was how he would see it.
She had woken to find him gone and in his place a wad
of money, along with the telephone number of a local
taxi company. Lucien had bought her services and, in
fairness to him, considering her lack of experience, he
had rewarded her well.

How red was her face now? Staring at herself in the
mirror, she patted her chipmunk cheeks, remembering
how, in her innocence, she had asked the man behind
the hotel reception desk on that night two years ago if
the Count of Ferranbeaux had left a forwarding address,
or perhaps a telephone number she could call. The man

had smirked as he'd told her that the Count of Ferranbeaux had checked out some time before, leaving no forwarding address, but that everything was paid for—including her, his expression had clearly stated.

She must have been the talk of the hotel, Tara thought, staring at the cruel reflection in front of her. The hotel staff must have laughed their heads off when she'd left. She only had to remember how pleasantly surprised and pleased with her Freya had been when she'd reported back to the bedsit. And no wonder— Freya must have known it was a long shot that Tara would interest Lucien.

Freya had been packing to leave with Guy, Tara remembered, and the fear and hollowness she had felt then came back to her now. Contemplating life without Freya had been dreadful. She had had no idea that one day their parting would be for good. Freya had smiled that morning and said gaily that it didn't matter if Tara never saw Lucien again, for there were plenty more where he came from, and that at least now Tara would know what to do with them…

Even today Tara shrank with shame as she relived that moment. She had been heartbroken, and had refused to believe that what Freya had said to her could possibly be true. Surely she would see Lucien again? Life would be unbearable if she didn't.

And now it was unbearable, because she must…

The only good thing to come out of all this was the lesson she'd learned; the life Freya had mapped out for her wasn't what she wanted at all.

Tara stared at her reflection in despair. She could breathe in, but she couldn't hold her breath for ever, and she couldn't drop three dress sizes in ten minutes.

Running her fingers through her mass of bright red-gold curls did little to tame her hair, but perhaps a little make-up would help…

If she had brought some with her.

She agonised, realising that high factor sun cream for infants and baby powder would hardly improve her looks. But it was all she had…

Grabbing the bottle of baby powder, she upturned it and sprinkling some on her palms, she wiped them across her burning cheeks…

Better…

Not much better…and certainly not perfect, but not so shiny, not so red…

Raking her bottom lip with her teeth, she wished it would plump out like it was supposed to do, and that she could reverse the colour of her lips and her cheeks—one so ashen and the other so red, but everything the wrong way round…

She tried hard to breathe steadily when she went to see Liz, the young nanny she'd brought with her. Liz had been trained by the same childcare college Tara had attended. Tara had paid her college fees with the blood money Lucien had left her; it had helped the shame somehow. Graduating with honours from that college had been the proudest moment of her life, and she must hang onto that now. 'Could you look after Poppy for me while I see the Count?' she asked Liz.

Tara had been offered a job on the staff of the college before tragedy struck, and when she had asked for leave to come and see where Poppy would be living the head of the college had been compassionate and had insisted she must bring Liz with her to Ferranbeaux. Everyone who knew Tara had read the newspaper articles condemning her and, without exception, her friends and colleagues had refused to believe a word they said. If only Lucien could be like them.

He wasn't, and there was no point wishing she could change him. Lucien had descended on the hotel like an avenging angel and was clearly not in the mood for negotiation, and now she had to meet him.

With every part of her trembling with apprehension. Lucien frightened her. His power frightened her. Anticipating the fact that he might look at her and laugh at her frightened her most of all.

She smoothed her skirt for the umpteenth time—her cheap skirt. But at least it fitted this time; she'd made sure of it. She checked her blouse—her cheap blouse. It was so cheap the fabric was like tissue paper, but if she kept her jacket fastened you couldn't see her bra…but then if she did that the buttons bulged…

Her breasts again…

Too big…

Everything about her was too big…

Including the big fat tears rolling down her cheeks. She hated them. They were a sign of weakness she couldn't afford with Poppy to defend.

Dashing them away, she sniffed loudly. Working out what was for the best, she decided on fastening the middle button on her jacket and leaving the other two undone…

Better.

Passable…

Not smart, but not bulging quite so badly now.

She was ready for whatever lay ahead.

Including Lucien Maxime, the Count of Ferranbeaux.

Lucien might be the all powerful Count of Ferranbeaux and hold all the cards, but did Lucien have the skills necessary to raise a child in the warmth and security of a loving family home? She wasn't going to let Poppy live in Ferranbeaux, cared for by strangers, just as she and Freya had been. Lucien could buy most things, but he couldn't buy time, and his business interests took up a lot of time...

Hearing a tap on the outer door of her suite, Tara whirled around. Her stomach was in knots. 'Come in...' Her voice sounded small, tremulous, pathetic, even to her.

'Ms Devenish?'

Tension seeped from her shoulders when the door opened and the hotel manager walked in. 'Yes?'

'Monsieur le Conte has arrived, and is waiting for you downstairs...'

Having powered through the gates in his twenty-first century equivalent of a fiery black stallion. Yes, she'd seen him.

'Ms Devenish?' the hotel manager prompted.

She was panic-stricken. There were too many holes in her plan. She needed more time. She had brought Poppy to Ferranbeaux because her lawyers had said she must, but whose orders were they obeying? Tara wondered now. She had seen Lucien's contempt for her as he must have seen her feelings for him. He believed the newspaper articles; ergo he believed her unfit to care for Poppy. He had come to take Poppy away. He thought her one more conniving woman who expected to profit from his brother's death.

As the hotel manager cleared his throat Tara swiftly refocused. Words had never come easily to her, and before the accident she had been content to remain in Freya's shadow, but with Poppy to protect that part of her life was over now. Tipping her chin, she spoke firmly. 'Thank you for delivering the Count's message. Please tell him I would like a little longer—'

'A little longer' would never be enough. It was better to get on with it, get it over with.

The manager's huff of surprise suggested he thought so too. But this was all just such a leap from the quiet life she had shared with Poppy since the accident. *All the more reason to hold their first meeting here, rather than in a public arena where she might make a fool of herself...* 'Could you ask the Count to come to my suite in say...ten minutes?'

'Here?'

The hotel manager seemed astounded, and Tara guessed that only years of training in the art of discretion allowed him to keep his opinions to himself.

Her relief was short-lived when he turned to go, for now the clock was counting down the seconds before she saw Lucien again—the man she adored, the man whom, the last time they'd met, had paid her off like a whore.

She listened intently to every sound, waiting for Lucien... She stilled her breathing, waiting for his footfall on the stairs. She wished she wasn't so tense. If she'd been more skilled in womanly wiles she might have known how to soften him, or if she'd been feisty, rather than hapless, helpless and useless, she might have known how to stand up to him. Unfortunately, she was none of these convenient things. She was barely twenty, and pretty clueless when it came to men. She was also plump, plain and poor and even her own sister had called her boring. Finding the right words was the least of her worries when she couldn't launch a good argument to save her life. And when it came to clothes and social graces...

By this point Tara's teeth were chattering with fear,

which was no help when her body was thrumming with awareness at the thought of Lucien just a few strides away. She knew he wouldn't have been idle while he'd been waiting. He would have been using this time to finesse his plan to eject her from Poppy's life.

She must blank her mind of fear if she was going to get through this. It was no good talking herself into meltdown; she must think things through clearly.

But, try as she might, the only thought Tara could come up with was that if Poppy had been old enough to pick a champion, her Aunty Tara should be last pick.

But who else was there to champion Poppy's cause? Lucien?

He'd make a far better job of it than she could, Tara reasoned, though he'd do it remotely through his servants.

Crossing to the window, she flung it open and inhaled deeply, hoping for a miracle. But there were no miracles—there was just Tara, an orphaned baby, and the Count of Ferranbeaux. That was the cast and it was up to her to decide whether she was content to play a role, or whether she would write the play. It was certainly time to get a grip. She wasn't the girl of two years ago; she was trained in childcare now and where Poppy's happiness was concerned she would fight tooth and nail to preserve it. It helped remembering a tutor at the college telling her she possessed a natural air of authority, and that it would raise her tiny stature in the eyes of a child. Would it work on the Count of Ferranbeaux? Somehow, she doubted it.

Lucien paced the room. Servants hovered, anxious to cater for his every whim. He waved them away. He wanted one thing, and one thing only, which was to have this meeting over with. Only then could he take his niece to a place of safety. At least, that was what he had been telling himself for the past half an hour, but the truth was more complicated. He wanted Poppy safe, that was a given, but Tara had dug her neat clean fingernails into some hidden part of him, and he was impatient to pluck them out.

He glanced at his watch again. How dared she keep him waiting? Didn't she think this meeting important enough to be on time? He had imagined she would be keen to get to work on him. Perhaps she was too busy luxuriating in the suite of rooms he had provided to remember her manners...

He stopped pacing to rake his hair. Even he was prepared to admit that last thought didn't reflect the Tara he knew. She might be cleaning the suite. He still remembered her surreptitiously picking up the napkin Freya had carelessly dropped on the floor, and then mopping up a pool of wine Freya had spilled on the table in the same graceful sweep. That Tara certainly didn't live up the sluttish image the media and her sister had painted.

He'd only just reassured himself with this thought when the old newspaper headline bounced into his head: The Unexpected Mistress. And the images of Tara in Guy's arms that conjured up made him physically sick. Lucien thought back to his own night with Tara; when she had thought he was sleeping she had whispered that there would be no other lovers.

So much for such adoration and innocence!

What was keeping the hotel manager? Lucien's eyes narrowed with suspicion as he stared through the open door towards the stairs. It was time to remember that Tara shared Freya's tainted blood. It was time to confront her.

CHAPTER FOUR

IT WASN'T just the aura of danger surrounding Lucien Maxime that drew attention as he crossed the hall. Tanned by the sun, and hardened by experience, Lucien married menace with style, which was a compelling combination. His tailoring was the best, and his only adornment a wrist-watch and a pair of gold cuff-links engraved discreetly with his crest. A man whose estates encompassed thousands of squares miles either side of the French and Spanish borders felt no need for the show other men considered necessary to boost their status.

Halting at the foot of the stairs, Lucien saw the hotel manager hurrying towards him. 'Where is she?' he demanded.

'Ms Devenish will not be coming downstairs, Monsieur le Conte—'

A spear of concern pierced him. 'My niece—'

'Is quite well, as far as I can determine, *monsieur*.'

Relief coursed through him, but his thoughts switched immediately to Tara. 'Then why does Ms Devenish choose to remain in her room?'

'Mademoiselle Devenish asked me to inform you that she will be happy to receive you in her suite in ten minutes.'

She will be happy? *She will be happy?*

Anger flared inside him. Not only had Tara defied his explicit instruction, she had dared to issue one of her own. It was time to call her bluff. How much could she have changed? Was she cowering in her suite? Or exulting in it at the thought that her pay cheque was only a few steps away? Whatever her motive, his niece would be raised in the security and stability of his family home and would not be left to the careless affections of some woman on the make. 'No matter,' he rapped in a tone that caused the unfortunate manager to press back against the wall. 'I will go to her.'

'Yes, Monsieur le Conte…'

As he mounted the stairs he fingered the cheque in the breast pocket of his jacket. If he had learned one thing from his father, it was that life had a universal currency. Tara would have her price. He would pay her off and then forget her. He stopped at the half landing and turned to see the manager still hovering and eager to be of service. 'I take it Ms Devenish is alone?'

'One other woman is with her in the suite with the child.'

'Who is this other woman?' His hand tightened on the banister at the thought of anyone standing between him and Tara. 'Do you know her?' It was not unheard of for men in his position to be trapped by unscrupulous women; witnesses could be hired and paid to make false accusations.

'I believe the other woman is the child's nanny.'

His lips pressed down as he thought about it. 'I was told Ms Devenish was acting as my niece's nanny. I was led to believe that was her profession now.' It had been reported to him that Tara had been awarded a diploma in childcare, and he had imagined her running some sort of agency from her front room.

When the manager remained silent he was forced to draw his own conclusions. The 'nanny' was a useful prop Tara had brought along to enable her to put aside the child she said she cared so much about whenever it suited her. *Just as her sister would have done…Freya Devenish…* He formed the name silently with detestation as he continued on up the stairs. Freya Devenish, with her wild blonde hair and her careless outlook on life…Freya Devenish, a woman who had put her baby second to her own pleasure. If Tara thought she could trick him as Freya had tricked Guy— 'Don't announce me,' he told the manager grimly. 'It is my intention to catch Ms Devenish off guard.'

He would dismiss the nanny and find out Tara's true intentions as well as what it would cost him to get rid of her; no amount of money was too great to safeguard his niece's happiness. The way he felt about Tara right now, he couldn't wait to see the back of her, but was it that thought driving him on, or some baser need?

The fact that she was in no hurry to see him stung him far more than it should have done and urged him to brush every remaining particle of compassion he might have had for her aside. It didn't matter what he found inside that suite of rooms—cunning schemer or last chance saloon girl here in a bid to finish what she'd started two years ago—either way, he was paying her off.

She had been listening so intently with every atom of her being on full alert that when Lucien finally knocked on the door a cry escaped her lips. Only a thin piece of wood divided them. She knew it was him. She couldn't mistake him when the sound of that imperative rap rang with his strength and his steely will, as well as his determination to have this over with. The hotel manager had made barely a sound, but then he had been schooled in the art of discretion, whereas the Count of Ferranbeaux saw no need for discretion, and why should he, when this was Lucien's suite, his hotel, his country—?

Where she was under his command...

Tara's body responded violently to the thought, though she tried to fight it. She tried warning herself that it was safer not to be in an advanced state of arousal when she opened the door, but her body wasn't listening. Her body was eager to feel Lucien's hand again, which left her a quivering mass of fear and apprehension.

And lust.

Her mouth dried. Other parts of her weren't quite so cooperative. How was she supposed to forget that night? She would never forget it, and neither would her body.

As the door shook with the force of a second knock, her teeth chattered as her mind sculpted the muscular frame behind the door. As the sound waves rippled through her head she could sense Lucien waiting outside like a predator preparing to pounce.

While she was what? The mouse with nowhere left to hide?

She exclaimed in fright as another knock sounded. 'Just one moment, please...' She sounded so strained, so timid and apprehensive and could only be thankful that she had remembered to slip the lock. Lucien was undiluted power, and she got the distinct impression that his shoulder would follow his fist if she didn't rush to answer the door.

Gulping in air, she smoothed her hair...checked her

skirt…her jacket…her collar… If the devil was in the detail, goodness knew what was in this short, plain, overweight package. If only she could close her eyes and open them to find herself tall and slim and elegant, with all the right words on the tip of her tongue.

'Tara,' Lucien bellowed. 'If you don't open the door, I'm coming in—'

'No, I'm here… Sorry.' She was actually standing rigid in the middle of the room with her fists clenched by her sides.

'Well, hurry up…Open the door.'

That beloved voice… He sounded so…utterly furious with her. She stumbled forward, disappointment and disillusionment propelling her. It only took one step…two to close the distance between herself and the door. 'I'll just open up,' she informed him unnecessarily, in an overly bright voice that sounded totally false.

'Well, come on, get on with it.'

She must stand strong. She stared at the handle, trying to concentrate. *She must stand strong.* Freya's tragic life and death was the most terrible warning. That was why she had got herself educated—made herself a better life—wasn't that worth fighting for?

Her mind blanked as Lucien rattled the handle again.

'What are you waiting for, Tara?'

She had to believe that somewhere beneath all the bitterness he was still Lucien, the man who had been kind to her.

She freed the lock with trembling fingers. Keeping her glance firmly fixed on the floor, she flung the door wide. She felt Lucien intimately in every part of her. He transformed her. He transformed her life… 'Monsieur le Conte…' Even now she felt more alive, but her voice was shaking. She had prepared for this moment so carefully, or thought she had, but nothing could have prepared her for the reality of Lucien Maxime, the Count of Ferranbeaux in person, only inches away.

Lucien strode into the room, walking straight past her without even acknowledging she was there. Halting, he turned and stared around the room.

He had ignored her.

And she? What had she done? She had stood there suffused with emotion, unable to speak. But the well of feeling inside her wouldn't be contained. 'Lucien, I was so sorry about your brother—'

His look froze the words on her lips. 'I'm not here to discuss Guy with you.'

His words rang in the silence, each one of them a death knell to her hopes. They carried a world of condemnation. Lucien had nothing but contempt for her and believed everything he had been told.

He shifted position and stared down at her from his lofty height. He couldn't have made it more apparent that this was now his room and she was an unwelcome visitor. Not only was it his room, this was his land, where Lucien's rule and Lucien's law prevailed.

And she was a lovesick girl who was already regretting the fact that on the one occasion when she had found some words to speak they were the wrong words.

But those words had come straight from her heart, Tara reasoned, and she had to believe Lucien was suffering for his loss as she was over Freya. She couldn't think him so cold-hearted he felt nothing.

And still she loved him.

She only wished she could reach out and offer him support—a thought so crazy she knew that only feelings so deeply ingrained and so precious to her could have prompted it. This man didn't want her. Lucien didn't want or need anyone's love. He was more polished and confident than ever.

Tara felt her spirit dwindling into nothing beneath Lucien's scornful gaze. She felt her fat cheeks burning beneath their pitiable coating of baby powder. Meekly, she turned to close the door behind him with exaggerated care. When she turned around Lucien studied her with a face that registered absolutely nothing. If his eyes showed anything at all, it was that she was an impediment to his day, and one that wouldn't hold his attention for very long.

'Tara...'

The deep, familiar voice held only irony and distaste. She searched his eyes, hoping for something softer in them, while Lucien searched for flaws, more things to count against her.

He'd find plenty, Tara concluded. She was still overweight, still plain, gauche and out of her depth in every way; she was still smoothing her skirt with repeated strokes of damp, shaky hands. 'Poppy's in the other room,' she managed, hoping to draw Lucien's attention away from her.

This failed too. He continued to stare at her while her cheeks continued to burn until she felt a faint sheen of perspiration starting to break out unattractively on her brow.

'I'll see my niece in a moment.'

This was her worst nightmare come true. This meeting was so awful, so completely at odds with her childish daydreams of seeing Lucien again, she felt strangely disembodied, as if this couldn't possibly be happening to her, because it was far too upsetting—far too final a rejection of her.

But it was happening. Lucien was here and he despised her. There wasn't a spark of humour in that deadly gaze. This was for real. You had better not be a whore, he seemed to be telling her, or I'm going straight to that nursery and taking Poppy from your care.

Tara realised she must have shivered at the thought because Lucien suddenly rapped, 'Why don't you ask the staff to close the windows if you're cold?'

Hysteria rose inside her and she almost laughed. If *she* was too cold? The roll of money Lucien had given her two years ago flashed in front of her eyes. That roll of money condemned her. He must be pleased to think she had never attempted to return it. He must imagine it would strengthen his case against her in court. Only she had the satisfaction of knowing she had used the money to pay her college fees. Perhaps it was that that allowed her to hold his gaze now. 'I know what you're thinking—'

'Do you really?' he said.

His voice was so deceptively mild, but his smile was cruel. Menace hung around him like a garland of thorns. Tara paused, unsure of herself but then the thought of Poppy gave her strength. All she could think of was the little girl sleeping down the corridor who depended on her. She would always stand between Poppy and the loneliness of being brought up by servants, whatever Lucien chose to throw at her.

'You were about to read my mind, I believe,' he prompted coldly.

Two years ago he had been kind. Two years ago he hadn't looked at her as if she was something he'd picked up on the sole of his shoe. Two years ago she had lost her heart, her virginity and, yes, ultimately her self-respect. And perhaps she should have stayed out of his way, but she hadn't. How could she leave Poppy's future for lawyers to fight over? She couldn't. She had to fight for Poppy. And so Lucien's path had crossed her own again. 'Do you believe everything you read in the newspapers?' she asked him quietly.

'Are you suggesting those reports were a pack of lies?'

'I had hoped you would know the answer to that—'

'So they were lies,' he said, cutting her off. 'Told by your own sister?'

Tara flinched at the look Lucien was giving her but, however much he provoked her, she would never speak badly of Freya. 'Freya was mistaken,' she said frankly.

'And you can prove that?'

Each time she spoke Lucien stamped on every word she said and kicked it aside. But she had always known this would happen, Tara reasoned, and only her wild imagination had allowed her to believe this meeting might be different. But she would defend herself—she had to. 'Whatever you think, I didn't sleep with Guy—'

'And I have the word of the "Unexpected Mistress" for that?'

Tara paled at Lucien's use of the cruel headline. 'Believe what you will of me, but I know the truth.'

Lucien remained unmoved and the ugly words he'd spoken hung between them like a challenge until she couldn't stand the tension any longer. 'Why would I want to sleep with Guy, when I'd slept with you?'

There was a flicker in his eyes, but his face remained a frozen mask she couldn't read. 'Why would I, Lucien?' She raised her voice. 'Guy talked to me sometimes… He asked me about Freya. He wasn't a bad man, Lucien… He was just—'

'Don't you dare presume to talk to me about my brother.'

He took a step forward, his eyes narrowed to slits of pure venom. His voice was pure ice, his stare heated. The anger between them was like a living force. She made herself hold that terrifying gaze, and was horrified to feel the energy slowly turning into something different.

No…

No… She shook her head, denying the evidence of her own eyes, her own body… This couldn't be happening… It mustn't happen…

She wasn't imagining it. In Lucien's eyes there was a look of pure appetite, a look she had not the slightest wish to ignore. It was the look of experience, of expertise, of understanding exactly what she needed. Her body responded powerfully to him. A look was enough to banish her fears and turn her dreams into a raging inferno of pure lust. Lucien knew this, and the understanding in his eyes only stoked the fires inside her.

And her heart? What about her heart?

A great black hole had swallowed up her heart, and all her foolish daydreams with it. Standing outside herself in these last few moments while rational thought was possible, she could see that for all his money and immense power Lucien was emotionally bankrupt, while she had too much feeling—enough to spare for him, if only he would accept it. But Lucien didn't want her compassion; Lucien wanted release. This wasn't an exercise to test her moral fibre, it was a simple basic need.

It had been so long and yet the touch of his hands on her arms made the lonely months melt away, and she was instantly transported back to a night two years ago, with the pleasure he'd brought her then fresh in her mind. She went with him in every way, every step of the way, holding his gaze and believing in something that didn't exist. It was no use trying to will her softer feelings into him because, whatever Lucien could or couldn't see, he was incapable of feeling.

He was careful with her, because she was so much weaker than he was, but they both knew where this was going. There was no point in dressing it up as something more when it was appetite pure and simple on both their parts. He had come here with the intention of taking the child home with him. Wanting Tara was an addendum, an inconvenience, an appetite he would sate and then move on.

'Do you want this?' His look silenced her.

Her lips parted and she closed her eyes. He stared hard at her. Her chest was heaving and she was flushed. 'Do you want this?' he repeated harshly.

She opened her eyes then and stared at him. 'I dreamed of this moment for two years,' she whispered.

Her lips…her full, trembling lips tempted him. Was this the slut he had read about, or could he believe her explanation about his brother? He leaned his weight against her and felt her body respond—did she respond only to him? He pulled back again and stared down at her. She met his gaze levelly.

Her eyes had grown dark and slumberous. Brushing her hair back from her brow as if he would find something to steal his trust away beneath its silky weight, he dipped his head and kissed her.

It felt like coming home.

He had to remind himself that he had many homes and didn't stay long in any of them.

He took off his jacket and tossed it on a chair before

helping Tara to remove hers. From there it was a scramble on Tara's part to lose the rest of her clothes. Last time, she couldn't wait to lose her knickers, he remembered. He lowered his zip and freed himself. Then sank into her and worked his hips to the accompaniment of Tara's frantic urging cries. She felt incredible and took him to places he hadn't been for two long years. Shutting his eyes, he closed out the doubt and concentrated on the pleasure streaming through him. He moved deeply and firmly, ramming her into the couch with each long, powerful stroke and, as the furniture shook and their makeshift bed inched its way across the room, some part of him registered that this was probably the most action the creaking floorboards had known in four centuries.

And still she wanted more.

'More?' he demanded, as if that didn't please him. 'More?' He worked his hips against her, upping the pace until she was shrieking with excitement.

'Yes!' she cried, unable to stop herself biting his shoulder like a wildcat as her fingertips raked his buttocks. 'Yes…!'

He finished her off, and was astounded by the strength of her climax. When she quietened there was no question of him soothing her down; he simply extracted himself with the least possible fuss and, standing up, arranged his clothes, before heading for the bathroom.

CHAPTER FIVE

TARA lay on the couch where Lucien had left her. Numb with disbelief that she could be so stupid. She had fallen at the first hurdle. She had betrayed Poppy. She had betrayed herself, proving herself to be no better than Lucien thought her. She was a weak and sorry excuse for a woman, and she despised herself thoroughly. It had taken her less than a moment to give way to carnal hunger. And to the pathetic longing to be loved and to be close to a man who could only think less of her. And what was she left with now? You couldn't wait for love, you had to earn it, and she had just thrown that chance away. She had thrown away her chance to be part of Poppy's life on a man who couldn't feel love, and all Lucien had proved was that he could get sex anywhere, any time, any place he wanted.

Realising the shower had been turned off, she quickly got to her feet and, hearing movement in the bathroom, she made a grab for her clothes. Lucien stormed into the room in a cloud of warm air and fresh soapy smells. 'Use the shower,' he said, towelling his hair.

His shirt was unbuttoned, his trousers unzipped...

She looked away. The moist and swollen place

between her legs was a humiliating reminder of the pleasure those strong, hard hips had dealt her. She still throbbed for him and, yes, if Lucien had wanted her now, she would have lain down for him again. Instead, muttering something unintelligible, she clutched her clothes as tight as a shield and hurried past him.

He rubbed his hair whilst absorbing everything around him, not least of which was a scent that took him back to boyhood and beyond. Baby powder. That was a bit different from the last time they'd met when Tara had been drenched in cheap perfume. He hadn't noticed the delicate scent before, but that was because he'd been consumed by rage, suspicion and contempt.

And now?

Now he was consumed by a different kind of rage. If Tara's intention had been to impress him with her newfound wholesomeness, she had just shot herself in the foot.

He finished fastening his clothes and, having folded the towel, stood by the window, waiting. He was impatient to see his niece and he hadn't met the nanny yet to approve her. He wouldn't scare the girl. He would wait for Tara to emerge from the shower and then she could introduce them. He was in no hurry. He felt quite relaxed now. Apart from the obvious, Tara had given him more than enough grounds to take the child to a place of safety…

But, regret—that was a different matter.

When Tara came back into the room he swung around, trying to fathom the attraction between them, for it was still there.

'Sit…'

She raised a brow, her gaze both wounded and defensive. She had lovely eyes, he registered as she went to sit on the edge of a sofa. She was more composed than he might have expected. Who would think she had been moaning in his arms only minutes before? He realised then what it was she had gained in the past two years that he hadn't been able to identify—it was presence and dignity. He weighed these two attributes against Freya's assertions regarding her sister. Tara could hardly be mistaken for Guy's usual bedmate, either, which could mean she was shrewder than her sister... Or it could mean that what she was telling him was the truth.

Concentrating all his attention on the unexceptional face, he attempted to rationalise his attraction to it. Apart from a scattering of freckles across the bridge of her nose, Tara's skin was as delicately tinted as the finest porcelain and her smooth brow was framed by kiss curls of bright gold hair. There was an appealing curve to her mouth that suggested she tried to see the best in things. She was quite a bit like Freya, but not nearly as pretty. He might liken it to paint running on a portrait, making the fine features a little less fine and the full lips a little fuller. Tara's eyes were quite different from her sister's too, and it wasn't just their striking colour; they lacked Freya's flickering distraction and betrayed a depth of thinking Freya had most assuredly lacked. That should have been a warning not to trust Tara any more than he would any other woman, but as he looked at her lips all he could think was they promised more than deceitful words, given the right circumstances. He knew he wasn't ready to let her go yet.

'Can I offer you something to drink, Lucien?'

Lucien? Her boldness intrigued him. 'No, nothing, thank you... We have another appointment in a few minutes.' How long would that boldness last then? he wondered.

'We do?' She looked at him curiously. First confusion and then hope flared in her eyes. She thought he was taking her somewhere nice, perhaps.

He got up and moved away, turning his back on her. It was impossible to be this close to Tara without wanting more of her. His appetite, far from being sated, had merely been revived. He couldn't remember the last time a woman had affected him like this. Before he'd arrived at the hotel he had told himself that Tara Devenish was everything he despised. But seeing her again had fired a memory, and that was of a girl he'd known two years ago, a girl he had mistakenly believed to be an ingénue.

'I'll see my niece now.' He spoke brusquely in an attempt to shut out the past.

Tara rose from her seat without comment and led the way to the door. She put her finger across her lips when they reached the nursery, as if he needed reminding that his niece was sleeping. Perhaps it was this combination of the angelic and the sensual that intrigued him. Brushing that thought aside, he walked in as she held the door for him. He noticed her capable hands then. Tara's nails were blunt and clean. She wasn't frightened of hard work, he gathered, which explained why Freya had decided that Tara must take charge of Poppy while Freya tried her hardest to spend Guy's fortune. Freya's hands had been thin and had fluttered aimlessly, he remembered. They had always been carefully manicured, each bony finger tipped with blood-red acrylic.

'Isn't Poppy lovely?'

As Tara distracted him from these unpleasant

thoughts, he stared down at the sleeping baby. She was right—his niece was lovely… Baby Poppy was sleeping the sleep of the innocent, and he felt an overwhelming urge to bring the infant under his protection. But, after what had just happened between him and Tara, he wasn't ready to discuss his brother's child with her, and so he merely hummed agreement, refusing to be drawn.

As she had suspected, losing Guy had marked Lucien deeply. Because he shunned feelings he was determined not to show an Achilles heel to her, but she could feel his pain. She could feel it as she could feel his love for Poppy.

'I'm ready to meet the nanny,' he said, pulling back.

That was her all over, wasn't it? Tara thought, as she practically sprang to attention. She always waited to see what would happen and then reacted to it. At some point she must seize control of her life or be content to remain in the shadows for good. For now she was the same moth fatally attracted to a scorching flame, only now that flame was Lucien instead of Freya. And it wasn't enough to tell herself to be strong if she didn't have a plan…

So far no plan had occurred to her, Tara realised, as she introduced a clearly awestruck Liz to the Count of Ferranbeaux. Her sense of dread only increased when Lucien leaned over the cot to adjust Poppy's blanket. The look on his face told her all she needed to know. Lucien had assumed control of Poppy's life, while she was on the sidelines, shortly to be dismissed.

But wasn't Poppy more than worth fighting for? Having identified the missing element in Lucien's make-up, was she going to abandon her niece to such a cold, hard man? It wasn't enough to hope and believe that everything would turn out right; she must make it so.

'I beg your pardon,' Lucien said politely as he brushed against her when he pulled back from the cot. He might have been speaking to a stranger.

'No problem,' Tara replied in the same bland tone. If she wanted to remain in contact with Poppy, she would have to fight. If she wanted to see Lucien again, she had to wise up.

He was standing by the door, indicating that she should leave the room before him. It was another example of Lucien asserting his authority, Tara realised, but she wouldn't fight him here in the nursery where they might disturb Poppy. She didn't have the resources to fight him anywhere, she reasoned as they left the room.

Closing the door silently behind them after leaving Liz in charge, Tara concluded that calm persuasion was the only weapon left to her. But would it be enough? Hadn't she seen the consequences of taking the line of least resistance? Sometimes you had to fight for what you believed in.

'You might want to brush your hair before we go downstairs.'

'My hair?' She patted it self-consciously. 'Why?'

'For the press conference…'

Tara's throat closed in terror. *A press conference?* She was hopeless in a crowd let alone in the spotlight.

'There have been enough scandals,' Lucien said calmly, as if meeting the press was an everyday event for him. 'Anything I do now must be seen by everyone to be scrupulous and above reproach, particularly in the run-up to adopting my brother's child—'

Tara's mind blanked. Lucien might have said something more, but she didn't hear it. She vaguely registered the fact that his lips were moving, but she couldn't hear, or think, or speak, or do anything other than stare stupidly at him as panic ran riot in her head. A press conference to announce the adoption? Since when? And what else would Lucien announce at this press conference? Her immediate return to the UK? He hadn't run anything past her, or even given her the courtesy of prior warning.

They'd been otherwise occupied, Tara remembered grimly.

'You knew about the adoption,' he pointed out.

'Of course I did… But you could have warned me about the press conference, Lucien.'

'I saw no need.'

No, he wouldn't. Lucien was used to this sort of thing; she wasn't.

'The child must have a father—'

'What did you say?' Tara's thoughts switched instantly from her own predicament to Poppy's future. And when her mind had computed Lucien's last few words she wanted to rail at him, *Poppy…Poppy* needs a father.

'It's for the best,' Lucien stated flatly.

For the best? There was a world of argument to counter that bold assumption, but as usual the smart words wouldn't come to her. And if they had, Lucien was already halfway out of the door.

'Wait, Lucien, please—'

As he opened the door and the noise of a crowd swept over her, Tara's courage failed. She had been pursued and pulverised by the media since Freya's death and the horror of it was still an open wound.

'Come along,' Lucien said impatiently, giving her no chance to refuse, unless she wanted to appear completely ineffectual in front of the world's press, that was.

Tara tried desperately to rake her hair into place before going downstairs, conscious that Lucien demanded the highest standards. She found an elastic band in her bag and, dragging her hair back, secured it, doubling up the wild curls and pulling them into a tight bun at the nape of her neck. Well, at least she looked a little bit respectable.

Polite as ever, Lucien waited for her, but she could see the brooding disapproval in his eyes and knew she hadn't got her hair nearly right. She also knew he wouldn't touch her, not even to smooth her hair. Sex was one thing, tenderness another, and that night of tenderness two years ago was all she was going to get from him. It was all she deserved. She was beginning to agree with him. No wonder Lucien had lost patience with her, when she was constantly proving herself to be such a clumsy, time-consuming handicap.

As they walked downstairs Tara could hardly believe the number of people who had crowded into the hotel, and all their faces quickly blurred into one hostile mask. No doubt basing their enthusiasm on past scandals involving the Maxime family, journalists had flocked into the town at Lucien's bidding. And no wonder, when between them Freya and Guy had probably sold more copy than any other celebrity couple on earth. Freya would have handled something like this with aplomb and even enjoyment, whereas she couldn't possibly...

'Lucien... Please... Wait...'

'For what, Tara?' he snapped impatiently, turning to face her.

'I'm sorry,' she said for the umpteenth time that day, self-consciously removing the hand she'd recklessly placed on his arm. 'It's just that I—'

'Not now, Tara,' he cut across her. 'And let me do the talking,' he instructed. 'All that's required of you is a pleasant smile and a nod of agreement from time to time. You can manage that, I take it?'

She remained mute. Lucien had dismissed her out of hand, and why wouldn't he when she had nothing of value to say? She followed him meekly down the stairs, trying to persuade herself that this was for the best and that Poppy would be far better off without her. She couldn't influence a decision, let alone the Count of Ferranbeaux. Why would any little girl want to be burdened with an aunt better known as an adulteress than as a childcare specialist?

As the swarm of faces in the lobby came into sharp focus it didn't help Tara's confidence that she was still throbbing from sex with Lucien. She was sure everyone must know every intimate detail of their relationship, and that just coming downstairs with the Count of Ferranbeaux had confirmed everyone's most salacious suspicion. They would think she was there as a convenience to be used. She should have thought things through before going along with whatever Lucien suggested. She should have thought about the consequences of having sex with him. She should have thought about the consequences of loving him, but it was far too late for that. She had no pride; there were no boundaries as far as Lucien was concerned and she had no strength to resist him. And, sure as the hell into which he'd plunged her, she had no common sense left.

They must have been halfway down the stairs when Lucien turned to deliver yet another instruction. 'However you feel about this situation, Tara, I'm asking you to keep your emotions in check. I ask this for Poppy's sake, as well as for the people who work for me on the Ferranbeaux estates—there have been enough scandals.'

As he broke off and passed a hand across his eyes, she told herself yet again that it was grief for his brother making him behave this way. Once again, her impulse was to reach out and comfort him, and she only just managed to stop herself in time.

'Are you listening, Tara? Do you understand what's at stake?'

As he spoke Lucien speared a look into her eyes, as if his harsh voice hadn't been enough to jolt her into the reality of their situation.

'Yes, of course I do.' She understood the Maxime family had become a source of ridicule, thanks to the notorious Devenish sisters, and she also understood that Lucien hadn't been given time to mourn his brother and that people needed time to grieve.

She tried to walk by his side, but Lucien quickened his step to get away from her. He radiated hostility, and as a path formed for them through the crowd of people in the lobby he continued to stride ahead of her. There were even people outside the hotel, standing on the steps, hoping to catch a glimpse of them, she noticed, and no wonder when Lucien was a grand Count from an ancient line and she was the wretch who didn't even know who her parents were. What a scandal! Tara guessed everyone must be saying. Lucien was such an imposing figure, which only made her more the mouse at his side—the dull little mouse with nothing to say.

She could feel herself growing hotter and more uncomfortable by the second, and knew she was attracting sideways looks. She could even hear some of the whispered comments. She was the Devenish sister who had slept with her sister's husband. She was the woman who had charge of Count's baby niece. How much longer before Lucien Maxime had charge of her? How long before he cast her off and forgot her?

In complete contrast to Tara's self-conscious scuttle across the crowded space, Lucien appeared completely at ease, even stopping to exchange the occasional pleasantry as he recognised one person or another. Tara marvelled at the way his pale linen suit barely seemed to have a crease in it, and the fact that his shirt looked as crisp as the moment it had left the shop. Lucien exuded class and money and confidence, and was every bit the elegant French count, with not one hair out of place to hint at the vigorous sexual activity he had been indulging in only a short time before. While she felt hot and wretched and completely out of sync as she hung back in the shadows, watching him talk with a body still singing from his touch, and the respectable outfit she'd put on earlier suddenly shrunk two sizes, or at least that was what it felt like.

As Lucien turned to glance at her, as if to check she was still there, she snapped to attention like a guardsman on parade. Perhaps he thought she'd run away and, goodness knew, she felt like it. Lucien had called this meeting to restore his family name, not hers, and she didn't doubt that he would. She knew the part she was expected to play. She was the ace up his sleeve, the disgraced sister who, having seen the light as shone by Lucien, had recognised the type of life the Count of Ferranbeaux could offer their niece and was prepared, not just to stand back, but to support him at this meeting and then conveniently disappear.

CHAPTER SIX

BUT even Lucien couldn't smooth all the snags away, Tara reasoned, as her wait continued. Yes, he could adopt Poppy, but what then? He'd have no alternative but to farm Poppy out for other people to look after. She must do something…say something…

At that moment the paparazzi swarmed and a barrage of flash bulbs exploded in her face. Her mind blanked and nothing but sheer black fright could get through. Holding her arms in front of her face, Tara tried to shield herself, and in doing so she almost tripped over the bottom step. She would have lost her balance completely had not someone caught hold of her, and it took her a moment to realise that the strong hand guiding her was Lucien's. He escorted her into the room that had been set aside for the press conference and asked her if she would like a glass of water before they began.

'Thank you…' No one could accuse Lucien of falling short on good manners. Who could say a wrong word about the Count of Ferranbeaux?

Lucien held a chair for her right next to his on the raised platform. She sat behind the long table dividing them from their audience, conscious that just being seated so close to him gave the impression that Lucien was controlling her. That was probably the right impression. The journalists were already filing in, while she waited apprehensively with her shoulders hunched and her head down, waiting submissively for whatever would happen next.

When Lucien rose to his feet the room went immediately quiet. He had no need of props or even a microphone to stamp his authority on their audience. With little more than a confident smile and a relaxed manner he put everyone at ease, and that command only increased when he responded fluently to questions in a number of different languages. She had *no chance* of standing against him, Tara thought as Lucien, having just wrapped up her final humiliation, turned to look at her for confirmation.

'Ms Devenish will, of course, be fully recompensed for her good care of my niece to date…and will use the money to start up a childcare agency…'

She found herself nodding agreement. She could see people thinking, how appropriate, how respectable, and knew that once again Lucien had saved the day. She was grateful, wasn't she? Of course she was. She nodded like an obedient child.

'And you, Ms Devenish?'

'I'm sorry…?' Tara's face flamed red as the attention of the room was drawn to her. Everyone was staring at her. She had been so lost in her thoughts that it took her a moment to rattle her brain cells into some sort of order and realise that someone other than Lucien was speaking to her. 'I… I'm not sure I heard your question…'

A number of disapproving sounds and knowing looks were exchanged before a quietly spoken man from a national television company repeated the question for her, but before she had chance to answer him another reporter chipped in with, 'Surely you must have some opinion on your sister's little girl coming to live so far away from you. Don't you worry that you'll never see her again?'

'Of course I do—' Icy fear twisted a knot in her stomach as Lucien stared down at her. What was it he had said she must do?

Inclining his head in a gesture only she would see, he flashed another heat-free smile, no doubt meant to encourage her to remember his instruction.

Nod your head and smile pleasantly—that was it!

She lifted her chin as a puppet might when the strings were drawn tight. The next move of her head must be downwards, and the nod must be accompanied by a re-assuring smile and a relaxed air, as she stared like everyone else in awe and admiration at the man who would take care of everything…

'Ms Devenish… Ms Devenish…'

Tara's hesitation had provoked the reporters into baying her name with increased urgency and, seeing Lucien was on the point of silencing the uproar, she knew this was her one and only chance to speak up. Unless she liked the look of the back seat in Poppy's life, that was.

Rising clumsily to her feet, she stood, face on fire, wishing she'd thought to loosen the waistband on her skirt. It was so hot in the room, and while everyone cla-moured for her attention she felt as if she were slowly expanding and becoming more a figure of fun than ever. Some of the hardened hacks were laughing openly at her, whispering together with their hands covering their mouths, and their eyes were so cruel. And the women were so thin. Why was that? How could she stand against them? A massed *them* against solo *her*. Not even Lucien was on her side; she had no one.

She couldn't stand against them. Where would she begin?

By waiting for silence, Tara's inner voice counselled.

It took much longer for silence to fall for her than it had for Lucien, and throughout every moment of that time Tara knew she was being laughed at. But there came a point when she realised it couldn't get any worse and so she held her ground. She also held the table, so tightly her knuckles showed white beneath her skin.

At least she'd had plenty of time to list the things she'd never done by the time the room finally went quiet, along with the things she never would do unless she spoke up now. She had put herself through college and had been awarded a scholarship to continue her education. She had been offered a place on the staff. If she could do that, surely she could handle a press conference? If she wanted to remain part of Poppy's life she had to, and if she wanted to see Lucien again, she must.

'Thank you, ladies and gentlemen…'

Perhaps it was her clear voice that shocked everyone into silence. Consciously relaxing her hands, she let go of the table. It took her a moment, but she got there. Sucking in her stomach at the same time as her breath, she continued, 'I'm sure you all appreciate what a difficult time this has been for both of us—' She glanced at Lucien then, but was careful not to let her glance linger. Having fought so hard for composure, she wasn't about to squander that composure on the altar of the Count of Ferranbeaux's smouldering mystique. 'But, hard though it is for us to speak so soon after losing people we loved, I know I speak for both the Count and myself when I say we have only Poppy's best interests at heart—' In her peripheral vision she was surprised to see Lucien nodding agreement.

'Absolutely,' he murmured.

She made the mistake of looking at him again, which prompted a minute nod, as if he wanted her to know he was pleased with her for toeing the party line: his party line.

'Pretty words,' one of the reporters interrupted. 'But what does this actually mean, Ms Devenish?'

The woman's voice was so cold that Tara's heart began to race again. She knew this was the defining moment when she must speak up or sit down. 'Nothing has been decided yet, but until a formal adoption order is made by the court…' she steeled herself for what she was going to say next '…I shall be travelling with the Count and our niece to the Count's family home in Ferranbeaux—'

The room exploded into uproar. It seemed like forever before the press pack quietened again, and when they did Tara was surprised to find that she felt much calmer, as if for once in her life she had hit on exactly the right thing to say. 'I will be staying in Ferranbeaux until it is decided how to ensure the best outcome for our niece,' she repeated with more confidence.

As she sat down cries of 'Why?' and, 'Is this right, Count?' nearly deafened her.

As Lucien stood to answer the questions, Tara was sure she wasn't the only one who felt the immense power he exuded, and the immediate silence proved this.

'Is this right?' he repeated mildly, directing his words at the acid-tongued woman. 'That was your question, wasn't it?'

Tara felt the anticipation in the room increase, provoked by the Count of Ferranbeaux's magnificent, yet brooding presence. 'I think Ms Devenish is quite capable of speaking for herself,' he said with a casual gesture.

Had Lucien really said that? Tara stared at him, unsure of the evidence of her own ears. She didn't know what to make of it. Was he endorsing her stand? Was Lucien supporting her? He certainly wasn't making a fuss about her visiting his home, which was so much more than she had hoped for.

Her body responded predictably to this new development, thrilling to the news, while doubt lost no time attacking her. The harsh words would come later, she reasoned. She had disobeyed Lucien's clear instruction to keep her thoughts to herself. As he leaned across to say something to her, she started in alarm, expecting the worst.

'They're waiting for you to speak,' he murmured. 'Surely you haven't finished yet?'

Was that a hint of humour in his gaze? She stared up at him, transfixed.

'Perhaps you'd like me to speak for you?' he suggested dryly.

This time there was doubt in her mind that Lucien was not only surprised by her stand, but rather approving of it. Her heart thundered in double time when she registered another flicker of amusement. If it hadn't been combined with such a hard set of his mouth she might even think the Lucien of two years ago had returned to her.

She couldn't hope for that, Tara decided sensibly. She had to stand on her own two feet. Determinedly, she did just that. She felt better this time—stronger. It was up to her to decide what she took from this room.

'I expect you all think this is an unusual arrange-ment…' Singling out the most influential reporters, she directed her comments to them. 'But I'm equally sure you can all understand that I have to be certain that Poppy will be happy here in Ferranbeaux. I've been caring for my baby niece since my sister's tragic death…' She paused for a moment to collect herself, aware that this was no time for a show of emotion. 'I'm very close to Poppy,' she admitted quietly, 'and the Count of Ferranbeaux understands that…' This time she did look at Lucien and, holding his gaze, she missed the murmur of approval in the audience.

'And how do you intend to do that?' the woman who had clearly cast herself in the role of Tara's nemesis demanded.

'By making sure that this—Poppy's first visit to her uncle's home—is made with those Poppy knows and trusts around her.'

'Are you accusing the Count of neglecting his niece?' the same woman called out.

Tara refused to be provoked. 'No, of course I'm not saying that.' How many lies had been told and believed about her? Would she condemn Lucien to the same fate? 'The Count has worldwide responsibilities and many calls on his time, and our niece is very young. For those reasons alone, he has not been able to see as much of Poppy as he would have liked—'

'Is that true, Count?' the woman called out.

Lucien smiled faintly. 'Ms Devenish seems to have everything covered—'

'Ms Devenish?' the same woman barked, 'do you have anything else you'd like to say?'

'No, I think that's it—'

'You wouldn't care to elaborate on your visit with the Count?' the woman pressed in a way that hinted at something seedy.

Tara kept a pleasant look on her face. She had no intention of losing her temper or inadvertently supplying some juicy detail that could be used to underpin the flagging sales of some red-top scandal-rag. 'There's nothing more for me to say, other than the Count will be seeing a lot more of his niece in the future—'

This time even Tara couldn't silence the storm of questions and one voice, predictably, rose above the rest. 'Is this right, Count? Your press office led us to believe that you would be taking over *full* responsibility for your niece and that Ms Devenish would be returning to England without the little girl, but with a rather sizeable cheque?'

This time even the most hardened reporters fell silent. They all knew that what had been said was a terrible slur on Tara's character. Tara tensed as she waited to see how Lucien would handle it.

He levelled a long, considering stare at her.

She must hold his gaze. *She must.* Lucien's expression held fire and ice, but which of those was for her? He could hardly have been expecting her to invite herself to his home, after all.

The menace in the air increased as he stood up and she could have heard a pin drop as he began to speak. 'Ms Devenish has explained the current situation as well as anyone can, and I confirm that the arrangements are exactly as she has stated. If a different version of events is reported *anywhere* it will be rigorously fought by my legal team in court.'

This time the silence had a different quality; no one

wanted to risk their job by exposing the company they worked for to the expense of defending a high profile libel case.

Tara was stunned by the fact that Lucien had chosen to defend her and that he had issued a threat that no one in the room could afford to take lightly. He had fought fire with fire and had done so with his customary compelling charm, but she was willing to bet no one had missed the underlying threat in his words.

'If that's all…?' He barely paused to take breath before adding, 'I'm bringing this meeting to a close. Are you ready?' he added, turning to her.

He had never seemed more magnificent to her, and all the people she had been so scared of paled into insignificance in the face of Lucien's reassuring presence.

'I'm ready,' Tara confirmed, standing up.

She walked out of the room at his side, but when the door closed behind them she became aware of the tension he'd hidden so well. Lucien had put on a good act for the press, but she had thrown him a curving ball. He might be escorting her through the crowded lobby as if she were minor royalty, with one arm outstretched in front of her face and his hand in the small of her back, but his grim expression wasn't solely directed at the most persistent of the hacks following them. Lucien hadn't expected the girl in the shadows to take a step forward and make a statement, and was only now taking on board the fact that where Poppy was concerned Tara had a mother's instinct and a woman's guile, and when it came to making sure her niece's childhood was very different from her own there were no dragons fierce enough to frighten her away.

'Wait there for me, will you?' he said distractedly as

a reporter for one of the major television companies waylaid him.

Tara stared at the chair Lucien was indicating. It was stuck away in a corner out of the way and she didn't want to go back to the shadows. The bare truth was, she wanted Poppy *and* Lucien, but Lucien wasn't some prince in a fairy tale on a quest for a winsome bride; he was one of life's leaders, and if he was searching for anyone it was a soul mate, not some compliant drip content to sit where she was told. If she wanted Lucien, she had to fight, and she didn't have any God-given right to care for Poppy, she had to fight for that too. But if she had to prove she had a backbone then Lucien must prove he had a heart; Poppy deserved nothing less. Fate had offered them both a chance to mend the past and provide Poppy with a happy future, and she had no intention of throwing away her side of the bargain through self-doubt.

Which was easier said than done when you looked like a dumpling tied up with string, Tara reflected dryly, having caught sight of her reflection in one of the many gilded mirrors. What she saw was all grey and putty-coloured and overweight, with red-gold hair bundled back as if to try and prove how respectable she was. She looked a mess. It was time to smarten herself up and not be content with what she thought people expected her to be.

Be herself? The shadows seemed tempting suddenly. Who was she really? It was early days in the rapidly changing world of Tara Devenish. Hanging onto who she wanted to be was proving harder than she had imagined. But she could work at it. Losing Freya had drained her emotional bank and she was only just be-ginning to understand how depleted that had left her. If she fell back to pathetic status, it was understandable, but it wasn't something she could afford to do. She had to stay on red alert and recognise those wimpish tendencies and kick herself out of them, if she had to.

While Lucien was still talking she took the opportunity to return to the nursery. She stood outside the door of her suite for a moment composing herself. No way was she taking the remnants of her self-doubt inside. There would be no scenes in the nursery, and no alarm caused to Liz or Poppy. Whatever she felt inside, whatever doubts assailed her, she'd keep them to herself.

Taking a deep breath, Tara opened the door and was instantly filled with happiness and relief to find Poppy gurgling happily in her cot. Wasn't this all that really mattered? Poppy's happiness was everything to her. She might have her setbacks, but she would never allow them to impinge on Poppy's life.

Having explained what had happened downstairs to Liz, Tara started to help her to pack up their things. 'Do you have any make-up?' she asked when they were almost finished.

'Make-up?' Liz looked at her.

Tara put down the sensible knickers she'd been folding, realising that her request must seem odd, but she had the idea that if she faced the world with a more confident-looking face she would be treated differently, even by Lucien. Anyway, she was going to give it a try. 'I've forgotten mine,' she explained.

Since when did Tara use make-up? Liz's surprised look seemed to say.

'Mascara, blusher, lip gloss?' Tara suggested hopefully. Well, it had to be an improvement on baby powder.

'Hypo-allergenic, for sensitive skin?'

'Perfect,' Tara confirmed. It was time to experiment. She might make a mess of it, but what harm could it do? She could always wash her face.

CHAPTER SEVEN

TARA'S courage under fire during the press conference had impressed him but why had she disappeared, and was it impatience or desire surging through him as he mounted the stairs to find her? He had been on the edge of his seat throughout the meeting, ready to spring to his feet and bail her out the moment it proved necessary. It hadn't. She might have been at a disadvantage and vulnerable on any number of fronts, but she had handled everything with cool aplomb. Just when he had cast himself in the role of white knight, she hadn't needed him. That had thrown him, but now he was prepared to consider that he might have made an arrogant miscalculation where Tara was concerned. The least he could do was to congratulate her on a job well done. She had shocked him, that was for sure, but by the time he turned onto the corridor leading to her suite he had calculated that she must be out of surprises.

Wrong.

She opened the door at his first knock and said calmly, 'Come in, Lucien.'

The surprises didn't end there. She had let her hair down in more ways than one. 'Tara...' His expression must have given him away but, as always, she kept her cool.

'Would you like to sit down?' she said, affecting not to notice his double take. 'We're almost finished here…'

She went to turn away, but something in his gaze must have held her. 'Yes?' she said, displaying the composure he'd seen downstairs, but this time with a slight edge of apprehension clouding it.

'You look different,' he said. That was a major understatement. She had freed her hair so it bounced round her shoulders like a wayward cloud of red-gold curls, and had put on some make-up. Not too much, and not expertly applied either, but enough to frame her turquoise eyes in a smudge of black, and to outline her lips with some gloss that caught the light.

'Different good?'

Now he understood her apprehension. 'Good,' he said, nodding with approval. He saw her relax and thought how pretty she looked, or maybe he'd never looked at her properly before, he decided.

She relaxed enough to give him a rueful half-smile. 'Welcome to the land of milk and vomit and no sleep, Lucien—'

He laughed and then stopped abruptly, wondering what the hell he was doing.

As Liz bustled past with an armful of baby clothes, he stood aside. In every other way he was swept up into the hustle of packing up and shipping out. 'Can I help you with that?' he asked as Tara hefted a box full of baby equipment onto the table.

'You could carry it downstairs for me—unless you'd like to call a member of your staff…?'

The changes in her weren't so subtle. 'Give it to

me,' he said, thinking the press conference had done her good.

'Well, thank you...' Her smile was warm as she held his gaze. 'And thank you for defending me down-stairs—'

'Seems to me you did a pretty good job of that all by yourself...'

'But it was nice to have you back me up.'

'I can't stand bullies,' he told her frankly, 'and that woman was bullying you.'

They looked at each other for a moment and then her gaze slipped away. He knew what she was think-ing, because he was feeling it too, down deep in his groin.

'Don't thank me,' he insisted, conscious of the grow-ing pressure. 'I won't stand by and do nothing if some-one takes you on—'

'Someone other than you, you mean?' she sug-gested quietly.

Something was happening between them—her growing confidence, perhaps, shifting things up a gear. Whatever, he liked it. Tara's quiet strength sparked enough electricity between them to light a small town. But he didn't allow himself the luxury of feelings and could switch off as fast as she could switch on the light. He changed tack to the subject they should both focus on. 'At least you should be reassured now,' he said con-fidently and, when she looked at him, he added, 'You've carried the responsibility of Guy's child single-handed up to now, and I thank you for that—'

'Poppy was my sister's child too,' she said inter-rupting him.

'Of course,' he said, determined to find the path of

reason through all of this. 'But you can only agree that Poppy will have a happy and settled life with me—'

'Can I, Lucien?'

'I don't know what more you can ask.'

'A woman's touch would be nice.'

He hadn't expected her to question him, but he was learning that the surprise attack was Tara's strength. She had been so quiet and retiring up to the moment she'd made her statement in the press conference, he still expected her to fall in line. He would have to re-jig his thinking where Tara was concerned, quite considerably, starting now. He didn't trade in false expectations, and sometimes you had to be cruel to be kind. 'Until I take a wife, our niece will have the best nannies that money can buy.'

Her gaze flickered, but she stated calmly, 'Money can't buy love, Lucien.'

He hardened his heart. 'Clichés, Tara?'

A wounded shrug rippled across her shoulders.

'Love comes at a price in my experience—'

'Then I'm sorry for you, Lucien.'

'Save your pity.' He didn't like the way she made him feel.

The mood changed, darkened.

'Finish packing and then I'll carry those things down for you.' He turned his back on her and went to stand in front of the open window. The storm had rolled back to reveal a watery sky streaked with cirrus cloud. He was still with the storm clouds, tense and brooding. Bottom line: Guy was dead and nothing would change that, but he could do something about Tara Devenish. 'I'd like to leave as soon as we can,' he said without turning round.

He heard her leave the room and immediately felt

the lack of her. She had the knack of unlocking parts of him he'd rather not inspect too closely; he didn't thank her for it.

'We're ready,' Tara announced some time later. He turned to see her carrying Poppy in her arms. He quickly stifled any response the tender tableau provoked.

'Good,' he said briefly. 'I'll call for the limousine—'

'How will you get back, Lucien?'

'With you...' He could tell she hadn't expected that.

'What about your car?'

'Someone will collect it.' He guessed she had been hoping for some time alone with Poppy. He sensed her uncertainty about the future, but when she saw him assessing her she tipped her chin and firmed her jaw.

'Fine,' she said mildly.

He had to wonder then, why was he taking her to his stronghold? Ferranbeaux was more than a medieval city of national importance to him—it was his home. Did he really want to introduce Tara to his home, to his staff and to his people? If she really was this decent, caring individual, why had she betrayed her sister so spectacularly? Freya had hardly been perfect, but why would she have wrecked her own sister's chance of a decent life by dragging Tara's name through the mud? Was the truth exactly as the newspapers had stated? Had Tara found Guy, or rather Guy's substantial bank account, irresistible? As his suspicions mounted, he asked himself if he had just been smooth-talked into a corner for the first time in his life. 'I'll see you downstairs,' he told her brusquely.

Tara saw Poppy and Liz settled comfortably in the back of the spacious limousine before taking her seat. She was both excited and apprehensive at the thought of visiting Lucien's home. It was one thing standing up for Poppy in a press conference and vowing to change her personality, and quite another entering the lion's den. She had tried to imagine what Lucien's home might be like and just couldn't; there were so many layers to him, so much he kept hidden. Plus, she didn't have that many visits to medieval castles for her imagination to draw on. In fact, this one would be the first. If she pictured anything, it was towering grey stone walls and a forbidding interior with lots of animal heads staring down sadly from the walls. The only thing that mattered, Tara reminded herself as they waited for Lucien to join them, was to satisfy herself that the arrangements he'd made for Poppy were the right ones. It really didn't matter what she thought of Lucien's home, her only concern must be—was it the right place for a little girl to grow up?

Her only concern?

Tara's throat dried as Lucien came into view. She must be mad if she thought that. She breathed a sigh of relief when he headed for the front seat next to the driver, where the chauffeur was holding the door for him. A special car seat had been fitted for Poppy, and she was slumbering in the row behind Tara, with Liz sitting next to her. Not wanting to disturb them, Tara had chosen a row to herself in the stretch limo. It was a good choice, she congratulated herself now. In spite of the effort she'd made to spruce herself up, she felt exhausted and fat. She was into small pleasures at the moment, she realised ruefully as she lowered the zip on her skirt with a sigh of relief. Hitching it up, she sighed with the first real pleasure she'd felt that day.

She had barely had a chance to relax when the door

swung open and Lucien took the seat next to her. 'What are you doing here?' He'd shocked her into defensive mode.

'In my own car, do you mean?' He glanced pointedly at her thighs before leaning forward to tap on the glass, the signal for the driver to pull away.

What a perfect end to a perfect day, Tara reflected. Lucien was his customary elegant self, while she had her skirt hitched up ungracefully!

'I'm sorry to have kept you waiting—' he glanced at her thighs again '—but I see you've made yourself comfortable.'

'That's right, I have,' she agreed, struggling inelegantly to right her clothes.

'Can I help you?'

'No, thank you, I can manage... What are you doing?' she exclaimed as he leaned over her.

'Fastening your seat belt.'

As Lucien turned to look at her, their faces were dangerously close. She held her breath. And let it out in a ragged sigh when he pulled away.

The hairpin bends on the steep mountain road made it hard to spot the walled city of Ferranbeaux until they were almost on top of it. But as Tara stared through the tinted windows of the limousine into the gathering darkness she finally saw something rising out of the mist. 'Is that a castle?' She was excited in spite of her determination to remain calm. Calm was one thing, but when calm was challenged by a fairy tale kingdom... She could see slim shadowy towers topped with inverted ice cream cone shaped roofs. The terracotta pantiles coating them glowed faintly red beneath a purple sky.

It was like Cinderella's castle…though, just as she had feared, the fairy tale castle was completely enclosed by towering stone walls.

'That's my home,' Lucien explained. 'Do you like it?'

Did she like it? A walled city that took up a vast acreage on the summit of a sprawling hill with a castle set like a rough hewn jewel at its centre? She most certainly did like it, though, like Lucien, it held more secrets than she knew, Tara suspected. 'So this is your place in the hills,' she murmured.

'One doesn't like to boast,' Lucien said, responding to her subtle irony.

'Doesn't one?' She couldn't resist a small smile. 'Do you actually live in the castle?' she said, turning to him.

'I do.'

The look in Lucien's dark, mesmerising eyes shot heat through her. 'That must be nice,' she said, trying hard to concentrate on something other than his mouth.

'Very nice,' he agreed in a way that suggested he could read her mind.

And now she couldn't stop her gaze wandering back to him. He was looking out of the window, fortunately. Lucien and Ferranbeaux had the same mixture of magic and menace about them and couldn't have been better suited.

The limousine was forced to slow as it approached a wooden bridge that crossed an illuminated dry moat. As they rumbled beneath a towering stone archway the car was plunged briefly into darkness, and Tara thought it was like moving back in time. Certainly, with every yard she travelled she was moving deeper into Lucien's territory.

And ever more under his control? She shivered inwardly. Whatever resolutions she might have made, she was only twenty, with little or no experience of life and men, while Lucien was the mighty Count of Ferranbeaux, an older man who wielded immense power and had almost limitless wealth at his disposal— hardly a fair contest!

Added to which, her rebellious body never missed an opportunity to respond to her erotically charged thoughts. Lucien was a hard, sensual man who had awoken appetites in her she had barely guessed at. Realistically, how long could she resist him? She didn't need the buzz of sitting this close to him to remind her how enthusiastically she had succumbed to his dark arts in the past, and just revisiting these forbidden thoughts was enough to make her wonder if she was destined to live the life Freya had mapped out for her after all.

She stole a glance at Lucien's proud face in profile. Like the fortified city he called home, Lucien was a timeless force of nature, and one she craved. He blended seamlessly into the wild and rugged terrain over which he ruled, and she wanted his attention, though she realised she had no hope of touching his heart. She had no intention of being anyone's mistress either, Tara determined, firming her jaw. She had to find a way through this somehow... As she stared blindly through the window, something caught her attention and it was a distraction she welcomed. There were flags and bunting everywhere, suggesting Ferranbeaux could be a happy place too. 'Has there been a celebration?'

'Of course,' Lucien confirmed. 'The people of Ferranbeaux are welcoming Poppy home.'

Of course. Tara's heart sank. She knew that, but it didn't stop her worrying at the thought she would soon be separated from Poppy, and possibly for good.

Lucien's home might look like a fairy tale castle on a hill, complete with twinkling lights and mullioned windows, but it wasn't her home, Tara reminded herself sensibly as the limousine slowed to negotiate golden gates leading into a vast cobbled courtyard. Still, it was hard not to be just a little starry-eyed when the vehicle halted at the foot of a wide expanse of sweeping stone steps. It was impossible not to let her imagination have full rein and picture elegant partygoers alighting from their carriages…the ladies in silks and satins in all the colours of the rainbow, escorted by tall, elegant men…

'Tara?' Lucien murmured, pointing out the fact that his chauffeur was holding the door for her.

Covering for her distraction, she tried to climb out with a modicum of grace. Well, that was a pipedream, but fortunately Lucien's reflexes were as fast as his brain, and his arm shot out to save her. 'This is very grand,' Tara said awkwardly, regaining her balance to stare up at the imposing façade of the first castle she had ever visited. She didn't belong here, though Lucien, with his small party of two awestruck women and a babe in arms, was understandably relaxed—this was his home after all.

He shrugged after steadying her on her feet. 'So what do you think of Poppy's new home?'

Tara tensed and instinct brought her closer to Poppy. 'I'll take her now,' she told Liz. Tara felt as if her stomach had been stitched with a running thread and someone had pulled it tight. She didn't need Lucien reminding her that her time with Poppy was limited and each precious moment was running through her fingers like sand through an hourglass.

She slowly turned full circle after Liz handed Poppy

over to her, trying to take everything in. She guessed that unless you'd been brought up in circumstances like this you would never get used to the sheer scale of the place Lucien so casually called home. She couldn't even see the boundaries of the courtyard, and the forbidding walls were decorated with crenellated battlements where, centuries before, archers must have patrolled. It was quite a bit different from the orphanage where she and Freya had grown up…

'Shall we go inside?'

Tara was still staring in wonder at a stone fountain where glittering plumes of water spewed from the mouths of fiery steeds mounted by fierce-looking stone warriors when Lucien dipped his head to speak to her and it took her a moment to refocus. 'Did they model those statues on anyone in particular?' she wondered, speaking her thoughts out loud.

'I'm not that old,' Lucien informed her dryly.

Apprehension and heat rippled through her as Lucien held her gaze. She was so acutely tuned to him she couldn't pretend not to interpret that look.

'Well, are you going to come inside?'

Tara stared up at the double doors of the castle. The ancient oak looked thick enough to withstand a siege, and each door was studded with iron bolts. Those doors were sturdy enough to keep an army out, Tara concluded—or anyone they chose to in. She was shivering with apprehension even as she nodded and followed Lucien. For now she had nowhere else to go.

Embracing Poppy protectively, Tara dropped a kiss on her baby niece's smooth brow. She had to make herself believe that a court of law would not compare her modest rented home back in England unfavourably to this. She had to believe in miracles, in fact. She was very proud of the tiny nest she'd made, but her concern that it would be considered an unsuitable destination for the aristocratic niece of the Count of Ferranbeaux seemed entirely justified now.

'Can you manage to carry Poppy up the steps?' Lucien asked her.

'Of course I can.' She knew she sounded defensive, and she was, but she had to be careful not to communicate her fears to Poppy. 'This is your new home,' she whispered, gazing up the steps. 'Isn't it lovely?' And the castle was lovely. The ancient stone gleamed silver in the moonlight, and after the storm the air was cool and fresh. The ground had received such a good drenching she could smell the fragrant minerals in the earth and, however hard she tried to fight off the charms of Lucien's stern grey home, just as she found him mesmerising, Tara was fast discovering that the castle of Ferranbeaux had wasted little time in wrapping its magic around her heart.

But as she wouldn't be given a chance to grow attached to it, Tara reflected sensibly as she started up the steps, she should concentrate her mind on whether it was a suitable home for Poppy. She was just getting a hold on this common sense approach when Lucien took hold of her arm. She knew he was just making sure she didn't stumble, but electricity shot through her at his touch. She flashed him a smile of thanks, but as the double doors swung open in front of them and she saw the line of uniformed staff waiting to greet them Tara realised her ordeal had only just begun.

CHAPTER EIGHT

SHE must concentrate on the fact that Lucien's castle was a much better environment for Poppy than the flashy penthouse Guy had bought for Freya, Tara decided as her courage deserted her in floods. Every face of every member of staff was turned her way, and it took her a moment to register the fact that people were smiling at her as well as at the baby in her arms. The castle might be huge but, with the addition of some warm-coloured tapestries and a giant-sized rug in the marble entrance hall, could give the illusion of cosiness. Despite its size, her initial impression was that this could be a proper home, with a proper garden, even if that garden was the size of a park. The penthouse had slippery floors and no garden for Poppy to play in when she was older, though Freya had assured Tara it was the perfect venue for parties.

'I'll introduce you to the staff,' Lucien murmured discreetly, 'and then I'd like you to get Poppy settled in as quickly as you can—'

'Of course…' Tara's brow puckered, she was thinking that Lucien seemed in quite a hurry to move things along. Cut him some slack, she told herself firmly. He was being considerate. He knew how tired they must be. It had been quite a day for him, as well.

Adjusting Poppy's position in her arms so everyone could see her downy cheeks and tiny, deep pink rosebud mouth, Tara followed Lucien into the magnificent hallway.

The floor was a chessboard of black and white marble, and there were gilded cream, pink-veined marble columns reaching towards a vaulted ceiling far above their heads. Apart from the murmur of voices pitched at a discreet level, there was a stillness and even a majesty to their surroundings. She had never been anywhere quite like it, Tara thought in wonder, though she had seen similar palaces in books, of course. The ornate painted ceiling was like something out of the Sistine Chapel. It had obviously been restored quite recently, and the colours were luminous—aquamarine, cobalt blue, ivory and cream, soft rose and peach tones...

'Shall I take Poppy from you?' Lucien offered.

Tara was still gawping open-mouthed at the ceiling and quickly collected herself. 'No, that's okay, thank you.' Instinctively, she tightened her hold on Poppy when Lucien made as if to take their baby niece out of her arms.

'I'll introduce you to the staff, then,' he said.

She was full of concentration now, wanting to remember everyone's name, but there were so many people to meet, it was inevitable she lost track eventually. The line stretched right across the hall.

It would take this many people to care for such a large building, Tara reasoned. She would just have to seek out each member of staff in private later. She wanted to introduce herself properly and get to know everyone so she could reassure herself about the people who would be caring for Poppy.

After the introductions had been completed, Lucien led their small party to the foot of the sweeping staircase. 'Now you will let me take Poppy,' he insisted. 'These marble steps can be quite dangerous when you're not used to them.'

Tara's gaze tracked up the towering staircase. He was right. She couldn't afford to take any chances with Poppy, she concluded, handing over her precious cargo.

They mounted the stairs beneath a legion of stern-faced ancestors. An older woman with grey hair, dressed in a sober uniform was waiting to greet them on the first landing. This was the housekeeper, Tara learned. She looked kind, Tara thought hopefully.

'Refreshments for the ladies?' Lucien checked with her before moving on down the wood-panelled corridor.

'*Oui*, Monsieur, le Conte,' the housekeeper confirmed, bobbing a curtsey to him. 'Everything is ready,' she said, sparing a warm and reassuring smile for Tara.

If she had needed any more reminders of Lucien's exalted position in life, she was sure to get them here, Tara reflected wryly as she smiled back.

'This is the nursery,' Lucien said, handing Poppy back so he could open a heavy wooden door. He stood back to allow Tara to enter in front of him. 'I hope you approve…'

Approve? Tara's eyes widened. She only wished Poppy was older so they could explore it together. This was only the sitting room, she gathered, seeing more doors leading off. She walked deeper into the inviting well-lit space, noticing that everything a baby could possibly need appeared to be, if not in place, then in boxes, and everything had been sourced from the very best of stores. It was a dream of a room, decorated in shades of rose-pink and ivory, cosy and yet not too small. There was a beautifully polished wooden floor topped with a deep rug, and comfortable sofas and lots of book shelves. Some of the child-friendly furniture was still covered in the protective wrapping which must have been used to protect it during delivery, but she could see the potential. 'It's fabulous,' she exclaimed excitedly. She couldn't wait to start organising it.

'It's not quite finished,' Lucien admitted. 'But I think everything's here. If there's anything more you need—'

Tara just shook her head, smiling. 'I'll be sure to let you know,' she told him happily, but even as she was thrilled by the preparations he had made, something in Lucien's eyes evoked a *frisson* of alarm inside her, as if everything wasn't quite as it appeared.

'I thought it better to wait for the nanny to tell the staff how she would like things arranged,' Lucien explained.

And he made that explanation a little stiffly, Tara thought. Was Lucien trying to shut her out, or was his remark simply a result of his upbringing? She could imagine that when you had grown up in such grand surroundings and had your every wish anticipated by an army of staff, you would have a different mind-set to someone brought up in an orphanage, but she wanted him to know that she intended to get stuck in and do her share of the work. 'But I'm here now,' she pointed out, 'so you don't have anything to worry about.'

Lucien's 'Hmm,' was hardly reassuring.

He turned to Liz. 'And this is your room for the duration of your stay,' he explained to the young nanny, walking across the room to open another door.

Tara smiled to hear Liz's gasp of delight. Who could

blame her? The room was very prettily decorated, with gingham curtains and a bed dressed with cream lace and a bank of coral-coloured velvet cushions.

'I had an interior decorator fit it out,' Lucien explained. 'I hope it's satisfactory.'

'With the addition of a waste bin and a mirror, it will be just perfect—' Seeing Lucien's face, Tara wished she could keep her sensible self under wraps sometimes. 'I'm sorry; I didn't mean to—'

'I'm sure Liz will find what she needs in one of those boxes out there,' Lucien said, cutting across her.

Once again, Tara got the feeling she was being shut out. 'Don't worry,' she told Liz discreetly, realising the young girl must be tired. 'I'll help you sort it out. It's only a small thing,' she added, turning to reassure Lucien.

Seeing a muscle flex in his jaw brought the uncomfortable feeling back again full force. She told herself she was tired too, and threw herself into sharing Liz's excitement. The room was beautifully presented and carefully colour-coordinated, with natural oak floorboards washed with white and covered with a fluffy rug. There were so many cute accessories they could start a store, the two girls agreed, laughing happily together. It looked just like something out of a magazine. Which, in a way, it was, Tara realised. Liz's bedroom was more like a set than a room to live in.

She kept these thoughts to herself as they toured an amazing pink marble bathroom, and both girls gasped when Lucien took them into Poppy's bedroom. There was a white cot set up on a platform carpeted with thick white fur, and the canopy over the cot was draped with a drift of white lace that trailed down the steps and was trimmed with pink satin ribbons. Tara and Liz exchanged a glance. It was fabulous, but had clearly not been designed by anyone who was used for caring for children. It would be all too easy to trip on the fabric as you carried a baby down the steps.

Not to worry, Tara told herself. She and Liz would soon rearrange everything. They would even find somewhere safe to display the beautiful lace so that Lucien would know they appreciated it. At least there were lots of shelves on which to arrange the toys and books, and there were even musical instruments for Poppy to play when she was older. Her modest home would fit here twice, Tara thought with amusement. Most importantly, how could Poppy not be happy here? How could anyone not be happy here?

How could she not be happy here?

She brushed that thought aside right away. She was here to scout the arrangements Lucien had made for Poppy, and nothing more. But still…

'Have your tea,' Lucien said gruffly, 'and then we'll go—'

'Go?' The *frisson* was back again, only now it was a full blown quake of alarm. Lucien had gone to a lot of trouble, Tara reasoned, and maybe he thought she had been too lukewarm. He would expect a better reaction from her when he showed her the room she was to have. 'The main thing is to see Poppy clean, fed and settled,' she reminded him. 'And then I'll help Liz sort everything out. You don't have to stay,' she assured him, knowing he must be tired too. 'I'm sure someone will show me my room…' She fell silent. Lucien wasn't just tense now, he was glowering at her. But what had she done? Drawing Poppy close, she brushed a kiss across her sleeping brow.

Lucien frowned as he watched her. 'I realise it's been a long day for you—'

'And for you too, and for Liz—' Tara exchanged an understanding look with the young nanny.

Lucien turned for the door. 'The internal phone's on the desk. Let me know when you're ready and I'll have someone drive you over—'

She was still smiling at this point. 'Drive me over?'

'To the gatehouse,' Lucien explained. 'In fact, you could leave now and have your tea there. I'll send someone up here to help Liz. Well, she seems to have everything in hand here,' he added when Tara looked at him.

She wasn't hearing straight, Tara concluded, calling on her sensible inner self to calm the alarm inside her. 'There's a lot to do,' she pointed out. 'I can't just leave Liz to get on with it.'

'She'll have help.'

Lucien was growing impatient. And she was guilty of selective hearing. What was it he'd said about a gatehouse? 'Do you mean I'm to go somewhere else?' Her anxious gaze flickered around.

'Why don't you give Poppy to Liz now?' Lucien said.

Tara became aware of Liz hovering on the sidelines while the housekeeper silently poured tea. It was like a film she was watching and yet wasn't a part of, she thought, feeling panic rise in her throat. But she mustn't make a scene—not here, in front of Poppy.

'Would you take Poppy for her bath?' she said in a voice that was only slightly shaky as she handed Poppy over to Liz. 'And make sure you have something to eat too—'

'I will,' Liz said, glancing worriedly at Lucien.

The housekeeper spoke up. 'I'll look after your young friend for you, *mademoiselle*.'

'Thank you…' There was nothing else for her to do, Tara realised as the two women left the room with Poppy. She felt sick and uncertain. 'Lucien, what's going on?'

'Poppy's my niece, part of my family, and as such she will stay here at the castle with me. You will only be a short drive away—'

'A short drive away?' Tara repeated foolishly.

'That's right,' Lucien confirmed.

'You mean you're keeping me from her?'

Lucien shifted position impatiently. 'Don't be so melodramatic. I've just explained to you, you'll only be a short drive away—'

'I'm not going anywhere unless Poppy and Liz come with me. Poppy doesn't know you.' As Lucien's eyebrows shot up, Tara firmed her chin. She might be at a disadvantage here, but both Liz and Poppy were in her care.

'For the sake of propriety, you must—'

'For the sake of propriety?' Tara's voice rose. 'The rules of propriety didn't seem all that important to you back at the hotel,' she reminded him frigidly.

'Please don't make this any harder than it has to be.'

Lucien's eyes were as hard and as cold as she'd ever seen them. His decision was made—had been made—and for some time, she gathered.

'You can see Poppy any time you like while you're staying in Ferranbeaux—'

Everything in Tara railed against Lucien's actions. 'If I ask your permission first, I presume?' She had always known her time with Poppy in Ferranbeaux would be limited, but she had not expected Lucien to tear them apart without warning her first.

'You only have to call me—'

'And if you don't happen to be in?' There was a

shake in her voice she couldn't control now. The end had come so suddenly. How could she abandon Poppy? How did she know Lucien would treat Poppy as she deserved? Would he be too busy to notice if Liz felt trapped and isolated in a big old castle peopled by servants? Was this it? For ever?

'For goodness' sake, Tara,' Lucien snapped, seeing her face, 'try to be grown up about this—'

'Grown up? Or detached?' she demanded in a voice that cracked with emotion.

Lucien answered her emotional outburst with silence.

'Why are you punishing me? What have I done to you?' Clinging to her last hope of staying close to Poppy, she was determined to reach him somehow. 'Treating me like this won't bring Guy back—'

'Don't you dare speak to me about my brother—'

'Why not, Lucien? Am I not *fit* to do so?'

His eyes blazed a warning, which she ignored. 'I know how deeply you loved your brother, even if you can't bring yourself to admit it.' She stood her ground as Lucien advanced a menacing step closer. 'Guy needed you—'

Lucien eyes blazed with a deadly intensity. 'What do you know of this? And why do you think I should want to talk about it now?'

'Because I want to make you feel something…' She pressed her lips together, and when she realised she wasn't getting anywhere, she exclaimed with exasperation, 'You cruel, hard man…can't you see what you're doing to yourself?'

Shaking her head, Tara looked at him sadly. 'And you ask me what I know of Guy.' Encouraged by his silence, she went on, 'I know that your brother and my sister took drugs—'

Lucien cut her off. 'That was common knowledge after the inquest.'

She waited until he was silent again. 'Guy and Freya's so-called friends were as bad as they were, and there were dealers coming round to the apartment all the time. Do I have to go on, Lucien? Or do you know what happened to your brother's fortune?'

'I have some idea,' he said coldly.

'You knew?' The thought horrified her.

'Of course I didn't know at the time. I was too busy rescuing the business and the estates Guy had declined to take an interest in to know what was happening at home. I only found out when Guy died and all the vultures started circling—'

'But you must have known Guy was weak—'

'Perhaps you knew him better than I did,' he snapped back viciously.

'So you still think I slept with him?' Laughing a sad little laugh, Tara shook her head in disbelief.

'Do you deny it?'

'Of course I do. And, from a purely practical point of view, the drugs had taken such a hold, I doubt Guy was capable of sleeping with anyone. Have you ever seen anyone on drugs, Lucien, scratching and sweating as they wander aimlessly about, waiting for their dealer to deliver?'

'If it was so bad, you could have contacted me—'

'Do you think I didn't try?' Grabbing her head in frustration, Tara finally lost her composure. 'Your secretary would never put me through to you. It was only when Guy and Freya were killed you decided to acknowledge my existence at all. Two years, Lucien,' she reminded him tensely as he stared coldly at her. 'Two years you ignored me. And now you can't keep away from me. Well, can you?'

He wasn't about to be trapped into an admission of that sort. And now he was locked in the past, reviewing his actions and each conversation he'd had with a brother he had thought he knew so well. 'When Guy refused the title and accepted the money—'

'What, Lucien? What?' she demanded as he murmured these thoughts out loud. 'What did you think? That Guy was being noble?'

'He didn't always come to the phone when I called him—'

She laughed again, but it was an ugly sound. 'And you want to know why that was, Lucien?'

He focused on her face, concentrating on the woman who had probably known his brother better than he had. 'Why don't you tell me?'

'Guy was most probably soiling himself, Lucien!'

And, as he sucked air through his teeth, thinking no new revelation could cause him more pain, she proved him wrong.

'And who do you think cleaned that up, Lucien?'

'Stop!' he commanded.

'Why? Because the truth is unpalatable? Or because you can't bear to hear it from me?'

He grabbed hold of her with an angry growl, then let her go. Could this be true? He didn't want to believe what she had told him, but that wouldn't make it go away. And now a part of him was remembering snatches of conversation and voices in the background when he had managed to get Guy on the phone… And then there was the money he'd loaned to Guy when common sense should have told him that Guy must have plenty of money of his own. He had put it down to Freya's excesses. Only when Guy was dead had he learned the truth.

'And you want to part me from Poppy when I've kept her safe all this time. How can you say you don't trust me, Lucien?'

She had made it hard for him to dismiss her as harshly as he had before. After what she'd told him he wished he'd been there for her, but it was too late for regret now.

'So that's why you're sending me to the gatehouse while you keep Poppy here with you?'

Her eyes were wounded, but she was no more, no less wounded than he was. What she had told him about Guy had cut him to the core, and if it was true he would never forgive himself.

'What do you suggest?' he demanded coldly.

'That I stay with her—'

And, before he could counter that, she added, 'In the servants' quarters, if that makes things easier for you—'

Easier for his conscience, did she mean?

'I wouldn't mind, Lucien.'

'And the staff wouldn't think it strange?' he demanded cuttingly, though guilt plagued him at the thought that she would do just about anything to stay with the baby.

'Do you care what anyone thinks?'

'It would only make things worse.'

'For whom, Lucien?'

So should he consign Poppy's aunt to the attic rooms, or stick her away in the gatehouse? The Count of Ferranbeaux was never at fault, Lucien reflected, hating himself at that moment—or, at least, he must never appear to be so. And those long-harboured suspicions that Tara might have slept with Guy had just received a mortal blow.

When he looked at Tara this time it was through different eyes and he saw how tired she looked. There were dark circles beneath her inexpertly made-up eyes—eyes that were brimming with tears—tears he'd put there. He didn't think he could feel any worse until he thought about Guy... Poor, poor Guy...

Oh, yes, he was proud of himself.

She had no energy left to fight Lucien. She was completely drained after letting go of all the tragic memories. If she could have helped Guy she would have done, but Guy hadn't wanted anyone's help. As Lucien went on staring at her, Tara knew what she must look like. She had provided him with entertainment at the hotel, but she wasn't stupid enough to think those events had any currency here. She didn't want them to have any currency, because whatever had happened between them, on her part, at least, had been driven by love. She could only throw herself on Lucien's mercy now.

'If I did stay in the servants' quarters...' his face didn't flicker, which gave her the courage to carry on '...do you promise you'd let me see Poppy first thing every morning?' Her heart sank as he turned away. 'Lucien?' How pathetically desperate she must sound, but she would fight for Poppy until the last breath left her body.

'You could come here each morning from the gatehouse,' Lucien pointed out, still keeping his back turned to her. 'There's a park beyond the courtyard where you could push the pram...' With an angry sound, he abruptly stopped speaking and raked his hair. 'They used to be jousting fields—' His face as he whirled around to stare at her contained more passion than she'd ever seen in him.

'I wouldn't take advantage of your hospitality. Ferranbeaux is Poppy's heritage. I know that. I also know you're not a charitable organization—'

'Good of you to notice.'

'I'll pay my way, Lucien.'

The flicker of humour in his eyes held no warmth.

'So, can I stay?' she persisted.

'*If* you stay,' he grated out, 'you will abide by my rules. There will be no more outbursts, and you will confide in no one—'

'Other than you, of course?' She met his gaze steadily.

'I'm not a bully, Tara—'

'And I'm not a doormat.'

'Just try to keep your thoughts to yourself. Well?' he demanded when she didn't answer immediately. 'Do you want to stay here or not?'

'Thank you for your gracious invitation,' she said quietly, careful to keep her face deadpan. 'I'd love to stay.'

Now what had he done? Tara living under the same roof was the very last thing he wanted. Conscious of the fragile state of his family name after all the troubles, he had planned to house her in the gatehouse—if she stayed in Ferranbeaux at all. After the newspaper reports, he had truly believed she had grown into the type of woman who would pocket his cheque and leave Ferranbeaux as fast as her legs could carry her. The cheque was still in his breast pocket, he confirmed, patting it. He had forgotten all about it. She had made him forget it. He had massively underestimated Tara, but then he had also underestimated the effect she would have on him after two long years apart. And why was he surprised by her stand now, after the way she had rallied at the press conference? She had earned herself a second chance.

'I'll ask the housekeeper to make a room ready for you.'

'If you're sure it's not too much trouble—'

There was no suggestion of sarcasm in her voice, and he wasn't sure if what he was about to say was an instruction or a vain hope. 'No trouble.'

She gave him a faint smile of acknowledgement. She had parried each thrust with dignity, using mostly calm reason and steady determination, though there had been a flash of that passion he so admired in her. She stared right back at him when he looked at her now, and it took quite a force of will to remind himself that however appealing he found her, there was no place for Tara in his life.

CHAPTER NINE

DECIDING to let the dust settle, Lucien returned to the nursery after what he considered to be a reasonable period of time to find Tara with the nanny in Poppy's bedroom. They were busily reorganising the furniture, while Poppy slept soundly in her Moses basket. He noted the ornate cot had been stripped of all its decoration and moved closer to the wall.

'I have people who will do that for you,' he pointed out.

'But we don't need them,' Tara told him. 'Do we, Liz?'

The young girl, looking much reassured now Tara had returned, laughingly agreed, leaving him with little more to do other than check everything was safe before saying to Tara, 'A suite of rooms has been reserved for you.'

'A suite of rooms?' she exclaimed. Lowering the table the two girls had been carrying to the floor, Tara planted her capable hands on her hips. 'Please tell your staff not to go to any trouble for me. A small bedroom is all I need—'

In spite of his fabled self-control, his lips tugged up at that. 'Unfortunately, we don't do small here—'

'Uh-huh?'

She was mocking him, but in a nice way. Making her happy and more confident was both good and bad. His intention had never been to make her miserable, but he didn't want her getting her feet under his table either. 'Could you leave that for a moment? We need to talk. I'll send someone up to help Liz with the rest of it.'

Having checked with Liz, she agreed.

He took her into the sitting room and shut the door. Her cheeks had turned a deeper shade of rose with all the physical activity. He couldn't help thinking about the last time he'd seen her look so flushed.

'So?' She held out her hands as if waiting for his words of wisdom to drop into them.

He refused to be hurried. She looked relaxed, which transformed her. He felt reassured about his decision to keep her here, which transformed his inner state of mind. He studied the golden hair flying wildly round her face and noticed strands of it clinging to her forehead. She brushed them away. 'So, you'll settle for a suite?' he said dryly.

'Anything your housekeeper can arrange for me at such short notice I'm more than grateful for,' she told him candidly.

He didn't want her to be grateful. He wanted what a few hours ago he would have believed impossible, which was an ideal world where they were on equal terms and he could feel…anything. He hadn't bargained for a woman descending on him who, having assumed responsibility for her niece, had no intention of letting go without a fight. Tara had surprised him when she'd found fault with the ferociously expensive arrangements he had made for Poppy's arrival, but he was ready to accept she might be right about the practicalities that seemed to have escaped the notice of his interior decorator. As his frown deepened, she spoke up, no doubt with the intention of reassuring him.

'If it hadn't been for Poppy, I would have been happy to stay in the gatehouse—'

'If it hadn't been for Poppy,' he reminded her dryly, 'you wouldn't be here.'

She raised a brow at this brutal account of the truth, and when she levelled that turquoise gaze on him he thought her even more appealing.

'I realise this can't be easy for you, Lucien.'

'What can't?' he rapped, trying not to find the way she angled her face to speak to him quite so attractive.

'You've only heard such bad things about me,' she carried on, undaunted. 'And now, here I am, living in your house.'

'My castle,' he corrected her dryly.

'Your home, surely?' she prompted him quietly.

'Anyway, I'd like to thank you,' she said, before he had chance to dwell on it. 'I just want you to know I appreciate your generosity of spirit.'

He kept his face carefully under control. She was so young, and seemed so sincere, and as she brushed her hair from her face again it was such a childish gesture it made him long to reach out and sample the silky texture for himself. It wouldn't take much to throw them back onto a darker path than this one. He wanted her now.

'Your suitcase should have been delivered to your suite by now. If you need any help unpacking it–'

'Let me guess,' she interrupted, 'I only have to call downstairs and someone will come to help me.'

'That's right,' he said, thumbing the stubble on his chin.

'I don't think I'm the type of guest you're used to. I

don't have a lot with me. I doubt I'll need help with one change of clothes and a toothbrush.'

As she stared at him he couldn't help thinking that she was changing before his eyes. He could see the woman she would become, given half a chance.

The housekeeper chose this moment to interrupt them, saying that Tara's room was ready for her occupation. As he watched them talking together he thought the older woman and Tara might have been friends of long-standing to see them laughing and so relaxed. He had never seen his stern-faced housekeeper unbend like this before, but then, he reasoned, Tara's *joie de vivre* was infectious.

She wondered if Lucien was growing impatient with her. She was keen to meet his staff. She could tell they thought a lot of him, and she was eager to get to know them all by name so she could talk to them easily and understand the role they played in Lucien's household. She might not be staying for long, but she was looking to the future when Poppy would be cared for by these same people. So far she felt reassured. The people who worked for Lucien were different from those who had worked for Guy and Freya. Tara had secretly thought they must have had to sit some examination in snootiness before Guy would consider them, but there was no hint of pretension here.

Wanting to thank him for his change of heart, she caught up with Lucien at the door. Her heart thundered as he stared down at her. Was she seeing what she wanted to see, or was that another thread of warmth in his gaze? Would it disappear if she gave him another list of enquiries about his household? After all, she'd only just arrived.

'Don't,' he murmured as he opened the door.

What did that mean? Don't push it? Don't thank him? What? He didn't give her a chance to ask him. She would have to draw her own conclusions, Tara realised as the housekeeper approached.

'Are you ready, *mademoiselle*? Shall I take you to your room now?'

'Oh, yes, please…'

'Monsieur le Conte has asked me to tell you that he will be in his private apartment should you need him—and, of course, if you require anything more for yourself, or for Poppy and her nanny, please don't hesitate to call me.'

'Thank you, you're very kind,' Tara said sincerely, exchanging a smile with the housekeeper as she followed her out.

Tara thought she'd seen everything, but when the heavy oak door that marked the entrance to her suite of rooms swung open she gasped. The richness of everything was overwhelming and far too much to take in at a glance. She tried to concentrate on one thing at a time as the housekeeper gave her the guided tour, but she wasn't used to so much space, or so many *objets d'art* all together in once place, let alone such quantities of antique furniture, all of which was burnished to a mellow shine, leaving the faint scent of beeswax in the air. There were fabulous silk curtains at the windows in tones of kingfisher-blue and gold, and on the walls brocade in the palest yellow ochre, punctuated with gilt-framed mirrors and oil paintings showing ravishing beauties in flowing gowns, some of whom wore tiaras, while others sported wide-brimmed hats trimmed with feathers. The pretty rug on the polished wooden floor had to be Aubusson, Tara guessed, judging by the intricate floral design…And this was only the ante chamber to her bedroom, she discovered, as the housekeeper led her through to a second room where a large bed set in the centre of the room on a raised platform dominated.

The hall had been cosy, but all the other rooms seemed to be on such a grand scale she could only think that Guy and Lucien must have been lost inside them as small boys. She was already picturing them dressed by their nanny in miniature versions of their papa's silk dressing gown and pyjamas, with their hair neatly slicked back and monogrammed slippers on their tiny feet. Had the boys come downstairs to bow low and share a few stilted words with the Count before bedtime? If so theirs must have been a lonely and uncomfortable childhood not dissimilar to her own in many ways, Tara reflected, running her hand thoughtfully across the silk counterpane.

'Do you like the bed, *mademoiselle*?' the housekeeper enquired, reminding Tara that she was still staring at it.

'It's absolutely fabulous,' she said honestly, pulling her hand away, 'but do you think I could have some more pillows?'

'*Mais, certainement, mademoiselle*…certainly…'

The housekeeper probably thought she was mad. There was a bank of pillows three deep on the bed already, but the ornate sofas and chair looked so uncomfortable. And she had plans. Lots of plans. And those plans involved cushions and throws, and everything she could think of to make things more comfortable and homely while she was here.

'There are flowers in the garden, and in the hothouse, *mademoiselle*… But we weren't sure you would like them…'

'I'd love them!' Tara exclaimed. 'Thank you. And some for the Count too—'

'The Count, *mademoiselle*?' The housekeeper frowned.

'Oh, sorry, does he have an allergy?'

'Not to my knowledge, *mademoiselle*…'

'Then definitely for the Count and some for the nursery too. If you show me where I'm allowed to pick, I'll arrange them myself so I don't put you to any trouble.'

'It's no trouble, *mademoiselle*,' the housekeeper said, smiling at Tara's enthusiasm. 'Is there anything else I can do for you?'

'Do you have a handyman?'

'A handyman, *mademoiselle*?'

'To fit childproof locks for when Poppy is older, and to build fireguards. I've noticed all the open fires.'

'The Count prefers them.'

Then the Count was going to have to adapt to the new regime a small child would inflict on his household, Tara thought.

'We should have thought of these things in advance of your arrival,' the housekeeper said with concern.

'It's early days yet,' Tara reassured the older woman with a smile. 'I just want to be sure before I leave…'

'Yes, *mademoiselle*,' the housekeeper said gently as Tara's voice tailed away. 'Please try not to worry, *mademoiselle*…' And as their gazes met and held, the housekeeper touched Tara's arm. 'I can tell already that you're going to make a great difference here.'

Tara kept her feelings on that one to herself.

'This is my favourite guest room in the whole house,' the housekeeper confided.

'I'm not surprised.' Tara laughed, taking in the grandeur.

'And the Count is right next door...'

Ah. Tara's smile dimmed. 'Thank you,' she said quickly. 'I'm sure I'll soon find my way around.' It occurred to her then that perhaps the staff thought she wanted to be close to Lucien, and she couldn't cause any more disturbance for them than she already had by asking to be moved.

The housekeeper showed her the luxurious bathroom made for two, and Tara's cheeks burned red when she spotted the twin robes hanging on the bathroom door, and by the time she had been shown round the dressing room with its selection of silk robes and jewelled slippers all her pleasure in the suite of rooms had vanished and she was mortified.

'In case you've forgotten yours,' the housekeeper said lightly, as if there was nothing unusual in stocking such items in a guest suite. 'And if you need anything more you only have to ring down.'

'I'm sure there's everything I need right here.' Remembering her manners, she thanked the housekeeper. Did Lucien make a habit of this sort of thing? She was growing angrier by the minute.

'The Count wants people to have luxury during their stay...'

'He does?' How many of Lucien's house guests wore jewelled slippers?

'His father was just the same,' the housekeeper confided. 'It's considered part of the old world charm.'

Hmm, Tara thought.

'Well, I'll leave you to settle in.'

She would never wrap her mind around the sort of life Lucien led. But there was no point fretting about it. She was here and had to get on with it. Or she could always stay in her room and skulk in the shadows, a technique she had perfected over the years, and which had got her precisely nowhere to date. Besides, her curiosity was beginning to get the better of her. There was nothing to stop her finding out what all these sophisticated guests wore when they came to stay at the castle. She'd take a shower first, and then find out.

Having dried her hair, she cleaned her teeth and threw on a baggy top. Brushing her hair and twisting it into a no-nonsense knot, she could hardly wait to visit the Aladdin's cave that was her dressing room. But, of course, she was only going to look…

Oh…but this was rather nice…

Rifling through the rail of fabulous lingerie in the dressing room, Tara came across a robe exactly the same colour as her eyes. Deciding it wouldn't hurt to slip it on, she tugged off her top and carefully slid her arms into the diamante-sprinkled silk. What an exquisite experience that proved to be! The delicate fabric felt incredible against her skin. She inhaled with pleasure imagining the beauty who might wear it. When she finally plucked up the courage to look in the mirror, Lucien walked in.

'Oh, I'm sorry,' he exclaimed brusquely. 'No one could find you. I never imagined you'd be in here…'

No, and she could see why not. She knew she looked ridiculous in a robe meant for someone slim and hastily tried to cover herself.

'It might be better if you wait outside…' Clutching

the robe around her, she stared at him miserably, but Lucien refused to take the hint.

'Why don't you try this?' Searching expertly through the press of garments, he extracted a velvet robe in the palest shade of blue, trimmed with a froth of white lace. It was breathtakingly beautiful. 'And these,' he said, dipping down to retrieve what looked to Tara like the most expensive feathered slip-ons on the face of the earth.

'How do you know my size?' she asked as Lucien placed the dainty slippers in her hand, but then she blushed at his expression. There wasn't much they didn't know about each other's body. But as she hopped in ungainly fashion round the dressing room, battling with feathered mules, and attempting to swap robes, Tara's insecurities mounted. 'I really wish you'd leave me to get on with this,' she exclaimed, knowing her face was as red as a beetroot.

'Why?' Lucien murmured with a look in his eyes she knew only too well.

CHAPTER TEN

'I DON'T know how you can ask why I would like you to leave,' Tara said with a frustrated shake of her head.

'What do you mean?' Lucien appeared genuinely bemused.

'You can see me,' Tara insisted.

'And?'

'What part of stupid, fat, clumsy me did you miss?'

He shrugged. 'I saw *you*—'

'If you needed any more proof that Guy wouldn't want me…'

'Guy?' He frowned. 'I don't want to hear any more about Guy in connection with you.'

'You don't?'

'*I* wanted you.' He said this with a flash of the old humour, though his use of the past tense was hardly reassuring.

'And now?'

'I've seen you wearing fewer clothes than you're wearing now.'

'So you do believe me about Guy?'

'The only thing I don't understand,' Lucien admitted, as they were both clearing the air, 'is why Freya would say those things about you.'

'I've wondered about that too. It was only later I realised how frightened she must have been.'

'Freya, frightened?' Lucien clearly found that incredible.

'If Freya had lost Guy, she believed she would have nothing,' Tara explained. 'Freya knew Guy talked to me sometimes and that threatened her. Freya couldn't believe a man could look at a woman without there being sexual overtones. She didn't see what I saw…'

'Which was?' Lucien's eyes narrowed as he pushed for more information.

'In Guy's sick mind, drugs made things appear perfect until he came down again into his self-imposed hell. Guy wasn't just addicted to drugs, he was addicted to perfection and, well, I could never be that, could I?'

Tara said this so matter-of-factly that he was desperate to reassure her, but before he had a chance to do that she let the clothes in her arms drop and stood in front of him, completely vulnerable. 'I felt sorry for your brother, Lucien, and I tried—believe me, I tried. But Guy didn't want anyone to help him, least of all me. Why would he?' she pressed when he continued to stare at her. 'Well, look at me,' she insisted. 'I never even registered on Guy's sexual radar.'

He realised he was still standing rigidly like a fool, with his eyes narrowed as if Tara were talking to him in the one language he didn't understand. But he did understand how she must be feeling, and felt a wave of shame creep over him to think that anyone could have made her feel this way. Scooping up the discarded robe, he shook it out and handed it to her. 'Here—put this on. I'll turn my back…'

She didn't move to take it and, realising she didn't

want to move because she was so ashamed of her body, he unzipped it and went to her. With the same care as he might have dressed a child, he lowered it over her head.

Tara kept her eyes tightly shut. Was this the nicest thing Lucien had ever done for her, or the kindest? When he stepped back, she quickly swept up her discarded clothes and folded them neatly, desperate for something to distract his attention from her body.

'Haven't you forgotten something?'

'Have I?' She turned to face him, flinching as he reached towards her. It was as if everything that had happened between them counted for nothing, and they were starting all over again from this horribly embarrassing moment. 'Oh, the zip…' Realising what had attracted his attention, she quickly did it up again with a blasé, 'How could I forget that?'

'Because you were upset?' Lucien's head tipped to one side as he regarded her.

He had changed his clothes and showered too, Tara noticed, finally pulling herself together both mentally and sartorially. Smart black trousers cinched with a Hermes belt… Hermes loafers on his naked feet and a sharp blue shirt that had probably been custom-made for him. Even in the fabulous robe he'd selected for her, and which actually fitted, she felt more than a little underdressed.

'Better now?' he said.

'I will be when you stop looking at me.'

'Something wrong with the way I'm looking at you?'

She had never liked being in the spotlight and she didn't like the way he made her feel. 'You make me feel so fat,' she confessed, looking away from too much virile perfection.

'Fat?'

'Yes, you know…wobbly bits.' Actually, he wouldn't know, Tara realised as she turned around to confront Lucien.

His lips tipped up. 'Actually, I like your wobbly bits.'

She was supposed to believe him?

'There's only one thing wrong…'

'Yes?' She was still acting defiant, but inside she had just been reduced to a snivelling bunch of insecurities.

'Let your hair down…'

'That's it?'

'Let your hair down,' Lucien repeated.

She reached up but, before she had a chance to take the clip out of her hair, Lucien had done it for her. As her hair bounced onto her shoulders he smiled. 'That's better,' he said.

'Are you sure that's it?'

'What else did you think I was going to say?'

If he thought she was going to give him more ammunition than could be gleaned by the evidence of his own eyes, he was wrong.

'You have to stop this, Tara. If I say you're beautiful I don't expect you to argue…'

'Beautiful?'

'Don't play the fool with me; we both know you're too smart for that.'

There was just enough warmth in Lucien's eyes to convince her he was being serious. It prompted her to ask the question she should have asked him the moment he'd come into the dressing room. 'Why are you here, Lucien?'

He continued to stare at her and the longer they held each other's gaze, the less his motive seemed to matter. If it had been anything urgent, he would have told her right away, Tara reasoned. 'Don't,' she said, flinching as he ran the knuckles of one hand very lightly down her arm.

'Don't?' he queried softly.

'Don't you know I'm exhausted?' she tempered. And even that was feeble when Lucien only had to look at her a certain way and she'd instantly recover from anything the day had thrown at her. And he was looking at her that way, Tara realised, lifting her eyelashes the smallest amount. 'Are you laughing at me?'

'I'm not laughing at you…'

No, but he was stroking her arm so tenderly it made it impossible for her to concentrate. 'Lucien, please…'

'Please what?' he teased in a husky voice. 'If you wanted to be alone you could have stayed at the gate-house.'

'That's unkind…'

'Unkind?' Dipping his head, he stared into her eyes. 'Let me assure you that I only intend to be extremely persuasive, attentive and, ultimately, hugely satisfying…'

'Hugely satisfying…?' She sighed.

'That's right…'

This was the moment when she should reject him and play him for all she was worth, but that was another girl in another lifetime, and one who was much less in love than she was.

Lucien carried her into the bedroom, where he tossed back the sheets and laid her down on the bed. She barely had time to inhale the crisp clean scent of fresh air and sunlight rising from the bedding before he kicked off his loafers and joined her. Drawing her into his arms, he stretched out his length against her, and as his weight pressed into her she knew it wasn't her imagination telling her this was the safe harbour of her dreams.

Lucien's lips were a familiar and irresistible introduction to the pleasures in store for her, but he wouldn't be rushed. He wasn't in half as much hurry as she was, Tara concluded, but why would he be when the outcome was so certain? He felt so firm and warm and strong, and was everything she wanted him to be and more. She pressed against him greedily, but it wasn't enough; it could never be enough. She gasped with anticipation when he brought her beneath him, containing her with his powerful frame, and pacing her pleasure as his lips incited little flames of sensation all down her neck.

Capturing her wrists, he held them high above her head, resting them on the bank of pillows so he could enjoy kissing her as much as he wanted to without her interference. He had every intention of appreciating each glorious inch of Tara at a speed that suited him. That it suited Tara he had no doubt. Judging by her sighs and the way she writhed beneath him, she was enjoying it. She liked it even more when he whispered suggestions in Catalan, a language he knew she couldn't understand, though she certainly got his meaning. He loved the look in her eyes and he loved the way her robe fell apart, revealing all her lush perfection the moment he pulled down the zip.

'What an accommodating robe,' he murmured, stripping it away in one swift movement.

'You are…'

'Impossible?' he suggested. 'No.' He pressed against her, loving the way her cushioned form yielded beneath his hard muscled frame. If there was a more perfect woman on the face of the earth he had yet to meet her.

The more she pressed against him, the more Lucien answered her with those wicked words against her lips. She knew they were wicked even though she couldn't understand them. Why else would he have that look in his eyes? Why else would he be working his magic on her now? She loved this feeling of being safe in his arms, even when she was completely in his power. She loved the way he held her so firmly with one hand clasping her buttocks and the other securing her wrists. She could feel the shift of hard muscle beneath his smooth, tanned skin, and the power of his erection against her thighs. The way she felt now tempted her to believe she could have it all—Lucien and Poppy...a proper life, a proper family... And as he whispered her name against her neck she trembled with desire, and when he let go of her wrists she immediately captured him, linking her fingers behind his neck to drag him back to her.

'Kiss me,' she ordered him. Make me forget the truth of our situation, was what she meant. 'Kiss me,' she repeated fiercely.

Lucien made love to her so tenderly that emotion welled inside her. She hid it, of course, and was relieved when she was incapable of feeling anything other than the most intense pleasure imaginable. She was glad her breasts were so large—Lucien made her glad. She had worked out that girls with small breasts must receive proportionately fewer kisses, which led her on to wondering who would want to be thin. She'd worked all this out long before Lucien nudged his way between her thighs and if she had a complaint, it was that he seemed intent on taking her as if she were the most fragile thing on earth.

'If you stop now,' she warned him when he paused to lavish kisses on her belly, 'I swear I'll never forgive you...'

'Never forgive me this?' Lucien queried in the stern voice she loved above anything. Dipping his head, he delivered the most intensely pleasurable attentions with his tongue.

'Okay, I might forgive you that,' Tara conceded, gasping.

Lucien laughed the confident laugh of a man who knew his skills in bed came with satisfaction guaranteed. He was about to migrate down that bed when Tara dragged him back again. 'No,' she commanded, raising her hips seductively. 'You don't get away from me that easily…'

'What makes you think I want to?'

He pinned her to the bed with his weight and she responded exactly as he'd hoped she would. Whatever she said, Tara was the perfect woman. She would stay in Ferranbeaux. She would stay with him. She would see Poppy exactly as and when she wanted. As the mistress of Lucien Maxime, the Count of Ferranbeaux, who would stop her?

After their shower they returned to the sitting room in their robes. Tara settled on the rug in front of the fire, staring into it with a pensive expression on her face. With her knees drawn up to her chin and her hair lit by the firelight so it became a cloud of glittering gold to frame her face, she had to be the loveliest thing he had ever seen.

He went to hunker down beside her and, cupping his hand around her head, he drew her close. 'You're beautiful.'

'Don't be silly,' she said at once.

'I've never been more serious in my life…' He closed his eyes to allow his senses full rein. He could feel her soft curls springing against his palm, and inhaling her fresh warm scent he knew this was one of life's better moments. 'A much better moment,' he murmured, speaking his thoughts out loud.

'Sorry?' She turned to look at him.

'This is much better than fighting all the time, don't you think?' He nuzzled his chin against her neck and then realised she looked stricken.

When he pulled back, she said, 'Oh, Lucien, I'm so sorry I was brutal about your brother…'

'The truth is brutal.' And he was more concerned about Tara right now. Guy was beyond his help, but whoever had made Tara feel so self-conscious and worthless had given him a task he could do something about. Drawing her close, he kissed the top of her head. How could he convince her he'd never known such peace before? Just sitting with Tara resting against his chest in front of the fire was enough for him. But as he listened to the crackle of wood as the logs burned and shifted he felt his sleeve grow wet. 'Tara…?' When she didn't answer he held her closer still, determined to make everything right for her. But they came from different worlds, he reminded himself, and his was ruled by duty, so how did he intend to do that?

He decided she must be grieving for Freya, and instinct told him the best way to counsel her was to commune in silence so she knew he understood, and when she looked at him as if trying to read his deepest thoughts, he did the only thing that felt right to him.

As Lucien kissed her it was like the sun coming out after a storm, food after a siege. This was where she belonged. Lucien was everything to her and she gave herself to him again without reservation. The tenderness they'd shared over the past few hours was what had sustained her for two long years, and now he had come back to her…

So enjoy it while it lasts, the demon doubt inside her whispered spitefully.

CHAPTER ELEVEN

TARA woke at dawn the following morning to find Lucien had already showered and left her, and there was just a rumpled pillow and his indentation on the bed. Gathering his pillow to her, she inhaled deeply, wondering if she'd ever been so happy. They had turned a corner, she was sure of it. And all her doubts? Were left behind, she told her inner voice firmly.

After taking a shower, she dressed quickly in her old jeans and a T-shirt and, after checking Poppy was still asleep with Liz in the next room, she hurried downstairs to find breakfast…and maybe bump into Lucien.

Tara's first impression of Lucien's home hadn't changed as she walked downstairs. It was crying out for some homely touches. She didn't like to think of Lucien and Guy growing up here. She didn't like to think of Poppy growing up here, come to that. Biting her lip with concern, Tara glanced back up the stairs towards the nursery. The castle of Ferranbeaux was like a wonderful museum, full of priceless objects that no one must touch. But it wouldn't take a magic wand to turn it into a home. Maybe the scent of age and great wealth was omnipresent, but her imagination could easily conjure up a time when the castle had been a family home. The pockmarked stone could be draped with warm-coloured hangings, and with a little tweaking here and there and some well-chosen pieces of furniture even the vast scale of the building would seem less daunting. There were so many lovely features—the magnificent staircase for one, with its smooth roll-topped banister. It made her think about all the hands that must have brushed the polished wood to a patina so fine it felt like polished silk. The light filtering in through innumerable panes of jewelled glass was absolutely magical, and with a few more well-placed lamps to eradicate the shadows… How she would love to share the renovation of it with Lucien.

And now she really was dreaming, Tara told herself firmly as she reached the bottom of the stairs.

'The Count is in the breakfast room, *mademoiselle*,' a servant murmured to her. 'Shall I show you?'

'Thank you…' Tara's heart leapt. Would she ever get used to being part of Lucien's life again?

When she walked into the dining room the addition of plaster dust on the front of Lucien's thighs where the denim had been stretched across hard muscle told her he'd already been out early that morning working on the renovations.

'Hello,' she said cheerily, sure he must know how she felt—as if all her Christmases had come at once.

'Good morning,' he said quite formally, barely looking at her.

She told herself that his reserve was for the servants hovering round them. Lucien would hardly want to announce to the world that they had spent the night together. When he suggested they take breakfast outside on the terrace she readily agreed, knowing this would give them a degree of privacy they couldn't enjoy in the dining room.

'Coffee?' Lucien said, once he'd seen her comfortably settled on an attractive cane chair with a deeply padded seat. 'Or tea?'

'Juice, please…' She smiled up at him. She could hardly wait to tell him what last night had meant to her. Just being here with Lucien brought the world into sharper focus, though he did still seem a little distracted.

And no wonder, Tara thought, gazing out across the raised terrace. The formal gardens were fabulous, prompting the thought that maybe someone had to clip the neat little box hedges with a pair of hand scissors one leaf at a time to achieve such a perfect outline. The scent of roses and lavender drifted on the same breeze that rippled the glassy lake…and, on that lake, swans glided elegantly, giving no hint as to the furious paddling going on beneath the smooth surface of the water to sustain their forward momentum. She felt a certain comradeship with those swans, Tara mused as Lucien sipped his coffee in silence. It was impossible not to compare the grandeur of the parkland surrounding Lucien's home to the narrow street and small cinder playground in front of her small house back home. Maybe that was why he'd brought her here, to let her see what she was up against…

It was a relief when the waiter wheeled a trolley over and she was forced to choose breakfast rather than dwell on the comparisons a court of law might make. When it came to access rights to Poppy, surely love counted for something? She had to believe it did.

'If you don't like anything on the trolley you can order something else,' Lucien told her.

'Thank you, this is fine.' Tara's heart squeezed tight. She could pretend all she liked, but the truth was they were back to square one. Last night had meant nothing to him, and that hurt her more than she could possibly have imagined. Even out here in the sunshine she was in the shadows, perhaps now more than ever. 'Lucien…'

First he waved the waiter away, and then, with a faint air of impatience, he turned to her. 'Yes? What is it, Tara?'

'I love you,' she whispered.

'I thought I'd show you the city today,' he said, leaning back in his chair as if she had just asked him to pass the salt. 'I think you'll want to see it to reassure yourself about where Poppy will be living—'

'Didn't you hear me?'

Thrusting his chair back, Lucien got to his feet. 'Let's take this inside, shall we?'

Did she have an alternative?

Lucien walked into his study and she followed.

He shut the door behind them.

'Lucien, I—'

'Just listen this time.' He held up his hands with a grim expression on his face. 'And, for once, please, don't speak—'

She couldn't speak. She couldn't believe he would speak to her like that.

'I don't…I can't…I have never loved,' he told her with a decisive gesture. 'And I'm not about to start now. It isn't your fault,' Lucien informed her stiffly. 'That's just how it is. So please don't talk to me about love, or bring it up again. If there's anything I've done to lead you on—'

'Just a minute,' Tara said quietly. 'Are you telling me you don't believe in love, and yet you're intending to adopt Poppy?' There wasn't a part of her that wasn't trembling as she asked the question. She was suffused with fear for the future of the little girl she loved so deeply, and hurt that Lucien could be so unfeeling towards her. In those few words he had made her feel used and dirty and stupid.

'Don't be ridiculous. Poppy will get everything she needs from me.' Tara's expression irritated him. It was as if she didn't believe him. She probably thought emotion was everything, whereas he knew for a fact it was a dangerous distraction. Closing himself off from emotion had brought him success in life, and it wasn't that hard to do. He just had to remember how it had felt to be rejected by the Count, his father. When he remembered how he had dealt with that, the rest was easy. He had never been an attention-seeker like Guy and so he had shut himself off as a child, killing off his ability to feel in the process. This time he was doing it for Tara rather than for himself. He would give her no false promises or lead her on in any way. His only regret was that he had allowed things to go this far. He was mid-self-congratulation when a waiter came in with a tray of breakfast. He often ate at his desk and his meals were brought to him without ceremony so he could continue working.

'Monsieur le Conte,' the man murmured, 'you left the table so I had the chef prepare something fresh for you…'

Which, he had to say, smelled delicious…

'Let me take it,' Tara offered.

He was relieved when Tara spoke up and not a little surprised to see how quickly she had regained her composure. He was glad she had taken their little talk so well. After last night he had been keen to set things straight between them at the earliest opportunity.

Satisfied that everything was back to normal, he settled down in his swivel chair. 'Just put the tray down on the desk for me, will you?' he said, clearing a space for it. 'What about some breakfast for you?' he asked as the waiter was about to leave. He noticed then that her face was ashen, and waved the man away. 'What's the matter?'

'You…you and Poppy,' she said in a quiet voice. 'You caring for Poppy—'

'We both care for Poppy—'

She shook her head. 'No, Lucien. By your own admission, you're not capable of caring for anyone.'

'I'm more than capable,' he assured her confidently.

'I should have known,' she murmured as if she hadn't heard him.

'You should have known what?'

She looked at him steadily then. 'I should have known that the man who left a small fortune on my bed after taking my virginity before disappearing from my life—'

'What did you say?' he demanded, suddenly acutely tuned in.

'I think you heard me. And don't feel guilty. There was no way you could possibly have known. It was my choice to do what I did that night, but I did think I might have heard from you afterwards. I didn't realise people could just shut themselves off. That night was special for me, and I thought it was for you—'

She had given him an opening, and paled when he said nothing. Getting to his feet, he considered what to say next. He had to achieve a balance between raising her expectations unfairly and crushing her. 'You're wrong to think that night meant nothing to me—'

'I don't know how you can say that, Lucien, when you never once made any attempt to contact me.'

'You know as well as I do that life intervened. I lost my brother—'

'And I lost my sister, and I have yet to hear one word of condolence from you. Why should I think that sleeping with me meant any more to you than scratching an itch?'

'Tara!'

'I don't see why you should sound so shocked. That's what you've reduced that night to. But where Poppy's concerned your cold-blooded approach isn't enough; she must have love.'

'And she'll have it—'

'From you?' Tara flinched as Lucien's blazing gaze dared her to say more. How startlingly attractive he was, and yet how cold. She was close enough to detect the scent of his soapy shower and to see that his hair was still damp and curling tenaciously round his cheekbones, but she had more sense than to stay around and let him work his magic on her once again. 'I won't keep you. There's nothing worse than cold eggs,' she said instead.

'We'll talk about this later,' he promised, turning his attention to his rapidly cooling breakfast. It was better to let her calm down, he reasoned.

'Let me save you the trouble,' she said in her usual non-combative tone and, before he knew what was happening, she had picked up his plate and tossed the contents in the bin. 'Enjoy!' she snapped on her way out of the room.

Tara sought refuge in the nursery. It was the only place she felt she belonged. Being with Poppy and doing the little tasks for the baby filled her with so much joy it went some way to scrubbing out the anger she felt where

Lucien was concerned. He was a lost cause, Tara decided, swishing the warm water in the baby bath over Poppy's chubby legs. Reaching for a towel, she wrapped it around the adorable warm, wriggly body and exchanged some baby noises with her niece as she lifted her. Then she felt Lucien's presence in the room. She turned to face him. He was leaning against the door, watching her. She stared back, telling him without words that he had no place being here unless he was prepared to respect the haven of a small baby and the woman who cared for her and loved her.

'I wondered if you'd like some breakfast, after all?' he said dryly.

'No, thank you. Would you like to hold your niece?' She advanced fearlessly, holding Lucien's gaze all the while.

'Me?'

'Why not? She's clean, and she's lovely. It's a great privilege, Lucien.'

He could see that. He reached for the baby. Seeing Tara holding Poppy had had an effect on him, leaving him warm and calm. He wasn't ready to let go of that yet.

Tara transferred his baby niece into his arms with the greatest care. As she looked at him a flash of understanding passed between them that said he had pushed her in the study and she had shoved him back. Tara had put her stake in the ground, and he could only respect that.

Holding the baby in his arms was an extraordinary feeling. He didn't want to let the little girl go, and could have stared into the depths of those sapphire eyes for a long, long time. He only wished Poppy was old enough for him to reassure her that he would care for her and protect her all his life and that he would even learn to love, if she would show him. His gaze met Tara's over the baby's head and she smiled at him. 'Why don't we go out?' she suggested. 'It might do us all good to have some fresh air…'

'Why don't we?' he said, surprising himself, and they agreed to meet outside on the terrace in forty minutes.

She should have known Lucien would change his outfit for a walk about in the city. He looked every bit the Count in a crisp bone-coloured linen shirt, which he had teamed with an elegant summer-weight jacket, beautifully tailored trousers and nut-coloured designer loafers exactly the same shade as his hair. Tara felt a little awkward at his side in her jeans and simple top, but when she was with young children she knew better than to dress up and, with Lucien introducing her so warmly to everyone they met as his niece's aunt, it wasn't long before she relaxed.

Plus Lucien had a position to uphold, Tara reminded herself wryly as they walked along the cobbled streets pushing Poppy in her buggy, while she most assuredly didn't. The Count of Ferranbeaux was on show to his people, she reasoned as he stopped to chat with some men playing boules along the way. It was the first of many encounters, and it was easy to see how proud the people were of their Count—easy to see why they would be, when Lucien looked every bit the aristocratic with his proud features and his fabulous physique. While he stopped yet again to exchange a good natured conversation involving lots of hand gestures and exclamations, she excused herself politely and, pushing Poppy into a nearby shop, she bought some ice cream.

'You didn't need to do that,' Lucien exclaimed when she handed him a dripping cone.

'You carry money?' she challenged dryly. 'Or perhaps you're afraid of spilling some down your suit?'

Tipping his sunglasses down his nose, he gave her a look before settling them back in place again. 'I carry money,' he assured her, 'and I certainly don't have accidents.'

There was so much to see and now she was relaxed she was full of questions. Lucien brought everything in the city to life for her, and if there was a moment when his enthusiasm turned down a notch it was when he shared his disappointment at not finding an architect qualified to help him restore the rotunda of the ancient basilica. The circular tower required a specialist in medieval architecture, he told her, and to date his team had failed to find one who was sufficiently knowledgeable.

They moved on from the shopping area to a cypress-shaded avenue which Lucien told her was an alternative route back to the castle. Sunlight dappled the pavements and there were skylarks swooping back and forth. It was a picturesque area, and one of the oldest in the walled city, Lucien explained. There was even a small park here, Tara discovered, with a playground, and she found herself looking for signs that said, '*À Louer*', meaning 'to rent', though she knew it was only a daydream. But perhaps she should start planning to find somewhere else to stay, because the next time she came to Ferranbeaux to see Poppy it might not be convenient for Lucien to have her stay at the castle.

CHAPTER TWELVE

LUCIEN invited her to eat dinner with him that evening. She had to keep a line of communication open between them, Tara reasoned as she took a shower. They still had a lot to talk about where Poppy was concerned.

And that was why her heart was pounding with excitement and her head was full of dreams…

Yes, well, she would put her sensible head on now, along with the only dress she'd brought with her, a modest cream shift with a pretty coral-coloured edging and a lacy cardigan to match. Slipping her bare feet into simple sandals, she made two very important phone calls before going down for dinner. The first went well, but the second, which involved her viewing and then potentially signing the lease for a room in an apartment building in the city, made her mad as hell. Women couldn't do that in Ferranbeaux, she was told. She must have the lease countersigned by a man.

What sort of place was this?

He had the shower turned to ice. The temperature of the water matched his mood exactly. He had shunned feelings all his life, only to have Tara break through his reserve. Turning off the water, he stepped out of the shower. Grabbing a towel, he dried off roughly. Had she turned down his invitation to stay at the gatehouse because she was playing for higher stakes? Was he guilty of drawing a veil over the fact that she was out of the same mould as Freya because he wanted her? With so many people depending on him, he couldn't afford to make the same mistake as Guy had with Tara's sister. The citizens of Ferranbeaux were waiting for him to take a wife not a mistress.

Guy had refused the title, Count of Ferranbeaux, because of the responsibilities that came with it. Lucien had taken on those responsibilities, knowing they would colour his actions for the rest of his life. He wasn't about to forget his duty to his countrymen now. Guy had been left the family money and so Lucien had always known he'd have to prove himself, which he had, and now he was going to use some of that money to complete the renovations his city so badly needed. Would he risk everything for Tara, when he wasn't one hundred per cent sure of her? He had schooled himself to believe his inclination where matters of the heart were concerned was a selfish indulgence and if he married at all it would be in the interests of his people. That determination had never changed. He would always put Ferranbeaux first.

Planting his fists on the cold hard marble, he stared into the mirror at a man he didn't like too much. Life had made him suspicious to the point where he couldn't see the good in people any longer. Guy's associates had turned his stomach with their tales of bills unpaid and promises his brother had made before his death. He'd paid them off to get rid of them, but it had left a bad taste in his mouth and a lingering mistrust of others that he couldn't seem to shake off…though this afternoon with Tara and Poppy had given him something more to think about. But he had inherited control of a region where antiquated laws prevailed, and he should be devoting all his energies to redrafting them rather than indulging in a dalliance with Freya's sister.

Tugging on his jeans, he pulled on a clean top and, ruffling his hair into order, he left the bathroom. This time with Tara had made him restless. She was no longer the ingénue he'd met two years ago, or even the same woman who had been waiting for him so anxiously at the hotel. She had come alive under pressure, and he was glad of it for her sake, but if she wanted to stay on in Ferranbeaux his terms for that were clear.

The desire to blow some fresh air through her muddled mind had gone badly astray, Tara concluded as she clung onto an icy metal upright. She hadn't expected the wind to be so strong out here on the castle ramparts. She had been lured onto a part of the walkway that was being renovated by the promise of an even better view over the walled city at night time, and was standing on some wooden planks over a drop she didn't even want to think about—especially not when the wood creaked every time the wind blew, and the wind blew all the time. She suddenly wasn't so sure she was brave about heights. She thought about Poppy, warm and safe in bed. She wouldn't be much use to Poppy if she fell, and the media would have a field day if she did. She had no option but to let go of the pole and start edging gingerly along. But the first step she took met with empty air and as she shrieked a voice called out—

'Don't move… I'm coming to get you…'

'Lucien…' Her hands were welded to the pole and she didn't dare to turn around, but she felt the wood shift when he stepped onto it. 'Is it safe for us both to be standing here?'

'What do you think?' he growled. 'I'm tempted to leave you here.'

'No—'

'Next time you feel like taking a stroll out here,' he said, wrapping an arm around her waist, 'call me first. Come on—you have to move.'

'Can't—'

'You must.'

Her throat was so dry she could barely form words. 'Lucien…'

'You have to trust me. There's a drop of around a hundred feet below us, so just do as I say for once.' He started peeling her fingers from the pole.

'Please—no…'

The rest of her protests were lost in a gasp as Lucien swung her into his arms. 'There are times to argue and this sure as hell isn't one of them.' Carrying her inside, he kicked the door shut behind them. 'Didn't you see the notices warning that this part of the building is unsafe?'

Having been dropped unceremoniously to her feet, Tara was not at her most complacent. 'It was dark—'

'Forgive me for not anticipating reckless guests. I'll have lanterns placed there.'

'Good idea,' she agreed, still shaking with fright.

'What were you doing out there, anyway?'

'I needed time to think—'

'More time?'

'Yes, more time, Lucien. There are quite a few things we need to iron out—'

'Like safety measures? You could have been killed out there.' He stood aside to let her pass but, as she did so, he caught hold of her and kept her trapped with his fists planted against the wall either side of her face. 'No more adventures, Tara—'

She was so sure he was going to kiss her she gasped as he pulled away.

'You don't need to walk across unsupported planks to prove how independent you are.'

She shook her head. 'That wasn't it at all.'

Lucien wasn't listening. She could see the strain in his face that told her how much danger she'd been in.

'I care about your safety.'

'I know, and thank you—'

'As I care about the welfare of all my people,' he said over her.

'But that's just it—I'm not your person, Lucien.'

He was still rocked by the thought of Tara plunging to her death, and was in no mood for lectures. 'Save your stand-alone principles for someone who gives a damn. There is such a thing as teamwork and cooperation—'

'Which you, of course, champion,' she flashed back. 'Am I the only one here who should learn to compromise? Can you compromise, Lucien? No,' she said after a moment, 'I didn't think so.'

'You don't have to break away from everyone to prove you're not like Freya,' he rapped, troubled by the thought that, even at her worst, Freya could never have evoked this level of feeling in him.

'And you don't have to be so hard to prove you're not like Guy—'

As silence rang between them he had more than enough opportunity to contemplate how uncomfortable the truth could be.

'Lucien... I'm so sorry... You almost certainly saved my life.'

He looked at her, wondering who was saving whom here. 'Just make sure you don't take risks like that again.'

This time Tara held her tongue. Would it have occurred to Lucien that just being in his company was the biggest risk of all?

Lucien insisted Tara must warm herself in front of the fire and have a hot drink, and she didn't argue when he led the way back to his apartment. She noticed more this time, now there was no red mist of passion to distract her. It was a man's space with no unnecessary items or even family photographs, which surprised her. She had expected one of the Count, his father, at least. No wonder Lucien had called on the services of an interior decorator to furnish the nursery. She guessed that, having been brought up in the formal splendour of a castle, he had no cluttered family home references to draw on. But at least he had chosen autumn-coloured textiles to soften the effects of wood and stone, and the furniture was all designed to be comfortable rather than stylish.

Having closed the outer doors behind them, he drew a soft gold curtain across them, shutting out the windy night. 'Sit,' he invited, gesturing towards one of the two taupe-coloured sofas arranged either side of a roaring fire.

The fire proved a stronger incentive and she went to kneel in front of it, wondering if she would ever thaw out. When a few minutes had passed, all the thoughts that had propelled her outside in the first place came to the forefront of her mind. 'What if I accepted your offer to stay at the gatehouse?' she said without turning round.

She heard Lucien shift position on the sofa and sensed his interest. 'I'd be delighted,' he said carefully in a way that told her he knew there was more to come.

'It seems inevitable I'll be staying on here in Ferranbeaux—at least until the final details of the adoption are ironed out…'

'Go on…'

'But if I stay at the gatehouse you must let me pay rent.'

'Rent?'

She turned to face him. 'What's wrong with that?'

Lucien frowned. 'You're my guest. I don't expect you to pay your way.'

'But if I want to?'

'No,' he said flatly.

'So what will I do?' She thought about the phone call and the tiny place she'd found that she couldn't even rent without Lucien's permission. 'You know, don't you?' she said, seeing the way he was looking at her.

'Do I know that you tried to rent a property in the city?'

'There isn't much you don't hear about, I imagine.'

Silence greeted this remark.

'So you also know I'd need you to countersign the lease before I can rent anywhere—'

'There are reforms I have yet to make,' he said pointedly.

'But would you sign?'

'Would I sign so you could live in poverty? What sense would there be in that?'

'I'd make it work—'

'But you don't have to.'

He didn't have to say another word. She already felt humiliated, and saw the irony in that at the very moment when Freya would have been inwardly dancing with triumph. 'So what's your suggestion, Lucien?'

'I think you know…'

No! Everything in her railed against it. It would never work between them, Tara realised, forcing back her grief. She could never, *never* do as Lucien wanted.

'Become your mistress?' she asked him bluntly. 'Live in the gatehouse, where I'm on hand if you should need me? Don't you think Freya's example taught me anything?'

'You don't have to walk in Freya's shadow all your life. It's up to you if you step out of it—'

'That's easy for you to say when you sacrifice nothing to do as you suggest—'

'What other solution is there?' Lucien cut across her. 'What's your suggestion, Tara?'

As he held her gaze she realised this was the end of her pathetic daydream. Sharing her life with Lucien and Poppy was never going to happen, and it was time for her to face reality. She loved Lucien with all her heart. She wanted him. She wanted to spend the rest of her life with him and Poppy, and Lucien was telling her she could only have the scraps. But she was done with accepting whatever life threw at her.

'Who are you, Lucien?' she demanded angrily. 'Who are you really? When did you grow to be so cold?' Tara flinched as she saw something inside him snap.

'Do you really want to know?' Lucien demanded coldly, making her squirm at the thought of what might unfold.

'Yes, I do,' she said.

She remained absolutely still, afraid to breathe or move in case he shut himself off from her again.

'I'm a bastard,' he told her. 'I'm the bastard son of the Count of Ferranbeaux. Are you satisfied now?'

His smile was all cruel irony, but she wasn't nearly satisfied and firmed her jaw, determined to learn whatever else he had to tell her. 'I thought you grew up here at the castle?'

'You thought wrong.' Lucien's tone was clipped— to conceal those feelings her persistence had unlocked, Tara suspected as his stare blazed down into her face. 'I grew up on the wrong side of the tracks with a mother who always put her rich bene-factor first. Don't feel sorry for me. It made me the man I am today—'

Lucien's short, humourless laugh made her flinch inwardly. 'I had no idea,' she admitted softly.

'That I was the son the Count discarded?'

Hearing the pain of long years' standing, she said not a word.

'Discarded until my father's legitimate heir turned down the title, that is—'

Understanding flooded her brain. Now she knew why Lucien was so cold. She realised how frightened he must have been as a child when showing his feelings would only guarantee more rejection. She felt compas-sion for that child and knew Lucien the man was a hostage for life to the duties he had taken over from those who least deserved his help.

'Ferranbeaux means everything to me—'

She didn't need him to tell her that, or why. 'The people need you,' she said, stating a simple fact.

'Yes, they do…and I need you.'

She looked at him, wanting those words to echo in her head for ever.

'I want you to stay here with me in Ferranbeaux, Tara.'

She stared into Lucien's strong, dark face and shivered with desire when he seized her arms. He said the words she'd longed to hear, and yet she knew her hopes were fool's gold. 'As your mistress…?' Her lips were dry, her throat was tight; her heart was breaking as she stared up at him.

Lucien stared at her intently and when he spoke again it was in a low, firm tone so there could be no misunderstanding between them. 'When I marry, it will be for the good of my country.'

'And I have no heritage…'

Lucien didn't answer this; he didn't need to. And who was she to question him? He was a warrior who would be her protector. He was the man she adored—should she put a price on love? Lucien was a primal force it took all her mental energy to hold at bay, and he was the ruler of a kingdom who, for now at least, must stand alone.

'I can't…' Her voice barely made it above a whisper. 'I love you more than life itself, but this is the one thing I can't do for you, Lucien…so I'm sorry, but my answer has to be…no.'

CHAPTER THIRTEEN

'WHERE will you go? What will you do? What about Poppy?'

'That all depends on whether you'll sign the lease,' she told him steadily. 'I'll see Poppy every day, of course—nothing will change that.'

He was coming to feel more for Tara than admiration, but it was time to inject some realism into the mix. 'How do you intend to support yourself?'

'I'll work, of course,' she told him, frowning.

When he took in the keen bright gaze he didn't doubt for a moment that she would. Her red-gold hair was still windswept after her adventure, and in spite of the tension of the moment he almost smiled when his gaze landed on the stubborn chin. But it wasn't what he wanted. He wanted to take her tiny feet and warm them in his hands. He wanted to dress her in silk and satin, and see her smile with happiness when he kissed her. He wanted to spoil her and give her the life that she deserved, a life that would take those work-worn hands and make them soft again. He wanted to treat her like a Countess—in all but name.

They had reached an impasse, Tara realised. Lucien

might have started life in poverty and worked his way up to the very top of the tree, but he had traditional ideas of a man and woman's role in life. And, though she relished the thought of him as protector, the thought of jailer had a different connotation. She couldn't live where he prescribed in a way he considered appropriate. Even six foot walls, as there were at the castle, could house a cosy apartment like this one, or those same walls could become a prison. It all depended on the people living inside those walls, and the respect, or lack of it, they felt for each other. Ferranbeaux was Lucien's home, his sanctuary, and it could be her home too, if she was allowed to live her life independently, the way she wanted to.

Lit by firelight and with her hair billowing around her face like a cloud of gold, he thought Tara the loveliest woman he had ever seen. She was also, without doubt, the most aggravating woman on the face of the earth. Why did she have to make things so difficult for them? He found himself wishing she had remained the innocent ingénue, and had to remind himself that he was largely to blame for the change in her. Who knew what they were capable of until they were tested? And Tara had been tested.

He called for warm drinks as they sat on the sofa talking the tension away deep into the night. He had asked Tara to tell him more about her childhood. She made light of it, of course, though the reports he'd read about it had told him something very different. The beautiful sister Tara talked about with such love was a stranger to him, and he could only conclude that much of Tara's childhood was a fairy tale she had invented to make it more bearable. He had little admiration for

Freya, but he admired Tara's loyalty towards her sister. The two girls had managed to squeeze more fun out of their miserable early lives than seemed possible, and it was a tribute to both of them. If he could never come to terms with the way Freya had lived her adult life, he did understand Tara's love for her sister a little better now. He even found himself laughing when Tara described some of the innocent scrapes they'd got into. Making the best of things didn't even begin to cover it, he realised, when finally she paused for breath.

'You must miss her,' he said then.

Her eyes filled with tears, which she quickly dashed away with a gulping, 'Sorry…'

'Don't apologise…' Taking out his own clean handkerchief, he handed it to her. 'You should never apologise for showing how much you love someone—'

'Says the expert?' She looked at him ruefully mid-snuffle.

'I'm learning…'

'Thank you for listening—'

'Did I have any choice?' he teased her, leaning forward to flick the curtain of hair from her face so he could kiss the tears away. He felt warmed when she smiled at him, and when she laughed and her hair floated back again he brushed it away and cupped her face. 'I didn't mean to make you cry.'

'I'm not over losing Freya yet… She had such a big personality; she left a big hole—' She touched her chest over her heart and couldn't say any more. She didn't need to. He felt the same way about Guy. His brother might not have had Freya's larger than life personality, but he had left no less of a gap in Lucien's world. He hadn't allowed himself to feel this way since Guy's death, or maybe ever, Lucien realised, but just talking to Tara had freed something inside him.

'Come here,' he said softly, drawing her into his arms.

'Lucien?' Her voice was very small as she looked to him, and at that moment he knew there was nothing he wouldn't do for her.

'Yes?' he said, planting a tender kiss on the top of her head.

'Can I stay with you tonight?'

He should have known her demands on him would be very small.

The promise of Lucien's firm touch made her sob with impatience. The sweet pain was growing inside her, and as he lowered her to the bed she kept hold of him so that he joined her, kissing her deeply, passionately, hungrily, as she moved against him. It was a tender and poignant moment, marking her route to independence as well as heralding her departure from the castle, where she had so briefly enjoyed living with him.

To distract from these unhappy thoughts, she dug her hands down the neck of his open shirt, thrilling at the feel of his back, so smooth and strong. 'You look so severe,' she teased him when he held her away from him to study her face.

'Because there are things I cannot change,' he told her with shadows crossing back and forth behind his eyes.

She understood what he meant, because she felt that way too. But it wasn't long before the great sense of belonging to each other broke through. First they exchanged a look of understanding, and then they were laughing and tearing at each other's clothes. Buttons flew everywhere as she tugged off Lucien's shirt, wrenching it from the waistband of his jeans, while he brought her beneath him with such force the breath shot from her lungs. 'I love you,' she murmured, not even knowing if she had truly spoken or if he had heard.

Gasping with excitement to see Lucien looming above her, Tara gave her wrists readily to be held above her head, while Lucien impatiently pushed up her top.

And now it was Lucien's turn to groan with satisfaction as he gazed at her breasts. She had never been more grateful for the fact that they were nice, big breasts, soft and round, with nipples that strained towards him like brazen lozenges. In the unlikely event he'd missed their appeal she arched her chest towards him, displaying them proudly. 'Do you like them?'

'I love…' Lucien paused as if she had distracted him from some deeper thought. 'I love them,' he confirmed passionately.

Hearing nothing now, she bucked towards him, nipples straining painfully. 'Oh, please…' she cried out with pleasure as Lucien began to suckle and, lacing her fingers through his hair, she kept him close, succumbing to the magic of his hands. 'It isn't fair,' she pointed out. 'You still have your clothes on…'

'You'd better do something about it then, hadn't you?' Lucien suggested with deliberate calm.

She started with the buckle of his belt but, before she had chance to free it, Lucien whipped it off and tossed it onto the floor to join their mounting pile of clothes. It still wasn't enough. She wanted more. She was ravenous to touch him, to taste and feel him. She wanted to feel his hot flesh against her, smooth against rough… His chest was broad and strong, shaded with dark hair, and all of him was deeply tanned.

All of him?

Sucking in a fast breath, she quickly looked away.

'Surely you're not still frightened of me?'

Frightened? Where Lucien was concerned, not at all, it was just the thought of a future without him that frightened her. 'You have no shame,' she said in an attempt to distract herself from these unhappy thoughts.

'Should I, with you?'

Her answer was to fall back on the pillows. 'Make love to me…'

Cupping her face in his hands, Lucien kissed her deeply, making her feel like the most cherished woman on the face of the earth. If tonight was all there was, it would have to be enough.

She'd had the place a week when he stood grimly by while she turned the key in the lock. She had come to the castle every day to spend time with Poppy, while he had signed the lease on what appeared to him now to be a derelict building. The first time he had taken a look, his initial reaction had been to have it condemned and knocked down, until Tara had talked him out of it. She had chosen a simple dwelling in an up-and-coming part of town—more coming than up, as far as he could tell. Her small apartment was located on the fringes of the commercial centre, an area that had attracted some of the smaller artisan cooperatives and boutique businesses. Tara had told him she felt at home here, she would live upstairs and her childcare agency office would open on the ground floor.

Right now, her face was alive with anticipation as she prepared to reveal her Shangri-La, while he was already running a number of rescue scenarios that would allow her to leave all this behind and return to him with her pride intact. 'There are boarded-up windows either side of the property, for goodness' sake,' he commented, thinking of her safety. She didn't even hear him.

'I hope you like what I've done with it—'

Hard for him to answer when he had to snatch out a hand to stop her tripping over the rotten door frame.

'It'll be great when it's all fixed up,' she assured him confidently.

'Better start by fixing that door,' he suggested dryly.

'It's all in hand. I've got a handyman—'

'You've got a what?' He frowned. A muscle worked in his jaw. 'I'll fix it for you.'

'Would you?' she asked him sweetly—so sweetly he wondered if he'd just been set up.

'That's really kind of you, Lucien. I've got some tools—'

His look silenced her.

'Well, we'd best get on,' she said, moving ahead of him up the stairs. 'I know how busy you are.'

He was never too busy for Tara, he had discovered, especially since she'd moved in here.

'And don't worry,' she said, stopping on the stairs to turn to him. 'Clearing the garden out back so Poppy can play outside is a top priority. I'll have it finished long before she starts walking—'

'And Liz? Where will she sleep?'

'If she could stay at the castle for the time being with Poppy—'

He thought how beautiful she looked, how vital, as she continued to explain her vision to him. Her face hadn't changed, but her spirit had grown beyond all imagining since that first strained day at the press conference.

'Honestly, Lucien, it won't take me long to make the place feel like a real home—'

As they came into the large open space at the top of the stairs, he thought Tara's enthusiasm must have got the better of her. Where was she going to find the imagination to turn a rundown room with a naked light bulb into a cosy nest? As far as he could see, there was a kitchen in a cupboard, a bathroom that had seen better days—everywhere he looked the paint was peeling and the tap was leaking. 'Doesn't that thing drive you mad?'

'You could fix that too...maybe...' She looked at him hopefully. 'Seeing as you're here...'

'Perhaps I could,' he admitted grudgingly, looking away before her turquoise eyes could work their magic. Restoration was his passion, but he didn't live on the building site while things were being improved, and he wanted better for Tara. He wanted to sweep her up and install her in the gatehouse this minute, where there was no damp, no draughts, no peeling paint and the latest high-tech plumbing in every bathroom.

'Well? Come on...tell me... What do you think?' Turning full circle, she began to describe her vision. 'I can put the bed here, the table over here—'

'Tara—' he frowned as he interrupted her '—you can't go on living here.'

'Why ever not?'

'Because the whole building should be condemned.'

'Like your basilica?'

He firmed his jaw; she did too.

'When my business expands—'

'Your business?' He had to rein himself in. How could he take this from her when just talking about her plans made her face light up like sunrise?

'My childcare agency,' she reminded him. 'Another signature I need from you, apparently. When are you going to change these antiquated laws, Lucien?'

'When you give me time,' he told her dryly, peeling off some paint that brought a chunk of plaster with it.

'Hey, don't wreck the place—'

His lips tugged up as he stared at her. 'I could knock it down for you, if you like.'

'I don't like. You leave my house alone—'

He had to be content with a mocking smile that made her cheeks pink up.

'When Poppy's older, which hopefully will coincide with my business expansion,' she continued, 'I'm going to turn the whole of the ground floor into business premises. This whole area will be for us then, and she can play here and we'll do baking and—'

'On that cooker…?'

'You'd be surprised what I can do, Lucien—'

He doubted that, somehow.

'And look,' she said.

'Look where?' he said, searching for clues in the dismal room.

'Ta da!' she exclaimed, throwing out her arms in front of a dingy alcove.

'Yes?' His imagination was really flagging now.

'Can't you see?' she demanded. 'This is perfect for my desk. I'll be able to keep an eye on Poppy while I'm working—so much better than London, where I hated having someone looking after her while I had to work.'

'But Poppy will be living with me,' he reminded her.

'But I'll have her to stay here sometimes; she is my niece—'

'So you're going to be working with a small child in the room?'

'Like every other single mother, I'll manage,' she told him confidently.

'But you don't have to manage,' he reminded her patiently. 'And how much money do you think it's going to cost to turn this space into both a functioning office and a home?'

'I've got some savings. I'm not completely destitute.'

'I don't suggest you are, but—'

'But what, Lucien? Oh, I see. You think the niece of the Count of Ferranbeaux couldn't possibly come to stay in a modest apartment in the shadow of your castle.'

'I didn't say that.'

'You didn't have to, and I happen to think it's important to show Poppy the other side of life.'

'The seedy side?'

'The real side, Lucien… The side of life where people have to take decisions and don't have someone standing behind them ready to clear up the mess if they get it wrong. The side of life where you learn to live within your means—'

'You don't have to do that here, you can do it equally well in the gatehouse.'

'Other people want to move to this area,' she insisted, selling it hard, 'and there are families who have stuck it out here for generations. Do you want them to go on living with boarded up windows, because they will if we don't make a start on regenerating the area. Basilicas are important, but so are people—'

'And who do you think will be using the basilica?'

'All right,' she conceded, 'maybe we both need to give a little.'

Wisely, he declined to comment.

'Or maybe you can't bring yourself to admit I can make a go of this.'

'You may have found one solution, but it's not ideal—'

'Can you come up with a better one?'

His mouth curved. 'My gatehouse?'

'By your own admission, Lucien, you started with nothing. Are you denying me the same chance to prove myself? Or are you saying I'm not as good as you?'

Easing onto one hip, he gave her a dark look, and as he stuck his thumbs through the belt loops of his jeans he noticed how she blushed and how her gaze strayed where it shouldn't. He also noticed she had positioned herself in front of a cracked window pane in the hope he wouldn't see it. Perhaps it was that that made up his mind for him. 'Give me a list of what you need—'

'A list?' Her brow puckered attractively.

'Pen, paper—a list? I'm asking what you need to make this work.'

'I'll make this work,' she said quietly, and then her smile broke through. 'You're backing my decision to live here—'

'I'm giving you another week.'

CHAPTER FOURTEEN

THE week before Lucien was due to come and inspect her handiwork passed in a whirl of activity, and one big and wonderful surprise.

'Marian Digby!' Tara exclaimed, opening the door to an old friend from her college days. 'I knew you wouldn't let me down.' Of all the people she had met in the university canteen shared by all the colleges, the eccentric lecturer in historical architecture was one of her very favourite people.

After exchanging hugs and greetings, Marian revealed that she had gone to the castle first. 'I couldn't resist,' she confided, her bright, birdlike eyes twinkling. Lucien had found her wandering in the gardens apparently, and had arranged for his chauffeur to deliver her to Tara's new abode.

'This is wonderful,' Marian commented, wiping her nose on a large duster she had plucked from her pocket, scattering plaster dust as she examined the walls. Realising her old friend probably thought she was using a handkerchief, Tara quickly pressed a tissue into her hand.

'What a wonderful opportunity you've given me,' Marian murmured, without realising the exchange had been made. 'There are so many wonderful old buildings in Ferranbeaux... Isn't this a thirteenth-century siege stone?' she demanded of no one in particular, having forgotten Tara was even there as she wandered distractedly across the room.

'I wouldn't know,' Tara admitted as her friend scrutinised the ancient artefact.

'When you rang to say you had something interesting for me to look at, I had no idea,' Marian exclaimed, switching her keen gaze to Tara's face. 'Don't tell me that you and the Count—'

'Oh, no. No, no, no,' Tara rebuked her friend, whilst trying to adopt a serious expression. 'I wouldn't bring you all this way to offer your expert opinion on the Count—'

'More's the pity,' the older woman twinkled.

He brought a picnic with him for the second visit. He couldn't possibly imagine that things had changed so much that Tara could provide them with lunch.

She lost no time proving him wrong.

'I think you'll see some changes,' she warned him.

'I'll be surprised if I don't,' he told her dryly, following her up the stairs.

Some changes?

What Tara had achieved in her second week, with the help of a few workmen, was nothing short of a miracle. The unpromising space had been transformed. Richly patterned fabrics hung from newly plastered and decorated walls, and there was an attractive light fitting where a naked light bulb had hung. Matching table lamps toned with thick-piled rugs, and the floor was freshly sanded and newly polished. There were comfortable throws flung over the backs of sofas that faced each other across a low table in front of the wide stone hearth, and a gleaming brass fireguard to protect inquisitive children from the flames. The mantelpiece already boasted several photographs of Poppy, and on the sills beneath the tall sash windows an array of healthy looking plants competed for attention alongside examples of colourful local pottery.

'This is lovely,' he said, taken aback.

'I'm glad you like it,' she said with a teasing smile.

Tara had turned a dilapidated space into a home. But where had she found the money? He wondered sometimes if the suspicious gene was part of his genetic make-up. 'How—' He got no further because she knew him too well.

'One person's clutter is another person's treasure. So while I was canvassing opinion about the crèche I'm going to open, I came up with the idea of starting a second-hand stall to help fund it and buy the little extras we're sure to need—'

'A market stall?' He laughed when she nodded enthusiastically. 'I have to hand it to you, Tara Devenish, you're a tycoon in the making.'

'I'm just practical,' she said. 'Don't look so surprised; I wasn't born with a silver spoon in my mouth—'

'Neither was I,' he reminded her.

She had prepared a feast for him, which he had not expected. It made his picnic basket redundant and touched him more than he could say. The tiny kitchen had not expanded, but she had kept everything cool in the lock-up downstairs. She had even baked a cake for him in the tiny table top oven.

'Leave your food with me,' she insisted when he

made some comment about them not eating it, 'and then I'm sure you'll come back again,' she told him shyly.

'I'll come back,' he assured her.

At one time this would have been his cue to lean over and plant a kiss on her mouth, but something had changed. It was like starting over. He wanted to hold onto that feeling and see where it went. He'd underestimated Tara even more than he'd first thought, and he was only now beginning to appreciate the huge mistake he'd made.

'I spoke to your Mrs Digby...'

'Did you like her?' Her eyes twinkled with mischief as they got up and started to clear the dishes.

'She's mad, but brilliant—'

'She's a mad genius.'

'I tend to agree with you on that.'

'Marian's a specialist in Gothic architecture. When they need to consult anyone about Notre Dame in Paris they call Marian Digby. I thought she'd be just the person you need to help you with your restoration of the basilica...'

'You were right, and I thank you.' He'd offered her nothing, he'd treated her badly, and yet still she had been thinking of him all along. As his admiration grew he had to shift position to ease the pressure in his groin. 'I shouldn't have come straight from the basilica—' He slapped his thigh, more to deter this surge of interest than to dislodge any dust he might have collected. 'I apologise for not being more smartly dressed.' He indicated his frayed jeans, cinched with a heavy-duty workman's belt along with his ripped and faded top, which he knew together with his disreputable stubble must make him look more like a pirate than a Count. 'That woman is a demanding taskmaster—'

'I'm sure you'll cope,' Tara told him, pointedly not looking where she shouldn't.

'I'm sure I will,' he agreed. But he didn't want to cope with a groin in torment—he wanted to make love to her.

He admired her on so many fronts—for making a go of this apartment, and perhaps most of all for refusing to lower her standards. They were on heat in each other's company, and it would have been the easiest thing in the world for her to take him up on his offer and move into the gatehouse, where they could sate that passion every day and every night. How could he not respect her for holding firm? How could he not respect the fact that Tara was vulnerable and innocent and beautiful, and more than capable of standing on her own two feet, as she had more than proven here? Plus she was caring and astute...

Had he just drawn up the résumé for a Countess? he wondered and, if he had, had he left it too late?

'So you like the apartment?' she said.

'Now don't put words in my mouth,' he warned her.

She stared at his lips.

'Nothing you could do would surprise me, Tara.'

She put that assumption to the test right away. Reaching up, she locked her fingers behind his neck and, as she drew him down to her, the aquamarine eyes widened. 'How much have you missed me, Lucien?'

It was a situation that didn't call for words. They were alone and they wanted each other; even a day was too long, and it had been more than a week. Buttons flew, zips whirred and belts fell to the floor. He kicked their clothes away as he lifted her. They barely made it to the sofa before they were drowning in liquid desire.

Lucien had her dress up and her briefs down with her legs locked around his waist before she had even time to draw breath. And now she couldn't draw breath—at least, not evenly. If she hadn't needed him… If she hadn't wanted him so badly… If she hadn't loved him so deeply…

'Lucien…' She called his name and clung to him and, as always the only thing that mattered now was this moment.

When she finally quietened Lucien held her safe in the circle of his arms. 'We share a bruising passion,' he murmured.

'Do you think it will ever burn out?'

'I doubt it,' he said with satisfaction, teasing her lips with his teeth and with his tongue.

Reaching out, he laced his fingers through her hair, allowing himself a few moments of self-indulgent pleasure before positioning her.

'Lucien, behave… We should clear up… We've got lots to do.'

'Indeed we have,' he agreed, nudging his way between her thighs again.

'I've missed you,' she confessed in a ragged whisper, locking her arms around him.

'And I've missed you too,' he assured her as he lifted her on top of him to rock her rhythmically.

'I need this,' she gasped out as her excitement mounted.

'We both do,' he assured her huskily. He took her again, firmly, in one long ecstatic thrust. She felt so good, so tight, so warm and lush, better than she ever had. From now on it was Tara's needs all the way. Pleasing her came as naturally as breathing to him and when she called out his name and clung to him fiercely he didn't try to hold her back. He rocked her steadily in his arms until she quietened and when he felt her relax he saw the tears were back again. 'What's this about?' he asked her softly, dropping kisses on her swollen lips.

'I just feel so emotional all the time…'

'You're not pregnant, are you?' He laughed.

'No, don't be silly…' Her cheeks blazed red beneath his kisses.

He willed his strength into her. She had come so far and had achieved so much more than he'd expected, he couldn't bear to see her upset like this. 'Do I make you unhappy?'

'No, of course not,' she told him with a fresh flood of tears.

'Well, what is it, then, *ma petite*?'

'I don't know,' she wailed. 'Just make love to me and forget…'

Forget Tara? Hadn't he tried that before?

As the fire crackled and Lucien made love, Tara knew her common sense was firmly on hold. All those late nights and early mornings sorting out the apartment had been worth it, that was all she knew, and she was exhausted, hence the tears. And this was perfect; this was how it was meant to be. This was everything she had always dreamed a home would be, and with Lucien tending to her every need it was all too easy to take the next step and convince herself this situation would last for ever.

'You are the sexiest man alive,' she murmured in the brief interlude between kisses, 'and I love you…'

A golden haze of contentment surrounded them as they snacked on the food, and kissed and murmured their way through the champagne he'd brought with him. He couldn't imagine anything better than this, or that anything could spoil it.

'That was a contented sigh,' Tara commented.

'I'm happy for you. I'm happy the way things have turned out. The way you've made a life for yourself in Ferranbeaux will—'

'—Make things so much easier for Poppy as she grows up,' she supplied, cutting across him when he had been about to say that Tara living here would allow her to share in the exciting rebirth of a city and would make him happy too.

Always kind words, thoughts and deeds for anyone other than herself, he thought, brushing the hair back from her eyes. He saw the flicker in her eyes that said she would always be hoping for something more from him where their relationship was concerned, but instead of complaints she put her hand over his as if to console him.

'You have to bloom where you're planted, Lucien—' She said this lightly, as if she was resigned to the hand that fate had dealt them, but as a draught of cold air enveloped them she shivered, as if destiny had whispered in her ear.

The gust gave him the opportunity to turn to practical matters he could do something about. 'I must remember to get that window fixed for you.'

'Not now,' she said, cupping his chin to reclaim his attention.

'Not now,' he agreed, holding the lovely turquoise gaze. He was going to make love to her now.

CHAPTER FIFTEEN

SHE had been sick all morning and now she felt dizzy too. Could it be the food she'd fed Lucien? Tara paled until she decided it was time to stop fooling herself. Gripping onto the edge of the sink until she felt safe to move had given her plenty of time to mull over the possibilities. She would have heard from Lucien by now if he was ill and the changes in her body were undeniable. Her breasts felt tender and her emotions were in shreds. She was pregnant with Lucien's baby. A great swell of love and fear hit her concurrently as she stared down at the shiny cold porcelain, willing strength into her shaking limbs.

There was no point panicking; she had to think. Lucien had returned to the castle in the early hours, and she didn't kid herself—this was how it would be from now on. She would remain independent and live here where the Count would visit her—discreetly, of course—and in time people would come to accept their relationship. She would work hard for Ferranbeaux and hopefully prove to be a role model for Poppy in spite of her irregular circumstances.

Once she was feeling steadier, Tara took a shower

and dressed neatly before heading for town. This was too important to take chances, she had to be sure.

It would have been easier to keep her head down and focus on the job in hand if so many people hadn't greeted her along the way. There was an air of purpose in Ferranbeaux and Tara had thrown herself into it, taking on a restoration project of her own as well as planning ahead to provide a useful service with her childcare agency. This can-do attitude had won her a lot of friends in a short time, but now she felt as if she was letting those friends down. Her worst fear was that the people of Ferranbeaux might think she had engineered this pregnancy to snare their Count.

Would Lucien think that? Tara's stomach clenched as the cheery bell over the pharmacy door announced her arrival in the shop. She was greeted warmly by both the assistants and the other customers, but for the first time since coming to Ferranbeaux she felt embarrassed, and unworthy of so much affection. Too many hormones swirling round her body, Tara reasoned, feeling faint again as she approached the discreetly placed pharmacy desk. She stumbled over her request, and then hurried out of the shop to race back home to conduct the test. In spite of her concerns she was excited beyond belief, because this was just about the most wonderful thing that had ever happened to her.

The instructions on the box said that at this early stage of pregnancy she should be able to see a faint response in the test windows. The reaction in the first window would prove the test was working properly, and the second window would show whether or not she was pregnant.

When the test showed a positive result elation battled

with the anxiety inside her. There was only one certainty, which was she loved this baby already. Her child would be a friend for Poppy. Now she had two children to love.

And Lucien? Tara's inner voice prompted. What would he think about this?

The same as everyone else, Tara concluded—that a woman who prided herself on her independence had committed the modern woman's cardinal sin. What was her excuse for this, by the way? But would she change anything? Surely that was the only important question. Knowing the answer to that was a firm and unequivocal no made everything seem brighter. She had always wanted this, Tara reasoned, tracing the outline of her still flat stomach with awestruck hands, and she would handle the practical consequences the same as any other woman. Sluicing her face in cold water, she stared at her glowing reflection in the mirror. Would Lucien guess just by looking at her? She wasn't naïve enough to think the pharmacist might not say something and nothing spread faster than rumour—she must tell him right away.

She almost jumped out of her skin to find Lucien on the doorstep as she left the house.

'I couldn't stay away,' he admitted, trapping her between him and the door jamb, and staring down at her until every inch of her was consumed by desire for him. Her heart was thundering, with anxiety and excitement. She had imagined there would be time to prepare. She had intended walking to the castle and having a plan all sorted out by the time they met.

'Well,' he murmured, making her ear lobe buzz with sensation, 'can I come in?'

No book she had ever read had warned about the pheromones running riot through her body along with the rest of the pregnancy hormones. She was melting, yearning, lusting, and pressing herself quite shamelessly against the marauding pirate in her way. How was she supposed to resist him, when Lucien was dressed in his work clothes of close fitting jeans and a casual top and his sensual face was covered in coarse black stubble?

'Haven't you shaved yet?' she reprimanded him softly.

'Later…'

She swallowed deep, feeling an almost primal desire to claim her mate. 'You'd better come in…'

'You're not too busy to see me, I hope?' he murmured wickedly. Cupping her chin, he brushed her mouth with one of his devastatingly frustrating almost-kisses.

'Too busy?' She shuddered out a moan as he ran his fingertips down her spine.

'Give me the keys,' Lucien whispered, recovering them from her shaking fingers. 'Let's go inside.'

There were people on the street… She should tell him right away… She would, the moment they got inside the house…

They stood facing each other in the main room, Lucien leaning against the table like a sleepy tiger. He said something in his own language. She understood. She might not know the words, but her nipples peaked immediately. Lucien's skill in bed had made her insatiable and now she was focused only on that.

A single step bridged the gap between them. She took it.

Lucien took hold of her, but far too lightly. She moaned, softening against him, while Lucien stared straight into her eyes, telling her he knew she was ready for him.

He loved making her wait. He loved seeing the excitement and anticipation building on her face. He led her by the hand into the bedroom, where he undressed her with studied care. When he had removed the last shred of Tara's clothing he took a moment to appreciate a body that an artist such as Rubens would have fought to paint.

Tara might be young, but she was a proper woman with proper buttocks, and proper thighs to hold him in place. Her generous breasts weighed heavily in his hands, and as he stroked the soft swell of her belly she eased her legs apart and he felt the heat of her.

It must be the pregnancy, Tara thought wildly; she had never been so responsive to Lucien's touch. She should tell him now…right away…

One more time, and then she'd tell him…

Exhaling raggedly as Lucien ran his warm palms down her neck to her breasts, which he cupped, she swayed against him. One more time…

She thrashed her head about on the pillows as he worked steadily with concentrated intent to satisfy her ravenous demands. Would she ever get enough of this—of him? He had taken her slowly and carefully, the way she had always liked before, but today was different, she had been almost frantic for release though it was only hours since they had last been together. She called out to him now, holding herself as if she wanted to isolate the source of her pleasure and concentrate only on that, while he grasped her buttocks in his work-roughened hands and rocked her beneath him in a prolonged assault that no sooner resulted in a sustained firestorm of pleasure than the next build-up began. It was several hours before he felt a new ease in her and, feeling it, he withdrew carefully and, wrapping her in his arms, he watched her sleep.

When he was confident she was sleeping soundly and he wouldn't disturb her, he left her side to take a shower. Towelling down afterwards, he happened to glance across at the shelf where she kept her make-up and suddenly everything made sense. She had tasted different—sweeter, fuller, richer. She even looked different—there was a glow about her. Clutching the cold, unyielding sink he stared into the mirror. He was ecstatic at the thought that Tara was carrying his child, but concerned that she had excluded him. The sense of being shut out had dogged him since childhood when his father the Count had not wanted his illegitimate son cluttering up the picture, let alone distracting his mistress from her main responsibility, which the Count had considered to be him. A shudder of resentment ran through him at the thought that history was repeating itself, only now Tara was denying him the chance of loving his own child.

'Why didn't you tell me?'

'Mmm...?' Tara's eyelids fluttered as she moved slowly from sleep to full consciousness. All that activity had left her very groggy, but somewhere down the end of a very long tunnel she knew that Lucien was talking to her. His voice sharpened as he asked the question again, and this time she woke up to find him resting on one elbow on the bed, staring down at her.

He knew.

Her stomach was in knots as she struggled to read every nuance in his stern face.

'Why didn't you tell me about the baby? I thought you trusted me, Tara—'

'I do trust you—'

'So you trust me enough to sleep with me, but not to tell me about the single most important change in your life?'

'I only just found out.'

'When were you going to tell me? Oh, I see,' he exclaimed tensely before she had a chance to answer. 'After I slept with you.'

'Don't say it like that. You make me feel so—'

'Cheap?'

'Lucien, please—' When she tried to touch him he shook her off. 'I won't embarrass you. I'll leave Ferranbeaux—'

'What are you saying, Tara? What about Poppy?'

She shivered as the full extent of her foolishness came home to her. 'I'd never leave Poppy. I was half asleep… I wasn't thinking straight.'

'If you think I'd let you leave Ferranbeaux while you're carrying my baby, you aren't thinking straight,' Lucien agreed. Seizing hold of her wrists, he brought her in front of him.

'Lucien, no… Surely, you can't believe I would do that?' It was so far from the truth, it made her feel sick.

'Why are you denying me the right to know about my child, then?' he said, staring intently at her. 'Did you think I wouldn't sleep with you if you told me? Did you think I'd walk out on you? What?' he demanded angrily.

Colour drained from Tara's face. How could she tell Lucien the truth—that she loved him so much she would do anything to protect him from reliving the shame that had scarred him as a boy, only this time through their innocent baby?

'If you feel so cheap after sleeping with me,' Lucien

spat out with contempt, 'perhaps I should go...'
Swinging off the bed, he snatched up his clothes.

'Don't leave like this,' she begged him, dragging a
sheet around her so she could chase him to the door. 'I
won't cause you any trouble... I'll get a lawyer... I'll
sort this out.'

'Sort what out?' Lucien demanded, slowly turning
to face her.

'My rights...your rights...the baby...'

'Your rights to my money...?'

'Of course not,' Tara exclaimed in absolute horror.

'Then let's get one thing straight,' he said. 'Poppy
isn't leaving here, and neither are you.'

But it was all too much for her in her present state,
and as Lucien rapped this last command at her she
almost fainted. Brought up short, he caught her to him.
'I can't believe this is happening...' Her voice was
muffled in his chest, but in spite of his concern Lucien
felt stiff and unresponsive.

'You regret the fact that you are pregnant?' Lucien
rapped.

'No, of course I don't—'

'What, then?'

'I just feel—'

'Yes?'

'Foolish,' she admitted softly. 'With all my talk of in-
dependence and standing on my own two feet...' It was
Tara's turn to stiffen with surprise when she felt
Lucien's hold on her soften.

'Perhaps I'm a little more experienced than you,' he
suggested with formidable understatement, 'but, as far
as I recall, it takes two to make a baby.'

'So you're not angry with me?'

'I'm angry that you didn't tell me, but angry about your news? No. How could I be, when it's the most wonderful news I've ever heard?'

'And you're not embarrassed?'

'That I've fathered a child?' Lucien gave a short and very masculine laugh. 'It would take a lot more than your pregnancy to embarrass me, and the gatehouse will make the perfect family home for you and my baby.'

Tara froze. She should have known Lucien's reaction was too good to be true, and now who was making history repeat itself? 'I won't live there,' she said flatly.

'What do you mean?' Lucien was still in magnanimous mode and had yet to pick up on the fact that she was utterly serious.

'This is my home now…' She glanced around before walking back to the bed where she curled up, hugging a pillow.

'It's not good enough—'

For an aristocratic baby? She let Lucien's words hang for a moment, and then sat up. 'Don't you mean I'm not good enough?'

He frowned.

She discarded the pillow and got up. 'My expectations in life are very different from yours, Lucien. You have a sense of entitlement that I lack, plus you have everything rigidly sorted out in your head. I just want to be happy with the people I love. I want to be a good mother to Poppy and our baby, and to remain in Ferranbeaux, where I can work on the regeneration of the city with everyone else. I don't care about position or wealth or any of that. I just want a family…'

'A family,' Lucien murmured, as if she had mentioned the Holy Grail.

'Yes,' Tara confirmed softly and, sensing she might have landed on the one thing that could reach him she waited a few more moments and then, crossing the room to him, touched his face. 'All I want is a family—a family that's part of a wider family in a country that cares.'

He covered his eyes to hide his emotion as his anger drained away. He didn't deserve her. Tara was too good for him. She was painfully honest and far too capable to need the all-powerful Count to take care of his mistress and their baby. She had proved she could manage perfectly well on her own without him, which stung his male pride. But together...what a force they'd be then!

How wrong he'd been about the meaning of duty. He had thought his country needed a model wife, when what both he and his country needed was a woman who loved his people as much as he did, and who wasn't afraid to get her hands dirty. If his intention was to modernise Ferranbeaux, then the woman at his side must be a thoroughly modern wife. Even more than that, for all their sakes, she must be the woman who had softened him and taught him how to love.

He'd never been impulsive in his life, and it would be irresponsible of him to start now, but Tara had changed everything around him—she had changed his life, making him feel like a youth again, shining light into all the shadows.

'Will you marry me?' he said, driven by these imperative thoughts.

Her brow puckered as she stared at him in confusion.

'Will you marry me, Tara? Will you do me the honour of becoming my wife?'

'Are you serious, Lucien? Lucien, don't tease me,'

she warned him, turning her face away as if she was frightened of what she might see in his.

'If I had to choose a mother for my child, you would be that mother, is that clear enough for you?'

'So you're not angry with me?' she said, turning to him hesitantly.

'Is it usual for a man to be angry when he proposes marriage?'

'I don't know…' She shook her head, looking doubly bewildered. 'I've never been proposed to before—'

'Then let me reassure you…' He took her hand and brought it to his lips.

'You're sure you're not making allowances for my being pregnant?'

'You think I'd go this far?' Lucien's eyes over the back of his hand were black and wicked.

'I wouldn't put too much past you,' Tara said frankly.

'I might make allowances for you being a woman—' he held up his hands in mock surrender when she would have shouted him down, and added softly '—and hormonal, and pregnant. But would I propose marriage?' His lips pressed down. 'Oh, Tara—' his face broke into a smile '—don't you know me at all?'

She'd seen flashes of this new, relaxed Lucien, but memories of the cold, forbidding Count still haunted her. 'I want to believe,' she murmured, voicing her thoughts out loud.

'That I love you?'

She stared at him.

'You can't still be that lost little girl who believes she isn't deserving of love,' Lucien protested, 'or all my efforts have been wasted.' His lips tugged up in an irresistible smile. 'Tell me you believe in love now?'

'I do…'

'In my love,' he insisted.

'In your love…'

'For you,' Lucien prompted. 'Don't you recognise a man who adores you?'

'You…love me?'

'That's not a word I'd choose,' Lucien argued, framing Tara's face with his hands. 'I prefer the word I just used, which I believe was *Je t'adore*. I adore you, *ma petite*…'

CHAPTER SIXTEEN

'WHAT will everyone in Ferranbeaux think if you marry me?' Tara was still not quite ready to believe Lucien had asked her to become his Countess.

'Those we care about will be happy for us; does anyone else matter?'

'The journalists should be happy,' Tara agreed. 'Think how much copy they'll sell. But what about your duty to Ferranbeaux?' she added, frowning.

'What about yours?'

'I would never come between you and your people, Lucien—'

'And I would never ask you to. Is that a yes to my proposal?'

She studied him for a long moment. 'Yes…yes, it is. I will marry you, and I'll do everything in my power to serve the people of Ferranbeaux—'

Lucien greeted this announcement by tumbling her on the bed. 'My people love you already because of the way you have involved yourself in the city, and now it just remains for you to stay on and serve their Count—' His lips tugged up wickedly.

'I could do all that without you having to marry me,'

Tara pointed out, not struggling too hard when Lucien pinned her beneath him.

'I know I shouldn't tease you,' he admitted, brushing frustrating little kisses on her neck, 'especially now, when your head is full of hormones, but you make it so hard to resist…' His eyes glowed with passion as he moved up the bed. 'I want you,' he murmured, staring deep into Tara's eyes, 'and I can't wait. I can't wait for our baby to be born. I want Poppy and the baby and you more than I can possibly tell you…'

But he could show her, Tara thought, making a token push at the wide spread of Lucien's chest. 'You don't play fair,' she complained when he worked his magic on her.

'True,' he agreed, moulding her naked breasts with his work-roughened hands. 'But do you want me to?'

'Yes…no…don't stop…' Pleasure raged between her legs as he teased the tender tip of each nipple in turn. Her thighs were trembling by the time he locked them round his waist.

'Don't worry, I'll be careful,' he assured her, the love in his eyes telling her everything she wanted to know.

'It's a little too late for that.' She exchanged a mischievous look with him.

'And aren't you glad?' he murmured.

Her answer was to strain towards him, but as always Lucien made her wait…a few seconds at most, thankfully, and the hunger in his eyes matched her own.

'This is where you belong,' Lucien told her when she quietened. 'At my side in Ferranbeaux…'

'We'll have to get out of bed occasionally,' she teased.

'Occasionally,' Lucien agreed reluctantly. He kissed the very sensitive nape of her neck, her eyelids and finally her mouth. 'Stay and help me to change things, Tara. I want us to be married very soon.'

Tara's expression grew serious as she considered this; she was still concerned for him. 'Are you sure you don't have to marry someone special?'

'Forgive me,' Lucien murmured, 'but I thought that was exactly what I plan to do.'

EPILOGUE

THE most fabulous wedding Ferranbeaux had ever seen
was held in the newly renovated basilica. The marriage
of Count Lucien Maxime of Ferranbeaux to the much
younger and very pregnant Tara Devenish caused such
a stir, but the bride and groom were too much in love to
notice the interest they caused. Tara had changed a great
deal in the intervening months and walked confidently
down the aisle on her own to meet her groom, though
perhaps the greatest change of all was in Count Lucien
Maxime of Ferranbeaux, whose stern face was transformed when he turned to see his beautiful bride.

There were so many smiling faces waiting to greet
the bride and groom when the service was over, and first
of these was their newly adopted baby daughter, Poppy,
whom Tara carried so that when they went outside the
crowds could get a good view of the happy family. Even
Marian Digby had exchanged her customary dusty outfit
for a smart suit topped off with an extravagantly feathered hat. It was Marian who was ready with Tara's
second wedding bouquet of the day, the first having
been left that morning at a newly constructed memorial
to Freya and Guy. This second bouquet was all the

dearer to Tara's heart for being composed of simple flowers picked for their new Countess by the people of Ferranbeaux from their own gardens.

Lucien had indulged Tara in this, because she believed so strongly that they must only talk about Freya with love in front of Poppy. It had taken Tara some time to persuade Lucien to think better of her sister, but when she said that all Freya had really wanted was a home she had struck a chord with him. 'We're so lucky,' she'd pointed out. 'We've got each other, we've got a home for our family—for Poppy *and* the new baby...'

The rest did not need to be said; they had both lost people they loved, and Count Maxime was so deeply in love with his young bride he had chosen not to disagree.

Tara stood modestly on the steps of the basilica at Lucien's side in the gown he had insisted on buying for her in Paris. The world's press took their photographs, which the Count had made them pay dearly for to swell the funds of his beloved wife's newly founded charities. Composed of three types of Swiss lace, the elegant dress Tara had chosen for this special day was decorated with seed pearls and diamanté, and her filmy veil was sprinkled with tiny jewels that twinkled in the sunlight as it lifted in the soft summer breeze. Poppy crowed with contentment in Tara's arms as Tara reflected on a service she had devised with Lucien. Even the sternest face had softened when they'd exchanged their vows, and many of the women were weeping. No one could remember such a moving occasion, many would say later, for neither the Count nor his young bride had forgotten the tragedy that had brought them together.

When they emerged from the basilica into the brilliant sunshine a great cheer went up and it seemed to

Lucien that every citizen in Ferranbeaux had crowded into the square to wish them well. He gazed down with pride at the woman who had changed his life. The woman for whom he had decided that only a clear corn-flower sapphire as blue as Tara's eyes and as pure as her heart should grace her wedding finger. And that night would see them, not on some glamorous yacht, or foreign beach, but at home in the castle of Ferranbeaux, which they now referred to fondly as Castle Cosy since Tara had worked her magic on it for her family.

'I'm the luckiest man alive,' Lucien murmured into Tara's ear.

'And I'm the luckiest woman in the world,' Tara replied, gazing with love at Lucien and then at Poppy.

'To the family,' Lucien said and, as the people of Ferranbeaux applauded, he first kissed Poppy and then, in a manner that set the world's press alight, Tara, one of the notorious Devenish sisters, who was now not only a Countess, but Lucien Maxime's beautiful pregnant wife.

Untamed Billionaire, Undressed Virgin

ANNA CLEARY

As a child, **Anna Cleary** loved reading so much that during the midnight hours she was forced to read with a torch under the bedcovers, to lull the suspicions of her sleep-obsessed parents. From an early age she dreamed of writing her own books. She saw herself in a stone cottage by the sea, wearing a velvet smoking jacket and sipping sherry, like Somerset Maugham.

In real life she became a schoolteacher, where her greatest pleasure was teaching children to write beautiful stories. A little while ago, she and one of her friends made a pact to each write the first chapter of a romance novel in their holidays. From writing her very first line Anna was hooked and she gave up teaching to become a full-time writer. She now lives in Queensland, with a deeply sensitive and intelligent cat. She prefers champagne to sherry and loves music, books, four-legged people, trees, movies and restaurants.

For Gabi, Ben, Michelle, Jenny, Mirandi, Tina, Vicki, Terese and Shirley, with love and appreciation.

CHAPTER ONE

CONNOR O'BRIEN'S plane glided into Sydney on the first rays of dawn. The shadowy city materialised below, a mysterious patchwork of rooftops and dark sea, emerging from the mists of night. The comforts it promised were welcome, after the deserts he'd traversed over the last five years in the dubious name of Intelligence, but Connor expected no feeling of homecoming. To him Sydney was just another city. Its spires and skyscrapers felt no more connected to him than the mosques and minarets he'd left behind.

Once on the ground, he breezed through customs, courtesy of his diplomatic status. His honed blending-in skills spared him any undue attention. He was just another tall Australian in the Foreign Service.

The technicalities taken care of, he strolled across the International Terminal with his long easy stride, his single suitcase in tow, laptop case in his spare hand. From force of habit, with covert skill he scanned the groups of sleepy relatives waiting to embrace their loved ones. Wives and girlfriends beaming up at their men and weeping, children running into their fathers' arms. For him, no one. With his father gone now, he kept no personal connections. No lives at risk for knowing him. His precious anonymity was intact. Not a soul to know or care if Connor O'Brien lived or died, and that was how it had to be.

The glass exit doors opened before him and he walked out into the Australian summer dawn, safe and secure in his solitariness. The sky had lightened to a pale grey, washing out the street lamps to a wan hue. Even for the height of midsummer the morning was warm. The faintest whiff of eucalyptus wafted to him on the breeze like the scent of freedom.

Scanning for the taxi rank, he felt an unaccustomed buzz.

He rubbed his bristly jaw and contemplated the potential amenities of a good hotel. Shower, breakfast, relax with the newspapers, shake off the jet lag…

'Mr O'Brien?'

A uniformed chauffeur stepped forward from the open rear door of a limo parked in line with the exit. Respectfully he touched his cap. 'Your lift, sir.'

Connor stilled, every one of his nerves and trigger-sharp reflexes on instant alert.

A thin, querulous voice issued from inside the car. 'Come on, come on, O'Brien. Give Parkins your gear and let's get on the road.'

Connor knew that voice. With disbelief he peered into the dim interior. A small elderly man swam into focus, majestically ensconced in the plush upholstery.

Sir Frank Fraser. Wily old fox, *legend* of the Service and one of his father's old golfing cronies. But surely the ex-Chief had long since hung up his cloak and dagger and retired to live on the Fraser family fortune? As far as Connor knew, he was now a respectable pillar of the world of wealth and ease.

'Well, what are we waiting for?' The quavery voice held the autocrat's note of incredulity at not being instantly obeyed.

Curiosity outweighed Connor's chagrin at having his moment of freedom curtailed, so he handed his suitcase to the hovering Parkins and slid into the old guy's travelling suite.

At once his smooth, bronzed hand was seized in a wrinkled claw and shaken with vigour.

'Good to see you, O'Brien.' The ancient autocrat took in

Connor's long limbs, his lean, athletic frame, with an admiring gaze. 'And, my God, you're the living image of your old man. Same colouring, Mick's build—everything.'

Connor didn't try to deny it. Sure, like his father, he'd inherited the ink-black hair, dark eyes and olive skin of some tall, long ago Spaniard who'd washed up on the Irish coast from the storm-scattered Armada, but his father had been a family man, and there the resemblance had to end.

'And you've done well. What department has the embassy hired you for? Humanitarian Affairs, isn't it?'

'Something like that,' Connor allowed as the limo started and nosed into the road for the city. He smiled. 'Humanitarian Advisor to the First Secretary for Immigration.'

Sir Frank's aged face settled into thoughtful lines. 'Yes, yes, I can see why they need more lawyers. There'd be plenty of work involved there.'

A vision of the horror he'd had to deal with at the Australian Embassy in Baghdad swam into Connor's mind. Unable even to begin describing it, he merely shrugged acknowledgement, waiting for his father's old mate to spill what was on his mind.

Sir Frank sent him a glance that penetrated through to the back of his brain, and said with unnerving perspicacity, 'Isn't all that tragedy enough to keep you interested, without this other work you're doing? Your father always told me the law was your first and only love.'

Connor controlled every muscle not to react, though a little nerve jumped somewhere in his gut. 'Sir Frank, is there something behind this friendly chat? Something you need to tell me?'

Sir Frank drew a cigar from his breast pocket. 'Let's just say we have a friend of a friend in common.'

Connor's ears pricked up. This was agency speak for *contact*. So why the old lion and not some field operative? He was considering the possibilities when Sir Frank came in with a low hit.

'Heard about your losing your wife and child. That was tough. There's too many of these planes going down. How long ago was it now?'

Connor gripped his case while the dust and ashes settled back in his soul. The force of it could still catch him off guard, even now. 'Nearly six years. But—'

The elderly voice softened a notch. 'Must be time you tried again, lad. A man needs a woman, kids to come home to. It's time you stopped all this adventuring and settled down. Take up the threads again. This sort of work in Baghdad…' He shook his head. 'A man burns out fast. Two or three years should be the limit, and you're well past it. I hear you've taken some very close shaves. They tell me you're good—the very best—but a man only stays on top of the game for so long.' He slid Connor a glance. 'The man you re-placed ended up with a knife through his gullet.'

Connor gazed at him with a mixture of incredulity and sardonic amusement. 'Thanks.'

But the old guy was in earnest. As his enthusiasm heated up his gnarled hands gesticulated with increasing fervour. 'I wouldn't be doing my duty to Mick if I didn't say this, young fella. You're dicing with death.'

'You should know,' Connor fired back. 'You diced with it yourself long enough.'

'That's right, I did, and I've learned what's important. No one ever wins this game.' He grasped Connor's arm. 'Look, I could pull a few strings for you. Your dad's left you a wealthy man. You could set up your own firm. There's always a call for good lawyers in this country.' He thumped his creaky old knee with his thumb. 'Plenty of injustice *right here*. A big handsome lad like you won't take long to find another lovely girl.'

The permafrost that passed for Connor's heart since the real thing had been broken and scattered over a Syrian mountainside registered nothing. He knew what he'd lost and would never have again. He made his way now without attachments. Banter, the occasional dalliance with a pretty woman, were sufficient to keep the shadows at bay.

'Civilian life offers its challenges, too,' Sir Frank persisted. '*And its excitements.*' He waved his unlit cigar. 'What are you now—thirty? Thirty-five?'

'Thirty-four.' In spite of his discipline Connor felt his abdominal muscles clench. He understood well enough what the old guy was alluding to. To perform in Intelligence an officer needed to be as clinical and objective towards his contacts as a machine. Perhaps, for some, cracks could develop over time and emotion begin to leak in, but *he* had no need to be concerned. He was still as balanced and dispassionate in his work as ever. He'd quit soon enough if he had a reason. In fact, he needed the constant threat of death to realise he was alive.

'Sir Frank,' he said in his deep, quiet voice, 'your concern is appreciated, but unnecessary. If there's something you need to tell me, spit it out. Otherwise your driver can drop me right here.'

Sir Frank looked approvingly at him. 'A straightshooter, just like Mick. Exactly like him.' He shook his head and sighed. 'If only Elliott could straighten himself out.'

Ah. At last. The crunch.

Connor stared broodingly out at the familiar streets, riffling back through the dusty mental files of family connections. 'Isn't Elliott your son?'

'Now *that's* what I wanted to talk to you about. A situation has arisen.'

As far as he knew, Elliott Fraser was one of those wealthy, fifty-ish CEOs in the private sector. 'He's involved in something?'

The old man looked gloomy. 'You might say *something*. A woman.'

Connor drew an austere breath. 'Look, I think you may have been misinformed, Sir Frank. I'm here on leave.' His tone was cool, but it was necessary to let the old guy feel the steel edge of his refusal. 'I haven't been flown halfway around the world to sort out your son's love-life.'

Sir Frank's indignant weedy frame flared up like a firecracker. 'That's exactly what you have been flown here for, *mister*,' he retorted with spirit. 'Who do you think got you your leave?' He gestured vehemently with his cigar, pointing it in Connor's face. 'No need to get cocky with me, fella, just because I knew you when you had your milk teeth. That's the very reason I've chosen *you*.'

Before Connor could respond, Sir Frank leaned forward and pinned him with an urgent, beady gaze. 'It won't interrupt your break much, Connor. It'll take you a week, a fortnight at most, then you can enjoy the rest of your three months. Who knows? You might decide to stay longer. Anyway, I know you'll do your best to help me out. For the love of Mick.'

Ah, here it was. The old boys' friendship card. All those mornings out on the green. Boozy afternoon sessions in the clubhouse. Connor knew it for what it was—emotional blackmail, and impossible to reject. He closed his eyes for an instant, then resigned himself.

'All right, all right. Go on, then. Shoot.'

'That's better.' Sir Frank sat back, satisfaction momentarily deepening the cracks and crevices in his crocodile-skin face. 'Now, this is strictly between us. Elliott's being considered for a top job with the ministry. Very hush-hush. He can't afford any scandal. Not a whiff.' He held up a wizened hand. 'No, it's serious. Marla is in America on business for her firm. If she comes back and finds out he's been playing away from home…' He shuddered. 'Marla can be very forceful. I have a strong instinct about this, Connor, and my instincts are rarely wrong. The chances are that this little popsy he's got himself entangled with is a plant. The timing is suspicious. But even if she *isn't*…' He closed his wrinkled eyelids in deprecation. 'Do you see now why I've chosen you? I don't want the agency involved. This is my *family*…I can't risk some stranger.' He moved closer to Connor and lowered his voice. 'You'll be on your own entirely. It has to be strictly between you and me.' He waggled an admonitory finger. 'No logging into the agency's tech services.'

Connor shook his head in bemusement. 'But surely all you have to do is whisper in Elliott's ear?'

'You try doing that with Elliott. He thinks he's keeping her under wraps.'

Connor concealed his amusement. The old guy was clearly loath to reveal to his son that he was keeping tabs on him.

Sir Frank clutched at his wrist. 'Connor, for all his sins, Elliott's my *son*. And then there's my grandson.' His rheumy old eyes filled up with tears. 'He's four years old.'

Connor noticed a tremor in the frail, liver-spotted hand grasping his sleeve and felt the faintest twinge in his chest. 'Right,' he said, exhaling a long breath. Old people and children had always been his Achilles' heel. He might as well grit his teeth, agree to the task and get it over with. He straightened his wide shoulders, and, needing to rein in the excess of emotion lapping the walls of the limo, injected some professional briskness into his voice. 'Do you have anything on the woman?'

Sir Frank conquered his tears with amazing swiftness and switched into business mode. Reaching into an alcove set in the door, he produced a file. 'Her name's Sophy something. Woodford…no… Wood*ruff*. Works in the Alexandra.'

'Where's that?' Connor said, flipping the single page. The information was sparse. A few dates and times. Meetings with Elliott in coffee shops. A bar. An indistinct CCTV still of a slim, dark-haired woman. Her face wasn't quite in focus, but the camera had managed to catch something of the delicacy of an oval face, the lustre of longish, wavy dark hair. Employed as a speech pathologist in a paediatric clinic. A good, conservative cover. Like his own.

'You know Macquarie Street?'

'Who doesn't?' As the avenue in which both the Botanical Gardens and the Opera House resided, Macquarie Street was one of the finest boulevards in Sydney. It had long been the preserve of the high-fliers of the medical profession.

'Some rooms have been vacated for you there. Your law practice will be a perfect cover.' The old tycoon added slyly, 'If you did decide to stay, there'd be nothing to stop you hanging up your shingle there for real.'

The location was just around the corner from some of the wealthiest bastions of the legal profession. Connor supposed he could get away with setting up as a lawyer in doctors' territory. Just how dangerous did the old guy expect the assignment to be? He felt some misgivings at the amorphous nature of it. Sir Frank's reputation as a cunning operator was well earned.

He studied the clever old face. 'What exactly do you want from me?'

'Find out about her. Her background, connections, everything. She's almost certainly working for a foreign state. *Pillow* talk.' He shook his head in disgust. 'You'd think Elliott would have enough savvy to…' He broke off, ruminating on his son's naiveté with compressed lips. 'Anyway, if—*if*—you find she's just a little gold-digger looking for a lamb to fleece, pay her off.'

Connor winced. From what he'd heard of Elliott Fraser, his lamb-like qualities were highly doubtful. On the surface, though, it seemed a tame little assignment. Nothing like strolling to an evening rendezvous to meet a contact dressed in high explosives. Hardly in the same universe as drinking coffee with a smiling man who was preparing to slice open his throat.

'A good-looking lad like you won't have any trouble getting close to the woman.'

Connor flashed him a wry glance. He didn't do *close*. He was just about to set him straight on that issue when the limo turned into a tree-lined avenue, and he recognised the graceful colonial architecture of Macquarie Street.

Traffic was minimal at this early hour, and there was time to appreciate the street's pleasantness, enhanced on one side by the dense green mystery of the Botanical Gardens burgeoning with summer growth behind a long stretch of tall, iron railings.

Halfway along the street the chauffeur pulled into the kerb.

'The Alexandra,' Sir Frank announced.

Connor craned to stare up at a honey-coloured sandstone edifice, several storeys in height. A splash of scarlet flowers spilled from a third-floor window ledge.

'You'll find your rooms on the top floor. Suite 3E.' Sir Frank pressed a set of old-fashioned keys into Connor's hand. 'Mind you keep in touch with me every step of the way.' He sat back and pulled on his blank cigar, then added excitedly, 'You know, Connor, I have a very good feeling about this now. I'm sure you'll be just the man to stop clever little Miss Sophy Woodruff in her tracks.'

CHAPTER TWO

SHADOW. Just a touch to enhance the blue of her irises. Violet like her name, her father used to say. Her official name, not that she'd ever use it. Thank goodness it only rarely appeared, usually on government documents or bank statements. What sort of people would call their child something so schmaltzy?

Certainly not the parents she knew. They'd felt obliged to keep it, but everyone had preferred to call her by the name they'd chosen themselves. Sophy was her father's choice. Henry—her *real* father, not the biological one.

That uncomfortable feeling coiled in her stomach. Her biological father. Such a cold descriptor. But could he really be as cold as he seemed? How warm was any man likely to feel when he encountered the daughter he never knew he had? Or so he'd said. Still, if he'd been lying, why order the DNA test?

He was lying about something, though, she could feel it in her bones.

Her brows were dark enough, closer to black than her hair. One quick pencil stroke to define their natural arch. In an emergency it would have to do.

Mascara was mandatory. Lashes could never be too long or too thick. A quick brush of blush on her cheekbones to warm the pallor of her broken night's sleep, but a glance at the clock decided her to be satisfied with that if she wanted to catch the 6.03 ferry.

With the heatwave still roasting Sydney after three days, she needed to wear something cool. She slipped on a straight, knee-length skirt, turned sideways to check in the mirror. Flat enough. Her lilac shirt with its pretty cap-sleeves was fresh from the cleaners' and required no ironing. She snatched up her handbag and slid into her lucky high heels.

Something told her there'd be running ahead. Tuesdays were seldom her best, but she had a very strong feeling about this one. She was on the verge of something, she could tell by the prickling in the back of her neck.

Zoe and Leah, her housemates, were barely stirring. She battled her way around the pile of camping gear they'd assembled in the hall, flung them a hasty 'Bye,' and ran down the path to the gate, the sun barely up. For the thousandth time she retraced in her mind every step she'd taken since she'd picked the registered letter up from the post office in yesterday's lunch hour.

She'd taken it straight back to her office to read. And there it had been. Official confirmation. Elliott Fraser's DNA profile matched sufficiently with hers for the lab to attest that he was her father.

She'd placed it in her bag, and felt sure she still had it when she went to help Millie, in the office next door, pack up for her move.

It hadn't been until she arrived home that she'd realised it was missing. After the initial panic, she remembered pausing in the mothers' room on the way from the Ladies. That had to be right…Sonia from the ophthalmic clinic had been in there having a weep, and she'd dragged out a handful of tissues from her bag to help Sonia mop up. The letter could have fallen out then.

If she was to find it before anyone else, she needed to get to work before the Alexandra hummed into life. She supposed she could easily get the lab to send her a replacement copy. But that wouldn't help the confidentiality problem. A promise was a promise. If she didn't find it... If she didn't locate it *at once*, she'd have to inform Elliott. The thought of that made her feel slightly sick.

After that first meeting in the café—even before then, in fact, when she'd first laid eyes on him—she'd recognised he had a chill factor. Even his name, seen for the first time on her original birth certificate, had had a cold clink of reality to it. At eighteen, when the law had allowed, she'd gone through the procedures of finding out her birth parents' names out of curiosity, but probably would never have acted on the information. She doubted if she'd have contacted him at all, if it hadn't been for that Tuesday, exactly six weeks ago.

She'd been standing at the reception desk, checking a patient's file, when someone had approached the desk and said to Cindy, 'Elliott Fraser. I've brought Matthew for his check-up.'

Sophy's heart had jarred to a standstill. In a breathless kind of slow motion she'd looked up and seen him for the first time. Her father.

He was in his late forties, his hair already silver. He looked smooth and well-heeled, the image of a successful businessman. His eyes were a cold slate-grey, not like hers at all, and as he'd talked to Cindy his gaze hadn't warmed or changed in any way. Though Sophy had stared and stared to try to find a resemblance, she hadn't been able to see any.

There had to be one, though. People could hardly ever see likenesses to themselves. She supposed she might take after her poor mother, who, according to the records, had died from contracting meningitis, but there should still be points of resemblance with her father.

Her glance had fallen then on the four-year-old at Elliott Fraser's side. He had the most endearing little solemn face. In a rush of conflicted emotion she'd realised he was her half-brother.

How strange to see some of the actual people in the world who shared her blood, her genes. Even perhaps, if she were lucky, things in common. Though she'd loved her adoptive parents, they had a much older daughter in England from Bea's first marriage, and

Sophy had sometimes had the feeling she was being compared to her. Lauren was good at maths and science. While Sophy liked them, too, she preferred the arts. Lauren had done medicine, while Sophy had chosen to study child language development. Lauren went hiking and shinning up mountainsides, while Sophy liked growing things and browsing through bookshops.

Soon after Sophy had turned eighteen, it was as though Henry and Bea felt they'd discharged their responsibility towards their adopted child, for, even though there'd been lots of teary regrets and one long visit, they'd emigrated back to England to be with Lauren, Bea's *real* daughter, when she started her family.

Sophy often thought that if only she'd had brothers and sisters, she mightn't have missed her parents so badly. *Still* be missing them. That little brother…

As she remembered his big brown eyes her heart made a surge of pleasure, though it was tinged with concern. He'd been so sweet, but she'd had the most overwhelming instinct that he was lonely. Afterwards, going over and over the encounter in her mind, it had struck her clinical brain that, while Elliott Fraser had waited in Reception with him, he hadn't made one single eye contact with his son. There were books and toys for the children to investigate while they waited, but Matthew had sat all hunched up on the seat beside his father, as if hedged into his own little world. Elliott hadn't spoken to him once.

She saw that often in the clinic. Parents who didn't understand that their communication with their child was crucial. She wished there were some way she could help Matthew. Dreaming about it, she was so deep in thought that by the time she disembarked at Circular Quay she realised she hadn't noticed the early morning sights and smells of the harbour once in the entire trip. In Macquarie Street, she broke into a run, not easy in a pencil-slim skirt.

Thank goodness Security had already unlocked the building's heavy glass doors. Once inside, she pressed the button for the lift, but then decided she couldn't spare the time it took for the creaking cage to descend, and took the stairs instead.

The great domed skylight let in the morning, lighting the tiers of galleries where the doctors had their rooms. Tall, stained-glass windows at either end of the building tinctured the weak morning light with the faintest hues of rose and lavender.

Few people were in evidence this early, although the rich fragrance of coffee as she sprinted past the second gallery, mingled with the aromas rising up from the basement café, suggested that Millie, her friend and colleague, was there already, establishing herself in her new room.

Millie's old room was right next door to hers. It was bound to be unlocked, waiting to be refurbished. If she didn't find the envelope in the mothers' room, or even the washroom, it would have to still be safe in there.

At the top of the stairs she paused to regain her breath, and was faced with the sight of Millie's door, firmly shut. With a shock she saw a new sign emblazoned on it.

Connor O'Brien.

The words leaped out at her, bold and alive like a confrontation. Connor O'Brien. Who was Connor O'Brien?

She flew along to the ladies' room, praying Security had unlocked it. To her relief the heavy mahogany door gave at once. Turning first to the washroom, she pushed through the swing door and scanned all the wash units, checked the bins, then strode through to the innermost room and peered into all the cubicles. Nothing.

Disappointing, but no surprise. The odds were still on the mothers' room.

She hurried across the tiny foyer, swung open the door to the mothers' room and was brought to a sudden standstill. For a confused instant she was confronted by what looked like a dark pillar shimmering in the white-tiled space, until she blinked and her vision cleared.

It was a man.

Naked to the waist, he was tall and lean, with strongly muscled arms and pitch-black hair. He was standing at the sink, his face half covered with shaving cream. A jacket and shirt were draped over a briefcase at his feet. His powerful torso was tanned, as if he'd spent real time in the sun, and as he performed his task small ripples disturbed the sleek, satin skin of his back.

His feet were as firmly planted on the floor of the mothers' room as if they had every right to be there. Didn't the man have a bathroom?

As he leaned further in she caught a glimpse of an angry, jagged scar across the ribs on his right side. A breathless sensation shook her, like the moment of sudden uplift on a ferris wheel. The door escaped from her paralysed fingers just as he was laying bare a swathe of smooth, bronzed cheek. His hand halted in mid-swipe, and in the mirror his gaze collided with hers.

His eyes were dark, deeper than the night, and heavy-lidded, fringed with black lashes beneath strong black brows. What grabbed at her, though, and shook up her insides, was their expression.

At that first instant of connection a sardonic gleam had shot through them. As if he'd recognised her.

Except… She didn't know him. Why should he recognise her?

He half turned and she caught a glimpse of his profile, a devastating sweep of forehead and long straight nose. Then he faced her full on and…

Gorgeous. Even half coated with foam, strength and masculine assurance declared themselves in the symmetrical bone structure of his lean, handsome face.

'Hi. Connor O'Brien.'

His voice was deep, with a rich, smooth texture. A smattering of dark whorled hair on his powerful chest invited her mesmerised gaze to follow its tapering path down beneath his belt buckle to…somewhere.

'Oh, er…er…hi. Sorry.' She backed out again into the foyer.

Connor looked after the closing door with some amusement. He began to regret postponing checking into a hotel. The last thing he needed was to alert Miss Sophy Woodruff to the suddenness of his arrangements. But who could have guessed she'd be so early to work?

He felt an intrigued little buzz in his veins. For a first glimpse, she had been nothing like he'd expected. Big soft eyes and sensitive, passionate mouths didn't go with tough little operators.

Unless, of course, they were her stock-in-trade. Perfect for sucking in middle-aged pigeons.

Outside in the foyer, Sophy tried to unscramble her brain. Whew. It took a few seconds to get the chest image out of her mind. Who needed to watch reruns of *Die Hard* with men like him around?

But, for goodness' sake, who could do any kind of a decent search in the presence of a semi-naked man? He was a damned nuisance. The cheek of him, treating the ladies' room like his own private en suite, even if it was barely six thirty.

And why, now she came to think of it, had she given ground? Whose rooms were they? If any of her fellow members of the Avengers netball team had been present, they'd have been yelling, 'Attack. Attack. Evict the intruder.'

She braced herself, and walked back in.

He was buttoning his shirt. Too late, though. That first impression was already seared into her brain. He might just as well have emerged dripping from a plunge in a weedy pond, his shirt clinging and transparent, for all the good it was doing him now.

At the sound of her step he flickered a glance over her from beneath his dark lashes. She knew that look. It was the hunter's assessment of her curves and sexual availability, as automatic to wolves and other male beasts as breathing.

'This is the mothers' room,' she asserted. His dark eyes sharpened beneath their dark lashes, and a sudden tension in the room seemed to affect her voice with an unwelcome throatiness. 'In case you didn't know.'

'I did know.' He rinsed his razor under the tap and gave it a couple of shakes. She waited for some sign he'd received the hint, but he resumed shaving with cool unconcern.

So who was he, *what* was he, that Millie had been obliged to make way for him? He didn't look like any of the doctors she knew.

She made a quick survey of the floor and surfaces. The cleaners had already done their work by the time she'd come in yesterday evening, but someone else might have picked the letter up after she'd left and thought it was rubbish. She glanced about for the bin and spotted it tucked under the sink. Directly in line with the man's long, elegantly shod feet.

Right. She straightened her shoulders, cleared her throat and stated with cool authority, 'Look, I'm sorry, but I'm afraid you'll have to finish that up somewhere else. There is a men's room further along.' She opened the door and held it wide with graceful, though determined, insistence.

Seconds ticked by, until she began to wonder if he'd even heard what she'd said, then he flashed her a lazy, long-lashed glance. 'I don't think so.'

To her intense indignation he remained as immovable as a tree trunk, continuing to scrape the foam from his handsome jaw as if he had all the time in the world. After a charged second in which her brain was jostled by a million incredulous thoughts about calling the police or the state emergency services for back-up, he had the nerve to add, 'No need to panic.'

Panic. Who was panicking? Even if such tall, dark sexiness was a rarity at the Alexandra, Sophy Woodruff was perfectly well able to deal with it, in the mothers' room or anywhere else.

Forced to, if she didn't want to look like an idiot, she let the door swing shut, as, without the slightest interest in her wishes, he started on the moustache area. Naturally her eyes were drawn to watch the delicate operation. Before she could properly drag them away, he paused and the corners of his mouth edged up a little.

'I'll be out of your way in a few seconds. Don't let my presence make you nervous.'

His voice might have risen from some bottomless inner well of chocolate liqueur, so appealing its deep timbre was to the clinically trained ear. Or would have been, if it hadn't been for the subtle mockery in it.

'Nervous?' She gave a careless laugh. 'My only concern is that at any minute now mothers may need to come in here to nurse their babies.'

He glanced at his watch. 'At six thirty-six?'

'Well, certainly.' It was only a bit of a lie. In truth, the clinics didn't usually open until seven-thirty, but in an emergency they very well might open earlier. 'There could be early appointments. I think you should be aware that this room is intended for the sole use of mothers.'

'Ah.' A gleam lit his dark eyes. 'Then in that case we'd both better leave.'

Without waiting for her reply, he turned back to his reflection. Shaving foam outlined his mouth, highlighting its chiselled perfection, the top lip straight and stern, the lower one sensual in that ruthless, masculine way. Mouths could be deceptive, though. In terms of kissing, sometimes even the most promising lips could end up being a disappointment. It all depended on the proficiency of the kisser. And the chemistry with the kissee.

Connor O'Brien's razor hand arrested in mid-air and his eyes locked with hers.

'Missed a bit, have I?'

The depth of knowing amusement in his glance burnt her to the soles of her feet.

'Pardon?' she said, forcing herself to hold that mocking gaze and ignore the pinkening tide flooding to her hairline. 'Are you asking for my advice? I'm afraid I can't help you. I know very little about men's hair-growth problems.'

With supreme dignity, she turned away and made an emphatic effort to search.

Connor smiled to himself, noting Miss Sophy Woodruff's apparent sensitivity with a pleasurable leap of surprise. It was rare to draw a blush in a woman, and strangely stirring. If she was the cold opportunist Sir Frank suspected, her ability to colour up was quite an accomplishment.

She was paused now in the middle of the room, making a slow twirl in search of something, giving him ample opportunity to observe her undulating curves, long slim legs and slender, graceful neck. He wouldn't have expected Elliott Fraser to risk everything over a scrubber, but that grainy photo had hardly done her justice.

He wondered what she was searching for.

'I humbly apologise for intruding on your sacred female space,' he said, in a bid to tempt her to turn his way again, the better to drink in more of her oval face. Luminous blue eyes—or had her lavender shirt turned them violet?—fringed by thick black lashes. Rosy lips against pale creamy skin. Enough to make any man's mouth water. 'No threat intended,' he added soothingly.

Sophy sent him a sardonic glance. A man caught in flagrante shouldn't try to flirt his way out of trouble. She wished now she'd called Security and had him thrown out.

'Do you usually prefer the women's to the gents'?'

Beneath his black lashes his eyes glinted. The air she breathed suddenly felt charged with dangerous, high-voltage sparks.

'Nearly always. You know how it is. I like to network. And what better place to meet people?' His bold, dark gaze drifted from her mouth to her breasts, down to her legs and back again.

Skin cells scorched all the way to her ankles. She turned her back on him and bent to check the sofa where she'd sat yesterday, slipping her hand down behind the seat cushion and feeling around the perimeter.

There was nothing there except dusty lint. Hyper-conscious of *him*, she straightened up to skim the change table and benchtops. He was pretending to be engaged again on his task, but she wasn't deceived. He was tuned into her every move, or her name wasn't Sophy Woodruff.

Or…or whatever it was.

She eyed the leather case beside him on the draining board. He might, just might, have found the envelope and be intending to hand it in. 'Er…' It was a stretch now at this late stage, but she tried to crank some goodwill into her voice. 'Have you by any chance— found a letter in here?'

'A letter.' His expressive brows gave a quizzical twitch while he considered. 'This seems an unusual place to expect a mail delivery. It isn't a covert letter-drop for the CIA, now, is it?'

That sexy, teasing note again in his deep voice. And there was something hard underneath, almost as if he didn't believe in her sincerity.

In an effort to show she was in earnest, she ignored his tone. 'It's not a delivery. I've misplaced an envelope. I think it may have dropped from my bag somewhere. Over there where I was sitting, or…'

'What sort of envelope?'

'Just a plain, buff-coloured… You know, with a window in it, like—' Like any official communication to Miss Violet Woodruff, she was about to say, until it occurred to her then how ridiculous it was, having to describe it. How many envelopes was he likely to have found? 'Look, does it matter what kind it is? Have you or haven't you found it?'

In her frustration, she might have sounded a tad impatient, because he turned from the mirror and directed the full force of his dark, shimmering gaze on her.

'I don't know if I should answer that. It would depend to whom such an envelope was addressed.'

She felt a small shock, as if she'd come up against an unexpected concrete wall, but said, as pleasantly as she could, 'Well, obviously, it's addressed to me.'

'Ah. So you say.' The infuriating man had finished shaving at last, and turned to wash his razor under the tap. 'But, then, who are you?'

It was clear he was toying with her. 'I'm—' She drew herself up to her full five-seven in heels and asserted, 'You know, Security in this building is very strict. They wouldn't tolerate your intrusion in here.'

'Ah. Now, that's where you're wrong. The fact is, it was the Security guy with the freckles who unlocked these rooms for me, since the Gents is having some sort of problem with the pipes.'

'Oh.' Nonplussed, she took a second before she managed a come-back. 'Well, it's a pity he didn't explain that that sink you're using is intended for nursing mothers who want to make themselves a cup of tea. I hope you give it a good wash when you're finished.'

The man's eyes gleamed, but he continued, musing, 'Not all states feel the need to pursue this rigid segregation of the sexes. Take France, for example. A French woman visiting the mothers' room in, say, the Louvre, would be very unlikely to feel threatened by the presence of a man shaving. Though, I suppose any woman who's not used to being around men…a woman, say, who's never watched a man shave…never been kissed, as the saying goes…'

Never been kissed. Was he trying to insult her? She hissed in a breath through her teeth. 'Look, all I want to know is if you found my envelope. If you *didn't*…'

He put on a bland expression. 'I think I might be able to help if you could be more specific. For instance, if you could give me some idea of the letter's likely contents…'

'What?' She stared at him in incredulity. 'Are you for real? Look, why can't you just *say*—?'

She broke off, shaking her head in disbelief as he bent to splash his face, his composure unruffled.

Her heart started to thud. He must have found it. Why else was he being so obstructive? She breathed deeply for several seconds, wondering how to go about extracting the truth from him. Often she could sense things in people, but in his case she was aware only of an implacable resistance. Despair gripped her. What was left for her to try? An appeal to him as a human being?

He reached for a paper towel and turned to her, patting his face dry.

'Are you sure—absolutely sure—you didn't find it?' Despite an attempt to sound calm she knew the plea in her voice revealed her desperation, loud and clear.

He crumpled the paper towel and dropped it in the bin. Then he slipped a purple silk tie under his collar and tied it, practice in the fluid movements of his lean, tanned fingers. At the same time he turned to appraise her with his dark, intelligent gaze. Drops of moisture sparkled on his black lashes.

'It's beginning to sound like a very important letter.'

'It is. That is—' She checked herself. The more she talked up the importance of the letter, the more likely he would be to read it if he found it. Just supposing he hadn't already. 'No, no, well, it's not really. It's only important to me. Not to anyone else.'

He nodded in apparent understanding, his sardonic face suddenly grave. Perhaps she'd misjudged him. Perhaps he could even be sympathetic. Although, how safe was it to trust him? If he could only be serious for a minute…

She watched him shrug on his jacket, then slip the leather case into his briefcase, all the while continuing her theme of playing the letter down. 'It's nothing really. Just a small—private thing.'

'Ah.' His dark lashes flickered down. 'A love letter.'

'No,' she snapped, goaded. 'Not a love letter. Look, why can't you be serious? Why can't you give me a straight answer?'

He sighed. 'All right. How about this one? I haven't found your letter. You can search me if you like.' He spread his hands in invitation, offering her the pockets of his jacket, his trousers, then as she glared at him in disbelief he thrust his briefcase at her. 'Go on. Search.'

As if she could. She wanted to snatch the briefcase from him and whack him with it. But even without touching it, she knew there was nothing of hers inside. He was tormenting her, when all he'd had to do was to tell her in the first place…

'Do you know,' she said, an angry tremor in her low voice, 'you are a very rude and aggravating man?'

'I do know,' he said ruefully, wickedness in the dark eyes beneath his black lashes. 'I'm ashamed of myself.'

She felt her blood pressure rise as he moved closer until his broad chest was a bare few inches from her breasts. The clean male scent of him, the masculine buzz of his aura, plunged her normally tranquil pulse into chaos. She became suffocatingly conscious of the nearness of the vibrant, muscled body lurking beneath his clothes.

The dark gaze dwelling on her face grew sensual and turned her blood into a molten, racing torrent. 'And do *you* know that you're a very uptight little chick? You should learn to relax.'

His sexy mouth was uncomfortably near, and, involuntarily, her own dried. She glowered at him, anger rendering her unable to breathe or speak.

He flicked her cheek. 'I'll let you know if I find your letter.' His bold gaze travelled down her throat to the neck of her shirt, then back. 'You know, with those eyes your name should be Violet.' He turned and strolled to the door, and while she stood there, the cool touch of his fingers still burning on her skin, it swung shut behind him. Then the enormity of what he'd said hit her like a train. The incredible words resounded in her ears.

He knew her name.

He'd known it all along. That had been no coincidence.

But how could he know it? How, unless he'd found her letter?

CHAPTER THREE

SOPHY strode along the gallery to the children's clinic. Connor O'Brien's door was closed, but she had to steel herself to walk past it and breathe the air he was infecting with his intolerable masculine game-playing. He was probably in there now, gloating over her DNA profile.

Although, what could it possibly mean to him? What could he *do* with it? Apart from post it on the Internet. Take it to the papers. Contact Elliott…

She shut her eyes and tried to breathe calmly. The man could be a blackmailer. He looked bad, with that mocking dark gaze and that sardonic mouth. Just remembering his refusal to take her seriously made her blood boil all over again. She wished she'd said something clever and cutting enough to douse that insolent amusement in his eyes.

She used her pass key to unlock the clinic, relieved that neither Cindy, their receptionist, nor Bruce, the paediatrician, had arrived yet, praying that against the odds someone wonderful had found the letter and popped it through the mail slot. But no such luck. In her office she plunged into a frenzied search, her desk, her drawers, all around the children's table and chairs, the armchairs for parents, only confirming what she already knew—she'd lost it *after* she'd left yesterday.

Millie was her last resort. She'd spent a good hour in there yesterday, helping her friend pack up her files. Fingers crossed, she phoned her, but again her luck was out. Amidst all her files and books, Millie had been in too much of an uproar to find anything, let alone something so ordinary and unobtrusive as an envelope.

She slumped down in her chair. Perhaps she should alert Elliott, but she wasn't ready to give up yet. He'd seemed so paranoid at the idea of the news getting out. Not that she could blame him altogether. Her existence had come as a complete shock to him. She pitied him for what he must have gone through when he found out. Anyone—*anyone* would have been upset.

She tried to crush down a nasty feeling at how he might react when he knew the letter was out of her hands. Then, with some relief, she remembered he said he'd be out of town for a week, and brightened a little. At least that gave her a bit of breathing space. He might not have even received his copy yet.

And, honestly, what was the worst that could happen to him if the news got out? Thousands of people had given up their children for adoption, for all sorts of reasons. It was hardly such a shocking scandal anymore. His wife should be capable of understanding something that had happened twenty-three years ago.

And it wasn't as if she wasn't an independent adult. She hoped she'd made it absolutely crystal clear that it wouldn't *cost* him anything to invite her into his life—their lives. Only a bit of friendship. Not a relationship, exactly. She knew she couldn't expect that.

But there was no denying her disappointment. Elliott's utter dismay when she'd made that first contact had been almost tangible. He'd tried to disguise it with his smooth manners, but she'd been able to sense how he truly felt. In the subsequent meetings, in the coffee shop and the bar, he'd seemed more concerned to find out who she might have told rather than how she'd spent her life to date, while *she…*

Her heart had been so full, so brimming over with joy and hope, she'd wanted to know everything about him. And Matthew.

But she felt sure, when someone got to know him, he was a wonderful person. When he got used to the idea, he would come round to seeing the fantastic side of having a daughter.

Restlessly she got up and started tweaking some brown-edged leaves from her geraniums on the window ledge. She hadn't felt such confusion for years, not since Henry and Bea had told her they were staying on in England for a bit. Possibly for ever. She lifted her gaze to the Botanical Gardens across the street, wishing she could go across right now, before she saw the first of the children on her morning's list. Somehow the soothing essence of those cool, leafy pathways always managed to soak into her like balm.

Connor O'Brien was to blame for this turmoil. A wave of puzzlement swept through her. What was wrong with him? Why had he been so mocking, almost *distrustful* of her?

His behaviour had been so arrogant, so callous and indifferent, as if her anxiety had been a joke. And as for that crack about her never having been kissed…

Of course she had. Countless times. He'd only been teasing, using a typical male ploy to start a flirty conversation, unless he'd been suggesting… A chilling possibility crept in. If, by some quirk of fate, a woman still happened to be a virgin, surely that minor detail wasn't obvious to people? Could there be something about her that flagged her status to the world?

And if so, what? Could it be her clothes? Her conversation? The way she walked?

She'd never thought it worth worrying about before. It was just— the way things had turned out for her.

It wasn't that she hadn't had opportunities. Plenty of men had been keen to relieve her of it. And she had no philosophical objections to sex. In fact, she fully believed that every woman should drink deeply from the cup of life, although the values Henry and Bea had instilled in her had quietly insisted that the drinker should be in love. And there was the little matter of trust. She'd tried a few tentative sips once or twice, but for some reason the trust factor had always intruded and she'd stalled at a certain point.

Leah and Zoe, her flatmates, called her a late bloomer. Sooner or later, they declared, some ruthless hunk would send her completely overboard and she'd plunge right in. And that was where she needed to beware, because someone as dreamy and impulsive as Sophy Woodruff was at risk of a broken heart.

If she wanted to land a man, she needed to do her research, they'd said. Find a solid prospect with financial security and a career trajectory, and plan a campaign.

'But what if we have nothing in common?' she'd argued.

The answer was stern and unequivocal. 'Plan a campaign. *Build* things in common.'

What Zoe and Leah didn't understand—well, they did, but they scoffed about it—was that she had dreams. And dreams didn't go with campaigns. In fact, she preferred to rely on her instincts about people, though she couldn't always, she had to admit. She had been mistaken more than once, sometimes quite spectacularly. But she'd known definitely at once that those boys she'd turned down just didn't have the chemistry, and never, ever would.

As for her needing to become more proactive, with a plan and some cold, hard strategy, she doubted she could bring that off. Campaigns weren't her style. In the situation she was in right now, though, some cool, ruthless strategy was definitely warranted.

She felt a little shiver of apprehension.

There was only one thing for it. Whatever it took, she would have to find a way to seize her letter back. She couldn't allow Connor O'Brien to ruin her chance to know her father before it had even begun. And he wouldn't win any future encounter with her, either, dammit. He'd better learn that, kissed or unkissed, Sophy Woodruff was a force to be reckoned with.

Somehow, if it killed her, she would find a way into his office.

It gave her an eerie feeling to realise that at this very second he might be on the other side of her wall, gazing out at the very same view.

Connor frowned out across the treetops, beyond the Gardens, to where a strip of Walsh Bay glimmered under a hot blue sky. It occurred to him that not so very far away, as the crow flew, he owned a house. Most of his father's things had been auctioned for charity, as became the possessions of the extremely wealthy, but it might do, especially as it wasn't too far from the haunts of Elliott Fraser. He was sure he'd left some of his law books there. Slightly outdated perhaps, but he could pick up some of the current publications later. It might be interesting to see what had changed this side of his old profession.

He stepped back from the window and gazed appreciatively around at the high-ceilinged rooms with their ornate cornices. If he'd been setting up for real, he couldn't have found a more pleasing location.

He glanced at his watch. Organise a car, then take some time to pick up his books and some stationery supplies before the office furnishings were delivered. Consider his next encounter with Sophy Woodruff....

His pulse rate quickened. He wondered what the letter was she'd been searching for. The anxiety in those stunning eyes had seemed genuine enough. With her sweet low voice, the ready flush washing into her cheek, she'd seemed amazingly soft, too soft to be any of the things Sir Frank suspected. But he was too hardened a case to be sucked in by appearances. Women in the profession could be superb actresses...

Whatever she was searching for, his challenge would be to find it first.

He remembered the fire that had flashed in those blue eyes when he'd touched her, and his blood stirred. He could so enjoy a worthy protagonist.

* * *

At lunchtime, on her way down to the basement deli, Sophy saw Connor O'Brien assisting some workmen to manoeuvre a handsome rosewood bookshelf through his door. She grimaced to herself. No doubt he needed it for storing other people's private documents.

She queued at the deli for a salad sandwich, but instead of taking it to her usual picnic spot in the Gardens, headed back upstairs to finish some of the morning's reports. As she reached the top of the last flight her stomach flipped in excitement.

Connor's door was standing half open.

Her imagination leaped to the possibilities. The workmen must have gone to pick up their next load. Had the arrogant beast gone with them?

Except that would be too good to be true. Surely he wouldn't leave his office unlocked and unattended?

With a thudding heart, she slowed her pace, and as she reached his door hesitated, pretending to search for something in her bag. She could hear no sound from within. All she could see in the slice of reception office visible through the half-open door was an empty expanse of carpet and the corner of the built-in reception desk.

He could be in the inner room, though, skulking. She hovered there, straining her ears, trying to guess if anyone was inside. If he was in there, she reasoned, she should be able to sense his presence. A quick glance along the gallery revealed a couple of people waiting for the lift at the other end. She closed her eyes and listened, but the air seemed flat and empty.

Voices floated up to her from below. She darted across and looked over the balustrade. There were people on the stairs to the lower levels, but no sign of Connor O'Brien. And the lift must have arrived without the workmen, for the waiting people were now step-ping into it.

For the moment, the coast seemed to be clear.

It was too good a chance to lose. She made a small precaution-ary knock, then waited with her heart thumping fit to burst. Nothing disturbed the stillness. Feeling as guilty as a thief, she cast a last furtive glance about, then slipped inside.

Familiar with the layout, she sensed immediately that the entire suite, including both offices and the tiny tea-room inside, were unoccupied. She ventured through the connecting door into the larger room. Already Millie's comfortable presence had gone. The place had a different feel, as if it had been given over to some sterner god.

Daylight streamed in through the tall windows, and with it the view her office shared of the Botanical Gardens and the strip of harbour beyond. A laptop sat on a heavy rosewood desk beside a stack of new stationery—cardboard folder files, packaged paper and a selection of office equipment. The bookshelves were bare, a large tea chest of books beside them waiting to be unpacked. She tilted her head and read a couple of the titles upside down. *Policy and Practice of Human Rights Law. International Human Rights.*

She felt disconcerted. Connor O'Brien was a lawyer?

How ironic. If he was so concerned about human rights, what was he doing stealing people's private letters? For a second she experienced a doubt. It hardly made sense. Could she have leaped to the wrong conclusion and lost her letter somewhere else?

Even visualising the envelope made a hot and cold sensation of the most unmistakable immediacy sweep over her, as though all the tiny hairs on her body were standing on end. Her overwhelming instinct told her it was close by. If she closed her eyes, she could practically feel the texture of the paper in her hands. Without a doubt she knew it had to be here in this room.

The question was where?

A new filing cabinet stood within easy reach of the desk. She glanced over her shoulder at the door and, ignoring some warning prickles in her nape, tried the top drawer. It sounded empty, but it was locked. They were all locked. She felt a surge of excitement.

Why would he lock the filing cabinet if he had nothing worth hiding? She looked around for the keys. She tried the desk drawers first, but, finding them empty, turned to survey the room. Her eye fell on a briefcase, leaning up against the leg of his desk chair.

Ah. A thrill of guilty excitement shivered down her spine.

Should she?

She vacillated for a moment, but with the seconds ticking away it was no time for squeamishness. Her pulse drumming in her ears, she whisked the briefcase up onto the desk, pushing aside stationery to make room, and unzipped the main compartment intended for the laptop. It was empty, apart from a couple of memory sticks.

Increasingly conscious of the possibility of the workmen's return, she made a hasty search of the other compartments. Her letter wasn't in any of them, nor any keys. In fact, the case contained nothing except for a few odds and ends for the computer. That was when she noticed Connor O'Brien's jacket, slung on the back of his chair.

Having sunk this deep into crime, rifling a personal jacket didn't seem much more of a stretch.

Gingerly, suspense creeping up her spine, she slipped her hands into the side pockets, and came up with nothing. She had no greater luck with the breast pocket, although her fingers detected a bulge through the fabric. She turned the jacket to the inside and tried the inset pocket. Her heart bounded in her chest. There was no envelope in there. Only a passport.

She slipped it out, then put it straight back in. This would be an unforgivable invasion of the man's privacy. But then, how concerned was he about respecting hers?

With a bracing breath, she squashed down her scruples and took out the alluring little red book.

Probably it was her imagination, but the covers felt warm to her touch, as if the book vibrated with some vital energy. It was such a temptation. Surely it wouldn't hurt to examine the photo. Almost at once she gave in, opening straight to the ID page to be faced with Connor O'Brien.

She might have known. Other people took ghastly mugshots, but not him. She stared, riveted, as his face looked out at her, stern and unsmiling, but still with the faint possibility of amusement breaking out on his sardonic mouth. He was thirty-four, according to his birthdate. She flicked to the back pages, and widened her eyes in surprise. Connor was a frequent traveller. And a *recent* one, going by the last stamp in the book. He'd only just arrived in the country.

She'd heard of workaholics, but this was an extreme case, surely, if he came to work straight off a plane without going home first to shave. Unable to resist one more look at his picture, she flipped back to the identity page. Was it her imagination, or were his eyes piercing her now with that infuriating mockery as if he knew what she was doing and could see right through her?

Her heart suddenly thumping too fast, she snapped the book shut. She held it between her palms, swept by a confused mixture of conflicting instincts about Connor O'Brien. They couldn't all be true. Was she going insane?

She gave an alarmed start as the sound of approaching voices alerted her that she was about to be caught red-handed, and the passport slipped from her fingers.

She dived to pick it up as bumps and grunts began to issue from the reception office, suggestive of several men hefting some bulky piece of furniture through a narrow aperture.

In her haste to slot the little book into the pocket, she knocked the stationery pile askew, and sent manilla folders sliding across the desk and onto the floor.

She dropped to her knees, and as she scrabbled to gather the files and stack them back on the desk the activity outside ceased. Her heart nearly seized as she caught sight of the briefcase. Quickly she dashed it onto the floor. For a panicked instant she considered hiding in the tea-room, then dismissed the action as cowardly.

She could do this, she thought, her heart slamming into her ribs.

She'd just brazen it out. She straightened up and faced the door, steeled for the worst.

There was a brief exchange of conversation outside. She was straining to hear what was being said when the door to the room burst open. At almost the identical moment her horrified gaze fell on the passport, still lying on the corner of the desk.

She snatched it up, whipping it behind her back just as Connor strode in. When he saw her, he stopped short, an initial flare of astonishment in his dark eyes changing nearly at once to cynicism. Almost as if catching her there was no real surprise.

Without a word he stepped past her, seized a pen from the desk, and turned back to the outer room, where he signed something on a clipboard presented to him by one of the delivery men.

With no time to return the passport to his jacket, and nowhere to hide it, she popped it down the front of her shirt, just as Connor turned to stroll slowly and purposefully back into his office.

If he saw her surreptitious movement, he didn't show it. He shut the door gently behind him, then paused to examine her, his black eyebrows raised.

He looked taller, grimmer and more authoritative when he was annoyed. It was harder to imagine him plunging through the pond.

No. No, it wasn't.

Her mouth became uncomfortably dry, and she smoothed her skirt with moistening palms.

He didn't appear to be imagining her in as favourable a light. His speculative gaze swept over her while she waited in an anguish of suspense, realising from the hard glint in his eyes he wasn't about to let her off lightly.

'Did you want something?' His deep voice was polite, with just a tinge of incredulity lapping at its edges.

As if he didn't know. The sheer duplicity of the man.

She tried to assume a cool, poised demeanour. 'Oh, look, er, I should apologise. I probably shouldn't have walked in. I came to—

speak to you. The door was open, so I just—' she made a breezy gesture '—wandered in.' Her voice wobbled a little, but she kept her head high and forced herself to keep meeting his eyes, all the time conscious of her pulse ticking like a time bomb.

His eyes flicked to his desk, over the once rigidly neat pile of stationery, now listing dangerously to one side, and on—to her conscious eyes at least—to the neon-flashing space where she'd rested the briefcase.

In a brilliant move inspired by adrenaline, she did the only possible thing, and sat on the desk in the telltale space, stretching a hand back so she could lean, and once again knocking over the wonky pile.

'Oh, damn,' she said, trying to sound careless, 'that's the second time I've done that.'

Connor O'Brien didn't look fooled. His acute dark eyes slid over her in sardonic appreciation. She grew uncomfortably conscious of her breasts and legs, accentuated by her posture, and hoped the red passport didn't blaze through her shirt.

'What can I help you with, Sophy?'

She smiled, but her sexual sensors, to say nothing of the others, were all madly oscillating on panic alert. Somehow, though, the danger she was in gave her a reckless sort of courage. She hadn't spent lonely years of her life watching old black-and-white movie reels into the small hours for nothing. She knew how Lana Turner would have played this scene.

'Ah, so you've found out my name,' she said throatily, crossing her legs.

His glinting gaze flicked to them. 'I described you to the Security guy. He had no trouble recognising you.'

Something in his voice told her the conversation he'd had with the man had been a loaded one. She could just imagine the sort of things they'd said about her. If his passport hadn't been burning a hole in her midriff, she might have been incensed. As it was, her major concern for the moment, apart from escaping unscathed, was how she was to return it to its pocket. It was one thing to be suspected of snooping, another to leave behind glaring evidence.

What if he accused her of stealing? He could have her up before the courts. Her boss would be forced to sack her. Perhaps, though, if she owned up and produced the passport at once...

She examined Connor's face for signs of softening, but his eyebrows were heavy and forbidding, his mouth and jaw stern.

Lana would have known what to do. If ever there was a man who needed beguiling, here was the man. Her skirt had ridden up a little on her thigh, and she discreetly tugged it down.

Connor O'Brien didn't miss the movement. He prowled closer and stood looking down at her with his harsh, uncompromising gaze. 'Breaking and entering is a criminal offence.' She noticed his glance flick to her mouth. 'What were you hoping to steal?'

Her heart made a scared lurch at the '*s*' word. Somehow, owning up lost its attractiveness as an option.

'Steal? That's ridiculous.' She fluttered her lashes in denial. 'It was hardly breaking and entering... You left your door wide-open, and I came in to talk to you. Simple as that.'

He looked unconvinced. 'I should hand you over to that Security guy and make his day.'

'Oh, why? For coming in for a chat?'

'A *chat*.' His lip curled in disbelief. 'About what?'

She wished he wouldn't use that sceptical tone. It was rich, this distrust he had of her, when he was the one who stole people's confidential DNA reports.

'The weather,' she said, rolling her eyes. 'What else?'

She slid off the desk so she could bring more height to the exchange, but standing before Connor only seemed to illustrate how slight and insubstantial five feet seven of guilty woman was in comparison with six feet three of hard, cynical man. Still, after the way *he'd* behaved, his outraged morality act was too much to swallow.

'I felt a bit sorry about not being so friendly this morning.' She stretched languidly, then sashayed towards the door, casting him a long Lana-esque glance over her shoulder. 'But I see now that my first instincts about you were correct.'

She had just grasped the door knob when she felt a big powerful bulk stride up behind her. A lean hand closed firmly over hers.

'No, you don't, sweetheart. Not yet.'

She could feel his hot breath on her neck. As his raw masculine proximity washed over her, accelerating her pulse into a mad racing turmoil, it homed in on her that, while *she* might have been playing Lana Turner, he was no two-dimensional Hollywood hero on the silver screen. He was a big, dangerous, flesh-and-blood man, and he wasn't confined to a script.

Heat emanated from his body. She turned to face him, her back against the door, barely able to keep her rapid breathing under control, panting like a marathon runner. Her blood throbbed with a tense excitement. Still, as sexy as he looked with his black brows bristling, his intelligent dark eyes scouring her face, she reminded herself that he was the man who'd stolen her letter. It was imperative that she keep her wits about her.

She made an attempt to ignore the major chemical reaction effervescing inside her, and stiffened her spine.

He stepped back a little to study her, frowning, his dark eyes burning with a curious intensity. 'Empty your pockets.'

In spite of her bravado, she felt her cheeks flame with the insult. 'I don't have any.'

A dark gleam lit his eyes. 'Ah. Well, then, I'll have no choice but to search you.'

Her stomach lurched. The silkiness of his deep voice couldn't disguise the determination in the set of his chiselled jaw.

It was a seminal moment. If she allowed him to make the attempt, she was lost. His stern, masculine mouth, not so far away from hers, relaxed its unforgiving lines, as though Connor was enjoying his mastery of the situation. His mastery of *her*.

Suspense coiled her insides.

On a rush of adrenaline, she leaned back against the door, her breasts rising and falling, and breathed huskily, 'But…would you feel honourable about violating my person? A woman who's never been kissed?'

His eyes flickered over her face and throat. She could sense his hesitation, his struggle against temptation. It gave her such an exhilarating feeling to see that she could tempt him from his intent. And he *would* succumb, she realised with a thrilled, almost incredulous certainty, her heart thundering.

Beneath his black lashes his pupils flared like a hungry wolf's.

He curled his lean fingers under her jaw. 'That can be fixed,' he said. Then he brought his lips down on hers with deliberate, sensual purpose.

At that first firm touch, a fiery tingling sensation shot through her veins like an electric charge, and sent an immediate swell of warmth to her breasts.

A shudder roiled through Connor's tall frame, as with a gruff little sexy sound he increased the sizzling pressure and sent her blood temperature soaring.

She tried to remember he was her adversary, and made a half-hearted attempt to cool her response, but he drew her in closer. Then, like the cunning devil he was, he softened the kiss to clever, gentle persuasion, until the fire on her lips ignited her bloodstream and aroused all her secret, intimate places with erotic yearning.

Though he was a big, powerful man, he held her tenderly, his lean, tanned hands on her waist. His touch was so seductive that, instead of her putting up a sound resistance, her own hands went sliding across his ribs. Even through his shirt, the heat of his hard, vibrant body under her palms was so thrilling, she couldn't restrain herself from writhing with pleasure.

Just when she was ready to swoon at all the intoxicating sensations of hot, strong, tender man, he tempted her lips apart with his tongue.

The taste of him exploded in her senses like a sunburst. Faint tangs of coffee and toothpaste were overridden with another flavour, some arousing primitive essence that was surely unique to him. His devilish tongue slid through, teasing and stroking erotic tissues inside her mouth she hadn't been aware existed. The sheer pleasure of his artful, gliding tongue lit her with a fever that infected every little corner of her being.

Her insides went into involuntary meltdown. Boneless, she had to clutch at him for support.

And he was so satisfying to the touch. He was all hard muscle, bone and sinew, as strong and unyielding as steel. Through his shirt, the solid reality of him under her clinging hands felt *right*, and her breasts strained against her bra for—*something*.

As her brain swam in a drugged delirium the hot, panting hunger of desire stalked through her feverish body like a ravenous panther. She had little doubt Connor felt it, too, for on deepening the kiss he pulled her even harder against him, as though to experience more intensely her softness in arousing friction with his lean, sexy body.

His restless, seeking hands caressed her breasts, the curves of her waist and hips, and she burned for more. She let go of all her reservations about him and surrendered herself utterly. Lost in the escalating sensation, she hardly noticed a sharp little tweak of the shirt at her waist until she became aware of the scrape of his knuckles on the skin of her midriff. Then his hands came up to her shoulders, and he pushed her away.

The sudden cold shock left her gasping and adrift.

As she stood struggling to adjust to reality, her blood still heavy and inflamed, Connor stepped away a pace. He was breathing hard, his darkened eyes ablaze. An angry quirk curled his mouth. He held up his passport and waved it at her.

'Did you really think you'd get away with this?' The clipped words were like a face-slap.

'Oh. Oh, that.' Impossible, considering how flushed she must have been already, but she felt her ears grow hot enough to spontaneously combust. 'Look, I did intend to put it back, but you—you came in too soon.' As his expression impinged on her brain her breathless, husky voice grew more strained. 'I couldn't think of what else to do with it. Sorry.'

'*Sorry.*' Several conflicting emotions warred on his handsome face. Astonishment, bemusement and—judging by the compression of his stirringly sexy mouth—contempt. He gave a sardonic shrug. 'Well, I hope you were satisfied with what you discovered.'

Stung by his disdain, she was reminded of his callous behaviour when she'd been so anxious over her letter, the letter he'd *stolen*, and felt her own anger flare.

'Well, I'm not satisfied,' she snapped. 'And I won't be satisfied until I get my letter back.'

'What?' He stared at her, then his face changed and his dark eyes lit with amused comprehension. 'Oh, your *letter*. Of course.' To her absolute fury he had the insensitivity to laugh. 'Still searching for that, are you?' His smile slowly faded and his gaze softened as he read her hot, flushed face, her heaving breasts. 'Ah, but it was worth getting caught, though, don't you think?' He reached forward and brushed her mouth with his finger. 'Delicious, Sophy.' His deep voice was velvet with sensuality. 'You must come and search again.'

She felt the strongest desire to murder Connor O'Brien.

She turned on her heel and yanked open the door, and had to restrain herself to walk with dignity and not run. When she reached the clinic, she strode blindly past Reception without seeing a soul, then stalked through her room to the window, where she stood gasping in air and trying to cool her face.

She was in a confused daze for minutes, then thoughts finally seethed to the surface in her brain. She absolutely loathed that man. She would get her letter back. And she would make him *suffer*.

Later on, though, after she'd cooled down and had time to analyse her feelings, she realised her humiliation was not so much about being caught. She didn't feel as guilty as she should about breaking in. The circumstances had demanded a bold move and the opportunity had been too good to throw away. She didn't really even feel bad about the passport. That had merely been the result of an unfortunate sequence of events.

The thing that was tearing at her, eating her up, gnawing at her soul—was that kiss.

She covered her cheeks with her hands. If she hadn't responded to him… She felt herself grow hot all over again at the thought of her undeniable enthusiasm. She hadn't seemed able to help herself. And he… *He* had seemed equally involved during the—event. She couldn't forget, though, how quickly he'd regained his cool, while she'd still been so hot and aroused to the bitter end.

What was truly humiliating was not knowing why he'd kissed her.

Had it only been because he'd known she had the passport?

Or—because he'd wanted to?

Connor finished shelving his books and closed the glass doors. The latest developments in his field as they applied to the rules of war had been his daily practice for years. Now, seeing the tomes lined up so proudly, his curiosity was aroused about what might have changed in human rights practice on the domestic front. This would be a good opportunity to catch up.

He glanced about him with satisfaction. His short-term hired furniture looked quite impressive. He could almost imagine what it would be like to set up here for real, with Sophy Woodruff in the room next door.

She was a puzzle. If Sir Frank's suspicions had any foundation, she was the most unusual operative he'd ever encountered.

He made a wry grimace at himself, still getting over his astounding lapse of judgement in leaving his passport unsecured. All at once Sir Frank's warning about him reaching his use-by date had a prophetic ring to it.

He would have to assume she'd have noticed the difference in his passport, forcing him now to some further embroidery of his cover story. Still, the lapse could work in his favour. Only a man with nothing to hide left his office door unlocked.

He smiled to himself, remembering her petrified expression in the first instant he'd surprised her search. Her clear blue eyes, alight with mingled horror and shame—that hint of a laugh dying to break out.

The question was whether she was inept, or very, very clever.

Whatever she was searching for now assumed crucial dimensions. With her being prepared to risk being caught in his office, she had to be near desperate, although there was no doubt she'd played her role of nervous bravado to perfection.

Of course, she still might have done if she were Sir Frank's other possibility—a rapacious predator seeking to lift a besotted middle-aged man from the marital nest.

That wasn't how she'd tasted, though. His blood stirred at the memory of her response. Her surrender had felt genuine. Fresh, and sweet… He had to admit he'd surprised himself. It had been a long time since he'd come so close to losing control.

His instinct for self-preservation made a belated attempt to drag itself off the floor and assert its presence. He should never have done it. There was a price to pay for kissing sensitive women with soft, ripe lips. That sort of addiction could grow cruel.

Squaring his shoulders, he reminded himself of the rules taught to him in the hard school of grief and loss. He must never allow a woman into his life. His code must be absolute. No woman could ever cross the threshold of his domain, and whoever she was, however tempting, he would never enter hers. An occasional rendezvous in some anonymous hotel room, a partner who gave the minimum and expected nothing in return, were the most he could ever risk, for the woman's sake, as well as his own.

Connections, emotions, attachments—all off-limits. Fraught with every kind of danger.

It occurred to him that Sophy Woodruff might simply be what she looked—an innocent—then he dismissed it at once. Sir Frank's hunches were legendary. He wouldn't have been so rattled over a non-threat. And why would a young speech therapist in a children's clinic be tangled up with a cold-blooded bureaucrat like Elliott Fraser?

Unless Elliott was suffering his mid-life crisis. Connor shrugged cynically. Understandable, in Elliott's case, but what could be her excuse? Wouldn't there be plenty of virile lads her own age to appreciate her charms?

Strangely, instead of the boredom he'd expected, he felt intrigued enough to find out.

Surveillance wasn't his favourite activity, but he was as skilled as the best at the essential basic levels of tradecraft. His ability to blend into any crowd, or vanish in an instant, had saved his life, as well as others, from more than one assassin. If there was anything to uncover, he had absolute confidence he could do it, silently and undetectably, without a whisper of him ever having been there.

His blood quickened. Keeping an eye on her would be too easy, hardly work at all. He could still find time to catch up with his reading and keep the lines of contact open with his department on the other side of the world.

And he'd find that letter first.

CHAPTER FOUR

'SOPHY?'

Her grip tightened on her office phone. 'Oh. Oh, Elliott, I've been intending to call you. There's something—'

The curt, dry tones cut her off. 'I haven't time to chat. Look, er…now that we have something concrete to go on, I think we need to—discuss our situation.' The words were crisp and impersonal. 'Might as well get it out of the way. Dinner tomorrow evening a possibility for you?'

Her hopes leaped up. 'Oh.' Dinner…at his *home*? Visions of meeting Matthew and Elliott's wife opened out a golden vista of more dinners, family occasions, outings… 'That would be just—just *lovely*, Elliott. I'm so looking—'

'Good. The reservation's at The Sands. You know Shellwater?'

Her heart slumped back down. A hotel. Not exactly a welcome-daughter-into-my-life gesture. Still, it was dinner. An entire meal with the chance of real conversation, not a hasty coffee in some obscure café. She was making progress.

There was still hope. There was always hope.

'Meet you at seven.' He disconnected before she could say anything to warn him about her copy of the report. At least no one had approached him with it yet, perhaps because he'd been out of town. If Connor O'Brien planned to do something with it… Her insides clenched. If she couldn't get it back before she met Elliott, she'd have to confess to letting him down.

Although, she had to acknowledge her chances of retrieving it now had sunk to levels around the zero mark. She flinched from the notion of any further attempts at breaking in. Not that it would even be possible. To her mingled shame and amusement she'd noticed a locksmith at Connor's door the very same afternoon of the kiss. Locking her out.

Over the last week she'd encountered Connor several times in the gallery. The first time, the morning after the kiss, she'd been saying goodbye to one of her families at the top of the stairs. She'd been bending to talk to the child when she'd looked up to see *him* in his dark elegant suit, briefcase in hand, in the act of unlocking his door. He'd paused to watch the small transaction with his dark, unreadable gaze. As her eyes had met his, some electric frisson had crossed the space between them and she'd felt that hot, suffocating rush in her veins.

A couple of times he'd passed her, on the stairs or coming out of the coffee shop in the basement. Once he'd said, 'They're like the sky today.' Other times she'd tense as he approached, prepared for some mocking assault, but just like any ordinary acquaintance he'd say easily, 'Hello, Sophy.'

Except he wasn't ordinary. Every time she saw him it was a shock, and her pulse went into a dizzy race. He disturbed her dreams, and threw her senses into disarray. And she'd started imagining things. A couple of times, walking in the street, or queuing for the ferry turnstile at Circular Quay, she'd found herself looking around, unconsciously seeking his tall figure.

Even in the clinic, she couldn't ignore him. Cindy and the other receptionist had noticed him, and were always talking about him, relating sightings, *drooling*. Of course, they'd never had the experience of kissing him. They were lucky.

'Guess what, guess what? I asked him and he isn't married,' she heard Cindy screeching on one occasion. No need for Sophy to ask who she was on about. Who'd ever dream of asking him a question like that?

Sophy tried to close her ears to their fantasising, but it never worked. Like an addict, she found herself listening for news of him. She was ashamed to admit she'd even searched for him on the Internet, but hadn't found his name in particular, though there had been pages of references to some old Australian billionaire with the same surname who'd died the previous year and must have been a great benefactor, since he'd donated a whole wing to the Royal Children's Hospital.

That passport had been intriguing. According to the government Web site, the fact that it was red rather than the same blue as everyone else's meant he was a diplomat, or at least that he worked in foreign affairs or in some foreign embassy.

From what she'd glimpsed in her quick flip through, he'd certainly done a lot of travelling. She'd always pictured diplomats as being ultra smooth, sophisticated people with excellent manners and social savoir faire. She couldn't really imagine Connor O'Brien flattering women at embassy receptions, rushing to get them drinks or charming them on the dance floor. He was much more likely to be scowling at them from the sidelines. Unless…unless he was outside with them in the shrubbery. Kissing them.

But what was he doing in the Alexandra?

After Elliott's phone call she couldn't wait for her lunch hour so she could escape to the Gardens to think. As soon as she'd waved off the last of her morning clients, she threw her sandwich and a book into her bag, took the lifts down to the ground and braved the midday heat.

It was another scorcher. She stepped from the relative cool of the Alexandra straight into the merciless blaze of the sun. Heat rose from the pavement in a wave. As she waited for a break in the traffic the soles of her feet nearly fried inside her shoes, and she began to regret her impulse. Quite often friends from the Alexandra accompanied her to congregate under the trees, but today they'd had the good sense to shelter inside.

Still, the moment she passed through the iron gates and plunged into the labyrinth of shady avenues she felt the cooler air on her face and the deep, almost mystical feeling of peace green places inspired in her.

The usual lunchtime workers lazing on the grass were few and far between, preferring their air-conditioned offices. A couple of patient mothers stood wilting by the ponds as their children threw crumbs to the ducks, but Sophy bypassed the popular spots to walk further, beyond the rotunda and the central café to quieter regions, where the greenery was dense and lush. She chose a narrow, twisted path through the rainforest, paved with the rich, loamy leaf-fall from overhanging branches twisted with vines. The earthy scents of mulch and vegetation mouldered in the shimmering heat. The forest opened to a lawn where willows cast a deep shade, sweeping the grass with their long, graceful boughs, their luxuriant midsummer foliage shivering and trembling with every breath of air.

She sank onto the grass, then moved further in under the canopy to lean back against the trunk and dream in the aromatic, willow-scented air, her book face down on her lap, long leafy wands drifting around her. She imagined herself going to Elliott's house, feeling familiar there, being welcomed by his family and friends, treated like a daughter, a sister…

A tiny, niggling worry she'd been holding at bay forced its way forward.

Maybe she should cut those dreams off. Her own experience suggested that real life didn't necessarily work that way. People couldn't become like family unless they'd been raised as family. Unless… Really, perhaps she should face it. Unless they *were* family. Despite the kindness of her adoptive parents, they must have felt a barrier.

It was all about the bonding, Millie always said. Sophy had bonded with Henry and Bea, but they hadn't bonded with her. She didn't want to be ungrateful, but sometimes she wondered… Would they have just moved away and left her if she'd been their real daughter?

She'd wanted to go with them when she'd come to realise they were staying on with Lauren, but Bea had talked her into remaining behind to finish her uni course. Since she'd been well into her second year by then, and her clinical hospital practice had been organised, she'd seen the force of Bea's arguments, and stayed.

By the time the four years were up and she'd received her excellent job offer at the Alexandra, the urgency to follow them had diminished.

They'd paid her fare to fly over there for a visit once, and it had been fabulous, though too short. They wrote often, phoned at Christmas and on her birthday, and she'd been saving to fly over to see them again in her next holidays, but she still couldn't seem to get over the hole they'd left in her life.

Surely children were precious. She couldn't imagine abandoning a daughter if she had one. Giving away a child.

She let her mind drift, and as usual ended up dwelling on Connor O'Brien.

What did he hope to gain? Was it something she'd said that day in the mothers' room that had made him want to taunt her? Almost as though it had been mental telepathy, a movement made her glance up, and her heart skidded to a halt to see him standing there outside the tree's canopy, his dark eyes intent on her with that unfathomable expression.

It was such a shock she froze momentarily, hoping the wild fluttering inside her didn't show.

He was wearing casual trousers and a white, open-necked shirt, and carried a bag from the university bookshop.

'So this is where you hide yourself,' he murmured. 'I wondered.' He ducked under the hanging foliage and stepped into the shelter of the canopy, dropping onto the grass a metre or so away from her.

Her heart thudded into the mad erratic rhythm he always provoked, but she managed to say coolly enough, 'Doesn't seem to have worked, does it?'

Still, his words had pinged straight to her weakness. He *wondered* about her. Did that mean she was as vivid in his imagination as he was in hers? But he was an experienced man, sophisticated in the art of kissing. He would hardly have given her another thought, not in that way, anyway. Although why he had any interest in her at all was a mystery. Then she remembered the way he'd looked at her in the gallery, and felt the warm surge to her breasts, the shortening of her breath.

He rolled back his sleeves. She tried not to watch, but the exposure of his forearms, their scattering of black hairs, was a reminder of the glimpse she'd caught of his naked chest at their first encounter. She felt scorchingly aware of every small thing about him, the crisp black hair crinkling slightly at his temples, his lean, elegant hands, their nails clean and manicured.

He lounged back, one arm resting on his bent knee. Her eyes were drawn to a faint mist of moisture gathered in the bronzed hollow at the base of his throat. *Salt to taste.*

His dark gaze rested on her face with sensual appreciation. 'They're the colour of the sea today. Cool and deep and mysterious.' He drawled the words to give them added impact.

Mysterious. Thank heavens for that at least, though she didn't feel very mysterious. She felt—bombarded. That sexy note in his voice. He was being definitely flirty. No, bolder than flirty. Seductive.

She raised a cool, mysterious eyebrow. 'So what's a diplomat doing in the Alexandra?'

He answered at once in his deep, smooth tones. 'Ah, well, I'm not strictly a diplomat. Not what you'd call a career diplomat, anyway. I'm a lawyer. I was hired by the government as extra staff for the embassy in Iraq. My contract with them is finished, so I'm doing some reading to catch up on the domestic scene before I open my doors. Not that I would ever need to open them to you.'

She ignored the gibe. 'Why do they need a lawyer?'

He hesitated. 'They have quite a few lawyers in various departments. My field is humanitarian law. That means…well, in the international sense it deals mainly with the fallout of war. Prisoners, refugees, etc. Because of the war, the embassy in Baghdad has a heavy load of people requiring assistance. Some apply to come here as refugees, or Australians who get caught up in the war need advice.' He flashed her a mocking glance. 'I thought you'd have found some of this out when you were snooping.'

'Certainly it *looked* as if you were a lawyer.'

He didn't reply at once. She glanced at him and his acute dark eyes were fixed on her face, calculating, assessing her. Then he said with a quirk of his eyebrow, 'Only looked?'

She shrugged and plucked at a blade of grass. 'I'm not so sure you feel like one.'

He blinked, but his dark gaze didn't leave her face. 'To kiss, you mean?'

Her nerve jumped and she felt heat wash through her. She knew it showed in her face, but pride wouldn't let her lower her gaze. 'No,' she said, keeping her voice steady, conscious of her pulse beating in her temples. 'That's not what I mean.'

It was hard to appear cool when her heart felt as revved up as a Formula One racing engine. Her last words seemed to throb in a silence that stretched and stretched.

Connor, on the other hand, looked relaxed, his long limbs at ease. As though unaware of the tension, he said easily, 'What's that you're reading?'

She hesitated, then with the utmost reluctance flashed him the cover of her book, hoping he'd miss the couple engaged in the hot clinch. He screwed up his eyes and leaned forward to read the title aloud. 'What is it? A romance?'

'As a matter of fact.'

He smiled, as though to himself. As if he were amused by her choice, but accepted it as typical. 'Not my kind of thing.'

Unreasonably annoyed, she retorted, 'Maybe you should read some. You might learn how to treat a woman.'

He gave her a long look and the amusement in his eyes deepened. She felt her face grow hot and had to turn away to avoid that knowing, sinful scrutiny.

Oh, God, why had she said that? She knew now why he had that scar on his ribs. Other people besides herself wanted to kill him.

He plucked a willow frond from the tree and put the end between his lips. 'Found your letter?'

'You know I haven't.' There was a raw note in her voice.

'How would I know?'

'Because you have it.' She'd never meant to come straight out and accuse him, but the words slipped off her tongue before she could stop them.

He was silent. She could feel him choosing his words. 'Why do you think so? Why would I do something like that?'

'To torture me.' As soon as she'd said it, she flushed again, knowing how melodramatic it sounded.

She felt his eyes travel down her throat, to where her shirt opening hinted at the valley between her breasts. She lifted her gaze to his and recognised in his eyes' dark depths the desire that couldn't be concealed.

'Torture can be a two-way street,' he said softly.

She turned her face away and fought to calm her tumultuous pulse.

Connor noted the quick colour in her cheek and couldn't repress a small, dangerous surge of triumph. It was seductive to draw a response, and he instantly regretted the words. Temptation was always easier to fight unacknowledged.

'I told you the first time we met I haven't found your letter,' he said, to quell the vibrations he'd let loose. Anything to silence his conscience. He was rewarded to see hesitation in her face. To further convince her he added, 'If I had, I'd have given it to you. I have no interest in your correspondence.'

He felt unexpected remorse for having to deceive her. There was vulnerability in the creases of her smooth, pale forehead, but the truth was there was nothing he was more curious about now than the contents of that letter. Was it from a lover? Instructions from her controller? Although what situation would require the use of hard copies in these days of slick communication? He took in the soft flush of her cheeks, the rapid pulse in her throat, and his resistance to the idea of her being a player rose up again.

He couldn't imagine her as Elliott Fraser's mistress. His glance fell on the slim hand clutching the book in her lap. The nails were trimmed short, as if the hand was unafraid of dirt. Hardly the talons of a predator. Everything about her seemed—natural.

His palms tingled with an urgency to seize her slim, smooth arms, pull her across to him and taste her again. Her ripe mouth, the feel of her soft breasts. That delicious moment of her surrender had stayed with him. Remembering it now, he felt himself stir.

He made another attempt to initiate a peace move. 'Why do you think I have it? Was it because I—teased you the other morning?' He held out his hand to her. 'I shouldn't have. I'm sorry.'

She met his eyes with a clear intelligence in her blue gaze that shook him. Her voice was low and earnest. 'Whatever you say…whatever you *say* your intentions are—I *know*, I have a very strong feeling that you're lying to me.'

Stunned, he failed to react at first when she stood up and snatched up her book and bag. Then he wanted to grab her hand and pull her back down beside him, convince her he meant well. Kiss her. But she flung through the screen of willow fronds and walked quickly away, almost at a run.

His muscles tensed in the almost irresistible male compulsion to pursue her, sweet-talk her, force her to acknowledge the attraction, but he knew he must restrain the urge. Once desire had been spoken of, sooner or later consummation would follow, then all the inevitable madness—passion, addiction, obsession…

The *hell* when he had to leave her.

He shouldn't have succumbed to the temptation today to hear her voice. Already he'd allowed his discipline to slip, and now he'd be haunted by the vision of her dreaming here under the willow tree.

With an effort he forced himself to concentrate on the task in hand.

Though his surveillance had been necessarily limited without the benefit of back-up, he was pretty sure she hadn't met Elliott since Monday of last week. Her routine was fairly predictable, divided between the Alexandra and her home in Neutral Bay. No evening rendezvous to date. Apart from one evening playing netball at a local club with her friends, she seemed to spend a lot of her time in her garden greenhouse.

It was time to focus some attention on Elliott. Where did he go in the evenings?

CHAPTER FIVE

WHAT did a woman wear to dine with her father? Something modest, but elegant to show she thought him worth it. Pretty, so he could be proud of her.

Sophy had quite sickening butterflies, partly from excitement, and partly from dread at having to tell Elliott the truth about losing the letter. Nearly every piece of clothing she owned was strewn across the bed before she settled again on her initial choice, a slim dinner dress in purple silk georgette with narrow straps.

Demure enough, she hoped, even though the dress fell short of her knees, and cool, even for the heavy heat hanging over the city. The shade enhanced her eyes, and in the right light somehow managed to find violet highlights in her hair. She twisted the dark mass into a loose chignon and secured it with a tortoiseshell clasp.

Should she confess to him at once, she wondered, fastening in a dangly earring, or wait till the meal was under way and some genuine rapport had been established?

In the beginning she'd planned to drive there, but the possibility she'd be drinking wine decided her in the end on taking a taxi.

She left it late to phone for one, then had a nerve-racking wait while the minutes ticked closer to seven. Would Elliott still be there if she arrived late? He always seemed so pressed for time, so impatient to get away, her chances of getting to know him could be ruined by this one ridiculous hitch.

'Wow.' Zoe paused when she saw her, her green eyes widening. 'Hot date? Come on, Soph. Who is it? *Spill.*'

Normally she'd have told everything. So when she hedged with, 'Er…just meeting a friend,' her flatmate's curiosity shot up along with her eyebrows, but, without lying, it was the best she could do until Elliott gave her the all-clear. Then she'd happily shout her secret to the world.

The taxi came at last, too close on seven for comfort, and carried her through the dusk that was still warm, even for midsummer. As they turned into the Steyne and drove along the beachfront, the full moon had just announced itself on the south-eastern horizon, a soothing relief after the angry sun. The cab slowed, and they drove in under the portico of a large hotel with several balconied storeys.

The Sands.

Sophy paid the driver and got out. Even this close to the sea the air was unusually still and warm, but, after the searing heat of the day, comfortable on her skin. She took a moment to smooth her dress with her palms while she surveyed the hotel entrance, her pulse ticking along too fast, every nerve and instinct on edge.

At one end of the hotel, tables and chairs spilled onto a terrace strung with coloured lights, and she could hear what sounded like the hum of a crowded bar. A flickering neon sign announced a casino as part of the complex's attractions. It was a resort, and she felt some surprise. She'd never have imagined Elliott dining in a place like this.

Inside, there was an excited buzz to the busy lobby as people came and went to the various entertainments. A careful scan showed no sign of Elliott among the patrons seated in the lounges. From somewhere came the strains of a band and occasional applause, while through an archway a wide bar thronged with the noisy pre-dinner crowd. Beside it, separated by a barrier of palms and cycads, was the hotel restaurant, already filling with diners.

She approached the entrance and looked eagerly for Elliott. The large room was inviting, all gleaming wood surfaces, with candles on the tables catching the sparkle of crystal and cutlery. Down a step, a lower level opened to the beach terrace, where a tiny dance floor had been laid under the lights.

There was an energy to the place, and she felt a surge of pleasant anticipation. Had he chosen it to please her?

This was it, she thought. Make or break time with her father. Conscious of her thudding heart, she was about to take her turn at the desk and give Elliott's name to the head waiter when Elliott materialised beside her.

'Miss Woodruff is my guest,' he cut in before she could say anything.

There was a moment of awkwardness when she half expected him to kiss her cheek, but it didn't quite come off, though he greeted her with courtesy. She held out her hand but he seemed not to notice. He must be nervous, too, she thought, curling up her fingers, though she suffered a faint twinge of anxiety. Still, realistically, how could he be expected to know how to behave with a new daughter?

They'd work it out, she told herself. It would come with time.

'This way,' he said smoothly, almost touching her arm, but not quite, as he indicated a table on the upper level by the bar.

She smiled her thanks as the waiter pulled out her chair, and placed the linen napkin on her lap. While Elliott made bland conversation, about the heat, Sydney traffic, she kept smiling her responses, barely able to speak for trying to control a sudden, irresistible wave of emotion pricking at the backs of her eyes. To think she was actually dining with her father.

The menus were presented, and she read hers through a mist. She hardly knew what she ordered. But Elliott's discussion with the waiter about the wine gave her a chance to recover some poise. She listened with pleasure, though she wasn't surprised he was so knowledgeable. Everything about him, his articulate command of language, his clothes and grooming, suggested he was an experienced man of the world.

It wasn't her first meeting with him, but the previous ones had been rushed and rather furtive, in places with poor lighting. He'd seemed stressed and curt on those occasions. Now he was more relaxed, and while they conversed she had a better opportunity to study him, and see him for the person he truly was.

His hair had nearly all turned to silver, though there were still dark edges at the temples. His face was well-shaped, with regular features. His grey eyes looked cold, but he almost certainly would have been a handsome man when he was young. It wasn't surprising that her mother had been attracted to him, even if they had only made love on the one occasion. Although Elliott claimed he'd hardly known her, it nagged at Sophy that he *had* known that she'd died. So he must still have known her to some degree, or known *of* her, despite the way he'd told it. And he must have known she'd had a child. She hadn't been adopted by the Woodruffs until she was two years old.

She thought she could understand him glossing over the truth a little. And with all the tremulous emotion churning around inside her she decided to hold off interrogating him. He was probably just as much an emotional melting pot tonight as she was herself. He wouldn't have invited her here if he didn't intend for their relationship to develop. There was no use spoiling things.

The chardonnay arrived and was poured, the menus were removed and a small silence fell. Elliott Fraser sat with downcast eyes, taking a moment to gather his words. Then he said very quietly, 'I'm prepared to give you a cash payment of one hundred thousand dollars, once and once only. That's quite a sum for a young woman like yourself. In return, I expect you to sign a confidentiality agreement. My lawyers are drawing it up.'

The words broke through her blur as if from a very long distance.

She stared at him, uncomprehending, then leaned forward. Her lips felt suddenly numb. 'Do you think I want money?'

He studied her, frowning, a hard light in his eyes. 'Well, what do you want, Sophy? Why does an adult woman hunt down a man she has no connection with, apart from a mere technicality—an accident of birth?'

After a moment of shocked paralysis she shook her head. 'Oh. No, no. That's not—that's not it at all. Please…' Impulsively, she reached across and touched his hand, but he drew it away at once as if he'd been touched by a leper. Something like a knife stabbed her insides. In her dismay her throat became as hoarse as a dry gulch. 'I…I only wanted to—'

'To what?'

The ridiculousness of her hopes flashed in on her and her words dried up. As she faced the hostile reality of him an excruciating embarrassment invaded her. What a fool she'd been. As far as he was concerned she was a stranger. An accident of birth.

She mumbled, 'To—to get to know you.' She felt the heat crawl up from her ankles and creep to the roots of her hair. How dumb she must sound. If he ever had any inkling of the dreams she'd allowed to grow…

His mobile phone rang, and, still frowning at her, he took it out and spoke into it. He rose, the phone to his ear, and murmured, 'I must take this call. Excuse me, I'll be back in a minute.' He hesitated. 'We'll…er…talk.' Then he walked away, talking into his phone.

She clung to her chair, every muscle in her body clenched. A wave of nausea washed through her. Who'd have thought her evening would have ended so bitterly?

She felt an urgent need to get away. Find a cab, fly home and hide herself. Forget Elliott Fraser and the whole damn thing. It wasn't as if she needed a father figure in her life, was it? She already had one she loved quite extremely. At the thought of Henry her eyes filled up with tears. She wasn't sure she ever could bear to lay eyes on Elliott again.

Except…she wasn't a child, or a *nothing*. The pleasant, busy restaurant swam and she tried to will the tears away for fear of someone at a neighbouring table noticing her dabbing at her eyes. So what if she was the result of an accident? She was still a person. She had a heart and feelings, hopes and aspirations, affections, talents… Her fingernails dug into her palms.

She couldn't allow herself to be so dismissed without standing up for herself. She'd started the process, for whatever insane reason. It had seemed like the right thing, the *human* thing to do, almost like a sign from Fate the day she'd first seen him in the clinic. Other people sought their birth parents without this sort of reception.

Her disappointment turned to dismay on Elliott's account. What did his response show about him?

She must at least finish the evening with dignity. Make him understand that not everyone was eager to use their biological connections for financial gain. Although, a man who thought that way… Would it ever be possible to convince him?

The waiter brought the first courses, and her soup sat cooling in front of her. As often lately when she was alone, she had that strange sensation in the nape of her neck, as if she were being watched. She glanced around at the other diners, but they seemed blissfully unaware of her and her little problems. They were tucking into their food, chatting and laughing, at ease with themselves and the world. None of them looked to be suffering a crisis. Life was going on for people with normal family connections.

After a while the waiter appeared and suggested removing the meals, to keep warm until Elliott returned.

The call was taking some time.

It was none of his affair, Connor thought, hunching forward on his bar-stool. Sophy Woodruff wasn't his responsibility. If he leaned a little to the left of the shrubbery, he could see her quite clearly, reflected in the mirror behind the bar. She was sitting quite straight, a stiffness in her posture, like pride. Or hurt.

He glanced at his watch. Elliott had been gone nearly ten minutes. He realised he should have been more alert to Elliott's departure from his table. Though, surely he wouldn't have walked out on her? If they were lovers…

They couldn't be lovers. Where had been the touches, the lingering glances?

He considered the moment when she'd leaned towards Elliott. There'd been supplication in the gesture, pleading… Elliott was a chilly guy, by anyone's standards, but his response had been curious, to say the least. What man in his right mind would have resisted her?

Although, whatever had taken place between them in that tense little confrontation hadn't looked like a lovers' quarrel. Where was the fire and passion? He remembered enough about intimacy with a woman to recognise when it was missing. So how far had the affair gone? Had they slept together more than once?

Still, it did have all the hallmarks. The meetings, the place. He glanced about him at the mix of dress worn by the clientele. As if on cue an Elvis impersonator entertaining the crowd in the neighbouring bar smooged into 'Love Me Tender'. No fear of Elliott running into his acquaintances here.

An unpleasant thought assailed him. Surely she wasn't part-timing as an escort?

The bartender cocked an eye at him but Connor shook his head. His drink could last all night if necessary. As he could, occupying his corner with the chameleon skill he'd honed to a fine art.

He glanced at the bar clock. Thirteen minutes. Where the hell was Elliott? Was he imagining it, or was there desperation in the look Sophy Woodruff was casting about her? Was she starting to worry about her rich Romeo?

Not that it mattered to Connor O'Brien. He just wished he hadn't been cursed with this vivid imagination. He was only guessing she was distressed from the tension in her slender frame. So what if Fraser had hurt her? She'd learn from it and maybe steer clear of married, older guys in future.

Although he needed to be realistic. Why would a young woman

want a middle-aged man like Elliott, when she'd almost certainly have hot-blooded, younger guys lining up for a taste of those luscious lips, her warm, vibrant body, so soft and pliant to the touch—unless it had to do with the Fraser millions?

His musings about Elliott's age and virility suggested another possibility for his lengthening absence. Maybe the guy had some health problem. Connor got casually off the bar-stool and strolled around the corner to the men's room. There were a few men in there, but no Elliott. He walked out again to survey the lobby. The crowd was beginning to quieten, but he could see no sign of the ageing silvertail. He turned down the corridor to the car-park entrance and peered through the glass doors.

His car was still where he'd left it, parked a few spaces along from Elliott's. At least, from the space where Elliott's *had* been.

The rat had run.

He felt a dangerous quickening in his pulse as he strode back to his corner of the bar. He tried to cool it with an astringent dose of professional realism. Either she was a gold-digger, or she was infatuated with an older man, neither prospect very desirable.

So why did he so desire?

He shouldn't go over there. Revealing his presence would be a mistake. It would jeopardise his investigation. He didn't know enough yet to exonerate her from having a hostile agenda, did he? And she wasn't a fool. She wouldn't swallow the coincidence of his being at the same hotel on the same night.

Unless he could come up with a story.

Another glance in the mirror. He saw her look bravely about her, a bright little expectant smile on her lips, as if to signal to the world that her date would be back at any second, and his grip tightened on his glass.

The bastard, leaving her alone in a place like this, a plum ripe for the plucking to every sleazy opportunist.

God, he was playing with fire, and he knew it. She was a walking, breathing, flesh-and-blood temptation, a bigger threat to him than a dark alleyway and a sly stiletto blade.

His struggle intensified. He couldn't afford any involvements. Although if he just talked to her, maybe she'd give him a simple explanation for her association with Elliott. A little conversation could do no harm. It didn't have to lead to a night of passion.

Not unless…she wanted it to.

His brain filled with images of soft, firm flesh, slender, shapely limbs tangled with his among the sheets, but he pushed them aside. She wasn't the type.

He lifted his glass to his lips and drained it. Suddenly the hunch he'd had about her overwhelmed him with rock-solid certainty. She was no agent for any intelligence service. She was a speech therapist in a children's clinic.

Looking to improve her financial status with an older, married man, perhaps. Way out of her depth, undoubtedly.

But that was *all*.

'Sorry, I have an emergency I must deal with. Please continue your dinner as my guest. I'll be in touch. E. Fraser.'

Sophy crumpled the page of hotel stationery in her hand. The rejection slammed in deeper. She could hardly have expected Dad, but *E. Fraser*?

A band had set up down on the lower level, and a few people were gyrating about on the dance floor to an old Stones song. She could feel some nearby couples' curious glances at her as they speculated about Elliott's desertion.

She gathered up her purse to leave, then tensed in shock. The lean, athletic figure of Connor O'Brien was strolling through the dining-room entrance, with all the casual assurance of someone for whom The Sands was a second home.

Her pulse plunged into a wild racket, fuelled by a sure, instinctive knowledge. He was here, because *she* was.

He was following her.

She saw him lower his dark head to speak to the head waiter, then glance straight across at her. Tensing, she reached for the wine specials pamphlet tucked between the salt and pepper shakers and pretended to read, refusing to look up, as if the specials were of more importance than the missing fragments of the Dead Sea Scrolls. All the time she knew Connor O'Brien was advancing on her with cool, steady purpose.

'Sophy.'

The quiet resonance of his deep voice had its usual volcanic effect on her insides. It took a moment before she could gather the emotional energy to raise her eyes from the pamphlet, and when she did, her lashes seemed to join in the wild fluttering of the rest of her. He was all in shades of black—black dinner suit, black shirt and gleaming black silk tie. With his ebony hair and eyebrows and midnight-dark eyes it was hardly safe to look at him, he was so tall and lean and sinfully handsome, looking down at her with that faintly amused glint as if he knew, he *knew*, damn him, how he affected her.

'This *is* a pleasant surprise.'

'For you, perhaps,' she said, finding her voice. Comprehension flickered in his dark gaze and she had the horrible suspicion she might have let him know just how humiliated she was to be sitting there alone.

'What are you doing here?' As if she didn't know.

He glanced about, as if in search of her companions. 'Mind if I sit down?' He pulled out Elliott's chair, and dropped into it before she could protest. 'I was supposed to meet someone, but I'm embarrassed to say she stood me up.'

A jagged sensation assailed her in the midst of all her chaos. Who was this woman Connor O'Brien had wanted to meet? 'I can understand your feeling embarrassed,' she said softly. 'As I can understand her wanting to stand you up.'

A muscle moved at the corner of his mouth. 'It's not something I'm accustomed to. I must be losing my touch.'

'Your touch isn't so fantastic, if you want to know.'

Their eyes met and he smiled. Sophy felt the flush rise in her cheeks as the memory of her enthusiastic participation in that kiss shimmered in the air between them. She lowered her lashes, determined not to let his sexy, teasing gaze get to her, although her pulse had started a mad, erratic gallop. Her suspicion that he'd followed her grew even stronger. It was impossible to imagine a woman standing him up.

'What about you?' His voice was as smooth as silk. 'Are you with someone?'

'Of course. Well, I—*was* with—someone. My—friend was called away to an emergency.'

His eyebrows lifted. 'Pity. And he didn't take you with him?'

'No. Well, he—he couldn't.'

'Ah.' He took the chardonnay Elliott had ordered from the ice bucket and examined the label before putting it back. 'He must be crazy.'

She glanced quickly at him, but his dark eyes were warm, without the usual mockery that threw her so off balance. For a second she nearly gave him the benefit of the doubt, until he had to ruin it.

'He wasn't that silver-haired guy you were with just now, was he? Don't you think he's a bit old for you? He's probably past it. He saw you sitting here like a ripe little peach in the candlelight and realised he wasn't up to it, so he scampered.'

She drew a sharp breath, then leaned forward and hissed, 'I knew it. You've been spying on me, haven't you? Just what's your game, Connor O'Brien? Why are you stalking me?'

Something like shock flickered in his dark irises and a muscle twinged in his lean, bronzed cheek. '*Stalking* you?'

She was sorry she'd blurted it out like that, because he stiffened and his expression grew quite haughty and defensive, as if she'd insulted his very honour. With his high, austere cheekbones, his dark brows and lashes, he looked so stern, such a model of outraged decency, she wondered if she'd been imagining things again and overreacting.

With cool deliberation he poured a little of the chardonnay into Elliott's glass, swirled it about, inhaled its scent, then tasted it. 'I was here before you, as it happens,' he said. 'I was waiting in the bar, when who should come sashaying up to the restaurant but Sophy Woodruff? How do I know *you* aren't stalking *me*?'

'Oh. You know I'm not.'

'How do I know? You break into my office—'

'You *know* why I did that.'

'Oh, that's right,' he said, looking sardonic. 'You came to apologise. You wanted to kiss and make up.'

She gasped. 'Rubbish. I only kissed you that time because—I was—*desperate*.'

He laughed and she could have bitten off her tongue. *God*. Why did he always have to trick her into saying things that sounded so green? He must have thought she was the most naive and unsophisticated woman he'd ever met.

He plucked the wine specials pamphlet from her nerveless fingers and gave it a cursory glance. 'Fascinating ,' he murmured. 'I can see why you were so interested.'

The impulsive words burst from her. 'I really loathe you, Connor O'Brien.'

His eyes lifted to hers and she saw their amusement gleam with a sexual challenge that pierced through her flimsy defences like a sword through paper.

'Are you sure?' he said softly.

He wasn't joking now. She shook her head, scrabbling for some words to come up with a massive and convincing denial, but he forestalled her.

'Shh. Don't say anything you might regret. I'm sorry, all right? Truly. For everything.' With rueful charm he placed his hand over his heart, or at the least the place where it ought to have been. 'Isn't it time we let bygones be bygones? Come on, you know you want to.'

Then he smiled. He never really had before, not like that, though she'd noticed his eyes smile, or soften. Now, as his lean, handsome face illuminated with warmth, the breath nearly seized in her lungs and her interior melted like honey dripping through the comb.

Ravished to their entrails, all of her instincts made a wild, excited surge towards *'Yes.'* Well, nearly all. There was still that nebulous part of her that found something worrying about him, even though he was so straight and tall and gorgeous.

On the other hand, he had an honourable profession most people, including herself, found impressive. Zoe seemed agog to hear more about him every night.

It was hard to know how to trust him, he was so difficult to talk to, with his mockery and sardonic teasing. There were barriers around him she had no idea how to breach. And, of course, there was her letter.

Although in truth, after that day in the Gardens, she'd actually started to believe in his innocence about that. It just didn't make sense that a human rights lawyer would steal a stranger's DNA profile just for the hell of it. She'd even started to go soft on him in some of her other imaginings.

And right now he seemed sincere. The dark eyes dwelling on her face were intent, and so attractive, with golden shards of candlelight reflected in their depths.

She didn't want to give in too easily, though. She said stiffly, 'You'd have to change your attitude.'

His black brows twitched. 'What attitude?'

'You know very well. Always mocking people.'

'Oh, that. All right. I promise I won't mock. So…' He smiled and held out his hand. 'Friends?'

Somehow, despite the constriction of her lungs brought about by being dazzled by smiling dark eyes, she managed to breathe, 'I suppose. Friends.'

She allowed him to take her hand into his smooth, warm clasp. The glow in his dark eyes intensified, and it took him several vibrant seconds to let her hand go. When she got it back, it was still madly zinging.

'I like your hair up,' he said warmly. 'It makes me want to pull it all down.'

Did friends say things like that? Perhaps it was the aftermath of emotional upheaval, after her rocky start to the evening, but there was a dizzy, racing sensation in her blood.

She tried not to show it with a cool demeanour. 'Oh. Well, anyway, I'm about to go home now, so—'

He trapped her hand again. 'No, don't go.' He signalled a passing waiter and the boy changed direction and swerved their way at once. 'A menu, please. Miss Woodruff will dine with me. Won't you, Sophy?'

Perhaps she should have refused, but time was marching on, and what with all she'd been through, with Elliott leaving her to rot in a public place miles away from anywhere, she still hadn't managed even a bite to eat. It couldn't count as a date, exactly, but she'd hardly be human not to have felt the tiniest twinge of pleasure and pride to have such a prime example of tall, sexy masculinity looking at her like that.

'And we'd like one of those tables down there,' Connor informed the waiter, indicating the terrace. 'Wouldn't we, Sophy?' He bathed her again in one of those intimate, seductive glances and her bones melted.

Those tables did look inviting. The musicians had started an old Bee Gees number, and couples were swarming to dance under the coloured lights. While the waiter transferred their setting and darted away to find him a menu, Connor held out his hand to her and drew her down to the lower level and out to the terrace.

There was a magic in the vibrant midsummer night, or maybe it was the exhilaration of Connor's arm slipping around her waist. The warmer-than-usual air caressed her skin and made her feel pleasantly sensual. The moon had risen into its full glory, and hung seemingly quite close, the breathtaking golden orb glowing in silent mystery. There was the occasional white flash of a wave breaking on the sand, and always underlying the noise and activity of the restaurant the constant swoosh and fall, the rush of foam on the beach.

Connor saw Sophy Woodruff's lovely glowing face as she gazed at her surroundings and felt something inside him lurch. With an effort, he dragged his gaze back to the waiter and ordered the snapper. He wouldn't have risked it in some places, but he had complete confidence in Elliott's choice of restaurant. There was nothing wrong with his chardonnay selection, either, so he settled in to fill Elliott's shoes, drink his wine, eat his coquilles, woo his girl. It was, after all, a golden opportunity.

He'd had a twinge of doubt earlier, but seeing her now enjoying her tempura mushrooms, dipping them into their sauce with such naturalness and poise, he allowed himself to relax. He reminded himself that if she were Elliott's girlfriend, however soft she looked, she was no ingénue, likely to pin too much on a casual evening.

And she did look luscious, the lavender of her dress reflected in her eyes, her smooth, bare arms and shoulders meltingly soft in the candlelight. The soft fabric of her bodice made two graceful curves over the creamy swells of her breasts and dipped to the shadowy valley in between. His lips tingled at the thought of tracing those delicious curves, but he quelled the image.

This was work. There'd never be a better opportunity to broach the subject head on. Enough information tonight, and he could wrap it up and report back to Sir Frank.

He kept the conversation firmly on her, finding out what he could about the women she lived with, her schooling, her parents in England. Much of it coincided with what he'd already found out himself.

She seemed so frank and open, if she *were* acting and it was all a cover, she was good. But could she be? His doubts returned every time he met her clear gaze.

He had to know. It could risk the rapport he was building, but he had to find out, once and for all. He chose his moment when they were nearly through their main courses.

'There was something very familiar about your friend,' he said casually. 'He's not Elliott Fraser by any chance, is he?'

Her eyes flew to his. The slim hands wielding the salad servers jerked and remained poised in the air for a second.

'Do you know him?'

'Not exactly. But my father and his were great friends. They were in business together at one time.'

'No, really? Goodness, that's such a coincidence.' Sophy stared at him, trying to accommodate the notion of him knowing Elliott and his family, however remotely. What were the odds? she wondered, examining the likelihood from all sides. She shook her head. 'It's quite amazing.'

'Not really.' He gave an easy shrug. 'Not if you know anything about the old Sydney establishment. All those old boys know each other, join the same clubs, go to the same concerts, send their kids to the same schools. Dad played golf with Sir Frank every Thursday for thirty years. You've heard of Sir Frank Fraser?'

'No,' she heard herself say, raising her glass to her suddenly dry lips. 'Elliott hasn't mentioned him.'

'Oh. So—you and Elliott haven't known each other very long?'

She lowered her gaze, reluctant to be reminded of her disappointment. There was a painful raw spot inside her now with Elliott's name on it. Just thinking about him hurt. Still, she couldn't repress the craving for more information. After all, this was her *grandfather* Connor was talking about.

She sent him an oblique glance. 'No, we haven't.'

He was silent, a small frown creasing his brow.

'What's the matter?' she enquired.

'Just that…' He narrowed his gaze and hesitated, as though seeking a way into a difficult subject. Then he shrugged. 'I guess—Fraser may not have told you he has a wife.'

She looked sharply at him. His eyes were watchful on her face. Surely he didn't really think…

'Are you serious?' She might almost have laughed if the implications hadn't been so insulting. Her Lana Turner impersonation must have been better than she'd thought. She leaned forward, demanding, 'Do you honestly think I'm having an *affair* with Elliott?'

He paused in the act of pouring wine into her glass. 'Well, you tell me.'

She stared at him in amazement. People swayed to the music, lovers were whispering under the moon, but Connor O'Brien was gazing intently at her with a grim expression, waiting to hear what excuse she had about seeing a married man.

'Well, apart from the fact that he's—' She pulled herself up just in time. She'd come too close then to blurting out the truth. Without lying, though, it was hard to know what to say, or how much. She didn't want to risk alienating him and wrecking the new accord. Hedging, she said flirtily, 'Why should I tell you?'

He dropped his dark lashes for an instant, then said softly, 'Because I need to know.'

The words thrilled through her like a wave. Perhaps it *was* a date. Another realisation sprang to the forefront of her mind. If he'd truly suspected, even for a second, that she was seeing Elliott, then he mustn't have read her letter. He couldn't have stolen it. He'd been speaking the sincere truth.

As she contemplated his lean, strong face across the table her heart swelled with a joyous relief. She could acquit him.

A whole new world of possibilities opened up before her. She could trust him, they were friends now, he *liked* her… More than liked, judging by that hot little flame in the eyes flickering to her throat and breasts, rousing sparks in her blood and sending her pulse into a giddy race. Compared to him, the boys she'd known before had been just that. Boys.

She raised the last forkful of filet and salad to her lips and said carefully, 'Actually, Elliott did tell me he has a wife.'

'And a child?' he added, suddenly quite still.

She nodded. 'Yes. I saw Matthew—his little boy. He brought him to the clinic.'

He set down his knife and fork. 'Is that where you met Fraser? At the clinic?' There was a note of incredulity in his voice.

She hesitated, uneasily aware that if she made it sound too mysterious, she'd only fuel his curiosity. 'That's where I first saw him. I only met him later. There was something I needed to—speak with him about.'

'Oh.' His eyes lit up. 'So the boy's your client?'

That excuse would have been convenient, but regretfully she had to wave it goodbye. 'Well, no.'

It would have looked curious, she supposed, observing Connor's bemused gaze. She wished she could just be honest and tell the truth, but despite Elliott's treatment of her this evening, it would be such a betrayal. He might not want a daughter, but without her knowing the consequences he was so fearful of, how could she judge him?

With a little shake of his head Connor O'Brien complained, 'You're being very mysterious.'

'I know, I know. I don't mean to be. It's just that—I have an agreement. I've made a promise, and I must keep it.'

'Oh, a promise.' He nodded, his eyes narrowed. 'Right.'

Instead of being satisfied, though, he only looked more puzzled than ever. His black brows edged closer together. 'You're not in any trouble, are you, Sophy?' He spoke lightly, as though teasing, but the dark eyes on her face were keen. Surprisingly—though it might have been a trick of the candlelight—they seemed touched with concern.

'No, of course not. What do you mean, *trouble*? Just because I met a man for dinner?'

He sat back, contemplating her, his lean fingers toying with the stem of his glass. 'An older, married man. *Much* older, and much married, in fact.' He raised his glass to his lips and said meditatively, 'He'll be keen to make amends, I guess. I'm betting tomorrow he'll send you flowers, at least. Maybe chocolates. Who knows? He might even pitch for diamonds.'

'Diamonds. Oh, please. Get real.'

'Well, he *is* very wealthy.'

'*Is* he?' Her eyes widened involuntarily. She had assumed her father was quite well off, judging by his clothes and the fact that he looked like a successful businessman, but this made it seem as if he might be very well off indeed.

Her heart sank and she chewed her lip. It wasn't good news for her. If Elliott was rich and powerful, he probably had a lot more to lose by acknowledging a twenty-three-year-old daughter. Perhaps she should have found out more about him before jumping in feet first. She had looked for information about him on the Internet, of course, several times since she was eighteen, without finding him mentioned anywhere. He wasn't listed in any phone book. She'd had to rely on what he'd acknowledged about himself.

Import-export, was what he'd told her at that initial meeting. What did that mean? Probably just a smokescreen to hold her at bay. Like inviting her here tonight, then walking out on her because he thought she was an opportunist.

Diamonds indeed. What a laugh.

Then the full horrific implication of Connor O'Brien's meaning finally seeped through. Did he think she was a—*prostitute*?

Unfortunately, the insult came too close on the heels of the wound Elliott had inflicted. She met his gaze angrily. 'Oh, I get it. Thanks. It's good to know people think the best of you.'

To her absolute shame then, some emotional subterranean river

chose that instant to rise to the surface and attempt to flood its
banks. Tears sprang into her eyes and she had to turn her face away.
She tried to smile and say something offhand, but her croaky voice
was a dead giveaway.

How many magazine articles had she read that stipulated that
whatever a woman did, on no account should she weep in front of
a man? Especially one giving her a candlelit dinner. Her housemates
would have been appalled at her letting down the side so disgrace-
fully. Men only felt contempt for women who used tears. She hated
them quite heartily herself. If there'd been any members of the
Avengers netball team present, she wouldn't have blamed them if
they'd stormed across the room, grabbed her by the throat and
shaken her till her brainbox rattled.

In Connor O'Brien's case, there was a sudden rigidity in his posture. His fingers seemed to freeze to his glass. As she fought to regain
control his stunned dismay reached her from across the table. Even
in her moments of extremis, she forgave him his blunder. After all,
he wasn't to know what Elliott had said before he dumped her. She
blinked rapidly a dozen or so times and somehow forced the dam
back behind the wall.

He broke the fraught silence, treading gingerly. 'Er…you didn't
know the Frasers were wealthy?'

The dam wall threatened to burst again, and she lifted her shoulders in stiff denial. 'Whatever Elliott Fraser *has*, whatever he *does*,
is nothing to do with me.'

The lines of his lean, strong face tautened. 'Look, I…' He reached
over and gently grasped her arm. Shamelessly, despite her turmoil,
fireworks flared in her flesh. 'I'm sorry if I seemed to imply… I saw
you there with him and…well, I was naturally intrigued.'

She glanced down at his hand on her arm, and he released her
and sat back. It cost her a struggle, but she managed to keep her voice
cool and steady. 'Maybe you're just naturally suspicious.'

He shrugged and his handsome face hardened into its usual calm expression, though there was a slight darkening of the taut skin across his cheekbones.

He kept glancing at her, and the silence grew alive with vibrations, as though her small upset had generated some massive, underground repercussion. Her fault, she castigated herself, for showing her true feelings over what had been perfectly natural questions anyone would have asked.

Their eyes clashed accidentally and the hunger in Connor O'Brien's clutched at her breath and made her insides curl up at the edges. She glanced quickly away, her body absolutely zinging with awareness, and tried to keep her attention on the dancers, though all the time she was conscious of him lounging back in his chair, his long fingers loose on the stem of his glass.

She felt a smouldering heat surge to her breasts. It was as clear as the moon sailing over the sea. He didn't trust her.

But he wanted her. Sensing it stirred something primitive in her blood.

Since the kiss—why couldn't she admit it?—she'd dreamed of him. Kissing him. Now that she'd had first-hand experience of how very sensuous his lips could be, looking at them made something coil deep in the pit of her abdomen.

She felt a trembling certainty about him. With his beautiful hands, his long, lean limbs, so much about him was so attractive.

The waiter came to remove the plates, then offered her the dessert menu. Connor O'Brien waved his away and ordered coffee. She opted for a slice of chocolate truffle cake.

All through the exchange with the waiter she could feel Connor's hot gaze devouring her like a dissatisfied wolf, his sexy mouth grim, the dark shadow of tomorrow's beard adding to the little frown lowering his black brows. Dying to know more, she supposed. Weighing up what sort of woman she was. *Judging* her.

He lowered his glance, but not before she saw his eyes. God, that hungry little flame made her feel reckless.

'Anyway,' she challenged on an impulse to inject some lightness into the mood, 'what's it to you, Connor? You aren't checking up on me, are you?'

Something flickered in his expression, but he said smoothly, 'Hardly.'

But he was mad keen to know about her, she could feel it in him. And she could sense the desire simmering in him, connecting him to her like a burning fuse. Whatever this was, it was for real, she realised with an adrenaline lurch. It was nothing like the tepid attractions she'd felt in the past. Even being grilled by him on such an uncomfortable subject somehow fanned the fever in her blood.

The slice of cake appeared before her, a faint dew on the frosting, scrolls of flaked chocolate on top. Beside it was a strawberry in a swirl of raspberry sauce.

'Well,' she said, taking up her fork, 'however it might look, you're mistaken. My—association with Elliott Fraser is not what you seem to think.'

He hardly seemed to be listening. His dark, sensual gaze was devouring her face, lingering on her mouth. 'What is it, then?'

She sat up straight, admonishing him with a stern look. 'It's a private matter between him and me, and no one else.' She waited for him to reply, and when he didn't felt herself flush with annoyance. 'Oh. Do I look so *hard* to you?'

Connor roused himself from his sensual contemplation of her. The sincerity in her wounded blue gaze struck deep. He took in the defiant tilt of her delicate chin, the poignant little hurt smile on her lips, and his suspicions fell in a heap.

After all the lies and deceits he'd lived through in the last few years, he should know truth when he heard it. He cursed himself for a fool. He'd been seeing her as a suspect, when the blindest idiot could see… Whatever the private matter was, she was an innocent. Sir Frank had got it wrong. A desirable, tantalising innocent.

'No.' He heard his own voice growl up from his depths. 'You don't look hard.'

She smiled at him then, with such sweet generosity he felt like the biggest bastard on the eastern seaboard. She waggled her fork at him and said huskily, 'That's just as well if we're going to be friends.'

He leaned back in his chair and watched her slide the fork through her truffle cake and lift it to her mouth. Each time her lips closed over a morsel he imagined the chocolate melting on her pink tongue, trails of it trickling off into the moist slipstream of her mouth. His loins stirred into dangerous life.

She picked up the strawberry in her slim fingers and bit into it.

He closed his eyes briefly, his body a torture chamber. Why were the most desirable women always the most forbidden? It was against his rules, it was a gigantic bloody risk, but he did what any red-blooded man would have done. He pushed out his chair, stood up and smiled down at her.

'Do you feel like dancing?'

CHAPTER SIX

KISSING Connor O'Brien had been thrilling. Dancing with him was a wild, erotic rush on a dreamy floating ride to…

Desire.

'How deep is your love?' the song called to Sophy's blood, as irresistibly as the moon beckoned the sea. She allowed him to lead her onto the tiny crowded dance floor, and for a breathless moment faced him, the night an elixir in her veins. O'Brien surveyed her with his dark, seductive gaze, then slipped his arm around her waist and pulled her close.

His familiar feel and scent thrilled in her senses in a potent reminder of the kiss. At first, remembering what a fool she'd made of herself then, she tried to hold herself aloof, not to inhale his thrilling, spicy maleness, not to be so conscious of his lithe, athletic body, the long, powerful thighs burning into hers.

'Relax,' he murmured against her ear, his hand firm and sure in the small of her back. 'Just dance.' His mouth brushed her ear, her senses swayed, and she surrendered herself and melted into him. He gave a deep sigh, and drew her closer.

And it was intoxicating. His chest against her breasts. His fingers caressing her spine, stealing into her nape, his hard, angular frame, the occasional brush of his knees, his lips in her hair.

Dancing was such a good excuse for touching. She'd heard of

women who could dance all night held in a man's arms, suspended in a dream. She must have been made of different stuff, because for her it became too difficult. Too—sexual. Or maybe those women hadn't been dancing with Connor O'Brien.

He gazed down at her, his eyes heavy-lidded and aflame, and her lips dried in yearning for his sexy mouth.

His shadow-roughened jaw grazed her temple, and inside her strapless bra her nipples swelled and peaked with shameless longing. All at once she felt the thrust of his arousal against her and her desire ignited as if she were drunk and out of control.

She panicked and pushed him, broke from his arms. 'It's too hot,' she said breathlessly, turning away from the dark flame in his eyes, 'much too hot.'

She stood still amidst the noise and motion of the crowd, her heart thudding, smoothing down her hair and dress with trembly fingers, then with a glance at him threaded her way from the dance floor. He followed without touching her, but in some intangible way she felt the arousing textures of him on her skin as if she were still in his arms.

Back at their table, while she poured the last of the water into her glass, Connor signalled the waiter. With cool efficiency he settled the bill, avoiding looking at Sophy. To her intense disappointment, he stood up and drew out his car keys.

'Ready to leave?' he said, finality in his decisive tone. 'I'll take you home.'

She shrugged and collected her purse, regretting her ridiculous flight from the dance floor. Why had she done it? How uncool he must think her. How naive, when it had felt so fantastic, being held in his arms. It was barely even midnight. If he took her home now, the evening would be over, and there'd never be another one.

She could hardly suggest another dance.

Rising from the table, she turned to look down at the beach. The moon had climbed higher now, and its golden glow had paled to a silver shimmer, finding an occasional glitter in the dark sea. Below the beach wall the sand gleamed softly white.

Connor started to move away, and on a sudden breathless impulse she said, 'It is a shame, though, to go home early on such a beautiful night.'

She saw him pause, tension in the set of his wide shoulders. After a couple of thumping heartbeats he half turned, the keys jingling in his hand, and she felt the flare of heat as he flicked her a glance from beneath his black lashes. His voice was deeper than ever. 'Well…what would you like to do?' His eyes followed her gaze to the beach.

'Perhaps—a walk?'

He hesitated. She could sense conflict in him, the tensing of muscle, the struggle against hard-headed purpose, but with a deep nervous tremor of excitement she knew he would come. After a moment he slipped his car keys back into his pocket, and her spirits rose, along with her anticipation.

Without touching, they descended from the terrace and crossed the grass verge and the beach walk. On the steps down to the beach she paused to slip off her heels, then stepped onto the sand, wriggling her toes, sighing with the bliss of its cool, silken feel under her feet.

'Gorgeous,' she exclaimed. 'Don't you want to take off your shoes?'

His face was shuttered. 'What for?'

'*Well,*' she said, spreading her arms, and twirling, 'to enjoy it all to the utmost.' She held her face up to the moon and inhaled the salty sea air. 'Smell the smells, hear the roar, feel the spray on your face. Isn't this the ultimate sensual experience?'

His eyes glinted. 'It's *one* ultimate sensual experience. Don't tell me you're one of those people affected by moonlight.'

'Well, I *am* a Piscean.' She smiled at him. Though his eyes burned, they were deeper than ever, mysterious pools. She held out her hand to him, and he shoved his in his pockets. Her heart gave a nervous lurch. She felt suddenly out of her depth. What would she talk about to him, a man she hardly knew, on a beach?

She strolled along with him, away from the hotel and the bright lights. The tide was low, and she followed his lead down to the hard-packed sand on the water line where walking was easier.

Occasional voices floated on the air as people strolled up on the walkway, enjoying the cooler air after their restaurants and entertainments, but the beach itself was deserted, apart from herself and Connor.

The moonlit angles of his face gave him a moody, remote beauty. Even without touching him she could feel the electric tension in his big, lean frame. It connected with hers, in every nerve cell of her body, despite the wall he'd put up. And she could sense his reluctance. Maybe that was why she needed to fill up the space between them with a stream of reminiscence about the Woodruff family holidays, good times she'd had at the beach with Henry and Bea, funny things that had happened to her as a child.

Listening to her chatter he thawed a little, asked the occasional question, even allowed himself a laugh once or twice. Whatever was eating him, the real Connor was there below the surface, the one who'd charmed her just a few hours earlier and rescued her from her social embarrassment. And all the time she was conscious of the silent conversation underlying the one they were having. The magnetic pull that tautened with every wave that broke on the shore and filled her with an exhilarated suspense.

They had almost reached the big rocks at the foot of the headland, when she was startled by the icy shock of foam rushing to kiss her bare feet.

'Oh,' she shrieked. 'Look out. We've come down too far.'

'The tide's on the turn. Come.' He motioned her away, to follow him further up the beach, into the shadow of the rocks at the base of the headland where the sand was cool and deep.

She ran clumsily after him, sinking ankle deep into sand, giggling when she accidentally stumbled against him. He took her arm and steadied her. The brief brush with his body, his firm grip, sent a yearning shiver though her. For a second his intense dark eyes held her breathless, then she moved away from him, into a patch of moonlight.

She could feel his desire as tangibly as the sand under her feet. And his grim resistance.

Night gave the place a primitive, magic quality that infected her with fever. Every sound and texture—the rush and ebb as little runnels of sea water found their way back between the cracks and crevices of the rocks, the shadowy places in between, the warm, caressing dark—in some way they all connected to her and infected her with excitement. Or perhaps it was Connor O'Brien.

A wildness inhabited her. She overflowed with the need to do something reckless and fantastic. Her limbs, her breasts, were languorous with longing. She felt as if the silver moonlight were inside her, as if her skin should shimmer like the scales of a fish.

She held up her face to the moon and stretched out her arms. She could feel Connor's hot eyes on her, sultry embers in their brooding depths.

'Are you ready to go home yet?' His deep voice sounded strained, as if he longed for the answer against his will.

'No.' She laughed giddily, and tilted her head back, stretching out her arms and closing her eyes to bathe in the magic light. 'Don't take me away yet, Connor. I'm drinking in the moonglow.'

'What are you? A witch?' A huskiness had crept into his voice.

With a thundering heart she heard him draw near. She opened her eyes and her pulse skidded as she read the desire in his burning dark gaze.

For a moment he stood as rigid as the rock-face, his handsome face taut and intent, then he reached out and touched her arm with his finger. The vibrant connection sparked an immediate leap in her flesh. As though unable to tear his hand away, he traced her arm and the line of her shoulder to her neck, sparking a trail of fire in her quivering skin.

'You're made of alabaster.' She could hear the dark turbulence in his voice, in his heavy, controlled breathing.

She had no hope of controlling hers. She was trembling, her heart pounding with a tumultuous beat. 'No,' she breathed. 'Just flesh and blood.'

His hands closed around her arms, then he pulled her against him and brought his mouth down on hers in a searing, hungrily possessive kiss. Her blood leaped in immediate response, madly coursing to inflame her nipples and her private, intimate regions.

This was it, she thought. Her time had come.

Wildfire danced along her lips, inside her mouth, wherever his marauding tongue touched the tender, erotic tissues. The taste and scent of him, his big solid body pressed against her, felt so voluptuously sensual she writhed in his arms, grasped at his powerful shoulders, clutched restlessly at his silky, thick hair.

She was ablaze. Her skin felt so sensitised, she thrilled to every touch of his hot, urgent hands caressing her nape, arousing her breasts, roving over her hips. The delight of his big, firm hands on her body was a sensual revelation. She'd never experienced such arousing pleasure.

And her palms ached for the feel of his bare skin. Tentatively, she released a couple of his shirt buttons and slid her hand in to touch his chest. The heat of his skin scorched her palm. Her fingers found the jagged scar over his ribs and she felt a deep tremor rock his big body.

She drew back, searching his dark face, but he was in the grip of a primitive concentration. He pulled her hard against his pelvis and ground his hips against her so she could feel the rigid length of his erection. Desire flared between her thighs. It was so intensely arousing, she couldn't have run now if she'd wanted to. Mesmerised by the dark magic of his mouth on her throat, her breasts, his hands on her wild, feverish body, she clung to him, thirsting for more.

She'd never been touched so intimately. He slipped his hand under her dress and stroked her bottom through her pants. The tingling fire rippled through her flesh and made her crave for his questing fingers to travel further and satisfy her delicious ache.

He kissed her again, open-mouthed, tongues teasing, then when she was nearly ready to faint with the pleasure of him drowning her senses with his heady masculine flavours, he drew back to gaze at her, his dark eyes flaming with a piercing sensuality, as if to appraise how ready she was for further delights. 'You're gorgeous,' he said, breathing hard, his deep voice rough with the passion contained like a powder keg within his powerful body. 'Who could resist you?'

He drew her further into the shadows and she went willingly, thrilling with anticipation as the passion momentum prepared to escalate.

He pulled her down onto the sand with him and slipped her straps from her shoulders, kissing the places where they'd been. Then he trailed tender, sizzling little kisses along the bodice-line of her breast, down to the dip at her cleavage. The sensation of his lips and shadow-roughened jaw on the tender skin of her breasts sent her wild. Half swooning while he stroked her with one hand, she felt him pull at her zip with the other.

Her bodice slipped a little and she felt the air on her naked breasts. He drew back a little, then sighed and gave a deep groan. 'God, Sophy Woodruff. You're too beautiful.'

He stroked her breasts, then took them in his hands and kissed them, tasting the hard nipples, to her amazement nipping them with his *teeth*. Astonishingly, her desire fanned to such a blazing inferno she kneeled up and clutched his shoulders, kissing his mouth and pressing wild, passionate kisses into his strong, bronzed neck and all over his gorgeous powerful chest as if she were a starving virago, ready to eat him alive.

He gave little shudders of pleasure, groaning and half laughing at the same time. Suddenly he put his arms around her and pressed her to him. Then he laid her down on the sand with him and kissed her mouth with such fierce, tender passion she felt as if he were drawing her very soul from her body.

'Connor,' she whispered urgently when the kiss broke and she'd dragged in some air. Her body was on fire with a reckless yearning. 'Do everything to me.'

He gazed at her intently, then sat up. 'Here. Lie on this.' He took off his jacket and spread it on the sand for her.

He stretched beside her, leaning up on his elbow while he un-buckled his belt. In the shadowy light she saw the hot gleam in his dark eyes, but she felt shy about watching him lower his trousers, and looked the other way.

With a potent, sensual touch his hand travelled up from her knee, under her dress, then paused when he connected with the edge of her pants. Thrillingly, he traced the elastic edge around her thigh with one finger, pausing when he reached her inner thigh. She stilled with the tingling anticipation, not daring to move in case he stopped. Then he stroked her with his fingers, through the flimsy material. The pleasure was so intense, she gasped and panted in quick, shallow breaths. Just when her excitement mounted to an almost unbearable pitch, he bent to kiss her from her navel down to her pants, igniting fire wherever his lips touched. He paused at her pants' upper edge. The delicious suspense became excruciating, then he suddenly tweaked them down, right down over her knees to her ankles.

She lay on the sand, naked from the waist down, her heart thun-dering in her chest. She'd never felt so exposed, and was glad Connor O'Brien couldn't see her blushing like a teenager. Even in the dark, though, she could see the flame lighting his eyes, and appreciated with tremulous gratitude that this was her moment to be a real woman, to make an adult exchange with a man without fear or shame.

And such a man. The moonlight cast certain planes and angles of his face into relief, highlighting the severe lines of his hard, mas-culine beauty.

His slumbrous gaze rested on her nest of dark curls, and he began to stroke her there. After what she'd participated in already, she knew her reluctance to part her thighs was unreasonable, but she kept them pressed firmly together. Connor didn't seem to mind, though. His eyes just gleamed the brighter.

Casting her a seductive, smiling glance, he bent to, oh, so softly kiss the dark tangled curls. Then gently, teasingly, he slipped his hand between her thighs, and she let him part them.

He paused to search his trouser pockets, then after a muttered exclamation glanced up at her. 'Do you have anything with you?'

His deep voice was darker than the shadows in the cliff-face. She heard a wave crash with what sounded like increased ferocity, the surge and retreat of swirling foam as it was sucked irresistibly back into the boiling surf.

'What do you mean?'

'Protection.' He spoke softly, but there was an urgency in his tone as he added, 'Condoms.'

She widened her eyes. 'Me? No.'

Breathless moments ticked by while he scanned her face with his hot, hungry gaze, then he drew away from her and sat up. 'Ah…hell.'

She leaned up on her elbows and touched his arm. 'Don't you have any?'

'I thought I did, but, no.'

His disappointment was so apparent, she exclaimed, 'I'm sorry, Connor. I didn't expect… I've never thought to… I've never had any reason to carry them.'

He gave his head a wry shake. 'And you a feminist.' Then he cast an appraising glance over her and smiled, lilting his brows. 'There are, of course, other ways.'

'How do you mean?'

She flushed then, realising how naive the question had been. For goodness' sake, how many issues of *Cosmo* had spelled it all out? How many fascinating post-mortems had she sat through with the girls over the breakfast table?

She corrected herself swiftly, 'I mean, of *course*. I know there are.'

His eyes glinted and narrowed on her face. She felt the sudden blood beat in her ears as a small frown gathered between his brows.

'What did you mean when you said you've never had any reason?'

She supposed she'd have to admit this sooner or later. She sat up and pulled down her dress, held her bodice up with one arm to cover her breasts. 'Just that I...' Her cheeks felt hot. Lucky it was quite dark. 'Well, you know, I haven't actually slept with anyone before.'

He stared at her, blinking. 'What?' He stilled to rigidity. For a second his lean frame could have been carved in stone. Then he let out a groan. 'My God. Tell me you're not saying you're a virgin.'

She'd always known there'd be a moment to admit this, and it might be embarrassing. Shaming, even. She was probably the oldest virgin in Sydney, possibly Australia. But, ever the eternal optimist, she'd always hoped *he*, whoever he was, would just accept it.

Gazing at him now, he looked anything *but* accepting. Her heart was pounding, but this time with an accelerating anxiety. Loath to show it, though, she said, 'It doesn't make any difference, does it? I mean, as you say, I can still... We—*we* can still make love, however you say... I'll—I'll do—whatever... Whatever you...'

Connor heard the tremor as her voice trailed off. The rock-hard, throbbing reality of his desire hardened further to taunt him. He saw her mouth swollen with his kisses, saw the sudden lowering of her lashes over her glittering gaze, and burned to have her.

But, God almighty, whatever his sins, he had some sort of a conscience. He forced himself to turn sharply from her and dragged himself to his feet, disappointment eating into his soul like bile.

'Connor...' He heard shame in her voice and his gut squirmed as his pain reached a crescendo.

'Don't talk to me. Don't look at me,' he ground out. 'Go away from me. Take yourself away.'

In the raw silence that followed as she stood up behind him and fixed her dress, his thought processes clicked in and helped a little in the cruel dousing of his erection.

How could he have allowed himself to succumb? Once he'd had her, he'd never keep her at arm's length. She'd want more. For God's sake, *he'd* want more. Impossible visions flashed through his mind—seeing her every day at the Alexandra, picking her up at her place, taking her to his place…

Familiarity, intimacy. Involvement.

And the things she'd said. *Make love*, as if they were a couple. Hell, she'd expect him to be her boyfriend.

An unbidden image of her nude body lying in that big empty bed flashed through his brain, and he struggled to banish it. As he buttoned his shirt, fastened his clothes over his aching arousal, he forced himself to concentrate on non-sexual things. On seaweed, and rocks and the creeping tide. On his rules and his unwavering commitment. On responsibility, and broken bodies and his hollow, broken life.

He picked up his jacket and shook it. Her innocence had been plain to see from the start. When had he ever got it so wrong? It was all his own fault. He'd seduced her to this point and now she had hopes of him. *We can still make love* echoed in his brain like a reproach.

He should never have given into temptation. He deserved to be shot.

When it felt safe enough, halfway at least, he looked around to see where she'd got to. She was a long way down, walking up the beach towards the steps, shoes dangling from her fingers. Her proud head, her slender neck looked so achingly vulnerable in the moonlight he felt something twist in his chest.

He caught up to her before she reached the hotel steps. 'I'll drive you home.'

'I'll get a cab.'

'No, *I'll* take you home,' he said, cool and ruthless as he had to be, knowing he was a brute. He would rue it all in the tortured night to come, cringe when he recalled his necessary savagery. 'You'll never get a cab out here at this hour.'

Ignoring her refusal, he guided her with brusque purpose through the hotel to the car park. He asked her for directions, although of course he knew the way.

The trip to Neutral Bay was silent with strain, but he made no effort to alleviate it. The more she suffered, the better for her in the long run.

He drew up in the silent leafy street in front of the old federation-style house, as if for the first time. He felt her glance as he pulled on the handbrake, and saw her hand reach for the door handle, ready for a quick escape.

'Thanks…'

'Don't thank me,' he said harshly, shamed by her good manners. He got out and went around to open her door, watched her slide out, walk past him to the gate without looking at him.

'Don't bother to come in,' she threw over her shoulder.

Stung, though he knew he deserved the worst, he still felt the need to insist, 'I'll walk you to the door.'

He followed her up a honeysuckle-scented path at the side of the house to where a light glowed on a porch. She bent to retrieve her key from a flowerpot. Even this evidence of her sweet humanity added to the black weight building in his chest. As she struggled with the lock he saw that her slim hands were shaking, and his darkness intensified.

'I won't come in,' he said when she'd got the door open, in case she still harboured expectations.

She gave him a withering look and started to close the door.

'Wait.' He shoved his foot in the crack and reefed his fingers through his hair while he tried to think of an exit. 'Sophy—let me explain.'

Her eyes glittered in the shadowy light. 'Don't,' she replied in her low, husky voice. 'You don't need to explain. I should thank *you* for dinner.'

'Oh, Sophy.' Guilt riddled him with holes. 'Look… You are a—a very beautiful woman. I shouldn't have allowed your charms to overwhelm my good sense tonight. I think we were both affected by that damned moon.'

She made to close the door, but he caught her and pulled her towards him.

'Sweetheart.' He held her arms, feeling the trembling of her smooth body in his hands. He had the shamed sensation he was crushing something fragile. Why did she have to be so damned desirable? He watched the play of shadows on her face and felt himself being drawn back on the same wild riptide, almost unbearably tempted to kiss her and start it all over again. 'I don't want any kind of… I don't *do* involvements. I'm not the guy for you. It's—nothing personal.'

She twisted from his grasp. 'And there was I, thinking you were the man of my dreams. What a let-down.'

The gentle sarcasm triggered a slight rise in his blood pressure. He was glad it was too dark for her to see his sudden flush. He resisted the temptation to shift his glance, and stated with grim finality, 'I'm not a man for anyone's dreams.'

She stayed silent. That discomfiting light was in her eyes, as if she could see straight through him.

'Look,' he asserted, 'we'll forget all about tonight. Put it out of our minds. Nothing happened. There's no harm done. All right?'

Gently, but very firmly, she closed the door in his face.

CHAPTER SEVEN

SOPHY saw him the morning after, far too soon for her lacerated feelings. She was at the top of the stairs directing one of her parents to the basement coffee shop, when her stomach clenched. Connor O'Brien appeared, elegant in a charcoal suit, briefcase in hand, strolling along the gallery towards his office. In the same charged instant he saw her. His long, easy stride almost checked, then continued on, as fluid as ever.

He flashed her a smooth, untroubled greeting as he unlocked his office door. Somehow she forced herself to respond with her own punishing brand of cool.

It took ages for her galloping pulse to slow down. She retreated to her office and tried uselessly to concentrate on a report she needed to write about the young child she'd just seen. It was a strain, with her insides so sore and aching.

Unfortunately, she couldn't think of anything else except Connor. Typical, she supposed, for someone as green and gauche and naive as she'd been on that beach. Much as she wished she could wipe the excruciating events from her mind, she couldn't eradicate him from her senses. Everything he'd said, every kiss and caress, seemed branded into her.

She wasn't sure why she should feel such a sense of failure. Certainly, she was the only woman in Australia who could go to a moonlit beach at midnight with a sexy man and come home *virgo intacta*. It was a pity about the condoms, but it hadn't needed to have ended there. She'd have done anything he wanted if he'd only explained a little.

But, oh, *God*... She covered her face with her hands. If only she hadn't *told* him that.

She cringed to think of how put off he'd been. It was clear she'd disgusted him with her over-enthusiasm. And why had she behaved that way, like a wild, obsessed creature? Her insides squirmed in mortification as she remembered some of her wanton behaviour, and she had to get up and pace the room with her hands on her burning cheeks to walk the agony out of her system.

He had fancied her at the start, she was certain. There was no mistaking that. Even now, remembering the scorching desire in his eyes made her insides curl over. According to all the women's magazines she'd ever read, men *liked* passionate women. Even if they were virgins.

So why not her?

And why had he said those things to her at the end? All that stuff about involvement. It wasn't as if she'd asked him to marry her, was it?

A thought she'd been fending off since her agonised walk back across the moonlit sand clawed at the vital depths of her feminine being. She'd always understood that males were so driven by their passions, a man would be unlikely to refuse sex when it was on offer. Yet last night...

Could it be that at the critical moment, when it had come to the crunch, Connor O'Brien hadn't found her sexy?

Dismay sank through her like icewater. If only there were someone she could talk to about it. But, no, even if Zoe and Leah weren't away on holiday now, she could never admit her debacle. She could never talk about it to anyone, not even Zoe.

Elliott Fraser phoned during the morning, with apologies that for him were quite profuse. He explained his housekeeper had been called away on a family emergency and there'd been no one at home to look after his son. She felt mollified, in a listless sort of way. There could hardly be a better excuse than that. At least he'd put Matthew's safety first.

What he said next, though, might have given her wilting optimism a boost, if she hadn't been so good at listening between the lines. Elliott still felt the need to discuss their 'situation', and he wondered if she would be prepared to visit him at his home.

He went on to explain that since the housekeeper's availability was uncertain, and since it was urgent to lock down the 'problem'— *her*, Sophy supposed—and since they couldn't be seen meeting at their places of work and needed a private venue for a longer discussion, his house was the most reasonable available meeting place.

His house.

Great. Maybe.

For once, possibly because of the ache weighing on her heart, she had trouble keeping up her spirits during the conversation. The language Elliott had used clearly signalled his intention to tidy her away like an embarrassing nuisance. At one stage, as he'd talked, her pride had nearly propelled her into snapping, 'Oh, look. Forget I ever bothered you,' and hanging up on him.

She was glad she'd controlled the impulse, though. If she'd given into that one, she'd have lost all the headway, if any, she'd made so far, and any chance of getting to know her little brother.

So she agreed. Dinner, he'd said. He'd phone her again with a suitable night. She wondered who would cook it if the housekeeper wasn't there. Somehow, she couldn't imagine Elliott doing something so comfortable and hospitable himself.

After lunch, once the sun had gone off the window ledge she took a few minutes to water her drooping geraniums. It was then that she was shaken by another realisation.

The letter.

With all her anguish over Connor O'Brien, she'd forgotten about it. She tried to imagine confessing to Elliott, but after his hostile tone last night the thought made her go cold. The beastly thing was almost certainly still hiding in Connor's office where she must have lost it the day Millie moved. How long before he found it? And he *knew* Elliott's father. If he read it... She nearly went faint as the connections slotted together with lightning speed. Connor would inform the older man. Of course he would. He'd tell him his son had a daughter.

How repulsed, how unforgiving Elliott would be if his father told him he knew all about his love child, and he'd heard it from an old friend of the family.

She started to sweat, and it was nothing to do with the heatwave. For an insane moment she even considered asking Connor to search for the letter for her. Thank goodness her pride clicked in before she succumbed to that fatal impulse. With a sharp ache she realised she could never talk to him again.

There was nothing else for it. Somehow, whatever else happened, she'd have to find a way to retrieve it herself.

'So what's she like?'

Perhaps because of all the trees and shady pathways, Taronga Zoo seemed like an oasis in the heat. The air had turned more humid, and a few lowering clouds were bunched on the horizon, as if the long-awaited change might be in the offing.

Connor paused with Sir Frank to watch a giraffe's graceful floating glide across its enclosure on long, spindly legs. Legs that yearned for wide-open spaces. He frowned, troubled as always by helpless creatures. Beyond the animals' prison a snapshot view of Sydney Harbour shimmered in the searing sun, the iron span of the bridge hanging between two shores like a gigantic cat's cradle. Could a view compensate for freedom?

Sir Frank walked with the aid of a stick, his shrunken frame barely reaching Connor's shoulder. An excited seven-year-old tearing down the path ahead of his family group nearly barrelled into them. Connor grabbed the old guy and moved him out of harm's way.

'Don't they love it, even in this heat?' the old man marvelled when Connor had steadied him and the kid had been retrieved by a young woman with another child in a stroller. 'I could have brought Matthew if it hadn't been a pre-school day. This is one of our favourite haunts.' He popped a mint into his mouth and turned his beady gaze back to Connor. 'What did you say she was like?'

A virgin, was Connor's first knee-jerk response. Unavoidable, really, since lately he'd been giving virgins a great deal of thought. Not that he was a man who'd ever cared about such things. He wasn't sure he'd ever actually *had* a virgin.

He gave Sir Frank a straight look. 'Slim. Five-seven. Dark hair.'

He tried to fight it, but his thoughts insisted on returning to their honeyed trap. Translucent skin, softer than a peach's. Ripe breasts, exactly the fit for a man's hand. His fingers curled involuntarily into his palm. Sweet raspberry nipples…

'Beautiful? She'd have to be to compare with Marla.'

Connor forced himself not to react. 'Attractive enough, I suppose.' But a pang at his grudging admission sliced through him as the image that tortured his nights flashed into his head. Sophy Woodruff's face, her eyes shadowed with desire, lashes heavy and languorous, her smiling, edible mouth, meltingly eager for love.

Sir Frank shot him a glance. 'Well? What have you found?'

'She was born in Brisbane, family moved to Sydney at nine.' Conscious of the old guy's almost supernatural perspicacity, he carefully cut all expression from his tone. 'Grew up in Neutral Bay, still lives in the same house. Educated at local schools, attended Sydney University. Her parents are modest people, Beatrice and Henry Woodruff, currently out of the country. No siblings. She shares the house with two friends. Both nurses. I've checked and they're clean of all known connections. All of them.'

'*All?*' The old man's brows rose, then he nodded, accepting Connor's word. 'Right, right. I see. So?'

So what? Was she Elliott Fraser's lover? Not unless she was an Oscar-worthy actress. He hunched and shoved his hands in his pockets, tried not to think of the beach.

'It's not an affair,' he said curtly, anxious to move on from what was not his finest hour.

'What?' The old guy stopped, clearly surprised. 'Are you sure?'

Connor looked squarely at him. 'As sure as anyone can be.'

Perhaps he sounded a little terse, but the heat alone would make anyone short of temper. An urgency to call the whole thing off seized him. He felt a sudden anger that his precious isolation was being threatened by what was, after all, just an old man's suspicions. Wasn't he supposed to dedicate his skills to the security of his country? Who cared if Elliott Fraser made a fool of himself? Would the country be worse off?

Sir Frank frowned and shook his head. 'Then *what* is it? If it's not an affair— Are you definite she's not an operative? Have you searched her home?'

Connor bunched his fists in his pockets. He'd put off that distasteful task. For God's sake, what was he, a spook in some television show?

'She's a speech therapist in a children's clinic. She's bound by some kind of commitment not to speak about her connection with Elliott. Whatever it is—he's the one calling the shots. My guess is— it's something to do with the boy.' He paused in the shade of a mulberry tree overhanging the wombat enclosure and drew out the keys to his rooms. 'Here, Sir Frank.' He held them out. 'This is hardly my field. Hire a private investigator. Some bloke who doesn't mind peeping into windows and taking photographs.'

The old man eyed him for a moment, then waved the keys away. 'No fear, matey. What are you saying? You can deal with terrorists and assassins, but you haven't the stomach to check up on a girl?'

'A woman,' Connor corrected sharply. 'She's a woman.' He

glanced at Sir Frank and saw the old guy looking at him with that curiously penetrating stare he was famous for.

'*Is* she? Well, then. Do what nature cut you out for. Sweet-talk her. Use a device on her phones. Bug the woman's bedroom. You're so edgy, fella, a bit of feminine company might be just exactly what you need.'

Connor's intestines clenched, everything in him repulsed by the thought of spying on her as if she were some dangerous criminal. As if she were the one at fault. As if…

As if, for God's sake, after his treatment of her she would ever look at him again with anything except contempt.

Though he knew very well that, on the other hand—certainly in his case—fruit once tasted, then forbidden, only grew sweeter in the memory. His eyes drifted shut.

Sweeter, more irresistible, more mouth-wateringly desirable. And how much more would that obsessive hunger tug at her, a woman who'd tasted passion for the first time?

A virgin.

He crushed down a pang of shame at his brutal behaviour on the beach night. A woman's first experience with love was supposed to be so powerful as to be unforgettable. Hell, he could even remember *his* first time. What would Sophy Woodruff be likely to associate with her first real taste of sex? Until…

Oh, God. He let out a sudden breath.

Until some new guy came along and wiped the mess from her mind. There'd be someone along, soon enough. Some guy who was freely available to get involved. Hopefully, one with some finesse as a lover. Unaccountably, his gut tightened at the thought.

Virgins required tenderness. Sophy Woodruff needed a lover who could take her in hand and teach her gently how to enjoy her body. How to wring every ounce of pleasure from that luscious arrangement of curves. Someone who could take the time to arouse her properly, and take her to the heights…

He hoped the old guy's eerie prediction wasn't coming true. In an unnerving flash he visualised his precious objectivity as a fine porcelain plate, revealing the first fine, microscopic line that presaged a crack.

He clenched his hands. The only honourable way forward he could see now, the only safe way, was to leave town. Remove himself entirely from the scene, let her get on with her life, while he got on with his.

Such as it was.

He opened his mouth to inform Sir Frank he was bailing out, but the octogenarian must have been reading his mind, for he pursed his lips, nodding his head and musing, 'I suppose if the worst happened and you pulled out, I *could* pay some private detective.'

'*No.*' Connor's immediate reaction burst from a visceral level before he could control it. But the idea of some other guy striking up an acquaintance with her, tailing her, invading her bedroom, rifling through her things with his grubby fingers—her sweet, feminine, virginal things—was intolerable.

Surely—better himself than some sleazy amateur.

Noting Sir Frank's look of surprise, he made a swift effort to recover his cool, and injected some sense into the discussion. 'You don't want a stranger checking up on Elliott, do you? Who knows what he might find out?'

'That's true, that's true,' the old man replied, nodding sagely. 'You're right, Connor, it had better be you. And, look, son, choose any method you like. I know you'll get results.' His brow creased into a thousand worry lines. 'You know, however innocent it might look on the surface, I've got a very strong hunch there's something significant going on here.'

Sir Frank's driver hoved into view, walking towards them to collect the ancient and carry him off for his lunch. Connor waited a moment to watch Parkins aid the old guy's slow progress up the path in case he needed a hand, then, satisfied, turned down the slope towards the ferry wharf, lost in reflection.

Instead of relinquishing the task as he'd intended, somehow he found himself sunk in even deeper, like a man caught in quicksand. He would just have to ensure he was never alone with her again. The temptation was too great.

She might avert her face now when he passed her by in the gallery, but he could recall only too vividly the fire that lay buried beneath that ice.

He gave a rueful shrug. Virgins might believe they could douse the flames of desire by freezing a man out. It only went to show how much they had to learn about the male animal.

The breath suspended in his lungs at an unbidden thought. How—how very easily he could reignite that blaze.

Not that he would. It was simply a case of self-discipline.

CHAPTER EIGHT

ANOTHER Friday dawned, heavy and humid. Fog had rolled in through the night and wrapped the world in a shroud. On the ferry across to Circular Quay Sophy felt as if the damp had seeped into her soul. When the cloud finally dissipated, it left behind a sultry, brooding heat, as if some sullen fury were building and plotting to vent its vengeance on the world.

Even the Alexandra was overly warm. In fact, her very computer felt hot when she switched it on, as if it had already done half a day's work before she arrived. For a second she wondered if Cindy or one of the doctors had been in there, searching her files for something, then dismissed the notion. They'd never do that.

At morning tea she considered not going down to the basement to buy coffee, but couldn't sacrifice the opportunity to walk past Connor O'Brien's office and find out if he was there.

Maybe—she allowed herself the shameful admission—she'd run into him. She wished she could cut him out of her mind and go back to being her ordinary careless self, but now her awareness of him seemed to infuse everything she did, had turned her into a vessel of yearning. She kept imagining she could see his lean, handsome figure in crowds. Once, returning early from netball, she'd even thought she spotted him driving down her street. Another night, lying curled up on her bed in sleepless longing, she felt such a powerful and haunting sense of his presence that when she finally did drop off to sleep, she dreamed of him there in her room, picking up her pillow and burying his face in it.

Crazy. She was turning into a madwoman. It was just as the girls had predicted. She'd gone completely overboard, and was utterly unable to swim.

Whenever she encountered Connor's tall figure approaching in the Alexandra, one look at his moody, darkly handsome face and her insides suffered a seismic shock. By the time she'd pulled herself together to say something coherent, he had passed by, and the moment was lost.

It was clear she needed to be more prepared. But how was she to behave? She felt as if he were holding her at a distance with his will, and there was nothing she could do about it. The rejectee could hardly take the initiative.

What she needed was a plan. A way to show him she was not succumbing to humiliation over the beach thing. Not a campaign, exactly, so much as a statement of confidence in her sex appeal.

She started with clothes. She'd read dozens of magazine articles that showed how a woman could project her sensuality in the workplace while still appearing demure and professional. Fitted shapes, rich colours and sensuous fabrics could swathe the feminine body in elegance while subtly calling to the male. Higher heels, lipstick, perfume and, above all, a cool, tranquil attitude. It was too hot to plant anything in the garden, anyway, so she'd actually spent the previous weekend combing the shops.

She introduced the new items sparingly into her daily wardrobe, so as not to alert anyone's suspicion. Most of her efforts were wasted, though. However cool and sensual she appeared in her sashays along the gallery, Connor was too often away from his office to notice. He seemed to be out most days, and only appeared late in the afternoon when everyone was leaving.

The truth was, he was avoiding her.

She knew she shouldn't let it, but it hurt like hell. Only yesterday she'd been lunching under the willow in the Gardens with a few of the girls from the next floor down, and looked up to see him strolling through, heading somewhere. He'd seen her and swerved away to take another path. She'd felt such a savage stab in her chest then she'd scarcely been able to breathe.

But she knew she had to conquer the feelings and stay in control of her life. She had clients depending on her, her normal contacts to keep up, and now that she'd started the Elliott Fraser process there could be no turning back from that. However difficult, she had to grit her teeth and see it through.

Her decision to go for coffee that morning paid off, in one way, although it cut her to shreds in another. When she walked out into the gallery, Connor was outside his office in conversation with Cindy. He had his briefcase in his hand, looking devastating and sophisticated in a charcoal suit. Despite everything, it would still have been such a charge to see him, if he hadn't been smiling and listening intently to something their receptionist was telling him. She supposed she could hardly blame him. Cindy *was* very pretty and bubbly. And now she was calling him 'O'Brien', as if they were mates.

Friends.

As Sophy approached the two of them Cindy broke off talking. It almost seemed as if they'd been talking about *her*. When Connor glanced up at her, his smile faded and his dark eyes grew intense and impenetrable. There was something so hungry and primitive in that look her body plunged into a wild surge of bittersweet excitement.

But for once she managed to ignore her blood's sudden frenzied pounding to smile coolly and glide by like the Queen of the Nile. She felt glad to be wearing high heels and a cherry-red silk dress like a cheong-sam. It fastened demurely to its mandarin collar, and had a longish hidden split in the side that allowed occasional flashes of leg. She didn't have to look around to know his eyes were following her.

* * *

Afterwards, to banish the image of Sophy Woodruff in a red dress, Connor took refuge in his office and updated his case notes on the progress of the 'Djara Djara People versus New South Wales'. The claims and counterclaims of the case had drawn on for years. He could see at a glance that the Djara Djara needed stronger representation if they were to win in the High Court. They'd never be able to afford someone like him, so the work would have to be donated. But how fantastic it would be to help them to reclaim their traditional lands. At one time he'd actually been keen to dedicate his own skills to their cause.

Before he was headhunted by Foreign Affairs. And then a plane had crashed over Syria, his world had turned into a charred ruin, and everything had changed.

On a sudden, rare impulse he felt for his wallet, opened it and drew out the photo taken in Paris six years ago. Somehow the portrait had captured the sunshine lighting their blonde heads and wrapped them in a joyous halo, though the effect wasn't as noticeable now as it once had been. He grimaced to himself. For a long time he hadn't been able to bear to examine it at all, now it seemed he'd grown out of the habit of trying.

He frowned at the faces, familiar now he had them before him. Strange though, how even the most beloved faces could fade in the recollection.

He laid the photo on the desk and returned to the Djara Djara. Their case was compelling. If he hadn't chosen to complicate his work for the embassy with the challenges of covert operations…

Still, it was done now. He'd accepted the agency's recruitment invitation, plunged into the gruelling training regimen—telescoped into a third of the time normally required of agents—and made the commitment to file intelligence reports. He hadn't diverged from his career path, merely taken on another that had led him into some strange and torturous situations.

After the crash there'd been a weird sort of symmetry in signing up for more danger in one of the most hazardous hotspots on the planet. He'd avoided admitting it to Sir Frank, but now, from this distance, the tightrope he trod over there was starting to look like sheer lunacy.

Still, nothing felt as crazy as the nights he'd spent sitting parked in a street in Neutral Bay, while Sophy Woodruff slept, imagining her luscious curves and the rise and fall of her breath.

Admit it. *Burning* to be with her in that bed.

If he were free to do as he wanted…

Dammit, if she weren't a virgin. It always came back to that. If she were an experienced woman who understood that a kiss and a night or two between consenting adults didn't have to mean for ever, he might consider reopening negotiations.

But there was no way around it. With her willow trees, her beach walks, her moonglow, she was clearly crazy for romance. Exactly the type to get sucked in deep, while he was honour-bound to maintain his singularity.

Thank God she was keeping her distance. He didn't need any more people on his conscience. He just wished he hadn't seen her in that red dress.

On her side of the wall, Sophy ploughed on through her work. She'd decided to skip lunch in the Gardens. The trouble was, she couldn't get the morning's encounter out of her mind and needed to brood over it. Besides, it was too hot to eat. If it hadn't been for the delightful moments with the children, she doubted if she could have lasted the day.

In the afternoon, clouds started to build on the horizon, and there was the occasional rumble, like a somnolent giant almost ready to surface from a deep, deep sleep. For the first time in days a breeze fanned her cheek.

All through the afternoon the image of Connor O'Brien's disturbing gaze tortured her mind. The distraction slowed her down, so that by the time the others were packing up and leaving for the weekend, she still had reports to finish.

How long could the madness go on? It was affecting her entire life. She'd hardly slept for a week. Twice at netball people had thrown her the ball and it had sailed right past without her even noticing.

If he would only speak to her, about any small thing. Anything to defuse the intolerable suspense. There had to be some way they could talk to each other.

There was, of course, the letter. If she couldn't talk to him, how else was she to retrieve it, still ticking away somewhere in his rooms like a time bomb? Elliott could phone at any moment. What if he chose *this* weekend to invite her to the Fraser home?

At first inconceivable, the last-ditch, desperate possibility of making a bold frontal approach that had been simmering in her mind for days began to take on a seductive appeal. What if she went to Connor's rooms, knocked on his door, and simply asked if she could search? How could he refuse?

They were adults, weren't they? Surely she could request something of him without him assuming she was attempting to lure him. If she made it *absolutely clear* she was no longer attracted... If she could somehow correct the humiliating impression she'd left him with, show clearly that she wasn't a love-sick, sex-starved nympho, yearning for any contact with him, however minuscule.

She returned to her report and tried to concentrate, knowing she couldn't take the risk. His contempt at what would seem like an obvious ploy could destroy her.

Although, if she didn't do *something*, another weekend would go by without any improvement in the situation.

At some level, though, the impulse must have been solidifying in her subconscious, because all at once she whipped around to her bag and raked through it for her comb and lipstick, then rose to check her appearance in the children's wall mirror. She retouched her lips to a rich, ruby red, and retied the ribbon in her nape.

Bracing herself with a deep breath, like an automaton she walked through Reception and out into the empty gallery. Just short of Connor's door her feet slowed like a coward's, but somehow she forced them on.

Standing outside his office, her heart racketing a drum roll, the excoriating thing he'd said at the beach came back and threatened to slay her all over again.

Go away from me. Take yourself away.

For a second her nerve nearly failed. But what was she, a timid child?

She winched up all the courage she possessed, rapped firmly and waited, barely able to breathe, every muscle clenched. She was just considering making a frantic dash back to her office and pretending she'd never left it, when a shape loomed behind the opaque glass, stilled a moment, then the door opened.

Connor O'Brien's dark eyes clashed with hers, then slid over her with a heart-stopping, sensual intensity. But even as his raw, animal magnetism reached out to pull her in and trap every strand of her being in a giddy, yearning coil, his black brows drew together. His expression smoothed into inscrutability and he drew back a little. 'Sophy. Hello.'

She angled her gaze away and managed to articulate, though her throat felt dry and her lips were stiff, 'I hate to take up your time, but I need to get that letter back. I was hoping I could come in for a quick second and look for it.'

He continued to block the doorway for a moment, long enough for her heart to plunge as she registered his reluctance, then he opened it wide. 'Sure.'

He shoved his hands into his pockets, as if to avoid touching her, and she walked past him, careful not to brush against him, and headed through the reception office into his inner sanctum. Her heart was pounding so hard she could hear the beat in her ears. She drew a deep breath, and attempted to fill up the fraught space with words. 'I know I lost it in here. I think it could be—behind something.'

She sensed the high-voltage electric force of his attention, but she kept her face averted so as not to risk being annihilated by meeting sardonic amusement in his eyes. All the time her breathless words continued hurtling forth. 'I helped Millie pack up in here the day before you—moved in. I suppose it must have fallen from my bag. I have a very strong feeling it might have been caught up behind a piece of your furniture.'

She ran out of breath, and there was a jumpy little silence.

She cast a glance about. The room looked more lived in since her last visit. He'd hung some certificates on the walls asserting his credit as a lawyer and a member of the Bar Association. A couple of them displayed his right to practise in the Supreme Court, and the High Court of Australia. The string of letters after his name looked impressive.

He must have been working when she'd interrupted, because the breeze through the open window was gently riffling a pile of papers on his desk. Beside it was an empty coffee cup and an open notebook with notes written in a bold, flowing hand. She couldn't help ogling his things with an insane hunger, and wished she could have touched them.

'Ah. So you have a very strong feeling.' He strolled over to lean his wide shoulders against the wall. 'Well, in that case, it must certainly be in here. Where would you like to start?'

His velvet words couldn't mask the steel implacability of his resistance to her. She felt so conscious of invading his territory, of him being in absolute control. He folded his arms across his chest and she tried not to remember that powerful chest, lit by moonlight, the whorls of masculine hair brushing her breasts.

'Oh, well, the—the filing cabinet, I guess.'

She risked a fleeting glance at him, and the dark eyes dwelling on her face were grave, not at all mocking.

He moved out of the way with extreme politeness, and she approached the cabinet, kneeling down to look behind it without seeing anything there except darkness. She got up then, dusting down her dress, and stood in front of it, grasping the solid piece in an ineffectual attempt to pull it out from the wall. 'What on earth have you got in here?'

Realising her hands were shaking, she quickly lowered them from the cabinet.

'Files. Here,' he said smoothly, and she realised he'd noticed. 'You'd better let me. You wouldn't want to spoil that dress.'

Had there been a sensual note in his deep voice? She dismissed the notion at once as wishful thinking.

She stood aside while he dragged the cabinet out with apparent ease, but when she looked there was nothing behind it except a rind of dust.

He shrugged and pushed it back in place. 'No good. What next?'

It occurred to her then that he didn't believe her instincts about the letter, and was just humouring her. She was seized with the challenge to find it, and prove herself right. Anything to acquit herself of his almost certain assumption that she'd visited him purely because she couldn't stay away.

Energised to succeed, she moved away to check behind everything large and small around the perimeter of the entire room, conscious of his eyes following her.

After a second he said, his deep voice a little hesitant, 'So—how are you? How've you been?'

'Fine, thanks.'

'You *look* very well.'

She didn't answer.

'That…er…that dress suits you.'

She lowered her lashes to hide her heart's leap. 'Thanks.'

'I thought earlier…wondered if you had shadows under your eyes. Has the heat been affecting you?'

She gave him a sardonic glance. Maybe he thought *he* was affecting her. Well, maybe he was, but how dared he assume it?

'I mean, you always look cool, but I just wondered…'

She gave a cool shrug. 'I've been having some late nights.'

His brows lifted. 'Have you? You mean—workwise, or…social?'

She met his gaze full on. 'Purely social.'

His dark eyes scrutinised her face, glinting. For a moment she almost had the feeling he knew exactly how much of a barefaced lie that had been.

She'd reached the massive bookcase. There was a gap of a few centimetres between it and the wall. Pressing her cheek against the wall, she could just make out something on the floor behind the case. It looked promising.

'There is something here.' In her excitement her voice rose a little and she lost some of her constraint. 'Hey, look, this could be it.'

She tried shifting the heavy piece herself, but had no hope of budging it an inch. Connor quickly stepped in to push her out of the way, shoving his shoulder against the case and bracing his powerful legs to ease it from the wall, the tendons straining in his neck with effort until the aperture was wide enough.

As the space opened to the light she saw an envelope with one badly scuffed corner, and with a little cry of triumph pounced on it. 'It *is* it.'

She straightened up, examining it almost with disbelief, turning it over and over. There was her name in the window, Violet Woodruff. She slid the folded letter from inside, and it was exactly as she'd last seen it. 'Well, there you are, now. I told you, didn't I? I was right. What a relief. This is it. This truly is it.'

Connor O'Brien pushed the bookcase back into position and turned to watch her, an enigmatic expression on his lean, handsome face.

'Oh, and look, I'm sorry I accused you of—taking it.' She flushed a little with guilt. 'Of course, I realise you would never do anything like that.'

He lowered his dark lashes to screen his gaze.

The fitful breeze snatched up the papers on his desk and she sprang to secure them, tidying them back into a pile and placing the cup on top to hold them. Her glance fell on a small photograph, partly hidden by the notebook.

Connor must have spotted it at the same time, because he swiftly moved to pick it up and tuck it into his shirt pocket. Their eyes met, and he hesitated for a second, as though about to say something about it, then turned away and went into the front office, murmuring about speaking to the cleaner.

Somehow, though, the breath was knocked from her lungs. She'd only caught one glimpse of the photo, but she'd seen enough to know what it meant.

He was married. Married with a child.

Why hadn't she guessed? It was clearly impossible for a man like him not to have been snapped up long ago. With a dreary inevitability, in her mind she scrolled through every encounter she'd had with him, from that first time in the mothers' room. He didn't wear a ring, and hadn't he told Cindy he was single? So perhaps the photo meant he was divorced. Although, did men keep pictures of their ex-wives handy? Unless…

Unless he was a cheat. A cheat, a liar and a scoundrel who made love to other women besides his wife. Maybe that explained the sense she'd often had that he was concealing something.

She walked across to close the windows, placing her letter on the sill while she knelt on the desk to reach out for the window catch. Just as she leaned out a gust of wind snatched the letter up and wafted it off the sill.

Thank goodness it only landed on the ledge outside. Grateful for her split, she half straddled the sill, and stooped to pick the thing up. But the instant before her fingers connected with it, another gust lifted it and skidded it along the ledge a little way past the window casement.

In a split-second reflex she climbed gingerly out all the way, and edged along the ledge until she'd nearly reached it, clinging to the window casement, then beyond that the wall. Each time she was nearly upon the letter, it moved on a little further. That beastly letter had become an allegory for her life, she reflected. Just when she thought she had it all, it slipped from her fingers and she had to go after it again.

The surface of the sandstone was amazingly rough. She dug her fingers in, conscious of the stone scouring her fingertips, grazing her cheek, adhering to the silk fabric of her dress.

At last the letter remained stationary long enough for her to reach it. She pinned it with her shoe, and was about to ease down to pick it up when she made the horrendous mistake of looking down at the street.

Bad move.

Her head swam with vertigo, her stomach heaved and the world veered crazily. Panicked that she was going to fall, with the hairs rising on her nape, she huddled to the wall and waited for the building to stop spinning, the fear and nausea to recede.

The world eventually righted itself, but she couldn't risk another move. She'd just have to stay there, frozen to the spot for the rest of her life.

Without the casement to cling to, her grip on the rough stone felt frighteningly tenuous. The window seemed miles away.

It dawned on her that she might not like heights. The ledge might have been nearly a metre wide, enough to support large pots of geraniums and whole generations of pigeons, but, three storeys from the Macquarie Street pavement, it seemed like a tightrope, a mere sliver of projecting stone.

The sky was darkening, the purple clouds making a rapid advance. She could feel the chill on the air as the temperature dropped. The wind buffeted her, her fingertips hurt and she all at once felt exhausted.

Tiny drops of rain on the wind stung her cheeks like grains of sand. How long would she last once it started properly? Already she was chilled to the bone, judging by her chattering teeth, although in some part of her brain she realised that was probably just the result of concentrated terror. But the force of the breeze in her face tired her and made her eyes water. She'd drop off the ledge soon with exhaustion. She imagined it on the news, the blazing headlines. WOMAN FALLS FROM LEDGE. CAT-WOMAN CAUGHT IN STORM.

How ironic. Killed by a change in the weather.

She realised with remorse that she hadn't spoken to Henry or Bea for a couple of months. Not since she'd contacted Elliott Fraser, in fact. What would they think when they heard? They'd be so hurt. She imagined them at the funeral, Bea weeping, Henry's face pinched with grief.

'Oh, my God.'

Connor's shocked exclamation broke through her musings from a great distance. She didn't dare turn her face towards him for fear of losing her balance and falling backwards.

After a moment he spoke to her. This time he sounded very calm. 'Sophy. Are you all right?' He was trying not to scare her, she realised dimly. 'Can you hear me?'

She had to strain against the wind to hear him, but there was no way she could risk the effort of replying.

He must have understood, because he said, 'Stay there. I'm going round to the other window.'

She supposed he felt furious. His tone, though, was merely brisk and capable. 'Stay quiet, don't jump and don't look down.'

Despite her fear, a measure of optimism revived. He must want to rescue her. And if he thought he could, then there must be some chance of her survival. There was hope. God. There was still hope.

After what seemed like an age but was probably a few seconds, she heard her own window open. She saw him lean out and lift a geranium pot inside, shift another one along out of the way. Then he tested his weight on the ledge, placed a foot on it so he was half in, half out, and stretched his hand out to her. She only needed to move a little way to be within touching distance, but her limbs were stuck in a sort of paralysis, in fear of letting go of this one safe spot.

Tying her heartstrings in knots, Connor didn't look furious, or mocking. His expression was calm and focused, the lines of his sexy mouth composed. Anyone would have thought he rescued daredevils from life-threatening situations every day of the week. The haven of his big body beckoned, exuding such solid competence, such safety and security, it seemed silly not to just throw herself into his arms at once.

If she hadn't already, in the most shaming way.

'Come on,' he cajoled, his deep, quiet voice confident and persuasive, as if he understood her fears exactly and sympathised. 'Just a little step further. You can do it.' His eyes were so warm and compelling, so trustworthy, her feet stirred into life and edged along an inch, halting abruptly as a sudden wind gust threatened to blow her into the street.

To her extreme relief, Connor repositioned himself, then managed to reach out far enough to grab her. His strong, warm hand closed around her arm. 'There, I've got you. Don't worry about the wind, just keep moving towards me. I won't let you fall. Trust me.' His eyes were so urgent and compelling, his deep, soothing voice so earnest and sincere, every fibre of her being wanted to be there with him. 'I won't let you fall,' he kept repeating. 'Come on, sweetheart. Come on.' His powerful frame, his open arms looked so warm and secure and inviting.

Sweetheart. In the exigency of the moment she pushed aside her wounded pride over the matter of the beach. Nothing mattered for the moment except for his dark eyes and his deep, mesmerising voice. The indignity of being wrapped safe in his strong arms would be better than trembling on a ledge for the rest of her life in a storm. She edged an inch towards him, hardly aware of the drag of her fingers on the rough sandstone.

'Come on. Just another step.'

She shuffled sideways. When she was close enough, he knelt back on her desk, which he'd shoved up against the window, and gripped her waist with sure, firm hands.

'Got you.'

As he helped her climb over the sill one of her shoes slipped off and disappeared.

'My shoe,' she cried, twisting round to see where it went.

Connor O'Brien didn't waste any time soothing her shattered nerves. 'Forget your shoe,' he said tersely, lifting her down to the floor with him and holding her against him so fiercely that mega-bolts of electric vibrations poured from his big, angry body into hers, and made her tremble all over like a willow frond.

But he felt so safe and solid and smelt so wonderfully male, being pressed furiously against him hardly seemed like punishment.

'I'm sorry for being a nuisance,' she whispered into his neck. 'Thanks for saving my life.'

Her abject apology only seemed to inflame him. He held her tightly to his chest for a further minute while the steam gathered, then released her as if she were an explosive device. Even though her legs felt like jelly, and she had to grab at her desk to support herself, her body sang with the sensual textures of the contact with his hands and clothes and hard-muscled body.

The muscles in his face worked with the need to say something. She didn't need to do a clinical assessment to realise he was having a temporary word-finding problem.

At last he got some together. '*Look* at you.' He raked her with his ferocious gaze, shaking his head in incredulity. 'You're a mess. What the hell did you think you were doing?'

She clung weakly to the desk. She wished he'd stop yelling. As if she'd wanted to freeze with fear on the ledge. 'It was too narrow,' she explained, conscious of a bone-deep fatigue. 'It looked all right until I got on there and moved away from the window.'

His eyes flashed. 'I find it hard to believe an intelligent person could have done anything so stupid. Look at your hands.' He seized them.

She looked down and saw her fingers, grazed from the sandstone, the skin broken in some places. His hands were strong and lean, brown against her pale skin. It felt so good, so comforting, having her hands held, she wished he'd just go on holding them, but he dropped them in disgust to pace the room, flinging his arms about while he thundered.

'I can't for the life of me believe… What possessed you? That ledge is by no means secure. Bits of it are crumbling—*crumbling*, for God's sake—all around the building.' He paused to draw breath, his lean, handsome face taut, his mouth even more sensual and stirring than usual, set as it was in such severe lines. 'One minute you were there inside, safe and sound, the next you were…' He shook his head.

'It was the wind. It blew the letter outside and I was trying to retrieve it.'

He stared at her in thunderstruck incredulity. 'We are three storeys above the ground. Is a scrap of paper so important you'd risk your life?'

'I didn't think I *was* risking my life. I told you. The ledge looked…'

Did she really need to explain? She began to feel nauseous, and strangely detached from herself. She put her hand on his sleeve. 'Connor, I might need to sit down.'

She backed into a hard chair and sat down. For a while the world looked a bit woozy.

'Sophy.' Connor's face materialised and she saw he was kneeling before her chair, the lines of his face taut with concern. Remorse flickered in his eyes, and something else that made her shut hers quickly. 'Are you all right?'

'I could do with a drink.' Her voice was croaky, as if her throat needed lubricating.

He sprang up and came back with a glass of water, watching as she took it and drank. 'Thanks.' She handed back the glass.

She made a move to stand but he restrained her with a hand on her shoulder. 'Steady,' he warned, then gave a rueful sigh. 'Sorry. I shouldn't have been so… You're in shock. Stay quiet for a while. I thought you were about to keel over.' His voice rasped a little, and she realised he was in shock himself. 'What you really need is brandy.' He placed a gentle hand on her arm. 'God. You're as cold as ice.'

Her skin cells roused to his touch and she moved her arm away. He lowered his black lashes as turbulent memories stirred.

'I'm all right now.' She scrambled to her feet, ignoring her unsteady head, and the world swayed horribly. 'I'm fine.'

'The way you look, I find that hard to believe.' He steered her into an armchair, then took off his jacket and slung it around her shoulders. He gestured towards the door. 'Is there any kind of staff-room in there?'

She indicated and he went away, then returned in a few minutes with hot tea.

As she took the cup he murmured, shaking his head as he surveyed her torn fingers, 'Where's a doctor when you need one?'

'Who needs one? Just because I needed a little rest? I missed lunch today, that's all. All I want now is a good soak in a hot bath and a piece of toast.'

She supposed it was her weakened state, but the dark velvet eyes scrutinising her were so warm and concerned, not at all like the furious Connor O'Brien's of a moment ago, that in a rush of tremulous emotion she forgave him everything. Well, nearly everything. For smiling at Cindy, at least. Although, if he were married, she couldn't possibly forgive him that.

She sipped the tea without complaint, though it was a little on the strong side and had sugar in it. The truth was, it felt wonderful being pampered. Perhaps she should have thought of dancing on the ledge before. Just remembering it, though, must have been a mistake, for the world swam threateningly again.

Connor, keeping a watchful eye, immediately noted her change in colour. Experience told him that the overbright spark in her eyes would be shortlived and she would soon need to sleep. Still, something was nagging at him.

He said casually, 'You know, er…some people who weren't aware of your obsession with that letter might have wondered if you were planning to jump.'

'What people?' She rolled her eyes. 'Idiots? If I'd wanted to jump, don't you think I'd have picked something higher? Do you think I want injuries?'

He felt reassured enough to go back to his office to lock up. That small worry subsided, at least. Sure, her face had more colour since the near faint, but it was a tenuous improvement. She was still white with exhaustion, the shadow under her eyes now purplish hollows.

She might not have been planning to jump, but she needed some sort of attention. A hospital waiting room with its lacklustre service would hardly be useful. He remembered then with quick relief that both her housemates were nurses. Excellent. She could go home safely enough. He should be able to drop her at her door and make a clean getaway. Although…

He hoped they were reliable.

For God's sake, it was none of his concern. It was just that he knew too much about the aftermath of a crisis. Friends might bathe her wounds perhaps, but there was the night to come. Too well he knew the horrors waiting to torment the small hours after a near-death experience. He grimaced, and a dangerous thought flashed in.

Who would hold her through the night?

With a mental shake he brushed the temptation aside.

Finished locking up, he strode back into the clinic, and frowned to see her up and struggling to lift the potted geranium off the table.

'Hey, give me that,' he growled, snatching the pot from her and setting it down. He turned to her for a swift examination. She looked fragile, her exhaustion apparent, and he felt remorseful for the time he'd taken next door. 'It's time I got you home.'

Reading his glance, Sophy remembered what a wreck she must look. Her hair was a mess, she couldn't stop trembling, her hands hurt—she couldn't wait to escape from his sight and clean herself up.

She slung the strap of her bag onto her shoulder and held his jacket out to him.

'Thanks for your help.' She spoke stiffly, trying to stop her teeth from chattering. 'I'd better hurry now if I want to catch the ferry before the storm breaks.'

His brows shot up. 'The ferry! I don't think so.'

In all honesty, she did feel as if she were at the end of her strength, but she still had some pride. He'd been helpful—too helpful, really, for a man who'd made his position on involvements clear. The next thing she knew he'd be turning on her again the way he had at the beach. With as much dignity as any woman could be expected to muster without having shoes on both feet, she asserted, 'The ferry will be fine. All I need is a soak in a long, hot bath with some essential oils.'

For just the tiniest fraction of an instant he hesitated, then shook his head and started to make vigorous objections. But the protest came too late. Whatever he said now, she knew his first reaction had been relief. Relief at the notion of getting rid of her. She made a dignified attempt to move around him towards the door, but her uneven feet stumbled and she bumped into him.

He caught her arm. 'I'll drive you to the ferry.'

'No, no. You have your own concerns. I don't want you to put yourself out. There's absolutely no need for you to involve yourself any—'

His lips thinned. 'Pride isn't your most sensible option right now, Sophy.'

She froze for a second, then allowed herself to relent. 'Well, all right, then. Thanks. That would be quite—very generous of you.'

He paused to wait for her while she locked the clinic's outer door. In the gallery he had to slow his stride to match her limping gait. In the end she took off her one shoe and went barefoot, though it still felt like the longest mile she'd ever walked.

Waiting for the lift, he stood in brooding silence, then on the ride down, as she sagged, grateful for the wall, he said suddenly, 'I'll drive you all the way home.'

'Oh, heavens.' Her voice was faint with the effort of talking. 'There's no need for that. What's a bit of rain?'

His lips compressed, but all the walking must truly have worn her out, because when they stepped out into the basement car park, and she'd put her shoe on again to protect at least one foot from the greasy surface, Connor turned to her with an exasperated sigh and said, 'Oh, look. Here, hold this.' Before she had time to react, he thrust his briefcase into her grasp, wrapped his jacket around her and hoisted her up in his arms.

She gasped and stiffened, trying to control her overwhelming sensory response.

'What do you think you're doing?' she cried in a suffocated voice, conscious of his warm chest through the fabric of his shirt, his gorgeous mouth and masculine jaw, dark with five-o'clock shadow, close enough to graze her forehead. 'I *can* walk. There's no need for this—this—'

'I'm in a hurry,' he said curtly.

She knew she should have protested more strenuously. If the Avengers had been lurking in the car park, she knew they'd have swarmed over and wrested her from his arms and shrieked, 'For God's sake, Woodruff, stand on your own two feet and act like a *woman*.'

But, to be honest, it was fabulous to be in his arms, even so temporarily, and under what was clearly, for him, duress. Though he avoided looking down at her, he felt so strong and comfortable, and the close proximity of his hard, vibrant masculinity sparked up her flagging blood better than any swig of brandy could have done. While she might have still been feeling woozy, she savoured every second.

Then she let him swaddle her in the luxury of his big car and float her across the Harbour Bridge.

Darkness had descended. There were intermittent lightning flashes around the rim of the horizon, and the air felt heavy and expectant, as if the storm had made up its mind at last and was awaiting its moment to blow the sky apart.

Or maybe it was in the vibrations in the car. Even when she wasn't looking at Connor O'Brien, she was so tangibly aware of him, a few centimetres away from her.

They were nearly all the way to her place when he said, 'Will your friends be in this evening?'

'No.' She sighed. 'It's just me at the moment. They've gone on a camping holiday to Kakadu.'

He fell silent, his black brows heavy with thought. Suddenly he slowed, swung the car into a side street and pulled over. He turned his dark gaze on her. 'Look, I really don't think you should be alone tonight. You're in shock. Is there someone you can stay with?'

She shrugged. 'Millie, I suppose, only she lives at Penrith.' She wrinkled her brow. 'I'm not sure she'll be at home, though. They go out on Friday nights.'

'What about Fraser?'

'Who?' She stared at him aghast. 'Elliott Fraser? Are you serious? I hardly *know* him. He's a—a stranger. He doesn't even *like* me.' She became agitated, in her distress breathing very fast. 'For goodness' sake, Connor, just drop me at home, will you? I told you I'll be fine.'

He gripped the wheel, staring ahead into the night as though he were locked in battle with some inner demon. At long last, just when she was considering getting out to walk, he gave a long, fatalistic sigh, and muttered, 'No one could accuse me of not trying.'

Then he turned to look at her, and his posture relaxed a little. He started the car, swerved it into a neat U-turn, and headed straight back into the city.

She looked about her in alarm, afraid he was going to do something absurd like dump her in some hospital emergency room. 'Now what? Where…? Where are we going?'

'My place,' he growled.

His profile was grim, his stern, sexy mouth resolute. Normally she'd have been agog to visit his place of residence. Face it, hardly anything could have been more fascinating. She could find out for sure if he had a wife there, for one thing.

It only went to prove how shaken up she must have been by the ledge experience, that, although it was quite a short journey, she actually dozed off on the way. She only started from her stupor when she felt the car slow and make a sharp turn. They were driving along a tree-lined street in one of those wealthy suburbs. On either side, the lights of multi-level mansions glimmered richly behind high hedges and walls. There were some grand apartment buildings, with expensive cars parked in front. Above the rooftops on the lower side she could see the city lights.

'Wow,' she exclaimed, blinking, 'I can see the city. This looks very... Isn't this Double Bay?'

He drove them right to the end of the street. 'Point Piper,' he said, swinging the car into a gravelled drive.

Point Piper. Higher up the market than Double Bay. Only the most expensive real estate in Australia, home of bankers, billionaires and filthy rich property tycoons. At the end of the drive, right on the very point of the Point, they came to a pale, thirties-looking villa with rounded edges and three levels of balconies. No lights showed in its perfectly round windows. In the dark, it reminded her of a cruise liner with portholes. A ghost ship.

A garage door slid silently open, and automatic lights snapped on as they drove in. Connor O'Brien stood by while she got out of the car, and took her arm to steer her to the lift.

Normally, when given a choice, she preferred to bound up flights of stairs, but on this occasion she felt grateful the people in Point Piper had lifts in their car parks. Once inside the lift, though, the space seemed very small. Connor leaned against the opposite wall, flicking her the occasional smouldering glance from beneath his black brows. There was a tension in his lean frame that communicated itself to her with a skittery, jumpy excitement.

She noticed him loosen his collar and yank his tie free. Even in her weakened condition it was impossible not to appreciate how, with his tie undone and the dark shadow roughening his moustache and jaw, his quality of brooding sexiness seemed intensified.

'Maybe I should have just gone home to my place,' she said, her cool slipping a little.

His eyes glinted. 'Does your place have brandy?'

She admitted the lack of alcohol with a shrug.

'Look on the bright side.' He gave a low, sexy laugh. 'At least tonight there's no moon.'

She lowered her lashes. It was clear what he was worried about. He was afraid she might take advantage of the situation and throw herself at him again like a ravenous, sexually voracious virago. As if she could, in her state. Although, if she were forced to drink brandy…

The lift opened to a foyer with a parquet floor, and Connor O'Brien stood back to allow her entry.

She crossed the threshold, into his domain.

CHAPTER NINE

CONNOR reached for a switch and a soft light illuminated the bare foyer. As he ushered Sophy forward into a dim, cavernous space his arm brushed hers and her skin thrilled to the contact.

She was in a large empty room that flowed to other shadowy spaces. The effect of vastness was enhanced by high ceilings and wide windows. Through the glass she could see harbour lights blinking beneath the troubled sky. The place looked deserted.

One thing was certain. No wife lived here.

'What happened to your furniture?' Her voice echoed in the gloom. 'Have you been robbed?'

'No. Sit down and I'll get you a drink.'

'Where?' She peered into the shadows. 'Where do your guests sit?'

'Oh, er…' He hesitated, and glanced about in mild surprise as if he'd only just noticed the lack of the home comforts. She was looking down at the floor, thinking that would have to do, when he said, 'Come this way. Through here.' He led her through another dim room and paused to flick a switch.

A kitchen materialised in the light. It was spacious, with heavy, old-fashioned benches and a floor of chequered tiles. There was a grand old gas stove side by side with some more modern appliances. A sturdy kitchen table in the centre of the room looked as if it had seen long service, and there were a couple of high-backed chairs. There was a graceful long-legged stool at the wide counter, and she slipped onto it. Connor opened his fridge and peered inside. From where she sat the fridge was a repository of wide-open spaces. He gave a shrug, then went in search of his first-aid kit and the brandy.

'You're not married, then, Connor?' she said when he came back, as offhand as she knew how to be.

His hand paused in the act of pouring, and he sent her a deep glance. Of course he knew she'd seen that photo. 'Not currently.'

'But you were.'

'I was, yes,' he said easily. 'They—that picture you saw was of my wife and son. They were in a plane that crashed into a mountainside several years ago. In Syria.'

'Oh.' The appalling tragedy sucked the wind from her lungs. What was there to say? 'I'm so sorry. That's—that's truly terrible. You must have been through a dreadful time.' She flushed at the inadequacy of the words. 'I wish I could say—say *something*...'

He dropped his gaze. 'Don't worry, Sophy. There's nothing anyone can say. Here.' He handed her the glass with a warning murmur, 'Take it easy now.'

She took a bigger sip than she meant to, then coughed as her lungs seized and the liquid burned her throat. Connor poured himself a shot and leaned on his side of the counter, watching her recover herself with a wry expression.

'Do you ever take anything carefully?'

'Of course,' she gasped through watery eyes. 'I'm normally a very cautious person.'

'That's not my experience.' The warmth in his amused dark gaze was a dangerous temptation, playing on her longing, inviting her to drop her guard. On the other hand, surely there were moments between men and women when they should be able to come clean? But how was she to guess when it was safe?

'Well...' She traced her name in the dust on the counter.

'Lately…since I've known you, in fact…I've had—some exceptional circumstances.'

'What circumstances?'

'Well, there've been—things. Millie's move from next door. And then you… The things *you've* done…' She saw his brows shoot up and her heart skidded in dismay as she realised she was flirting with disaster. How close she'd come to spilling her guts and laying herself open to emotional slaughter. Leah and Zoe would have been horrified.

'Things.' He'd rolled his sleeves up to his elbows, and leaned lazily on his side of the counter, glass in hand, contemplating her. Doing it again. Charming her. Devastating her with his dark, velvet gaze. 'What sort of things? You mean, like making love to you?'

Her heart plunged and she turned her face quickly away. 'No, no,' she mumbled huskily. 'Not—that. I wasn't thinking of that at all.'

'Sophy.' He reached over and softly brushed her throat with his finger. 'This little pulse here tells me you're lying.'

Gentleness from a harsh man was so weakening. Her skin tingled where he touched, rivulets of fire in her willing flesh. She longed to respond to him honestly, but all the painful emotions of the beach churned up inside her and couldn't be denied. Did he think she could just carry on as though it had never happened?

She slid off the seat and headed for the blessed shadows of the empty sitting room. After a few tense moments he followed and reached for the light, but she stopped him. 'No, please,' she said, constraint in her voice. 'There'll be lightning soon. Let's—just enjoy it.'

The storm was building, but it wasn't the only reason she wanted to avoid the light. That casual little touch had roused the wildfire that resided in her blood for him, and thrown her into emotional uproar. The signals were all so conflicting. The things he'd said that night were seared into her brain, but the vibrations told a different story. Either he wanted her or he didn't. Or at least—somehow he wanted her, but at the same time he didn't.

It was a tightrope. She might as well have been back out on the ledge. Any false step and she could plummet straight to another debacle. And despite the strengthening prop of the brandy, she didn't think she was up to another one.

The night beat against the glass, pierced by the fretful lights of the marina, masts bobbing restlessly in the sullen dark.

Connor moved to stand beside her, wondering how he'd ever imagined it would be a simple matter to bridge the breach. How could he have forgotten the mysterious workings of the female mind? Now he could remember occasions with his wife when he'd been brought to a halt by that complexity. How had he managed then?

Of course. Sex. The great soother. But in the case of a *virgin*... Especially a virgin who'd been spurned by a damned fool...

He surveyed her tense profile. Instinct—dammit, every blood cell in his body prompted him to kiss her, unfasten that red dress and carry her straight to his bed. What else did a man do with a woman in an empty house? But he'd erected that barrier against himself.

He turned to her at the same instant as she turned to him. In the half-light the hollows and fatigue in her face made him piercingly aware of her fragility, despite the overbright sparkle in her eyes.

For God's sake, what sort of an animal was he? She'd just been through an ordeal. He couldn't just grab her and throw her on the bed.

'Have you ever seen *Last Tango in Paris*?' As soon as the words were out Connor closed his eyes, wincing at himself. Get a grip.

'I've heard of it. Was Marlon Brando in it?' He made a slight nod, and she added, 'What was it about?'

A man. A woman. An empty apartment.

Sophy heard his sudden hesitation and her insecurity increased. 'Look, Sophy...'

'This is such a fantastic house,' she exclaimed. 'I'd have expected it to belong to some billionaire.' Even to her own ears her voice sounded unnatural, echoing around the walls with nervous haste. Without giving him a chance to start again, she hastened to add, 'I don't mean to be rude, but is it that you can't afford furniture? Because I know some great little second-hand shops I could show you.'

He turned to examine her with an intent scrutiny, his black brows drawn. 'It's not that. This was my father's house for the last ten years of his life. Most of his stuff went to auction when he died.'

'So it's yours now?'

He gave a shrug.

Gosh. The O'Briens must be really up there. 'Your father wasn't that O'Brien who donated the wing to the children's hospital, was he?'

'That's right. I think he did do that. He was always very concerned about—charity.'

She nodded, trying to look nonchalant. 'Are you buying some furniture?'

'Haven't thought about it.'

'Er…don't you want to make it comfortable?'

'Is it uncomfortable?'

'Well, I was only thinking that if your friends come to visit…'

'You're the first.'

She was silent for a couple of heart-thuds. 'But what if your family…?'

'I don't have any more close family in Sydney. Just cousins and aunts I don't really know. No one even knows I'm here.' He smiled and his eyes gleamed with a seductive light. 'We have it all to ourselves.'

'Right.' Her heart started to thunder louder than the percussion section of the Sydney Symphony. She swallowed. 'Do you mind if I—look around?'

'Be my guest.'

She wandered from room to room and he followed, switching on lights for her. The rooms were nearly all empty, gracious bedrooms with wide windows looking onto the harbour and large, old-fashioned bathrooms. A staircase led to the upper storeys, but Connor admitted he never bothered to go up there unless he was scrounging for bits and pieces that had escaped the auctioneers.

There was one room with a desk and media equipment, as well as a new-looking leather armchair with a standard lamp, and she noticed a stereo and a pile of CDs in one corner. And there was his bedroom.

She stood poised at the door. The bed was large, necessary for a tall man, with side tables and a matching chest of drawers. It looked like the sort of furniture that could be bought from a warehouse catalogue, something you could phone up for and have delivered. But to her exhausted self it looked so inviting, all at once, with its deep red-and-gold covers, plump pillows with snowy white cases. She ached to plunge into its softness and surrender her aching limbs to its embrace.

Her glance fell on a suitcase on the floor. She stared at it for seconds.

Connor O'Brien was watching her, his eyes veiled as her eyes switched from suitcase to bed. 'Would you like to try it?'

'Oh, no, no, thanks.' She backed from the room.

'You should rest. Those shadows under your eyes are deeper.' He reached out to brush them lightly with his thumb. 'You've been through an ordeal.'

She lowered her lashes. 'It's all right. I'm fine now. I'll—phone for a taxi in a minute and go home.'

He was silent for a few seconds, his brows drawn. Then he shrugged and shoved his hands into his pockets. 'You don't have to phone for a taxi, Sophy. If you'd really prefer to go home I'll drive you.' After a second he added with a shimmering glance, 'You would be quite *comfortable* in that bed.'

She looked quickly at him. He looked grave, but had there been the hint of a smile in his voice? She wished she'd had a string of lovers and could read men's minds. What did he intend? If there was only one bed…

The stormy sky over Sydney Harbour mirrored her inner turbulence. The truth was, in recent days she'd have thought there was nowhere in the world she'd rather be than in an empty house with Connor O'Brien, but that had been when she thought she didn't have a chance. Now there seemed to be the glimmer of a possibility, she wasn't sure. After the last disaster, was it worth taking such a risk again? He couldn't just turn her on and turn her off when he felt like it. A woman had her pride.

On the other hand, she'd always felt very affected by storms. Perhaps the atmospheric disturbance had jammed her sexual sensors into the *On* position. He might, in fact, just be acting the Good Samaritan role. He'd already told her in the most devastating way that he didn't want an involvement. And if that wasn't enough, she'd just had the strongest possible cosmic flash.

This home was temporary.

He was going away.

It gave her such a hollow feeling. She wandered back to the shadows of the large room, Connor's thumbprint still on her face, a storm in her heart. Common sense told her she shouldn't be dreaming of him. Everyone knew it was easy for a man to make love to a woman, then just go away and forget her. But for the woman…

She supposed some women could take it in their stride. Shrug their shoulders and move on. Next, please, as Zoe always said. But in her case… In this case…

Moving on had never been her forte.

Outside the planet was holding its breath. Something was about to break loose. The first fat drops of rain spattered against the glass.

Just when the suspense reached an unbearable pitch a jagged fork of lightning zigzagged across the sky and illuminated the room in greenish neon. For a second she saw Connor's tall, solitary frame, outlined in the gloom of his empty house. A moment later a deafening crack of thunder split the air, making the windows rattle. He brushed past her to close the blinds and she felt the shock of contact with his bare forearm.

Silence reclaimed the room before the next onslaught and all she could hear was her pounding heart, the throb of her blood, or was it his?

He turned to her, his eyes burning with a dark flame in the half-light. For a breathless second she waited, yearningly aware of every part of him—the rise and fall of his chest, the masculine hairs curling on his long limbs, his heart beating its dark, mysterious rhythm. If he took her in his arms now, she wouldn't be phoning for any cab.

He reached out and smoothed his fingers over her left cheekbone. 'You've got a little graze here.' His voice sounded as deep as a gravel pit. His fingers travelled further, tracing the line of her jaw, rousing light rays in her skin. 'You look gorgeous in that dress.'

His voice was so deep she held her breath, waiting for him to seize her and press his beautiful, sexy mouth to hers. But he dropped his hand and his eyes narrowed.

'Are you sure you're all right? You're looking a bit fragile. I really think you should rest. And you need food. Have a little sleep then we'll find you something to eat.'

A *sleep*. Was he kidding? How romantic. Next he'd be tucking her up in bed with a hot-water bottle and a tray with a boiled egg and soldiers.

If she had been a sophisticated woman of the world, she'd give him a breezy wave now and sashay to the door. The trouble was, the thought of sashaying fatigued her through to her very marrow.

A wave of exhaustion washed over her. She slid down the wall onto the floor and leaned back. 'I'll just have a little rest before I phone for the cab.'

Connor looked bemused. 'No. No, for God's sake, you can't sit there. Come and lie down on the bed.'

Gingerly, she lay down on her side. 'It's just for a minute.'

He lowered his lashes for a second, then his eyes glinted with rueful comprehension. 'You're—welcome to use the bed, Sophy.'

'I like the floor,' she lied. 'I often prefer the floor. I'll just close my eyes for a second before I phone…'

His sensuous mouth tightened. Frowning, he shook his head. 'It's not a good idea to travel in a storm. We really should be looking at bathing those wounds. You need to rest properly. I don't think I have any spiritual essences on hand, but there's plenty of soap and hot water here. Towels and—everything.'

The bath sounded tempting, but she was just too tired. She stretched out, the hard boards ruthlessly crunching her bones at shoulder, hip and ankle. 'Maybe.'

He stared fascinatedly down at her as she pillowed her head on her arms. 'I suppose I should do something about dinner.' His gaze flicked to her bare legs and feet and hung there as though mesmerised. 'I'll order some in. What do you feel like? Thai, Turkish, Indian, Chinese?'

'Oh, what do I know?' She sighed. 'Is that what you do every night? Order in takeaway?'

'What's wrong with takeaway?'

He stood there, hesitating, then dropped onto the floor a little way from her. It wasn't so very far. He could have reached across to take her in his arms if he'd wanted to. Every fibre of her flesh and blood yearned towards him. But he only said, 'Sophy…won't you tell me what's got you in such a bind over that letter? It isn't some sort of blackmail, is it?'

God. If she wasn't sick to death of that stupid letter. She was glad it was gone now for all time. She never wanted to lay eyes on it again.

She felt the last of the spurious energy drummed up by the brandy drain away. Surrendering to the inevitable, she tucked her hands under her cheek and closed her eyes, mumbling, 'It's my DNA profile.'

She let herself drift. She stopped noticing the boards pressing into her, as if they'd developed grooves in the right places. After what seemed like an age she was floating, floating down that river towards a beckoning golden shore when she felt a strong arm, gentle and sure under her shoulders, another under her knees, and knew Connor O'Brien was lifting her off the floor.

CHAPTER TEN

SOPHY surfaced to the sound of clattering dishes. Smells tickled her nostrils, delicious cooking smells, and her stomach groaned. She was in a bed. It gradually homed in on her that it could only be Connor's. She opened her eyes. Sure enough, she was in a strange room and she could hear the comfortable sound of rain outside. She woke a little further and stretched with luxurious relish. Somehow Connor's mattress supported and massaged her every aching muscle. She spread out her arms and made a voluptuous little shimmy, soaking up every molecule of the personal O'Brien essence while she had the chance. A quick bodily survey made her realise she felt rested and alive.

Her optimism level made a surprising upward bound. It was amazing how invigorating a nap in his bed could be.

'Good. You're awake.'

She started and blinked as a soft light illuminated the room. Her eyes focused, then refocused on Connor standing at the door. Her insides curled over and she sat up. He'd changed into jeans and a dark casual T-shirt that outlined the athletic contours of his lean body. His hair glistened as if it was damp, and she wondered if he'd shaved, he looked so fresh and scrubbed and relaxed. And handsome, she thought, her heart surging. It wasn't fair. It just wasn't fair that a man should be so… She noticed his gleaming, dark gaze riveted to her in the bed.

Aware suddenly of her dress rucked up around her thighs, she scrambled to draw the tangled covers up to her waist and sat up.

'How long have I been asleep?' Knowing she must look all flushed and tousled, she made an attempt to smooth her hair.

'A couple of hours.'

His voice had thickened slightly as his gaze drifted below her chin. Glancing down, she saw her bodice twisted askew, drawn too tightly over her breasts, and made a hurried attempt to fix it.

'Are you hungry?'

'I am,' she said, her own voice nearly as husky. 'Ravenous, you might say.'

His lashes flickered and she saw the corners of his sexy mouth edge up. 'Good. I dropped down to the night market and picked up a few things for dinner.' He angled away, leaning his weight on one foot. 'Would you like me to—run you a bath?'

Had she died and gone to heaven?

As soon as he left she scrambled out of the bed, smoothed and straightened it back to its neat beginnings.

The old-fashioned bathroom was an indulgence of ornate mirrors and white marble surfaces, with that last word in roaring twenties-style decadence, a sunken bath. While she stood admiring it, Connor produced a comprehensive first-aid kit.

'What are they for?' she enquired, noticing a couple of lethal-looking clinical tools like tweezers, with little lights attached.

'Oh, you know.' He pushed in the little drawer in the kit that held them. 'Picking up things, small particles caught in your skin, etc.'

'Bullets.' The word whizzed into her head and popped out before she even connected with it.

His startled gaze flew to meet hers, then almost at once his eyes veiled and he said lightly, 'You know, you're a worry, with that imagination of yours.'

She kept reminding herself, as he moved the conversation on, giving her instructions about antiseptic and adhesive tape, showing her where the towels were stored—his two spare towels—that he might be very hospitable, but nothing else had changed. He was still a man who had some very mysterious layers. And he had rejected her on a beach.

'Anything else? Need to know where anything is?'

She screwed up her face. 'I just wish I had some clean clothes to change into.'

'Can't help you there. Unless…' He hesitated, then his face smoothed to become expressionless. 'I suppose you could try one of my shirts.'

The bathroom space suddenly shrank to the size of a cupboard. She avoided his eyes. Surely wearing something of his would be a dangerously intimate move. And then there was the problem of undies.

'I don't know,' she mumbled. 'I'll think about it.'

After a fraught two seconds he strode out and returned with a clean blue shirt on a laundry hanger, which he hung on the door. 'My last offer. Take it or leave it.'

As the voluptuous sunken bath filled and the steam rose, and the moment for him to withdraw from the room with gentlemanly grace approached, it occurred to her with a leap in her pulse that Connor was not altogether impervious to her charms.

There was still hope. There was always hope.

'Oh, and I forgot,' he said gruffly. 'This was all they had at the market.'

He thrust a package into her hands. Mystified, she ripped off the brown chemist paper and widened her eyes in astonishment. Oils. He'd brought her essential oils.

'Oh, my God.' Overcome, she blinked and shook her head. 'Connor! *Well*, this is just… This is *so*… So very *thoughtful*…'

'I'll leave you to it,' he said brusquely, removing himself. 'Don't be long.'

If the sleep had been invigorating, the bath was blissful. She lay back in the water, redolent of rosemary and clary sage, and let the soothing essences permeate her spirit with their healing power, while she considered Connor O'Brien. Could she be dreaming? Had the sense of emergency pervading the evening since her rescue changed something between them? Soon though, driven by hunger pangs, she rose and towelled herself dry until she tingled and her skin felt silky soft.

She tried on the shirt. It nearly came down to her knees front and back, although not at the sides. She considered the degree of thigh exposure, but, when she'd turned back the cuffs about twenty times, decided it was no less modest than most things. It just *looked* suggestive.

Connor seemed to think so, anyway, when she finally met him in the kitchen. He glanced up from stirring a saucepan on the stove. Instantly the hand that held the spoon stilled and his eyes flared with that hot, sensual gleam that made her nipples harden with yearning.

'Ah,' he said softly. 'You look much better. More like your old self.'

More like the old self of his fantasy, Connor thought, his heart rate escalating in erotic appreciation of the shirt hanging from her slim shoulders with surprising elegance. *His* shirt grazing *her* nipples.

There was only a glimpse of cleavage. If only he hadn't had such a good memory.

He poured her a glass of red wine with a steady hand, though his blood buzzed with every angle of thigh revealed and concealed by the shirt's uneven hem.

He clinked glasses with her, smiling, forcing his eyes not to drift below her chin. If she hadn't been a virgin, he might have trailed his hand up that smooth thigh and under the shirt. He turned sharply back to the stove, his jeans all at once tight.

Sophy perched on the stool and sipped her wine very sparingly. There was something very sexy about Connor's cooking style. He tasted his brew, threw in extra salt, slapped on the lid, stooped to check on something aromatic he was heating in the oven, his movements all with a swift, casual grace that was so essentially masculine.

At the same time her excitable senses attuned to a silent conversation pulsing in the air between them, drumming with the rain, underlying every spoken word and glance.

When he set her soup before her, the fragrant steam rising from it sent her weak at the knees. Or perhaps it was the wine infusing her bloodstream. Or him.

'Bon appetit,' he murmured.

The meal had an Eastern theme. There was tabouleh salad he'd bought from a deli, delicious little kofta meatballs with pine nuts, and flatbread with hummus. More than enough for a late-night supper, marooned on a rainy night in an empty house with a sexy, dark-eyed man.

After her last spoonful, she exclaimed, 'Delicious.'

And it had been. Lentils and spinach, lemon and coriander, cumin and some other Eastern spice. Heavenly nourishment for her grateful stomach.

'Have some more,' he urged. 'You need to build up your strength.'

'That's very good of you, Connor, but I can't fit any more in. I'm so impressed you went to the trouble of cooking. And such an exotic soup. Who'd have thought you'd be so domesticated?'

He smiled. 'It's one of the few things I can cook. It's a very common, ordinary dish in the Middle East.'

'Oh, of course. You were in Iraq.'

'You should know.' He made a wry grimace. 'After all your snooping around my office I've started to wonder if you're a detective.'

She smiled. 'Snooping. Now, there's an overstatement. I may, perhaps, have accidentally come across your passport while conducting my own affairs…'

'Ah, yes. Your affairs. I think that's what we should be talking about.' His dark eyes were gentle and teasing, piercingly sensual.

'I don't think so. Tell me more about Iraq. Did you live at the embassy?'

'Some of the time. Sometimes I travelled to other places.'

'It must have been terribly dangerous.'

The lean, tanned hands resting on the table curled, but he said evenly, 'Everywhere is dangerous. Nowhere more so than the Alexandra in Sydney.'

'Oh, now how is that dangerous?'

He said softly, a smile edging up the corners of his mouth, 'There are traps there for the unwary. Beautiful, lethal temptations.'

Adrenaline rushed along her veins like a torrent of the warm red wine.

'You mean, those danishes in the coffee shop? They *are* very appetising.' She leaned her elbows on the table and rested her chin in her hands. 'When are you going back?'

His eyes registered a hit, but veiled almost at once. 'Who said I was—' He broke off. 'Never mind that now. There's something I think we need to straighten out.'

She slumped back in her chair and heaved a sigh. 'Right. The letter, I suppose.'

'No, not the letter. I can guess what that's about.' He frowned down at the table for a few seconds, his forehead creased in seriousness, then reached across and took her hands with such an earnest expression that her insides clenched in anxiety. 'I—I've been wanting to say something to you. I'm not very good at this, but... You know that night at the beach... I shouldn't have... I—know I hurt your feelings. It's on my conscience. I'm sorry, Sophy. You didn't deserve that. I apologise.'

There was sincerity in his gaze and she felt herself flush. She knew she'd reached another seminal moment. But it was hard to bear him touching that sore spot, however carefully. Her heart was racing for gold, but it was time to stand up tall and act like a woman. Thank God for adrenaline.

'What feelings, Connor?' She flexed her hands in his strong, warm grasp so that her fingers laced through his. 'I'm a big girl. Isn't it time we left all that behind us and moved on? Now, what's for dessert?'

Connor's grip on her hands tightened. The sensual flame in his dark eyes intensified, and he said softly, 'Don't you know?'

His hands slid to her upper arms, and he leaned across and took her mouth in a searing kiss. Some dishes clattered at their elbows, but he seemed oblivious of them. He pulled her up out of her chair, still kissing her, and drew her away from the table into his arms, pressing her soft curves against his hard, angular frame.

She responded with all she had, and he deepened the kiss to a sizzling, sexual intensity, his tongue darting in to plunder her mouth. As the heady flavours of wine, lemon and him invaded her senses, her bones dissolved and she had to cling to his shoulders for support.

As his hands sought her breasts through the shirt, and slid down to her hips and thighs, her blood ignited with a heavy, pulsing turbulence like a fever, and she wanted to hold him, and experience him with every inch of her skin.

His erection nudged hard against her belly, and, unaccountably, a small rush of moisture pooled between her legs.

The kiss grew frantic, and when she was out of breath and drowning, he broke away from her, his powerful chest rising and falling.

'Is this what you want?' he said hoarsely.

She nodded, wondering if she hadn't given clear enough womanly signals. She took a step in the direction of the bedroom, glancing back to draw him after her with her eyes, but he didn't need any encouragement. He just swept her up in his arms. He'd done it before, but this time it was so thrilling, and romantic, and as he strode along with her, she reached up for another burning taste of his mouth.

He laid her on his bed, and stood gazing at her for a few moments, his eyes blazing like hot coals while she waited, barely breathing, excitement gathering in her like a storm. Then he sat on the edge of the bed and took off his shoes.

She hoped he wasn't getting cold feet again.

'I've got some condoms in my bag if you need any,' she said in an offhand tone.

He broke into a grin. 'Have you, now?' Then he grew grave, though his eyes glowed with tender amusement. 'Well, as it happens, I have some on hand. But if we need any more, we'll use yours.'

He opened the drawer in the bedside table, pulled out a handful, and laid them on the pillow. Her shirt had ridden up a little, and to her surprise he tugged at the edge of it to pull it down more demurely.

What the…? He *did* know what he was doing?

'So…' she breathed, 'what happens now?'

He stretched out beside her on the bed, leaning up on his elbow and gazing down at her, a flame behind the sultry smile in his eyes. 'Well, now. First, we have a little kiss.' He held her jaw lightly while he kissed her mouth, then he pressed his scorching lips in little feathery kisses across her eyebrows, cheeks and jaw. When he reached her throat, the heat of the kisses intensified, and she could feel her breasts swell with arousal and longing.

'Would you like to take off my shirt?' she panted, her voice husky.

His eyes shimmered. 'What do you have under it?'

She hadn't read hundreds of *Cosmo* articles for nothing. 'Isn't that for you to find out?'

He seemed to thrive on the challenge. He changed position, switching his attention to her feet. He lifted the right one in his hand, rubbed his thumb over the sole, and bent his dark head for a long, caressing kiss into the hollow of her ankle.

Oh, God. It was so *seductive*. Little rivers of tingling delight rayed through her foot and somehow settled in the lower regions of her abdomen. Who'd have thought feet and ankles could be so erogenous?

She sank deeper into the bed. 'The other one, Connor. *Please.*'

He obliged, this time with an even more sensual assault on her ankle, appraising her face with shimmering eyes. She was still thrilling as his lean, supple hand edged further up her legs, caressing them as if they were made of satin. When he reached her knees, he smoothed his hand over them as if their rounded shape gave him intense, sensual satisfaction. The more he stroked her, the more his hand seemed increasingly charged with some high-voltage current that radiated straight to her interior. While his eyes…

His eyes held her mesmerised. As his caresses travelled up her thigh, his hot, lustful gaze set her throbbing with a heavy, yearning pulse.

He was so cunning. Fire dripped from his fingers. His hand slid up under the shirt hem, stroking the soft skin of her upper thigh with a sensual intent that made her tremble with suspense.

'Aha,' he said, connecting with the elastic hem of her pants and giving it a playful tug. Then, just as she braced in expectation of him slipping them off, he slid his hand down to the inside of her thigh, just above her knee. She tensed, barely breathing, then he bent suddenly, and with his tongue traced an electric path along the silken skin, nearer and nearer to the flimsy fabric that hid her tingling, throbbing secret place.

Her mouth dried in anticipation. But just before he made the crucial connection he paused and raised his head, a wickedness in his eyes. 'Let's take that shirt off now.'

Now? She wanted it off, of course, it was making her so *hot*, but…

He sat up and pulled off his T-shirt. In the soft light his wide chest was satin bronze, the dusky hairs curling up on it an irresistible temptation. The scar at his ribs stood out in startling contrast, and she reached out to smooth her fingers over it, but he held her hand still. 'No.'

He stretched out on his side, leaning languidly up on one elbow, gazing at her with such sinful intent in his dark, slumbrous gaze that her insides turned to liquid. His hand slid below the shirt to undo her top button, then beneath his black lashes she saw the flare in his eyes as he gazed on the swells of her breasts. One by one he released all the buttons, so that the shirt edges separated. With a husky groan, he bent his burning lips to her breasts, cupping each one in his hand, stroking them until she nearly swooned with pleasure.

It was so fantastic and arousing, she couldn't resist moaning. Her breathing became increasingly hoarse and shallow. Then he trailed greedy little kisses of fire all the way to her navel, then on to the upper edge of her pants.

And there he paused.

But surely. Surely he would…

'Ah. Let's take that shirt all the way off.'

She sat up and he helped her off with the shirt. Then he gazed at her with a hot, intense gaze. She glanced self-consciously down at her breasts, wondering what he was thinking.

'Care to bite anything?'

His lustful face broke into a husky laugh, then he grabbed her in his arms and kissed her lips, tenderly at first, then with mounting fierceness. As his tongue ravished her mouth she could feel his big powerful heartbeat, thumping in electric communication with hers.

Her heart filled with emotion. She ached with everything in her to be close to him, as close as a human being could be to another person. Responding with fervour, she wound her arms around him and clung, aroused by the feel of his chest hair in friction with her breasts, craving for every form of contact as he pushed her down with him onto the bed.

He kissed her throat and breasts, and the yearning that was storming her blood set her every skin cell alight with erotic craving. Her nipples were so hard and aching, so throbbing with need for attention, that when he closed his mouth over first one, then the other and tenderly licked them with his tongue, *then* drew hard on them with his mouth, she nearly went wild.

'Oh, Connor,' she gasped, shuddering with pleasure as his passion moved on to rage over her prostrate body. Between her thighs, a searing hunger blazed, but his lips and devouring, inflammatory hands stopped short of that potent spot.

He leaned up for a second, motionless, watching her face.

She felt the air in the room tauten.

'What are we waiting for?' Her voice was nearly a croak.

He smiled, then all at once whipped her pants down to her ankles.

She heard the sudden quickening of his breath. 'You're—beautiful.' His voice was thick and unsteady. For her to have such a powerful effect on him filled her with thrilled wonder.

The room crackled with tension as he gazed at her nude body with rapt appreciation. But, in a sudden anxiety, she couldn't help thinking of the last time.

Swallowing, she ventured, 'Connor, you're not—you're not still worrying about me being a virgin, are you?'

For an instant his eyes closed. Then with a long, shuddering groan he bent his sensuous mouth to her soft nest of curls in a kiss more tender and arousing than she could ever have imagined. She made wild little gasping cries of sheer pleasure, parting her thighs for him, clenching and quivering as his lips and tongue flicked across the tender, yearning tissues. The sensation was so delicious, so exciting, she was in an ecstasy of wanton sexual rapture, until all too soon the erotic frenzy came to a halt. He paused, lifted his head to cast a long, smouldering glance at her, then rolled away.

He sprang off the bed and, without taking his eyes from her, unbuckled his belt and stripped off the rest of his clothes.

The breath caught in her throat at his power and beauty. He was so tall and strong and well made, the lines of his long, sinewy limbs and lean, muscled body as graceful and stirring as any classical sculpture. But when her gaze fastened on the robust length and thickness of his engorged penis, her eyes widened. For a second her courage nearly took a dive.

She tried not to show her momentary cowardice, but Connor's watchful gaze on her face was instantly aware.

'Sophy, Sophy.' He sat down on the bed beside her and kissed her lips very gently. Then he drew her hand to touch him. 'Feel the skin here,' he murmured. 'This is not designed to hurt you.'

She closed her hand around him, marvelling at the velvet texture of the skin encasing the rock-hard shaft, while he kept motionless, only a small tremor and the glitter in his eyes showing his effort of will not to react.

'Well,' she exclaimed. 'You are very… You're *very*… Who'd have guessed?'

A tinge of amusement crossed his face, but he gently removed her hand. Then he took her by her shoulders and laid her down. His smile slowly faded as his smouldering dark gaze feasted on her nude body with a fierce possessiveness that shook her.

He extracted a sheath from the packet on the pillow, and eased it onto his virile arousal as she lay motionless, pricking with anticipation, her breasts, her skin, every part of her aflame.

He turned to her and she whispered, 'So…?'

'So.' With one provocative finger he drew a line of fire in her sensitised skin from her collarbone to the apex of her thighs. Then he slipped his hand between her legs, parting them a little, and softly, with exquisite gentleness, stroked the tender, burning flesh until she moaned and gasped.

Then his clever fingers brushed the most aroused spot of all. 'Ah-h-h…'

He slipped a finger inside her, stroking her with patient concentration. Every part of her felt aflame with hunger, his every light touch was the most intense, searing pleasure.

Suddenly he paused, then rolled his big, lean body on top of hers, supporting his weight on his arms, and positioning himself between her parted legs.

She could feel the rapid beat of his heart, hear his heavy breathing as he contemplated her.

'Link your ankles behind my back,' he commanded.

She complied, and he gazed down at her, his eyes glowing with a dark flame. She felt the velvet tip of his hard penis nudge at her moist entrance, then he made a firm, insistent push.

She felt an uncomfortable pressure and dug her fingers into his shoulders, straining with tension.

'Easy now,' he ground out. 'Just relax.' Then he thrust again, a little more firmly.

This time she felt a sharp, raw tweak of her tender tissues. He was inside her, his face settling into an expression of absolute ecstatic triumph, while she clenched her entire body and cried, 'Hey.'

He froze, searching her face in alarm. Then he eased himself out of her, his eyes closing momentarily as if even the backwards movement was the most sublime pleasure.

'Are you all right?' His voice was a deep rasp. His brows drew together, and he said, breathing heavily, concern in his dark eyes, 'Are you hurting?'

She made a rapid review of her discomfort and realised she wasn't, not really, and made an effort to relax. 'Not now. It's all right.'

He still frowned, raking her face, and she said huskily, in an effort to tease, 'What do you think? Am I made of glass?'

He stroked the hair back from her hairline, his hand gentle and soothing, though unsteady, like his breathing. He grazed her cheekbone with his lips. 'We can stop if you want to.'

His dark eyes were so tender and at the same time so fierce and hot, a dark, heavy heat pooled deep inside her. 'No,' she whispered. 'Don't stop.'

His pupils darkened and he made a sharp little intake of breath, then bent his lips to hers in a deep, searing kiss. As her senses swam to the taste of him, the passion rose in her like a seething tide. With a little involuntary sound in her throat, she locked her legs around him.

He eased carefully into her, filling her, scanning her face with his hot, possessive gaze until she got used to the unusual feeling. Then he started a gentle rhythm of slow, controlled moves while she grew accustomed to the strange erotic pleasure, enjoying the curled hairs on his chest and legs brushing her smooth skin. With gradual care he increased the tempo, and her flesh ignited to the sexy rocking. Little streamlets of delight roused in her and spread like rays of the sun. She clung to his powerful, athletic body, arching and giving herself up to him, barely conscious of her own desperate, hoarse little cries.

As though hearing the fevered beat of her blood, Connor escalated the rhythm, thrusting faster and faster, until passion and pleasure entwined to propel her up a wild, exhilarating climb, higher and higher, to a peak where her wild, frenzied tension hung poised, then shattered and dissolved in a rapturous, blissful release.

His big, strong body bucked, and he emitted a deep groan that sounded as if it came from the very depths of him. He collapsed on top of her, and lay panting there for several seconds, his cheek against hers, while their bodies were slick with their efforts.

He rolled away from her, and after a time visited the bathroom. The dark felt soft and caressing on her skin as she lay there, listening to the running water, reviewing all the sensations of her body after her momentous initiation.

Connor returned and slipped into the bed beside her. He lay there silently for a while, his elbow crooked over his eyes. Eventually he roused himself and turned on his side to gaze at her, his dark eyes glowing into hers with such warmth she felt bathed in the light of the sun.

'Well, then, Sophy Woodruff?'

Smiling, she turned to face him. 'Well, then, Connor O'Brien.'

Softly he traced her silhouette with his finger, while her heart brimmed with a million tremulous, heartfelt things she needed to say to him. But he whispered, 'Shh, sweetheart,' kissed her lips, and pulled her close in against his big, warm body. 'Go to sleep.'

CHAPTER ELEVEN

BREAKFAST at Connor's was a casual affair. Sophy didn't have any clean clothes, so she was forced to stay in bed. At least, that was Connor's reasoning.

On first awakening, she gently disentangled herself from his embrace, and tiptoed to the bathroom. She borrowed his soap for a warm wash, cleaned her teeth with toothpaste on her finger, and, unable to locate her clothes, wrapped herself in a towel. When she emerged, Connor was lying awake, gazing out the window at the grey view of the harbour, dismal with misty rain. She hesitated at the door, uncertain of the etiquette. Wasn't it time to wave a sophisticated au revoir and saunter to the door?

Anyway, she had washing to do at home, her library books to return, and the house to clean before Zoe and Leah came back from their camping trip.

'Oh, good,' she said, a little breathless. 'You're awake. Do you know where my clothes are? I have some things I have to do at home. There's the—the housework, and…'

Connor turned to examine her, and leaned up on his elbow, as languid as a big, lazy panther. His dark, sinful gaze and the black growth of his beard gave him a villainous look.

'I have to…have to go to the library…'

He gave his brows a seductive lilt and lifted the bedcovers, patting the spot beside him.

Her bones dissolved. His bronzed chest with the dark whorls of hair looked so warm and inviting. With a surge of excitement she managed to walk primly back until the very last second, when she dropped the towel and dived, giggling, under the covers and into his arms.

At some later stage he got up and showered, leaving her body humming with pleasure and a certain amount of soreness, her heart in a state of thrilled suspension. Then somehow locating her clothes along with his own, he blew her a kiss and went out in his car.

What was a prisoner to do? She took the opportunity for a long, relaxing shower.

Connor returned with hot croissants, sour strawberry jam and double cream, lattes and golden peaches with rosy skins. 'I couldn't resist them,' he said, kissing her shoulder where the T-shirt he'd lent her kept slipping. 'They reminded me of you.'

The dearth of furniture was a blessing in some ways. On a rainy Saturday, the bed was the cosiest place for the breakfast feast.

It wasn't long before the conversation came around to her letter. Connor's quick brain had made the connection about her relationship with Elliott, of course. He kept shaking his head and saying, 'I should have realised at once.'

There was no point trying to conceal anything from him any longer, and she told him all of it, the meetings, the disastrous dinner at the hotel. She couldn't prevent her voice from wobbling a bit when she told him about Elliott's offer of money to buy her silence.

Connor looked grave. 'Not a very clever way to handle it. He must feel very threatened.'

She glanced quickly at him. 'I realise he must, of course. If he didn't know I even existed, then it's come as a terrible shock. Anyone would feel threatened. But it's funny, I have the strongest feeling he's lying to me about something. I wouldn't be a bit surprised if he *did* know. He knew that Sylvie—that was my mother—had died. Surely he would have known she left a child.'

'He might have known that, without knowing you were *his*

child.' He licked some croissant crumbs from where they'd landed on her thigh. 'That was a tragedy, your mother dying when you were so young.'

'It was,' she agreed, sighing. 'But I was so lucky, being adopted by the Woodruffs. They were wonderful parents, and so generous. You know, they haven't sold their house. They might still decide to come back.'

His brows knitted, and he scanned her face. 'That must have been hard for you when they left. How old were you?'

'Eighteen. It was hard at first, but I got over it. People have to move on and grow up, don't they? It did me good in some ways. Taught me to be independent. How many people move out of home at that age? It's really very normal.'

His eyes were pensive. 'How do they feel about your contacting Elliott?'

She lowered her lashes. 'Well, I haven't exactly mentioned it. To be honest, I doubt if they'll mind one way or the other.'

Connor frowned, considering. From all he'd heard, adoptive parents felt equally threatened when their children chose to search for their birth parents. And though it might be normal for people to leave home when they attained their adulthood, it wasn't all that normal for parents to be the ones who left the children. And the country. Such a total abandonment.

'Why did they go back to England?'

'Well, Bea has a daughter from an earlier marriage. She and her husband moved back to live in England. Lauren had some problems during her first pregnancy, so naturally Bea wanted to be with her. They only meant to visit for a few months at first. But the baby was born with some disabilities, so they decided to stay on to give Lauren support. And now other children have come along, and I think they love being grandparents. You know how it is. Blood is thicker than water, as they say. I guess that's why I feel so interested to know about my own parents.'

Connor felt a twinge. Could Sophy Woodruff truly feel so little bitterness about having been abandoned by two sets of parents, for whatever reasons?

He rubbed his jaw. 'It shouldn't be so hard to check up on all of it. Are you sure you want to go ahead? You might find out things you don't want to know.'

'I've considered that. Even if I discover that Elliott is not someone I particularly like, there's little Matthew. I'd love to have a little brother. And, you know, I suspect Elliott isn't really very kind to him. That has a huge bearing on a child's development, you know. He needs people to talk to him, be interested in him.'

'There might be—other people in the family who do.'

'I hope so.' She reached for a tissue to wipe peach juice from her chin. 'You know what? Sometimes I think…the way Elliott has reacted…it's all too hard. Maybe I should just drop it.'

It would save Elliott grief. And Sir Frank. Although…would it? Connor met her wistful blue gaze, and felt remorse. Did Elliott Fraser deserve to be spared? Surely every child had the right to know where they came from. And who was to say the old man wouldn't welcome the news of a granddaughter?

Once he got used to the idea.

'And listen,' she said, startling him with her uncanny ability to read his mind, 'I have to ask that you keep this confidential. I've promised Elliott.'

But *he* hadn't.

She gazed anxiously at him. 'You're not thinking of telling his father, are you? That would be shocking for poor Elliott if the old man finds out from someone else. Elliott needs to break the news himself. Please, Connor.' She put her hand on his arm. Her eyes were filled with such urgency, he wavered. 'Elliott might come round, he might see the light and realise it's lovely to have another child in the world. Let him be the one who tells his father.' She leaned forward and the T-shirt slipped and showed him an alluring creamy swell.

'Can't you see? If you tell Sir Frank, Elliott will blame me. He's bound to. And it will be my fault. You'd never have known at all if I hadn't lost that letter.'

Or if he hadn't been so tied up in knots with lust that his brain hadn't been working.

He hesitated. He owed Sir Frank the truth. The investigation had stretched on long enough and he'd used up weeks of his leave already. How much longer would Elliott Fraser stonewall? To Connor's mind, most good-hearted men in Elliott's position would have opened their doors to their lost child by this stage, discreetly, if not with enthusiasm.

But he concealed from her his cynical reading of the man. Sophy Woodruff seemed to have a boundless belief in people who had let her down, and he didn't want to be the one to damage it.

'Sir Frank's an old man,' he pointed out. 'He won't last for ever. If Elliott doesn't tell him, he might miss out on his chance to know you. Now *that* would be a tragedy.'

'No, but… Oh, promise me, Connor. Please.'

She smelled tantalisingly of peach. The pleading in her eyes dragged at something in his chest. With her soft, swollen mouth, the exposure of one smooth shoulder in the absurdly large shirt, she was too desirable for all these worries. What she needed was more kissing to warm her through.

Perhaps she was right, though, and Elliott deserved a chance. She might have a lot to lose if he blew the gaff. On the other hand, there was his commitment. The old guy was relying on him. He *trusted* him.

Either way, someone could get hurt.

He felt a chill misgiving at how it would be for her if Elliott Fraser rejected her.

In the end he compromised. 'Look, I don't feel as if I can promise. I might run into Sir Frank at some time, and then I'd feel awful for concealing something so important from him. But we'll see how it goes with Elliott. If by…say…the autumn…he shows signs of acting like a human being, then we'll see. Here, let me,' he said as she peered down her T-shirt and tried to mop between her breasts with a tissue. 'I can clean this up for you.'

Autumn.

The word sank through Sophy's conscious mind and into a deeper region, where instincts and inspirations combined with clues and intelligence to give her ideas that weren't always welcome. But she pushed this one away from her. Heavens, it was raining, the trees were getting a drink, it was Saturday, and she was in bed with a big, warm, sexy man.

She stayed there for most of Saturday. Connor O'Brien had much to teach her about the erotic arts, he said, and she was a willing pupil. The laundry service returned her clothes in the afternoon, but as it turned out she didn't need them until the next day, when the sky cleared to a joyous blue.

Connor's house wasn't gloomy in daylight. In spite of its neglected feel, it was full of light. The once lush terraced garden was overgrown with wild creepers, and, though there was a private landing stage for the O'Brien boat, no vessel was moored there.

From its location on the Point there were spectacular views in every direction, from the postcard view of the Opera House and the Harbour Bridge, right out to the Manly Heads. She glanced around at all the overgrown shrubs, their leaves plump and juicy with water, and wished she had some secateurs with her.

In the afternoon Connor took her strolling through the Sunday markets at the Rocks, where they gazed at exotic treasures and bought each other souvenirs from a stall that sold stuffed-animal toys. Increasingly conscious of the weekend coming to a close, and her time running out, Sophy secreted her precious koala in the safe zip section of her bag. Soon he would take her home.

On their walk he paused to stare through the window of a bazaar that sold oriental rugs. She tried to read his gaze. She could tell he loved the East by the way he talked about it. Were those foreign scenes calling to him, drawing him back? He surprised her then by striding inside and negotiating with the rug seller for an enormous Kashmiri rug. The man rolled it out on the floor. It was pure silk, in delicate shades of pinks and lavenders, blues and creams, the colours changing from whichever angle they were viewed.

She wished she could take off her shoes, and let her feet sink into its gorgeous pile and wallow.

Watching her with a knowing glint in his eye, Connor said, 'In case you feel like a nap. Let's take it home and try it.'

She was thrilled to the soul. This didn't sound like goodbye, Sophy Woodruff.

When he did take her home to her place, drowsy and languorous with love in the early hours of Monday, he didn't come inside. He kissed her lingeringly at the door, then turned and walked down the path while she watched his retreating back from inside the door, wonder in her heart. How could she, Sophy Woodruff, be desired by a man like Connor O'Brien?

The piles of gear were back in the hall, and she realised with delight that Leah and Zoe were home. Would they believe her fantastic luck? She tiptoed to avoid waking them, only stumbling and barking her shins once, then slipped into bed, hugging her happiness to herself.

Every summer day after that was a precious, golden day. She met Connor before work, on the mornings he didn't drive her there from his place after she'd spent the night. He walked across to the Gardens with her at lunchtime, his lunch, like hers, in a paper bag from the basement deli. Perhaps sensing they'd be intruders, other people stayed away from the willow lawn, and she and Connor had it all to themselves.

Revelling in their privacy, he teased and flirted with her, argued about movies, snatched her novel from her and read steamy excerpts aloud to make her laugh. Sometimes, though, hearing the evocative words in his deep voice would make her hot, and she'd sense from his thickening tones and the spark in his eyes that he was affected, too. Then he'd throw the book aside, grab her and push her down on the grass.

Lying in his arms in the grass, drowning in his kisses, was a dangerous pursuit, because now a kiss was never enough. More than once, passion leaped out of control, and they were forced to hurry back to the Alexandra, running the gamut of the lift and the walk along the gallery, avoiding touching each other while their burning bodies raged to be assuaged. Then she would slip into Connor's office with him for hot, urgent sex. With just enough of each other's clothes removed to make it possible, he would lift her onto his desk and thrust into her, every sizzling stroke a delicious, searing ecstasy, until he raised her to such a wild climax he or she had to cover her mouth to prevent her rapturous cries from exposing their forbidden delight.

At first, in the evenings he took her to restaurants, although increasingly, as the demands of their passion accelerated, it was easier, and more private, to eat at his place and cook for themselves. Connor's kitchen equipment was limited, so it became necessary to go to a kitchen store and buy utensils and a non-stick frying pan with a lid. She went with him, and argued over the merits of the different brands.

In the same week, out of concern for her comfort, Connor bought two rather sumptuous sofas to go with the rug, as well as a deep reclining armchair and a coffee table.

Life had never felt so fantastic. Somehow, the sheer, joyous excitement of being with Connor seemed to spill over and touch everything. The hours she spent with Leah and Zoe, though restricted, seemed more fun than ever, her work with the children more pleasurable.

She was living in an exuberant whirlpool, all anxieties on hold, when she lifted the phone one morning to hear the voice of Elliott Fraser.

Well, well. What had taken him so long?

He regretted the delay, he said in his dry, cool tones. Pressure of work, but he was eager to make good his offer of dinner and a proper discussion.

The night he suggested was her netball night, but she agreed without hesitation and wrote down the address. The Avengers would locate a stand-in for her without much trouble. Instinctively, she decided to keep the invitation to herself. It was a private contract between her and her father, and, depending on the success of it, she'd report back to Connor. She acknowledged something to herself then that she'd sensed in her heart. Though he'd never stated it, Connor didn't have a very high opinion of Elliott. If things didn't turn out well, she'd hate him to think she looked like a needy little loser.

Better to see how things went.

Since the address Elliott gave her was a fair distance from home, she chose to drive. She took along a bottle of wine, out of courtesy, although she wouldn't be indulging herself.

She felt mildly surprised by 221 Enfield Place. It was a modest brick and tile home with a small garden behind a high hedge. When she rang the doorbell, a woman in an overall with a pleasant face opened the door and invited her in, introducing herself as Marie, and explaining that Mr Fraser had been delayed. She showed Sophy down a short hall into a sitting room with an adjoining dining room. Marie took the wine from her and offered her a glass, but Sophy declined, accepting the offer of soft drink instead.

Savoury food smells suggested that dinner was well under way.

Marie brought her lemonade, then returned to her cooking, while Sophy sat on a stiff sofa with cylindrical steel legs and inspected the room. The carpet had an all-over autumnal pattern. The autumn theme was continued in the pictures on the walls, some lake and forest scenes in over-vivid shades that suggested mass production.

A cabinet stood against one wall, with a small lamp and a couple of photos in frames. One was of a much younger Elliott Fraser, the other was a magnificently gilded one of his wedding party, and looked as if it would be more appropriately placed in Buckingham Palace than this unpretentious suburban room.

Sophy got up and walked over for a closer look. The wedding

looked like the high-society occasion she might have expected, with the bride and bridesmaids in couture gowns.

The room held no sign of a child. Where was he? she wondered, turning to investigate the dining room. The table was set for two. Perhaps Matthew was being minded by someone, although…

Something about the place gave her a prickly sensation of discomfort. The furnishings were adequate, but somehow sterile like those in the first room. Not really what she'd have expected of the residence of the wealthy man Connor had described.

A depressed feeling descended upon her. All at once she knew with certainty Elliott didn't live here.

Following the aromas, she walked through to the kitchen. Marie had dinner plates on the warming hob, and was mixing some sort of sauce. She looked up in surprise.

'Sorry for intruding,' Sophy said with a smile. 'I just wondered something, Marie. Mind if I ask? Have you been cooking for Mr Fraser long?'

The woman paused her stirring. 'No, well, love, I don't stay on. I'm a temp, really. This is my first job for Mr Fraser. I think it's just for the one night, although he said there was a slight chance there might have to be more coming up.'

'Did he?' Sophy smiled, though she could feel the weight on her heart like a stone. More coming up. In case she wasn't convinced the first time. For a while her head swam in disbelief while she tried to process it.

Why had he attempted such a cheap, despicable trick? For fear she would contaminate his real home? Or…an even more contemptible possibility occurred to her. Was it a ploy to conceal his massive wealth from her, in case she got ideas? She felt enveloped in a choking shame. Where was his integrity? How could she be related to a man with so little honour?

'Look, Marie, the dinner smells lovely, but I'm sorry I won't be able to stay. Will you please tell Mr Fraser I'm not hungry?'

She let herself out the front door, and as she stepped off the small patio started when her attention was drawn by a man getting out of a dark, sleek car parked in the driveway. It was Elliott, looking grim-faced, his movements hurried and rather jerky as he stooped and reached into the backseat for something.

As he straightened he saw her and jolted upright, then closed the car door and strode along the cement path that crossed the lawn, smoothing back his silver hair. 'Miss Woo— Sophy.' He extended a hand, then his eyes focused on her face and he dropped the attempt. 'What're you…? You're not leaving?'

'I am, yes, but you don't have to worry, Mr Fraser. I won't cause you any trouble. You have nothing to fear from me.' She felt her throat swell, but held back the tears. 'I won't bother you again.'

He stood there looking thunderstruck as she turned to walk down the path, then he hastened to catch her at the gate. 'Miss Woodruff… Sophy…what's this about? Has something happened? What has my housekeeper been—'

She paused outside the gate and turned. 'Don't, please. Don't make it worse. I'd rather remember you as someone with dignity, at least.'

His face contorted and anger flashed in his chill grey eyes. 'Look, how have you missed out, just answer me that? You had good parents, from all accounts. A good family life. How could I have raised you on my own? After your mother died, it was the best option. You come after me, wanting answers, harassing me. Just *who* do you think—'

'Who do I think I am?' She faced him proudly, the barest tremble in her low, cool voice. 'I'm Sophy Woodruff. That's who. And whoever *you* are is nothing to do with me.'

All at once she felt sorry for Elliott Fraser. Without looking at him again she got into the car, started it at once and drove away. Away from his pathetic subterfuge, his decoy home and the flimsy hedge he'd erected against the monstrous threat she posed.

After a long while she realised she was shaking and travelling in the wrong direction. She had to turn back and drive around for ages, in and out of unfamiliar streets, before she could find any landmarks she recognised. At last, by accident, she stumbled back onto the road to Bondi Junction. She headed up the hill, through Woollahra, and joined the artery that would take her to Point Piper.

CHAPTER TWELVE

CONNOR O'Brien wasn't expecting her, that much was clear. When he opened the door he stood there with such a veiled, stern expression, Sophy's heart plunged, realising she'd never just dropped by before, and wondered if she'd crossed some invisible line. Then his lean face relaxed and he smiled. 'Ah. Come in.'

Too late, though. That first impression sank in like indelible ink. 'What's the matter, Connor?' she said in an attempt to smile it away. 'You haven't got a blonde in here, have you?'

'The blonde's just left. Now I'm ready for a brunette.' He spoke lightly, but his eyes were hooded. He gestured her in and she started down the hall ahead of him. They reached the sitting room and he stood with his hands tucked into the pockets of his jeans. There was an awkward moment, then he said, 'Is anything wrong?'

He looked more closely at her, then reached out to touch her, but she backed away, suddenly seeing how it would be if she broke down and sobbed on his shoulder like a whining wimp.

Without properly meeting his eyes, she gave a shrug. 'Just thought I'd drop by. See if you had plans. In case you felt like some gorgeous feminine company.' She smiled and fluttered her lashes at him, slipped off her shoulder bag. Her glance fell on his laptop, open on the coffee table.

He followed her gaze and made a swift, smooth movement to close it.

She remembered then that Connor had a life she wasn't privy to. An unpleasant realisation dawned on her. Being his lover didn't automatically give her rights. She shouldn't have assumed she could just drop in, and expect him to…what? Drop everything? Comfort her while she bled all over him like a needy child? More than ever this visit felt like a transgression. After all the fun and excitement of their daily contacts, she couldn't help feeling hurt, and a warning sense of panic. Heavens, what with having unrealistic expectations of Elliott, and now Connor, she had to wonder if she could ever trust herself to get anything right.

She could see him studying her, his black brows drawn, a question in his intelligent dark eyes, and she tried to conceal the black, leaden weight on her heart.

'Oh, look, Connor. I see you're working. Sorry. I shouldn't have interrupted you without warning. Very insensitive of me.' She took up her bag again, slung it on her shoulder and flashed him an unfocused grin. 'I'll take myself off.'

Recognising too late that his responses had been inadequate, Connor put out a hand to halt her. 'Hang on.' Her arm felt quite cold. In the stronger light he could see he hadn't imagined her pallor, the brittleness behind her smile. 'Isn't this your netball night?'

'Yes, well, usually. I…er…couldn't go tonight.'

He frowned. 'But—you always go. You love the Avengers.'

'I know.' She hesitated a second, her face working with the effort to conceal some inexpressible emotion, then she turned towards the hall, giving him a backwards wave. 'Anyway, I'd better go. See you.'

A quick succession of thoughts and feelings flashed through him. Consternation, remorse. Something was wrong, she'd chosen to tell him, but he'd been too concerned at being dragged away from his communication with the embassy, and failed the test.

He had to stride to catch up with her at the door. 'What's wrong?' She stood with her back to him, her hand on the knob, and he saw her brace her slim shoulders against some heavy weight. 'Sweetheart, what is it? What's happened?' Then he guessed. 'Oh, no. Don't tell me. You've been to see Elliott Fraser.'

She didn't answer. He gripped her upper arms and he could feel the tremor in them. He turned her to face him. She gave a twisted attempt at a smile that wrenched his heart.

'Connor…' She breathed in with difficulty. 'Would you mind just putting your arms around me for a second?'

'Sophy, Sophy…' He held her as close as it was feasible without crushing her, stroking her hair, wishing he could go to Elliott Fraser's house and confront the man with his cold, patrician face. Little by little he prised it out of her, the phony house, the confrontation at the gate.

He tried to limit himself to murmuring soothing things in her ear, but the fragrance of her hair and her supple, vibrant body had their inevitable effect, and before he knew it he was kissing away her tears, then kissing her for real.

The next thing he knew he was as hard as granite, stripping off her clothes with shaky hands, his heart thundering in his ears as he laid her on his bed and felt the passion rise to consume them.

As always, she offered herself to him with such ardent, unfettered trust he felt awed. Uncritical of his rough, masculine solution to every agony of the spirit, she returned his caresses with as much fervour as before. Her responsiveness as he tasted the treasures of her body were even more passionate.

It wasn't just his imagination. The playful eroticism of their previous couplings was swamped by a powerful emotional current that connected her to him at some deep level. The intensity moved him so deeply he felt shaken. In some way, the primitive core of him opened up to the harmony of two souls mingling, like a dry desert gulch welcoming rain.

His brain tried to warn him of the deadly danger of what had happened, what he was doing, but he was beyond reason.

As he positioned himself to take her, gazing down at her delicately flushed face, his lust was infused with the most overwhelming tenderness. Concepts like rules and responsibility were meaningless when faced with his poignant urgency to drive the shadows from Sophy Woodruff's eyes.

He plunged into her, groaning with the almost unbearable pleasure of sliding into her moist heat.

Then he rocked her, tenderly stroking the smooth satin walls yielding before him with such a delicious friction, all the time holding her fervent gaze. Unable to restrain his sinuous movements for long, he thrust faster and faster, deeper, harder, while she dug her nails into his back, her face and neck strained with the sweet tension.

With every stroke he felt himself wanting to bind her closer, his thundering heart awash with emotions he'd forgotten he could feel, passion and possession, and an aching need to somehow protect her from all the tragedies of existence.

With a massive effort of will he held back his own rising pleasure to keep pace with hers, until he was nearly ready to explode.

At last, he felt the convulsive tightening grip of her muscles, saw her eyes close, the wave of ecstasy ripple over her face, and allowed himself to soar to his own crescendo and let his searing-hot seed spurt in a fantastic, rapturous release.

Afterwards, though, while she slept snuggled into the curve of his body, Connor lay wide-awake and stared into the grim dark.

His body felt energised, fulfilled and at ease, while a hopeless dismay invaded his soul.

What had he done? The very thing, the *one* thing he knew he must not. He'd let emotion in, and lost his sense of perspective.

What a self-indulgent fool. He could see how, little by little, he'd succumbed. He'd turned every incident to his advantage to have her, a tender woman, a *virgin*, for God's sake. He'd played with her, seduced her, romanced her, and now…

His gut churned with the awful guilt.

Now she depended on him.

No use to remind himself she wasn't a child, she was responsible for her own actions, her own risks. At that first peal of the doorbell earlier that evening he'd recognised the damage he'd done.

He'd forgotten his code. Forgotten that people in ordinary walks of life needed the invisible tendrils of relationship to connect them, keep them safe and supported. Allowed himself to link with her. Encouraged her to trust him.

And who would she have when he was gone?

CHAPTER THIRTEEN

'OH, IT'S just so *mean* keeping such a beautiful animal in prison. Look into those eyes, Connor. Don't you wish you could set him free?'

Sophy glanced up at him but he wasn't looking at her. He was staring through the glass at the leopard, but with such grimness in his fathomless dark gaze she realised with a small tremor of fear that he was looking beyond the magnificent creature, at something remote and internal.

'What, Connor? What is it?'

She didn't expect an answer. Not a true one. And she didn't want one. Since the night she'd dropped in on him, Connor had changed. She blamed herself, of course. She'd done the thing Leah and Zoe had often shaken their heads over in regard to other poor, foolhardy women.

She'd exposed her true feelings. Not in what she'd actually said, but in so many other ways. And now he'd retreated to some distant region, and she felt helpless to change things back to the way they had been. She supposed she could try to pretend not to feel anything, but there was no fooling him. She read his comprehension of her weakness in every dark glance. It made her painfully unable to be natural with him.

Every time she opened her mouth, she could feel him tense, as if she might be about to blurt out the fateful word. And she could hardly trust herself not to. So often now, especially when they were making love, she longed to tell him, to somehow ease her soul of its aching burden. But it didn't take Einstein to know what would happen if she did, and how that gaping black universe might feel.

'Sorry? Come this way,' he said. 'Let's see what's down here.'

They strolled away from the big cats, and headed down a wide avenue where the sound of trumpeting and heavy shuffling were drawing a crowd. She'd brought a shady hat with her, for though the leaves were on the turn, the sun was still strong. She put it on now, grateful for the wide brim's usefulness in concealing her face when she needed to.

Her lover looked so lean, tanned and handsome in his jeans and a snowy white polo shirt, if it hadn't been for the tension in him she'd have felt proud. Every so often he took her hand and held it for short bursts, and she saw other women look at her with envy. If only they knew how tenuous her happiness was.

She felt so sorry for the poor elephant, rocking backwards and forwards like an unloved child, a heavy chain on its leg. She glanced at Connor to see what he made of it, but his attention was suddenly turned on some people approaching down the path from the other direction. He was watching the approach of an elderly gent with a stick, who was doing his best to keep up with a very small boy in a Spiderman costume. A man in a chauffeur's uniform followed them at a respectful distance.

As they drew near the old man spotted Connor, and his face lit up in recognition. 'Well, well, now. Connor O'Brien.' He halted and leaned on his stick. 'Now, isn't this a splendid coincidence? Good to see you, my boy.' His bright eyes darted straight to Sophy.

Connor stepped forward to shake hands, enquiring warmly about the old gent's health. The boy's gaze was fixed on the commotion surrounding the elephant, then he turned Sophy's way. With a severe shock she recognised the intense, eager little face of Matthew Fraser.

'Come and say hello to Mr O'Brien, Matthew,' the old man commanded.

With her head still spinning, she hardly heard Connor's murmured greeting to the child, and when he drew her forward and said, 'Sir Frank, this is Sophy Woodruff. Sir Frank Fraser, Sophy,' the words were so momentous, they took a while to connect.

So this was her grandfather. The old man nodded his head at her, and held out his wrinkled hand. He smelled of mints and eucalyptus. 'Well, well. So you're Sophy Woodruff.' He peered at her with curiosity. 'Do you like the zoo, Sophy?'

'I…I like the animals,' she hedged, not wanting to disappoint him. She glanced at Connor, but he'd slipped on his sunglasses and his eyes were inaccessible.

Sir Frank turned his attention back to him, though he kept glancing at her as he made elderly small talk. Connor's responses were smooth and respectful. She could sense that, despite the careful conversation, he and the old man were very familiar with each other. And she knew something else with absolute certainty.

This was a set-up.

She'd thought it strange when Connor had suggested an afternoon at the zoo. But how much had he told the old man? Was he aware she was his granddaughter?

Oblivious of the concerns of the adults, Matthew grew bored with the conversation and commandeered a park bench under a nearby tree for a game of climbing up one end, running along and jumping off, until his grandfather called him over.

'Sit down here with me awhile, my dear,' Sir Frank said, patting Sophy's hand. 'Here, young fella. Take Connor for a walk and show him that elephant.'

She allowed Sir Frank to usher her to the bench and commence a gentle, probing inquisition about her job, her interests and her friends. He was a charmer. Normally she'd have been enchanted, but there were so many vibrations and dangerous cross-currents on the air that, though she answered everything politely, she couldn't keep her attention from Connor and the boy.

True to his grandfather's instructions, the child took a couple of brave steps towards Connor, who stood in silence, his hands hooked into his jeans. He made no gesture of encouragement. She saw Matthew gaze up at his intimidating height, and wait for some sign from behind the dark glasses. The little boy's feet faltered.

He cast an anxious glance over his shoulder at his grandfather.

Sophy tensed and sat very still, her breath on hold as Connor surveyed the child in a sort of frozen immobility. At last he appeared to thaw. He relaxed his posture and held out his hand. 'All right, Spiderman,' he said, a smile in his deep voice. 'Show me an elephant.'

She heaved a secret sigh of relief, and became aware of Sir Frank studying her with a shrewd gaze. 'No need to worry about Connor. He'd never hurt a little one. He had a son of his own, you know. Things go wrong in families, my dear, as you'd know in your line of work.'

The old man rambled on, about fathers and sons and mothers and daughters, but all the time she couldn't take her eyes off Connor and the child. Watching him looking down at Matthew, listening to his chatter, strolling along and holding his hand, pointing things out to him, lifting him up to see over the heads of the crowd. She was overwhelmed then with the saddest, most poignant feeling of regret she could ever remember, a feeling so painful and intense she knew her heart would break.

Connor O'Brien was the perfect man for her. And she could see it all clearly now. She knew why he couldn't meet her eyes. Why he was introducing her to these strangers.

He was leaving her.

The journey to Point Piper seemed very long. She made a few listless enquiries.

'Does Sir Frank know everything?' she asked.

He glanced at her, then his eyes slid away. 'Look—I felt I had to tell him. It seemed—necessary. You don't really mind, do you?' She gave a shrug and he made an attempt at encouragement. 'You know, he's not at all the same person as Elliott. He's quite a—a grand old guy. My own father thought the world of him. And you're like him in some ways. Amazingly.'

'Really?'

He must have heard the lack of enthusiasm in her voice, because his brows lifted. 'I'm surprised. I thought this meant so much to you, getting to know your birth family.'

They'd turned down a street lined with plane trees. She noticed they had a sad, yellowy, autumn look. 'Yes, well, it's not as simple as I thought. Nothing ever is, is it?'

She felt his swift glance on her face.

'Are you hurt that I told him?'

She tried to smile. 'How could I be? I know why you did it.'

His jaw tightened and he was silent for a second. 'Look—look, sweetheart, it doesn't have to change anything if you don't want it to, does it? There's nothing to say you *have* to have him in your life.'

'Sounds as if you're sweet-talking me, Connor. But there's no need.' She gave a weary sigh. 'Let's face it. There's no saying I'll ever hear from him again. He's met me now and satisfied his curiosity. What more is there to expect, really?'

And to be honest, right then she didn't even want to think about the Frasers. All her hopes in that direction seemed like the naive, girlish dream of the person she used to be. Before she found what she really wanted. Before she grew up.

They lapsed into silence after that.

When they arrived at Connor's, he quickly disappeared to the kitchen to make coffee, then brought the cups in and set them on the coffee table. Props for the death scene. She wished she weren't so good at picking up vibrations.

Here it was. The kiss-off.

And so soon, she kept thinking. She'd known all along it was coming, but somehow she still wasn't prepared.

Connor invited her to sit. When had they become so formal with each other? He took the adjoining sofa, leaning forward and frowning down at his clasped hands. The world seemed to slow down, or perhaps it was her heart.

Luckily for her, adrenaline kicked in.

'Sophy. There's something I need to talk about…' He closed his eyes for an instant. 'To *tell* you…'

She raised her eyes to his. 'I know what you're going to say.' Her voice sounded as raspy as if she'd been living on dry biscuits for a year.

His gaze sharpened. 'You know. *What* do you know?'

'You're going away.'

'*How* do you…?' He closed his eyes again, as if meeting hers was too difficult. 'All right. It's true. I have a job on the other side of the world. And I have to go. It's as simple as that. This…this is what I do.'

It was her old dilemma. Whether to fight, to plead, cajole and manipulate to hold the people she loved, or to accept the verdict with dignity and let them go. Either way, they left in the end.

She tried to keep her voice firm. 'I thought you said your contract had finished.'

'Yes. I…did say that. It had finished. But I—I've been given the option to renew it.'

'I see.'

That was painful, but there was worse to come.

Connor's lean hands curled into fists. She could see the sinews ridging along the insides of his wrists. 'No, I don't think you—you really understand. I'm— This isn't easy for me. It's not easy for me to just—leave. To—leave you.'

She smiled at him, though it scraped the sore spot in her chest. 'Well, you could always stay. Save yourself some heartache.'

A muscle tightened in his cheek. Then he leaned forward and took her trembling hands, his dark eyes grave. 'My position as a lawyer is just one of the jobs I do at the embassy. There's another one I'm committed to, as well. I have to return to fulfil that.'

'What do you mean? What is it?'

'It's—intelligence. I collect information.'

She sat up straight and widened her eyes. 'What? Do you mean— like a spy?'

He flushed a little. 'Not exactly. Not like something you see in the movies. But I do—have to—keep contact with a—a network of people. Sometimes I have to meet people in quite dangerous locations.'

Ridiculous lurid scenes from James Bond, sadistic villains, dark alleys and spectacular car crashes flitted through her mind. 'Well, do you shadow people? Bug their phones?'

He was silent for a couple of heartbeats, then said, 'I can't really talk about this. It's serious business. National security. People's lives are at stake.'

Her life was at stake, but she didn't like to mention it, although she felt a sudden numbing roar in her ears. 'So—let me get this straight. This time you've been here now—were you ever really planning to stay?'

His eyes slid away from hers. 'Not really. I came out here for a break.' He shook his head and held up his hand as if to forestall her reaction. 'No, there's no need to say it. I know. I should never—never have… I had no right to get involved with you.'

'So all the time you've been here—you've been on *holiday*?'

He gave a cautious nod.

'But you took the rooms at the Alexandra. Well, then… I mean— have you been doing intelligence work here?'

He lowered his eyes and made a sharp intake of breath. 'Look…Sophy…'

A horrible possibility began to emerge from the mists, almost laughable at first, until it began to take shape.

'You know, it's a funny thing…' her voice sounded as husky as a soul sister's in a film noir classic '…but when I first knew you, I often had this really strong feeling that you were right there, close by, wherever I went. As if you were *following* me. I kept telling myself I was imagining things.' She gazed at him long and hard. 'Were you, Connor? Were you—what do you call it?—keeping me under surveillance?'

He flinched a little, but his dark eyes met hers with grim honesty. 'For a while.'

'Oh.' The pain was so extreme. As the blood drained from her heart the world as she'd known it for the past few months kaleidoscoped and reassembled itself into a new agonising pattern.

All the romance, the laughter and excitement, the passion. What had it been, really?

The answer sliced through her. A sham.

She closed her eyes, and the next word escaped as a croak. 'Why?'

He continued to meet her eyes with his grim, bleak gaze. 'As a favour to someone. Someone who mistakenly felt his family was under threat.'

She stared at him as the full, indigestible truth finally began to penetrate her numb brain. His rooms at the Alexandra. Getting to know her. Bringing her home with him. Making love to her. Securing her trust, her confidence.

Her eternal, undying love.

'Oh. Oh, I see.' Her eyes filled with tears, and through the mist she noticed the faintest sheen on his handsome forehead, but she had shock and betrayal to contend with, and didn't have room for pity.

She held her fists to her chest. 'I feel like such a fool. It was Elliott, I suppose. You were doing a favour for him. Keeping me occupied and away from him.' Her lips were nearly too dry to move. 'Goodness. He must be a really important man.'

'No, no, *not* Elliott,' he corrected swiftly, almost as if that would have been an insult. 'Look, I shouldn't be telling you this, but I'm trying to be honest with you. I owe you that much.' She flashed him a wry look and the stain across his cheekbones deepened. 'It—it was Sir Frank. He was worried—he wanted me to find out why you were meeting his son.' He made a jerky movement with his hands and said, 'And I was not *keeping you occupied*. You must know it's *not*—it never has been like that. I was with you for the same reason any guy would want to be with you.' His face was so stiff and controlled, she had to wonder what emotions were contained behind the rock face. Call her gullible, but she actually believed what he was saying.

'But—' his lean hands lifted '—I really can't stay. I tried to tell you that once before. I'm—not the man for you.'

She twisted her hands in her lap. 'I know. I remember… But that was before we…'

Fell in love.

'But, Connor, *maybe*…'

Maybe she was wrong. Maybe no part of his heart had ever been involved. She loved him so much she'd imagined it was recipro-cated, when what she was really seeing and feeling was a mere re-flection. Everyone knew secret agents were good at divorcing their emotions from their work. Look at James Bond. A different woman in every city.

With her pride, her life hanging in the balance, she hardly dared frame the words. 'Maybe there are children over there who need a speech-language pathologist.'

He sat very still, his lashes lowered while his sharp brain regis-tered her brazen proposal. What else was it, after all? Whoever heard of a diplomat turning up with a speech-language pathologist? He'd have to marry her.

Her hopes, her most secret dreams, her foolish love-struck heart all waited, quivering, beneath the guillotine.

'Sophy.' His eyes were cool and steady, and she could see he'd switched off his emotions to deal with her in secret-agent mode. 'It's the most dangerous place on earth. The work I do there— Try to understand. My wife, my *son* died flying out there to meet me. I— I really can't be responsible for another human being.'

She flushed at that. 'I'm responsible for myself, Connor.'

She didn't stay long then. She wasn't the woman to use her wiles to trap a man, even if she'd had any. Deceit wasn't in her repertoire.

To her mind it all came down to love, and the elusive nature of it. In her experience, there was no way of forcing someone to love you.

Connor didn't want her to drive him to the airport. Perhaps she should have been relieved, but that seemed as cruel as the rest of it. However hurtful it felt to see her lover leave, it was the *seeing* that mattered. Every tiny last fraction of a second of *seeing* him was precious, to be treasured and stored in a vaccuum-sealed part of her heart until she was too old to care or remember. He just mustn't have felt the same way about her.

After that final goodbye, not many mornings passed before she ran up the stairs in the Alexandra to see that his name had been removed from his door. His books and certificates were gone. Every trace he'd ever been there, ever teased her, laughed with her, kissed her under the willow tree…gone.

She'd expected it daily. But it was a blow.

The Alexandra was a desolate place.

There were some things a woman didn't feel like confiding, even to her best friends. By the way Zoe and Leah tiptoed around her at home, though, it seemed likely they guessed. Even the staff at work seemed to treat her with kid gloves. But people had to move on, even when they were broken and dying inside, and she still had children depending on her and a life to haul back onto the tracks. It was a lesson she'd learned before. To be happy again, she had to *be* happy. She needed to be positive and upbeat, and show the world she was fine.

Which was why, when she received an elegantly embossed invitation in the mail to attend Sir Frank Fraser's ninetieth birthday celebration, she sat down after a few moments, and wrote an acceptance.

CHAPTER FOURTEEN

WHAT was the perfect gift for a nonagenarian with a sharp, lively mind? In what Sophy hoped was an inspiration, she decided on a small volume of wry, clever verse from an Australian poet of the same extraordinary vintage as Sir Frank, and wrapped it in silver paper.

She started dressing early. For luck, as much as the exclusive Vaucluse address, she'd bought a new dress for the occasion. Its silvery blue chiffon clung to her curves. There was a faint shimmer in the fabric when she moved that seemed to lend a pale luminosity to her skin.

She'd had her hair straightened, and it hung below her shoulders, as glossy and silken as a shampoo model's. She just hoped she hadn't gone overboard.

All day long she'd experienced warning prickles up and down her spine, as if something portentous was about to happen, and sure enough, late in the afternoon, at the exact moment when she was thinking of phoning for a taxi, a man called to inform her that a limousine was on its way to collect her.

Heavens. She felt overwhelmed by such unexpected consideration. In truth, the surprise nearly brought on an anxiety attack. The old gent certainly knew how to roll out the red.

The limo arrived on time. She recognised Sir Frank's driver, and as he transported her through the gathering dusk, felt her nervousness subside into a taut anticipation.

Set behind high iron gates, Sir Frank's home was an imposing stone mansion. When she arrived, the party appeared to be already under way, with people spilling from the front entrance. As she alighted from the car more guests were being set down.

She was greeted by a middle-aged woman who directed her through the noisy crowd in the large, elegant vestibule to the morning room.

She threaded her way through and found her host surrounded by well-wishers, among a mass of presents and wrapping paper. When he caught sight of her, he broke into an elderly beam, and exclaimed, 'Ah, Sophy, Sophy. Here you are.'

She presented her small offering, and brushed cheeks with him. Then he turned excitedly to the people on either side of him. 'Now, this is Sophy Woodruff. Sit here beside me, Sophy. Hey, you there, matey, this young woman needs a drink.'

A white-coated boy bearing a tray sprang to instant obedience and brought her a glass of champagne. She found herself warmly greeted on all sides, though, of course, Sir Frank's friends and relations wouldn't have known who she was to the family. Elliott hadn't arrived yet, Sir Frank told her in a low voice. Something about his wife having returned from overseas.

She was relieved about that. The occasion was fraught enough for her as it was. In fact, it was really very emotional. Despite the evident wealth of his home, the fleet of waiters and caterers, she found a homely kindness in the old man's welcome that was so moving, a lump rose in her throat.

After a full-on thirty minutes of chatter and friendly enquiries she had to excuse herself for a brief spell, for fear of disgracing herself with tears. But, of course, these days she was an emotional *Titanic*.

She wandered outside, where tables and chairs were set on a terrace beside the pool.

Lights glimmered on the harbour, their glow intensifying in the deepening twilight. Below the balustrade of the terrace, a lush, softly lit garden flowed down to the water's edge. Steps built into the hillside led down to a picturesque, old-fashioned jetty where some of the guests had moored their boats.

This was how Connor's garden could look, she reflected, if anyone had been there to tend it.

A sleek motor launch, lights ablaze, nudged alongside the jetty. More wealthy people, she guessed, come to pay their respects.

It was wonderful, and so unexpected, to be one of the honoured guests, welcomed into the home of a bona fide grandparent. A few months ago nothing could have made her happier. And she *was* happy. She truly was. She had everything to be happy about. A wonderful job she loved, friends, and now a grandfather.

Her eyes grew misty and the cruiser's lights blurred. Face it. The trouble was, no matter how positive and upbeat she pretended to be, she couldn't move on from the terrible black chasm in her soul. In fact, celebrations only made her feel miserable.

Other people made her miserable.

Sunshine and birdsong made her miserable.

When she'd made a discreet dab at her eyes she saw that the man stepping up onto the jetty from the cruiser was really quite tall. From this distance, as indistinct as he was in the dusk, he looked a bit like Connor.

Another cruel twinge. When would she stop imagining him everywhere, dreaming of him, yearning for him? When would she ever get over this aching emptiness?

She strained to watch the new arrival, noting his long, easy stride as he headed for the steps and disappeared from her view.

The trouble was, the things that had eased her spirit in the past were unavailable to her now. She couldn't go to the Gardens. She had to avoid all parks and green places for fear of sighting a willow. Even the moon could make her cry. And there it was again, slyly swimming up over the headland, mocking her with its pale glory.

The man's dark head came into view as he climbed the steps.

She tensed, and her heart beat painfully fast. He looked so like *him*.

He lifted his head, and she felt certain he was looking straight at her. He *was* Connor. He had to be. Unless she was hallucinating again. She remembered then that actually she never *had* been hallucinating. He had been there all the time, shadowing her like a ghost. As the man drew nearer he quickened his stride, then broke into a run.

Her own personal ghost materialised from the indigo dusk, but at the very last his steps faltered. 'Sophy?'

He must have noticed her shocked, incredulous face, because with a little groan he surged forward, threw his arms around her and crushed her to his big, hard body.

'Oh, Sophy, my darling, my darling.'

It was Connor O'Brien, it really was him in the flesh. *His* hands, *his* lips, and his big strong heart beating against hers and making her burst into tears.

He kissed her wet face, and smoothed her hair, caressing her all over as if his hands had to reassure themselves of the feel of her, while her starved body hugged him to her, breathed in the familiar scent of him.

Eventually he stopped kissing her and held her away from him, while she issued a stream of barely coherent questions.

'Where did you come from? I mean, how long have you…? When did you get the boat? Why…why are you…? Connor? I thought you—had to… I'm in shock.'

'I'm so sorry.' All at once his dark eyes were uncertain, and he dropped his hands. 'I shouldn't have just assumed… I should have let you know. I should have given you time…' He ran a hand through his hair. 'Oh, oh, yes, the boat. I borrowed it from a neighbour. Quickest way here. Are you— Sophy, are you still…? You do seem quite pleased to see me.'

He glanced around then, as though noticing the surroundings for the first time. The crowd had started to trickle onto the terrace. People were noisily chatting, laughing, sipping their drinks, being served food by the platoon of waiters. It was hardly the place for a private reconciliation.

Connor slipped his arm around her. 'My darling, is there anywhere here we can talk?'

With the universe suddenly upside down in a state of joyous confusion, Sophy hardly knew what she said, or if any of it made sense. *My darling* was sounding very positive, though. 'I don't know. It's terribly crowded. Maybe the garden, or inside…'

At that moment Sir Frank, supported by Parkins, emerged from the house, and stood searching the terrace with his bright gaze until he spotted Sophy. 'Ah, there she is.' When he saw Connor, his wispy old eyebrows shot up as far as they could go. 'Connor. *You're* here.'

He shook Parkins off and limped over to them, making amazing progress on his stick, and exchanged an affectionate embrace with Connor. 'I thought you were on the other side of the world.'

Connor smiled and sent her an intense, heart-stopping glance. 'I needed to come back.'

'I knew you would,' the old man exclaimed. 'I had a very strong feeling. Didn't I, Parkins? Isn't that what we said? It's just what we expected. I told you, Parkins, didn't I?'

Not waiting for Parkins's endorsement, he beamed from one to the other of them with such obvious satisfaction, Sophy felt herself blush. It was clear he believed himself involved in a little matchmaking. Little did he know the raw undercurrents that connected her and Connor, for all that first spontaneous burst of joy they'd both expressed in seeing each other.

'Look, Sir Frank,' Connor said, taking swift charge. 'Sorry to rush off from your celebration, but we can't stay. I'm just off a plane, I'm jet-lagged, and I need to sort something out with Sophy. That's if…' He turned to her, his dark eyes soft and intent on hers. 'Will you— will you come home?'

Her heart skipped in her chest, and she nodded with a tremulous hope.

They took their leave, promising to come again, then Connor ushered Sophy down the steps, and along the jetty. She didn't feel dressed for a boat, what with her new chiffon and lucky high heels, but since that first moment of knowing it really was Connor bounding up the steps to her, her excitement had taken such a hold, she was prepared to rough it.

Once on the boat, though, she saw she needn't have worried. People from Point Piper didn't rough things. Connor settled her beside him in a seat that was as sheltered and padded as his big recliner, and wrapped a blanket around her knees. Behind them was a luxurious state room, with deep, inviting sofas cunningly fitted into the walls.

Once he was sure she was comfortable, he started the engine and steered them out into the bay. He seemed to know what he was doing. She felt the most exquisite, bittersweet longing as she gazed at his beautiful, lean hands, so sure and firm on the helm, and her eyes threatened to mist up again.

How she loved those hands.

Even with the moon in the ascendent, the lights around the Sydney shoreline had never glittered more brightly than on this magic night.

Once they were across Rose Bay and had rounded the Point, he cut the engine and she heard the rattle of the anchor chain seeking the murky depths.

In the sudden silence, broken only by the lap of the waves and the distant hoot of a ferry chugging back to the Quay, the cockpit felt as cosy and intimate as a fireside. She had the most thrilling, prickling sensation in the back of her neck.

Something wonderful was about to happen.

'Sophy…' He turned to her, then hesitated, frowning a little as though searching for the right words. 'My darling…'

Lucky for him he had a speech-language pathologist aboard. To help him get started, she said, 'Are you thinking of throwing me overboard? I can swim, you know.'

'I don't doubt it.' He smiled, but his eyes quickly grew serious. 'Sweetheart, I've been such a fool. I'm truly sorry. I know I've cost you—some pain.' He winced.

She lowered her gaze. There was no denying it. After all, she'd given him her all and he'd trashed it.

'I have to tell you something. I've been doing a lot of thinking. I don't want to stay in the Foreign Service.'

She stayed motionless, then said carefully, 'I thought you loved your job there.'

'I did, yes, but I've done it for long enough now. The other part— you know, the intelligence work—I don't want to do anymore. I've been missing out on too much, so I've packed it all in. Both jobs. Cancelled my contract. Left the Service. *Both* services. What do you think?' He looked seriously at her.

'What do *I* think?' Her heart was singing, but she wasn't sure she was entitled to an opinion. 'Well, I think you have to follow your heart.'

He smiled and gave her hands a squeeze. 'You know, until I met you— For years now I've been fooling myself… I *believed* that I could live without—people in my life.' The raw emotion she heard in his voice moved her unbearably. 'It was after the accident I took on the other work. In the end I stayed much longer than I'd ever intended. I guess there seemed no point coming home.' He gave her a rueful glance. 'In order to carry out that work I found I had to live more or less like a machine, with no personal attachments.' He shook his head. '*Crazy.* Thank God at least I managed to see my father before he died. So, when I was sent home on leave and Sir Frank asked me to check out your background—he did me the greatest favour of my life.' His grip on her hands tightened. 'I know it hurt you, but…I'm so grateful. You know, Sophy, from the first minute I saw you…'

'Oh, Connor,' she breathed. 'And from the first moment I saw *you*.'

He kissed her. 'What you saw was a very cynical man. A lost cause. And what *I* saw—' his voice softened '—was a beautiful, innocent girl.'

'Oh, *what*?' She rocked back in her seat. '*Innocent*? I beg your pardon, are you trying to insult me? Where do you think I've been living all my life? In a convent? You'd better realise that just because I happened to be a virgin when we met, it was nothing special. It was a perfectly normal state for me to be in, until I was ready to change it. Being a *virgin* does not have some mythical, magical *stuff* attached to it.' She grinned at him. 'Get with the real world, fella.'

He laughed and kissed her lips, and she felt the fire dance along them with the old rousing charge to her bloodstream.

'No, no, of course it doesn't,' he said smoothly. 'I know that, of course I do. It's just that…well, after I seduced you…'

Sophy gazed at him wide-eyed for a second, then couldn't restrain a laugh. It was quite a low, throaty laugh, probably because she hadn't laughed very often lately.

'So…what makes you think *you* seduced *me*?'

He blinked, then he smiled and his lashes flickered down. 'We-e-ll. All right, then. Perhaps we seduced each other. But what I wanted to say was…if you're ready to hear this…'

'All right. Please. Sorry. I'm just a bit excited. Go on.'

He drew a sharp breath and his lean, handsome face grew grave. She tensed, realising he was about to state some uncomfortable things. 'When we…when I… Look, I realised when I got on the plane—no, even before I was on the plane—that I was—walking away from my life.' He closed his eyes for an instant, as if in remembered anguish. 'My—love. I knew I was—hurting you. But I felt…' He tightened his grip on her hands. His dark eyes held a sincere, earnest light that made her heart tremble. 'I was in black despair. I felt you deserved better than me. You *do* deserve better. But, the truth is, I couldn't bear—*can't* bear—being without you. The further away from you I went, the more I needed to be with you. These last few weeks, I've been in hell. I hope you can forgive me for being such a bastard. And a fool.' The ardent glow in his eyes intensified. 'I love you, Sophy.'

'Oh.' Her eyes filled with tears. 'Oh, darling, I love you. You must know I love you.'

'Thank God.' He kissed her and held her so close, she could feel his big, powerful heart thumping against hers. 'You know, when I was flying back, I wondered if I still had a chance with you.'

'Oh,' she breathed into his neck. 'Now you *are* being an idiot. Anyway, you aren't all that bad. You are quite kind, when you aren't mocking people. And you do rescue damsels in distress.'

'Only if they're especially hot.' He gazed down at her, smiling, then a faintly guilty tremor crossed his face. 'There are some things I've done I'm not proud of.'

'Maybe we both have.'

Connor looked quite taken aback for a second, but she didn't give him the chance to enquire what she meant. She put her arms around him and kissed him. It began as a gentle, loving kiss, but somehow fireworks ignited and threatened to waylay any further conversation.

Fortunately Connor broke the kiss when the cockpit was so steamed up it was impossible to see through the glass, and held her firmly away from him. 'Before we do anything else, there's something I need to know. You don't really mind that house up there on the Point, do you?'

She laughed. *Mind* it? 'Not really, no.'

'If we were to buy a bit of furniture, fix it up, purchase a few paintings and make it like a *home*, what do you think? Could you bear to live with me there and be my love?'

She nodded, her heart aglow with joy. 'I think I could.'

'So.' His dark eyes smiled into hers, and she knew what he was going to ask next. She could feel it in her bones. She had reached a truly fabulous seminal moment.

'Well, then, Sophy Woodruff, will you marry me?'

Her heart overflowed with happiness and love. 'Oh, Connor, *yes*.' She showered him with kisses. 'A *million times yes*.'

After some time, thinking about that house on the Point, and the work that needed to be done in the garden, she interrupted Connor's passionate appreciation of her to pant, 'You know, Connor, I have a very strong feeling—'

'Good,' he growled, his eyes burning with a fiery hunger. 'Because *I* have a very strong feeling.'

All night long, the boat rocked on the bosom of the waves.

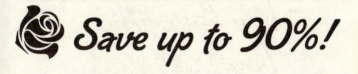

FREE Online Reads

Visit
www.millsandboon.co.uk
today to read our
short stories online—FOR FREE!

- Over 100 short stories available

- New reads updated weekly

- Written by your favourite authors,
  including…Lynne Graham,
  Carol Marinelli, Sharon Kendrick,
  Jessica Hart, Liz Fielding and
  MANY MORE

You can start reading these
FREE Mills & Boon® online reads
now just by signing up at
www.millsandboon.co.uk

Have Your Say

You've just finished your book.
So what did you think?

We'd love to hear your thoughts on our 'Have your say' online panel
www.millsandboon.co.uk/haveyoursay

- 🌹 Easy to use
- 🌹 Short questionnaire
- 🌹 Chance to win Mills & Boon® goodies